THE SECRET ROOM

Jane Casey has written fifteen crime novels for adults and three for teenagers. A former editor, she is married to a criminal barrister who helps to ensure her writing is realistic and as accurate as possible.

This authenticity has made her novels international bestsellers and critical successes. The Maeve Kerrigan series has been nominated for many awards: in 2015 Jane won the Mary Higgins Clark Award for *The Stranger You Know* and Irish Crime Novel of the Year for *After the Fire*. She also won Irish Crime Novel of the Year in 2019 for *Cruel Acts*, which was a *Sunday Times* bestseller, and in 2024 for *A Stranger in the Family*. Jane's standalone thriller *The Killing Kind* has been adapted for television.

Born in Dublin, Jane now lives in southwest London with her husband and two children.

Also by Jane Casey

THE MAEVE KERRIGAN SERIES
The Burning
The Reckoning
The Last Girl
The Stranger You Know
The Kill
After the Fire
Let the Dead Speak
Cruel Acts
The Cutting Place
The Close
A Stranger in the Family

STANDALONE NOVELS
The Missing
The Killing Kind
The Outsider (featuring characters who appear in the Maeve Kerrigan series)

THE SECRET ROOM

JANE CASEY

HEMLOCK PRESS

Hemlock Press
HarperCollins*Publishers* Ltd
1 London Bridge Street,
London SE1 9GF

www.harpercollins.co.uk

HarperCollins*Publishers*
Macken House, 39/40 Mayor Street Upper
Dublin 1, D01 C9W8, Ireland

First published by HarperCollins*Publishers* Ltd 2025

1

Copyright © Jane Casey 2025

Jane Casey asserts the moral right to be identified as the author of this work

A catalogue record for this book is available from the British Library

ISBN: 978-0-00-870225-0 (HB)
ISBN: 978-0-00-870226-7 (TPB)

This novel is entirely a work of fiction. The names, characters and incidents portrayed in it are the work of the author's imagination. Any resemblance to actual persons, living or dead, events or localities is entirely coincidental.

Set in Sabon LT Std by HarperCollins*Publishers* India

Printed and bound in the UK using 100%
Renewable Electricity at CPI Group (UK) Ltd

All rights reserved. No part of this publication may be reproduced, stored in a retrieval system, or transmitted, in any form or by any means, electronic, mechanical, photocopying, recording or otherwise, without the prior written permission of the publishers.

Without limiting the author's and publisher's exclusive rights, any unauthorised use of this publication to train generative artificial intelligence (AI) technologies is expressly prohibited. HarperCollins also exercise their rights under Article 4(3) of the Digital Single Market Directive 2019/790 and expressly reserve this publication from the text and data mining exception.

MIX
Paper | Supporting
responsible forestry
FSC
www.fsc.org
FSC™ C007454

This book contains FSC™ certified paper and other controlled sources to ensure responsible forest management.

For more information visit: www.harpercollins.co.uk/green

*For the up-all-night readers, the day-off-work readers,
the one-more-chapter readers,
the re-reading readers, the best-one-yet readers,
the favourite-series-ever readers, the first-one-I've-read readers,
the when's-the-next-one readers, the no-spoilers-please readers,
and the would-you-ever-cop-on-Maeve readers.*

Prologue

She walks into the hotel like she owns it. She moves fast, breaking into a little run a couple of times, her heels clicking on the marble floor. It means she gets to the reception desk just ahead of a large group of tourists from South Korea – eighteen of them milling around a guide, handing over passports and documentation before they all check in. No matter how efficient the receptionists are – and they're trained to be very efficient indeed – the tourists will take a long time to organise themselves and fill in their registration cards and find out which rooms they have been allocated and collect their keys. It's worth hurrying – worth being rude, in fact, and pushing in ahead of the guide, who was really at the desk first. She sidesteps him with a brilliant smile that cuts off his murmur of polite protest as sharply as if it was a knife. The reception staff greet her with manufactured warmth, wide smiles and blank eyes that hide their real thoughts. They are professionals.

She doesn't have to say anything to set one of them tapping at the computer in front of her. The other turns to leaf through the box of welcome folders behind the desk. There is one folder with her name on it – or the name she uses for them. There is no need to go through the welcome spiel, they acknowledge, with a conspiratorial nod that stops short of a wink. She is there every week and she has never stayed long enough to book a table in the Michelin-starred dining room on the top floor or the hotel's more casual restaurant next to the lobby, where a breakfast buffet is available in the morning between 7 a.m. and 10 a.m. She will not be there for breakfast, although the room is booked for the night. She will not visit the highly equipped gym or the swimming pool in the basement, not even to make use of the steam room or the award-winning spa facilities, which currently have a special offer for a half-price massage if you book any facial treatment. The receptionists do not bother to mention this. The woman has the soft, glossy hair, immaculate nails and flawless complexion of someone who knows her way around a spa, but she is not in the hotel to pamper herself. That has all happened already, in preparation for her brief weekly stay with them.

There is no need for help with luggage, either. As usual she only has a tote bag slung over one shoulder, this one jangling a gold C and D from the strap, a tiny reminder that it was made by Christian Dior. Her handbag is Hermès, in soft calf leather that is the delicate pink of the inside of a shell. Her shoes are buff suede Aquazurra slingbacks with towering heels and a bow on the back of the ankle, and the coat is the palest fawn cashmere, full-length, the sort of clothing that has never – even in nightmares – encountered the grime of an underground train. It is a coat for a world where cars come with drivers, where a taxi is a last resort, where public transport simply doesn't exist. There's a hint of white under the coat, a froth of lace at the neck and a delicately pleated skirt, but really there's no way to know what she's wearing might look like without the coat. It is a dress that cost more than the girls on reception make in a week, but soon it will be flung on the floor of room 412, the coat thrown over the chair in the corner, forgotten along with her memory of this brief interaction.

What happens at the reception desk is a ritual so familiar to her that she barely looks up from her phone now that they are preparing her key card and slotting it into the paper folder and murmuring the only information that interests her – *no, Ms Pusey, the other key has not been collected yet* – and she knows where the lift is, and how to get to the room that is booked every single week, that has been booked every Wednesday for the last eleven months, whether they could use it then or not.

She turns away from the desk with a small, private smile on her face that doesn't waver as the tourists edge out of her way. She walks straight across the lobby to the lift, and turns as the doors slide shut, looking out through the gap with ladylike composure.

Once she is on her own and unobserved – oblivious, like most people, to the cameras mounted in the corners of the lift – she drops the act for a moment. She leans in to get closer to the mirror, inspecting her eyes, running a fingertip under her lower lashes to smudge away some mascara, tilting her head left and right with a critical frown. Something catches her attention – some mark, some imperfection – and she gets close to the glass again, worrying at her cheek with a long nail, until she is satisfied it's gone. Then a step away and she considers herself, turning sideways, putting one leg forward and leaning back like a model. She sweeps the coat to one side and props a fist on her hip, posing more outrageously now, tipping her chin up so the bright overhead spotlight catches her cheekbones. Unexpectedly, charmingly, she pulls a face at herself as the lift slows to a halt. She abandons the mirror and turns to face the door.

The cameras pick her up as soon as she leaves the lift, her stride longer now, her impatience apparent from the way she is chewing her lower lip, and the quick, almost irritable movement that pulls her bag onto her shoulder when it slides down. She looks nervous, or possibly excited. Room 412 is at the end of the corridor, which is shaped like a T. The door is on the right side, facing room 411, slightly recessed so that the cameras can't see it, and this probably doesn't seem important to her, if she's aware of it at all.

She pauses at the door, framed against the blank wall, and fumbles with the card wallet to pull out the key. With one quick flick of her wrist (at 2.13 p.m. exactly, according to the timestamp on the CCTV image, confirmed by the hotel's own data from the electronic lock) she opens the door and then disappears from view. The camera captures only a flare of light from the room before the end of the corridor fades to dimness again as the door is closed.

The next time the camera in the corridor sees her, she will be lying on a metal trolley, zipped inside a body bag, as the undertakers wheel her quietly and discreetly past the closed doors of rooms that are now empty. No one will stay on the fourth floor until the police are finished, and no one will stay in room 412 until it has been comprehensively, thoroughly cleaned of every trace of what took place there.

First, it will be necessary to find out what actually happened behind that closed door. Much time will be spent watching the footage over and over again, especially for the period after the door closed. Much effort will be expended on identifying and assessing everyone who comes and goes on the fourth floor, even those who don't seem to pass anywhere near room 412.

But everyone who watches from the beginning – from the first moment that she steps into view, striding past the doorman as if he doesn't exist – will have to fight the strange, pointless urge to warn her, to call her away from the lift, to usher her out of the hotel and onto the street, to slip her back into her life again, as if there might still be a chance that someone could stop her from hurrying towards her death.

PART ONE

Curtain Up

'No two people see the same one thing alike.'
Harry Houdini
*The Right Way to Do Wrong: An Exposé
of Successful Criminals* (1906)

1

The job was never the same, and it was always the same. I walked into the hotel room – more of a suite, in fact, at the exclusive Governor Hotel – and it felt familiar, immediately. Death had arrived just ahead of me, and it greeted me like an old friend, which was fortunate because the welcome from the staff downstairs had been distinctly chilly. Here was the familiar nightmarish sense of everything normal having shuddered to a stop, the ordinary and everyday turned strange. I had had that feeling in small, grubby houses and immaculate mansions, barely habitable flats and filthy alleys, in car parks and woodland, and now here, in an elegant five-star hotel that occupied a sliver of expensive, exclusive Mayfair.

Ahead of me, there was a small dressing room, the cupboard doors open to show empty hangers. To the left, a bathroom, the door slightly ajar, and from inside the rustling movement of crime scene technicians. Light seared the air for an instant: a camera flash. Heat and steam seeped out through the gap in the doorway. I left it for the moment and went on into the bedroom.

If you ignored the crime techs, the clothes strewn on the floor and the scattered bits of disposable equipment the paramedics had left behind, it was a beautiful space. A huge bay window curved around two armchairs so you could sit and stare out at the heart of privileged, wealthy London, or look the other way at the enormous bed that your money had temporarily bought you. A tray stood on the table between the chairs. It held a single champagne glass beside a bowl of strawberries that scented the air with an unlikely breath of summer. The heavy curtains were still looped back with gold ropes and the lights of the building opposite gleamed in the November afternoon gloom.

The furniture was a combination of modern luxury and carefully chosen antiques. The sort of hotels I stayed in ran to a sheet of mirror glass on the inside of a cupboard door, or next to the door, inevitably in the darkest corner of the room. Here there was a full-length mahogany-framed mirror on a stand, so it could be adjusted for the best and most flattering reflection of the person using it. There was a tall glass-fronted bookcase opposite the bed filled with a curated selection of reading material and decorative pieces: a small model of St Paul's Cathedral, a bust of Charles Dickens, a porcelain shepherdess bending over her sheep. It felt unique and specific instead of exactly the same as every other room in the hotel, and that was part of what you were paying for too – the sense that someone had taken time and care in furnishing the space. It was a room you could fall in love with, a room where you could fall in love, if you had someone to fall in love with . . . I gave a small, unhappy sigh.

'Maeve.'

I jumped and turned to see my colleague Liv Bowen, elegant in steel-grey, her dark hair plaited and pinned into a neat knot.

'When did you get here?'

'About ten minutes ago.'

'Have you been in there?' I nodded to the bathroom.

'Only briefly. Too many people in there at the moment. The pathologist is waiting to have his turn.' She glanced around to make sure no one was close enough to hear her. 'Are you OK?'

'Fine. Don't I look it?'

'You look good.'

I knew. I was wearing a midnight-blue trouser suit and a long coat the same colour. My skin was clear and glowing, my hair was clipped at the nape of my neck and behaving itself, my head was high. Winning all round.

Until you looked into my eyes, which was where people who knew me well tended to start worrying.

'I hate sudden, suspicious deaths in hotels,' I said, which was true but not what she had been asking about. 'The more luxurious the hotel, the worse it is. Getting the management to cooperate is always a pain in the arse because all they want is for you to pack up and leave so you stop getting in the way of their precious guests.'

'This is an interesting one, though.'

'Is it? I don't really know what the case is. I got a call from Una telling me to come here.' Una was Superintendent Una Burt, a woman of great efficiency and no personal charm. She was never prey to self-doubt, which I admired, but on the other hand total conviction was only useful if you were always right, and Una was not infallible. 'All she said was a dead body and suspicious circumstances and the hotel had asked us to be discreet, which I was. Much good it did me. The concierge actually winced when I told him who I was and why I was here.'

'Well, you can see his point. A dead body on the fourth floor doesn't really fit with the hotel's image.'

'And that's my main priority, obviously. Tell me more about the dead body.'

'The victim is Ilaria Cavendish, who was a regular guest here,' Liv said. 'She booked the room under a different name – Anne Pusey. The first police officers who responded found her real ID in her bag. According to the reception staff, she met the same man here every week. They would stay for a couple of hours and then leave, even though the room was booked for the night.'

'It's just a wild thought, but maybe they were having an affair.'

'Do you think?' She grinned. 'Anyway, today she came up here on her own. She ordered champagne from room service, which was delivered to her room at 2.32 p.m. At 2.50, the man she was meeting – Sam Blundell – turned up. Nine minutes later he was on the phone to reception, telling them to call an ambulance. He'd found her in the bath and he couldn't get her out.'

I frowned. 'Why not?'

'The bath was full of scalding water. She was submerged. Still is. He said the water was still running when he came in. He turned the tap off, then tried to lift her out but all he managed to do was burn his hands.'

'Why did it take him nine minutes to get around to calling for help?'

'Good question. We haven't been able to talk to him yet. He's gone off to hospital to have his injuries looked at.'

'One champagne flute,' I said, looking around. 'Where's the bottle and the other glass?'

'In the bathroom. The champagne was in an ice bucket.'

'So she was having a bath and a drink and what – passed out and died? That's an accident, not murder.'

'She has a significant head injury.'

'She could have slipped getting into the bath and knocked herself out.'

'We'll have to see what the pathologist thinks, but it doesn't look like that kind of head injury.'

'And she was on her own here apart from the lover?'

'Apparently so.'

'We can confirm that with CCTV. Unless the manager is reviewing it right now. If it looks problematic for the hotel, he'll discover that, oops, the camera wasn't working and the maintenance team were supposed to have fixed it last Friday. Sorry, he can't think how it happened.'

Liv laughed. 'That's cynical, even for you.'

'Wait and see. But really the mystery here seems to be how she died, not who killed her.' I shrugged, frustrated. 'At least, it looks straightforward. Una could have told me all this on the phone.'

'What else did she tell you about this case?'

'Nothing. Why?'

Liv looked around, ultra-casual. 'She didn't mention who was in charge?'

I felt my stomach drop. 'He's not.'

'He absolutely is. The senior investigating officer on this extremely fascinating case is none other than Detective Inspector

Josh Derwent.' She leaned closer to whisper, 'He's only just got here. He was held up.'

A jolt of anxiety ran through me. 'Everything OK?'

'It must be, or he wouldn't be here.'

'Good point.' I swallowed, trying to loosen the knot that had suddenly tightened my throat. 'Una could have warned me.'

'I thought she was keeping the two of you apart.'

'She isn't, actually. He's the one who wants to avoid working with me.'

Liv looked surprised. 'Are you sure about that?'

'He told me so himself.' No room for ambiguity in it, either; it had been a straightforward statement that I couldn't interpret in any other way. 'I presume he had to take me this time because there's no one else, apart from you. Everyone else is tied up with the Russian gangsters in Chelsea.'

'Well, at least we're not on that one,' Liv said, trying to sound positive. 'It's a total shitshow.'

'Give me three tortured and disembowelled gangsters in a five-million-pound flat any day if it means I can avoid . . . certain people.' I looked around, half hoping to see his dark and glowering presence, half afraid he would be standing behind me. Derwent had a gift for appearing at the wrong moment. If anyone needed to arrive in a warning cloud of sulphur, it was him.

'It'll be fine.' Liv put her hand on my arm and squeezed it for a second. 'I know it's hard but you're both professionals.'

'Both professionals? That's generous. He might be a professional but he doesn't often act like it.'

If anything, Liv's sympathetic expression intensified. 'I know it's been a few months since you last worked with him, but you'll fall into the usual routine soon.'

The usual routine was the problem, I thought. The usual routine was why he had been avoiding me.

A white-suited figure emerged from the bathroom. He pulled his mask down so it hung below his chin, revealing the face of Kev Cox, my favourite crime scene manager. He was eternally cheerful even though he spent most of his days examining the worst things that people did to one another, in the closest possible detail.

'Maeve! I didn't think you'd be working on this one.'

'Why not?'

He looked evasive, which sat oddly on his open, honest face. 'Well. I don't know.'

I took pity on him. 'I do. Is he here?'

'He had to take a phone call from the hospital.' Kev looked around, checking the coast was clear. 'Have you heard anything about Thomas?'

'No,' I said. There was a knot of tension in my stomach. 'Nothing. And we'd better not talk about it here.'

'It's hard to ask him about it. I don't want to upset him.'

I nodded. I knew. 'What have we got?'

'She's still in the bath.' He brightened. 'You won't like it.'

'Why?'

'Skin slippage.' Kev's eyes narrowed with amusement at my reaction, which was unfeigned nausea. 'We'll be pumping out the bathwater before we lift her out. We'll sieve it for fibres and anything else that might be useful.'

'Liv, see if you can track down the CCTV. I'd better go into the bathroom and have a look,' I said with minimal enthusiasm.

'Suit up first,' Kev ordered. 'And don't touch anything if you can help it.'

I had started to walk away but now I stopped so abruptly that Liv walked into me. 'Kev, how long have we worked together? Do you really think you still need to tell us not to touch anything at a crime scene?'

'Better safe than sorry. I'm a scientist, Maeve. I don't take anything for granted.'

'I'll let it go, but only because I like you.' I was smiling as I got changed, and even as I slipped through the bathroom door, but that didn't last long when I saw what was waiting for me.

2

The bathroom was about the same size as my flat and most of it was marble. Chrome taps gleamed at the sink and in the glass shower cubicle, as well as beside the enormous bath. There was a crime scene technician preparing to pump the water out of the bath, and a short man I didn't recognise. He was wearing a forensic suit, his arms folded across his chest. The air was clouded with steam, but the mirrors were heated and therefore free of condensation. It was hard to avoid my own reflection: practically every wall was mirrored, which meant an infinity of versions of me looking around, trying to take in everything except what was lying in the bath. As Kev had promised, it was the stuff of nightmares.

'Are you the pathologist?' I asked, and the stranger nodded.

'Dr Alex Brown.'

'Maeve Kerrigan. I'm a DS on the murder squad. I don't think I've met you before.'

'I've only just started working in London.' He had a soft Scottish accent. From what I could see of him behind his mask I guessed he was in his forties. He seemed pleasant enough, but I was wary. I'd dealt with pathologists who were a delight, and those who had chosen the job because they preferred the company of the dead to the living, and I wasn't sure where Alex Brown landed on that social scale yet.

'Presumably you haven't been able to do much so far, given the water.'

'I've had a quick look and formed some initial opinions, but don't hold me to them.'

I had run out of reasons to avoid focusing on the body. Ilaria Cavendish was fully submerged in water that was cloudy, but not opaque enough to hide the details. She was naked. The skin on her hands and arms was loose, and there was something wrong with her head that I couldn't immediately interpret.

'Jesus, what happened to her?'

Dr Brown was at my elbow. 'We don't yet know how she died. My guess at this stage is that the obvious injuries happened after she died. The gentleman who found her tried to lift her out by the arms, which accounts for the degloving there. The heat of the water would have caused the skin to detach, you understand, and once he exerted force on it, it slipped easily. When he couldn't lift her that way, he panicked and grabbed her hair. As you can see, her scalp came away from the skull.'

'Thanks,' I said faintly. 'It was more of a rhetorical question.'

'No such thing for me. I'll have a closer look when the bath is empty, and of course I'll be doing a proper post-mortem this evening – I presume you'll be joining me?'

'I'll probably be there. I can't wait.'

He looked at me with a hint of amusement, picking up on the total lack of enthusiasm in my voice. 'Don't tell me you're squeamish, Sergeant.'

'It's not my favourite part of the job, but I've been to a lot of post-mortems and I've never fainted yet.'

'Always a first time.'

'This is not making me want to come along,' I pointed out, and he laughed.

'It shouldn't be that bad. I'll be looking at her lungs to see if she drowned or if she was dead before she went under the water. Hopefully I'll be able to give you a cause of death if not a time.'

'You people never commit to a time of death. Don't get my hopes up.' I didn't say what I thought, which was that the CCTV would be a bigger help than medical science in this instance.

The technician started the pump and the room filled with a loud hum that made conversation impossible. The pathologist moved back to stand next to the shower and I switched my attention to the rest of the room. A small army of bottles beside the sink looked untouched, and Ilaria didn't seem to have brought any toiletries with her. Crumpled towels had slipped from the heated rail to the floor, where they were piled up with a few scraps of very expensive, skimpy lace underwear that I took some time to examine without touching any of it. The champagne was sitting in the ice bucket, now full of water instead of ice, next to the sink which was clean and dry. The missing flute was beside the bath, a trace of champagne left in the bottom of it, as if the victim had drained it and then set it down next to her before she slipped under the water.

I was frowning as I came out of the bathroom and went to change out of the forensic coveralls. I was back in my suit, looking at my phone when the door to room 412 opened wide: Liv, followed like a shadow by Josh Derwent, and in spite of the fact that I'd been expecting him I felt jolted. He made eye contact with me for a half-second, if that, then looked away, which was exactly my reaction too. I dropped my phone into my pocket and concentrated very hard on tucking in my blouse where it had pulled out of the waistband of my trousers, adjusting the sleeves, generally focusing on everything but him. The glimpse I'd had of him wasn't reassuring. He was pale, with dark smudges under his eyes from sustained lack of sleep. More than that, he seemed to have withdrawn into himself, holding himself differently, not taking up space with effortless confidence as he had before. Unhappiness radiated from him.

And he wouldn't want me to mention any of it, I thought.

He went straight on the offensive. 'Busy?'

'Why?' I sounded flustered. *Hello to you too.*

'You were looking at your phone.'

'Just checking on something.'

'Have you had time for a look around?'

'Briefly.'

'And?' Liv raised her eyebrows.

'Well, I don't think this was an accident now that I've had a look at the bathroom.'

'The injuries were post-mortem, according to the pathologist,' Derwent said, dismissing it.

'Yeah, I know. He told me.'

He frowned. 'Did he find something else?'

'Not yet. But I did.'

'Go on.' There was no encouragement in his tone, which annoyed me enough to tease him a little.

'The bathroom didn't ring any alarm bells?'

An irritable shrug. 'Should it have?'

'Yes,' I said, feeling sorry for him suddenly. He should have noticed what I had seen too, and he would know that as soon as I said it. The Josh Derwent I knew would never have missed any of the jarring details I'd spotted. 'There's champagne in the bottom of the glass but no mark on the rim from her mouth. Even if she wasn't wearing lipstick, there'd be a print from her lip. And from the clothes on the bathroom floor she was wearing really expensive, show-off underwear – a garter belt, silk stockings, a lace bustier. You wear that kind of thing so someone else can take it off.' I was concentrating on not blushing and thought I was managing it fairly well. It helped that he was listening gravely, without the glint of enjoyment that he would once have had. It helped – and it killed me that he was listening with that flat concentration. 'She would never have stripped that underwear off for a bath before her lover arrived after going to the trouble of putting it on.'

'That's true,' Liv said. 'It's not as if those are comfortable things to wear.'

'I wouldn't know,' Derwent said.

'Also, having a bath – it doesn't make sense to me.' I frowned. 'If she'd been in the shower, she could have been freshening up after work, but a long hot bath when they're stealing a few hours from their lives and they're short on time? Why would she bother?'

Derwent looked sceptical. 'You think she worked?'

'I know she did. I looked her up. That's what I was doing when you came in.' I pulled my phone out and waggled it at him. 'Open-source search. You never know what you can find online.'

'And what did you find?'

'An article from *The Times* two years ago plugging her interior design business. The offices were in Soho, near Golden Square.'

'Convenient.'

'Well, if you're slipping out in the middle of the day to meet your lover, you don't want to have to go too far, do you?'

I didn't mean anything by it, but he frowned and I felt awkward and furious and unhappy all over again, none of which I was prepared to admit if he asked me. Why I felt that way was unclear. *We* had never slipped away from work to be together.

We had never actually been lovers.

He was studying the floor, concentrating. 'OK.'

'And her hair was loose. It would have been soaking wet after her bath, which would be annoying if they were going to bed. If she was planning to wash it, I think she'd have had a shower, and if she was washing it in the bath for some reason that I can't fathom, there would have been a bottle of the hotel shampoo next to the bath at the very least. She wouldn't have dunked her head in the water and left it at that.' I shook my head. 'Staged.'

'So why put her in the bath?' Liv asked.

'Forensics,' Derwent said. 'The heat will have destroyed any DNA that was on her. Or possibly in her.'

'OK, but we must be looking at limited possibilities.' Liv looked from me to Derwent. 'The only people who came into this room were the victim and the lover.'

'And the man or woman who brought the champagne,' I said. 'Or someone else we don't know about yet.'

'I haven't seen the CCTV but they're gathering anything that might be relevant so we can watch it now. I've requested everything from the last three hours – all the hotel's cameras,' Liv said.

'Make it the last twenty-four hours,' Derwent ordered. 'I'd rather have too much than too little.'

'And you won't be the one who has to watch it.' Keep it light, keep it normal, I thought. It was fine to tease him the way I always had.

He flicked a look at me but his reply was almost indifferent. 'Colin will be doing that.'

There was a thump from the bathroom and a clatter.

'What's going on in there?' Derwent leaned forward, trying to see.

'The undertakers are removing the body.' As I spoke, the pathologist came out. He unzipped his suit and took off his mask and I was pleased to discover I'd been right about his age. His features were more boyish than I'd expected – he had a nice smile and a snub nose which made him look youthful despite his greying hair. I wondered idly if he was married, and if so, what he told his spouse about his day at work. *Not too bad today, darling. Only one corpse seething with maggots.*

Dr Brown raised his eyebrows. 'So am I seeing you later, Sergeant?'

'What time?'

'Probably seven or thereabouts.'

'I'll be there,' I said, and he nodded and said goodbye to all of us, then headed off.

I watched him go, and then turned to find Derwent glaring at me. It was like walking into a wall; I took an actual step back.

'Really?' His jaw was clenched: he had absolutely and completely lost his temper, which baffled me. Liv muttered something vague and slid away.

'What's the matter?' I replayed the last couple of minutes in my head. 'Oh. He wasn't – he was talking about the post-mortem.'

In a way it was worse once I'd explained. He swallowed, hard. 'I'm sorry.'

'You don't have to apologise.'

'No. I do. It's none of my business.' He shook his head: disbelief in how badly he'd handled it, I deduced, and he was right, and maybe I should have told him it was none of his business myself.

I was saved from answering by the undertakers emerging from the bathroom with Ilaria Cavendish safely zipped into a black body bag. They had moved her onto a stainless-steel trolley so they could transport her to their black van. It would be parked, I guessed, next to the rear entrance of the hotel, out of sight. All unwanted items removed swiftly and discreetly, from rubbish and dirty sheets to bodies. I sidestepped to get out of their way and almost collided with Derwent, who was doing the same thing. He moved away, fast, and I felt myself blush.

How was it more embarrassing that he wasn't standing too close to me?

Because it's different.

Because it's how things are now.

'I'm going to take another look at the bathroom,' Derwent said as the undertakers continued into the hall. 'Coming?'

'I think I've seen all I need to.' I walked away. I'd had more than enough of sharing a small space with him for the time being.

3

Inevitably, the next thing I had to do was share a small space with Josh Derwent. This time it was the lift. I'd expected him to send Liv with me to review the security footage, or to let me go on my own, but he followed me. I waited until the lift doors had closed and we were alone for the first time in months.

'How are things?'

'Um, yeah. Waiting on results from the latest round of tests.' He kept his eyes on his phone where he was thumbing a quick message.

'Are they any closer to knowing anything helpful?'

'Hard to say.' A muscle flexed in his jaw.

'How's Thomas feeling?'

'Much the same.'

'I'm only asking, Josh,' I said quietly. 'I know you don't like talking about it, but everyone wants to help.' *For everyone, read me:* I *want to help.*

'There's nothing anyone can do, but I appreciate the . . . interest.'

'I'm not asking because I'm *interested*.'

After a moment he sighed. 'I know.'

I leaned back against the mirrored wall of the lift, my hands clenched on the bar behind me. Of all the things that could have happened, Thomas falling ill was just about the worst. Since May, Derwent had been fully, totally preoccupied with his girlfriend's son, especially since the doctors couldn't work out what was causing him to be unwell. I understood that it was agonising for him to see the little boy in hospital, in misery, and I understood that Derwent had to be there to support Melissa, the girlfriend I cordially detested. Thomas was very, very sick, and he was only eight. In the circumstances, my feelings didn't matter at all.

That didn't mean I could switch them off.

'I hate seeing you like this.'

He dropped his head. 'Maeve.'

'I know you don't want me to—'

The lift slowed to a stop and the doors opened on a family of five, complete with large suitcases and lanky teenagers. They shuffled into the lift, taking up most of the space, laden with backpacks and handbags as well as their suitcases. Derwent moved out of their way, making space, eventually finding himself boxed into the same corner as me. He turned towards me so my shoulder was against his chest, and leaned against the back wall of the lift with a grimace that I interpreted as: *I tried to keep my distance . . .*

'Three weeks travelling around Europe with two teenage girls and a boy – I didn't even attempt to pack light,' the mother said to me in a soft murmur that had the sweet lilt of the southern US. I looked down at the suitcases.

'You're from New Orleans?'

Her eyes went wide. 'How did you know that?'

'Just a guess.'

'Well, you must be a mind reader. Or Sherlock Holmes.'

I shook my head. 'Definitely not.'

'Mom,' the oldest teenager hissed. 'Stop. You're so *embarrassing.*'

I tried to keep my face straight. Down at my side, Derwent's hand closed around my wrist, out of sight: a warning.

If you laugh, I'll laugh.

The mother took the opportunity to share their entire travel itinerary with us as her children looked furious, bored and dazed respectively. Her husband's expression was resigned. I guessed this happened a lot. I listened, and smiled, and at long last we reached the ground floor. The family slowly, painfully extracted themselves and their luggage and the mother waved.

'So nice to meet you!'

'Safe travels.' I started to follow them out of the lift and Derwent tugged me back, reaching out and pressing a button at random. The doors closed again and the lift began creaking upwards.

I turned to face him, surprised. 'What are you doing?'

'Nothing.' He tilted his head, considering me. 'Just a guess, Sherlock?'

'Luggage tags,' I explained. 'They still had them on their bags and I recognised the airport code. They'll need to take the tags off before they go on the Eurostar. I should have told them.'

'What's the code for New Orleans?'

'It's a weird one. MSY, after the old name for the airport. They renamed it after Louis Armstrong, but I suppose LAX was taken.'

He raised his eyebrows. 'How did you know that?'

'I once got it wrong in a pub quiz.'

'And you never make the same mistake twice.'

'Not often.'

The lift bounced to a halt and the doors opened, saving us from having to consider whether our words had any other possible interpretations. It was the sixteenth floor. Derwent looked at it, uninterested, and pressed G again.

'Explain the round trip?'

'No reason, really.' A pause that felt like the silence between an arrow being loosed and thudding into the target. 'Except that I didn't want to let you go.'

The lift seemed enormous without the family and their belongings, but he was still standing close to me: close enough that it was easy for him to put a hand up to my face, his palm against my cheek. I found myself leaning and shut my eyes. For a moment, we might have been on a beach in spring sunshine, before everything had slid sideways.

'Maeve.'

The way he said my name brought me back to myself in a hurry. *You know I can't control myself*, he had said on that beach. No word of a lie. His mouth was so close to mine that there was no doubt about what he intended to do, and I reacted instinctively, moving without thinking about it. He ground to a halt, looking down at the hand I had braced on his chest to keep us apart. 'Maeve?'

'CCTV,' I said, and slipped away from him so we were a decorous three feet apart when the doors of the lift opened again on the ground floor. I was trembling but no one needed to know that.

We had very nearly started a relationship a few months earlier, waiting only so he could end things finally with his girlfriend, Melissa. And then, Thomas, and the health issues that had landed like a bomb to blow us apart. Not my fault that it hadn't worked out, and not his, but sometimes doing the right thing felt worse than I could ever have imagined.

Derwent took a deep breath, visibly shaken, and followed me out of the lift.

'Sorry.'

'Mm,' I said, which was all I could manage. I couldn't say it didn't matter when it did. I couldn't say I didn't mind.

'Forget that happened.'

'Forget what? Nothing happened.' I folded my arms and sought for a safer topic of conversation. 'My parents were wondering if they could help.'

He gave me a quick glance full of guilt. 'I should call them.'

'I can pass a message on. I'd like to tell them something. My mother's been lighting candles to Padre Pio. Apparently he's the go-to saint for healing.'

'Not the candles.' His face had softened, though; he genuinely loved my mother.

'They miss Thomas.' They had often babysat for Derwent and Melissa, because they lived in the same area of suburban London. So far they only had granddaughters, courtesy of my brother and his wife, and I wasn't exactly about to present them with a grandson, so Thomas had been a welcome addition to their lives. 'They'd love to see him.'

'I'll ask.'

'I can understand that Melissa doesn't want me around,' I said, with some difficulty given that he'd recently proved she was right to be suspicious of Derwent's feelings, 'but my parents haven't done anything wrong.'

'Neither have you.' He turned away abruptly. 'As I said, I'll ask. Now let's speak to the security team. Hopefully we can wind this up before too long and get home.'

'Excuse me.' A fair-haired woman in a pearl-grey suit had crossed the lobby. A discreet pin in her lapel announced that she was hotel staff. 'You're dealing with the issue on the fourth floor, I believe.'

'That's right,' I said, thinking that 'issue' was one way to describe murder.

'If we could encourage you to use the staff lifts rather than the guest lifts, that would be very useful in terms of managing the extra demands on the hotel's resources.'

Translation: *Please stay behind the scenes in the staff-only areas of the hotel so the guests don't start asking questions.*

'I'm sorry, I didn't get your name,' I said.

'Jeanette Lee.' She watched me write it down. 'I'm the hotel manager.'

I'd assumed the manager would be a man and that we would be unwelcome in the hotel. Half-right was better than nothing.

'We wanted to have a look at the CCTV from today,' Derwent said.

'Of course. Follow me.'

I was mesmerised by the way her staff glanced up, like sheep watching the sheepdog, as she walked in front of us. You could tell a lot about a person from the way other people reacted to them. Jeanette Lee was not to be underestimated.

We passed through a series of rooms behind the reception desk, each one a million miles from the luxury of the lobby: the cheapest office furniture, plain walls, no daylight. The final room contained a bank of screens and two men. One was watching the live feed from all of their cameras, and didn't look around when we came in. The other was wearing a well-cut suit and had a neat black beard. He jumped up and shook Derwent's hand enthusiastically.

'Mo Ramzan, head of security.'

'Ex job?'

Ramzan grinned. 'Does it show? Twelve years working for West Midlands Police.'

'And you left that behind for the glamour of a five-star hotel? Interesting choice.'

Ramzan laughed this time, his eyes bright. His handshake was firm and confident, I discovered. A people person, I thought, someone who could charm a difficult guest or calm an awkward situation.

'What can you tell us about Ilaria Cavendish?'

His smile faded. 'So sad. I saw them moving the body.'

'It's gone?' Jeanette Lee stiffened, alert. 'When am I getting the room back?'

'Not yet.' Derwent's tone did not encourage a discussion about when that might happen.

Jeanette sighed. 'I've moved everyone off the whole floor – we had enough space to be able to offer the guests an upgrade and they were happy to take it. The secret to a good hotel is hiding as much as possible from the guests. Anything ugly or functional has to be invisible.'

I wondered if we counted as ugly or functional. Perhaps both. 'How many rooms were occupied on that floor?'

'Only six. Mid-week, November – we're running at half-occupancy, but that's standard. One room was out of action because of a plumbing issue, but that's been resolved.'

'Did you tell the guests why you wanted them to move?' Derwent asked.

'They didn't need to know the details, and none of them asked.'

'I wouldn't ask too many questions if I was getting a free upgrade,' Ramzan said. 'And a bottle of fizz, I bet.'

'For anyone who drinks alcohol, yes. A fruit basket for the ones who don't.' A dimple dented the manager's cheek for an instant, transforming her appearance. 'Repeat business is worth it. These guests come to London several times a year.'

'What about Ilaria Cavendish?' I asked. 'She was a regular, I gather.'

'Oh yes. She stayed every Wednesday. The room was booked every week as far in advance as we would allow, which is eleven months.'

'Pre-paid?'

A nod. 'But she could rebook it if they needed to change the day.'

'And did they come every week?'

'No. Sometimes I assume they couldn't make it. They let the booking stand.' A shrug. 'If you have serious wealth, your time is worth a lot. Calling up to change arrangements wouldn't have been something they cared about.'

'Did they ever stay overnight?'

'No. They would always check in mid-afternoon and leave by six.'

'Ilaria checked in under a different name, didn't she?' I said. 'Anne Pusey.'

'That's the name of the person who booked the room. We only knew her as Anne until the first police officers who were here found her wallet in her bag.'

'And the man who was with her? Sam Blundell?'

'He never paid. It was always her card.'

'Any arguments? Any trouble?'

'They were easy guests.' She gave a tiny shrug. 'The Governor is not the kind of hotel that has guests who only stay for a couple of hours, but they were discreet so I turned a blind eye.'

'Was it always the same room?' I asked.

'Always.' She frowned. 'In fact, that was the only thing we ever had an issue about. It must have been three months ago. My assistant manager had put someone else in 412 from Saturday to Wednesday and they asked to stay on an extra night. I offered Anne – Ilaria – an upgrade to one of our best suites when she checked in and she refused. She was really angry that we asked. We moved the other guest instead and he was very pleased to be able to stay in our penthouse.'

That was interesting, I thought. The room was nice, but it sounded as if she'd turned down a better option. Maybe she had been sentimental about 412.

'What about the CCTV?' Derwent asked.

'Of course.' Ramzan gestured to a computer in the corner. 'We've sent everything to the address your colleague gave us, but you can review it here if you like.'

'I'd like to see her arriving at the hotel.'

'Here you go.' Ramzan selected a file and scrolled until he got to two o'clock that afternoon. On the street, people walked and talked, in groups or alone, unaware of being watched. 'She comes into view at three minutes past two.'

We watched as the blonde woman stalked down the street. I was trying and failing to recognise any aspect of the bloated, ruined corpse I'd seen in the bath. She walked fast, a phone to her ear.

'Did we get the phone?' Derwent asked me and I nodded.

She ended the call just as she arrived at the front of the hotel and pushed past the doorman without looking at him.

'Charming,' I said.

Ramzan tracked her through the hotel with the smooth skill of a professional, toggling between different views of her as she checked in, and went up in the lift, and walked down the corridor, and let herself into room 412.

'Is that the only camera angle we have?' Derwent asked, and Ramzan nodded.

'I'd never thought about the last two doors in the hall not being covered by our CCTV. I'm going to get small cameras mounted there on every floor.'

'Too late for us.' Derwent chewed his lip. 'And that's the last we see of her?'

'Yes. Four minutes after she goes in, the guests in room 408 leave,' Ramzan said, speeding through the frames where the corridor was empty. The guests were an elderly couple, fussing with his stick and her bag, and she returned to their room to collect something she'd forgotten before they moved down to the lift.

'We should talk to them,' I said to Jeanette, who nodded.

'Of course. I'll take care of that for you.'

It sounded like a phrase she said often, an automatic reassurance for needy guests.

'Then five minutes after that, the room service waiter arrives. His name is Abilo Braga, he's Brazilian and he's worked in the hotel for seven months. He came up in the service lift which is behind the door marked Staff Only, to the right of the guest lifts.'

He was medium height, medium build, with dark hair. He pushed a trolley up to room 412 and waited until the door opened. I peered at the trolley, neat with its white cloth, noting the champagne resting in the ice bucket, the glasses, the bowl of strawberries, and a narrow leather folder. He wheeled the trolley in, disappearing from view. Two minutes passed.

'Opening the champagne,' Jeanette Lee said, more or less to herself.

When he came out the trolley was empty apart from the folder and the champagne cork, still in its metal cage. He pocketed something with a quick, deft movement before he walked towards the lifts, steering the trolley with care. Jeanette watched him approvingly: he had clearly met her exacting standards.

'At least Ilaria tipped,' I commented. 'Then what?'

'Then nothing until Sam Blundell arrives downstairs.'

Unlike his lover, Sam nodded to the doorman and said something that made them both laugh. He was wearing an expensive coat with a suit under it and shoes that made Derwent shake his head.

'Chisel toes. Unacceptable.'

He was handsome in a square-jawed way, with white teeth and a broad-shouldered rugby-player build. The receptionists, both women, stood up straighter when he approached the desk, and their interaction was full of smiles on both sides. We watched him take the lift, with a brief glance in the mirror. Not vain, no need to preen. He sauntered down the corridor towards room 412, opened the door with his key card and disappeared from the camera's line of sight.

'What time are we up to now?' Derwent asked.

'Ten to three,' I said. I was scribbling a timeline in my notebook.

'So when does he call for help?'

Ramzan was speeding through the frames of still, empty corridor. 'It's a good nine minutes. He calls down to reception at a minute to three. One minute before that, this.'

The door of 412 opened and Sam Blundell reeled out of it, off balance. He had shed his jacket and coat, and his shirt was translucent as if it was wet. He was holding his hands up, palms facing him. His forearms were red, and his face was distressed. He yelled. I wasn't all that skilled at lip-reading, but it wasn't difficult to work out what he was saying.

Someone help me. Someone. Help.

None of the doors opened. He made it halfway down the hall towards the lift, then changed his mind, swung around and ran back, cannoning off the wall and disappearing into room 412 again.

'And that's the last thing that happens in the hallway before the paramedics arrive,' Ramzan said. 'You can watch that if you like but you don't see him, or anyone else.'

'No need to look at it now,' Derwent said to me, and I nodded soberly.

'I think he was crying.'

'You saw the state of her – and he loved her.' His voice was unexpectedly gentle. 'Can you really blame him?'

4

'Ilaria Cavendish's husband has been informed of her death but he's not in a fit state to speak to anyone – his doctor has given him a sedative, according to his lawyer.' Liv looked up to see our reaction.

'His lawyer?' I repeated. 'That's keen.'

'He seems like the kind of person who generally has a lawyer hanging around – he's something incredibly important in finance, as far as I can tell. More money than God. Devastated about his wife.'

'OK. Put him on your list for tomorrow,' Derwent said. 'What else?'

'Sam Blundell is in A&E and he's on serious painkillers for his burns so, again, no interview today, but he is prepared to talk to us tomorrow. He'll be at home.'

'I'll go,' I said, and Derwent nodded.

'Always useful to see them on their home turf. Where does he live?'

'West Ken,' Liv said.

'Posh people,' he said under his breath.

I raised an eyebrow. 'With all these luxury properties you'd think they wouldn't have needed a hotel room.'

'Part of the thrill,' Liv said. 'Neutral space, too. No embarrassing reminders of her husband or his girlfriend.'

'Oh, Blundell's in a relationship?'

'For now. I think a lot depends on whether she knew about Ilaria or not.' Liv tapped her pen against her mouth, her eyes gleaming. 'He asked if we could be sure to leave before six.'

'He's not going to be able to hide this from her,' I said. 'Not if he gets arrested.'

'No, but he lives in hope.'

'So who do we need to speak to today?' Derwent put a hand out and braced himself on the wall. He was swaying with exhaustion.

'Well, you don't need to speak to anyone. Liv and I can take care of it,' I said quickly.

'I'm fine.' He looked anything but. 'I didn't get a lot of sleep last night, that's all.'

'Inspectors get to run away to the office and engage with their paperwork until it's time to go home. I know you don't usually take advantage of that, but you should.'

'Maeve is right,' Liv said. 'We can handle whatever's left. I'll speak to the couple from down the hall, and Maeve can talk to the waiter who brought the champagne.'

I checked my watch. 'I'll probably go to the post-mortem too, or at least some of it. Everything else can wait until tomorrow.'

'OK.' The very fact that he wasn't arguing was terribly, horribly unlike him. I barely listened as he ran through the remaining tasks that he wanted Liv to take care of, and when he walked away I watched him until he was out of sight.

'He'll be all right,' Liv said. 'He's just tired.'

'I'm sure you're right.'

'Did he talk to you about Thomas?'

'Not really.'

'Come on.' She put her arm through mine. 'Work will take your mind off it.'

I didn't think it would be as easy as all that to distract myself, but actually, once I was sitting in Mo Ramzan's office opposite Abilo Braga, I felt a lot better. I couldn't say the same for Braga, who was sitting, hunched, on the very edge of the sofa that was crammed into one corner. In person he was younger than I'd thought, and obviously scared. Sweat glossed his forehead and his upper lip, and he had pinned his hands between his knees to stop them from trembling. He was smaller than he had looked on the CCTV too, below average height and slim with it.

'Don't think too badly of him,' Ramzan had advised me. 'I don't know how the police do things back in Brazil but he's got no faith in the Met. Probably thinks he's going to be deported if he fails any of your questions.'

'I don't want to deport him,' I said. 'I couldn't care less about his immigration status. I only want to know what he knows about my murder victim.'

'I'll pass that on,' Ramzan had promised, and maybe he had, but Braga was still terrified, his tongue passing over his lips every few seconds as if his mouth was dry.

I leaned over and poured a glass of water, sliding it across the coffee table to him.

'Try not to worry, Mr Braga. We're here to ask you about what happened this afternoon when you went to room 412.'

'Nothing happened.' His voice was soft, barely audible, and heavily accented, but his English was fluent. 'I went there with the champagne. She let me in. I opened the bottle for her – I asked, and she said yes.'

'Hang on a second. Go back. Did she order the champagne herself?'

A nod. 'It was a phone call when she arrived.'

'Had you ever dealt with her before?'

'Many times.' He was clenching his hands together and it made all the muscles in his arms stand out. 'Every week.'

'And it was always the same order?'

'Yes.'

'Was there anything different about today?'

'About the order?'

'More about how she was,' I said. 'Did she seem like herself?'

'Like herself?' he repeated. 'I don't know her. I just opened the bottle and left.'

'Did she tip you?'

'No.'

I raised my eyebrows. 'Really? You were putting something in your pocket when you left the room.'

'Oh.' He dropped his head. 'No, she did today.'

'You didn't remember?'

His voice was soft. 'I thought I might get in trouble for taking it.'

'I'm sure you earned it. Tips are allowed, aren't they?'

'At the guest's discretion.'

'But this lady didn't usually tip.'

He managed a kind of smile. 'Not usually. So that was different. That's what you mean, yes?'

'Why did she give you a tip today? Did you do your job very well?'

'She was in a good mood, maybe? I don't know. Sometimes people tip, sometimes they don't. I always do a good job.'

'I'm sure you do,' I murmured automatically, thinking about Ilaria, and the good mood that hadn't really been in evidence when she was checking in. 'I know you might find it hard to answer this, but do you think that she might have taken something?'

'I don't understand.'

'Drugs.'

'Ah . . . I don't know.'

'There wasn't any sign of it in the room when you went in?'

'No.'

'And how was she dressed?'

'I don't remember.'

'A dress? Her coat? A towel?' I smiled. 'Try to remember, Mr Braga. It's important.'

'Maybe . . . a robe? From the bathroom?' He shrugged. 'I don't remember. I don't know clothes. Something white.'

'And she was in a good mood.'

'Yes.' Emphatic.

'Did you notice anything else strange? Any noises or smells – or anything unusual, really?'

'Nothing. I knocked on the door. I pushed in the trolley. I opened the champagne. I went out. That's it.' He shrugged. 'She didn't like to talk so I didn't talk. She gave me money and I said thank you. That was all.'

'OK,' I said, taking pity on him. 'Mr Ramzan has given me your address and phone number. Is this right?'

He looked at the page of my notebook where I'd written it, and nodded.

'We might need to speak to you again, Mr Braga, so don't go anywhere.' I took out a card and handed it to him. 'If you're moving, let me know. I don't want to have to come looking for you.'

'I won't move.'

'Or change jobs.'

He looked startled. 'No. I love it here. This is the best place I've worked. In Brazil I worked in a hotel but it was . . .' He trailed off. 'Here, it's heaven.'

After he'd gone, Liv came in.

'How were the Glazers?' I asked.

'Adorable. He's in his eighties but spry apart from a knee issue, which explains the stick. She's fabulous – clearly had more than one facelift, giant pearl earrings, loves to shop. They always stay here but not in any particular room. They're loving their upgrade and I can't blame them – we sat in the sitting room of their suite for the interview and all I wanted to do was move in.'

'And did they have anything helpful to say?'

'Not really – they heard doors opening and closing but they didn't see Ilaria or anyone else. They always have a nap at midday and they didn't hear anything out of the ordinary – hotel staff moving around while they were cleaning the rooms, a chambermaid vacuuming the hall, and some banging from the room down the hall where they were fixing the plumbing. It was basically silent from one o'clock onwards. They both have excellent hearing and they were both really sharp – good witnesses. He said they were planning to go to an exhibition this afternoon but they were too tired so instead they had a drink in a posh wine bar and came back.'

'Silent from one o'clock onwards,' I repeated. 'I'm surprised no one heard anything while Ilaria died.'

'If there was anything to hear.'

I raised my eyebrows. 'The way the bathroom was set up doesn't bother you?'

'I don't know. I'm keeping an open mind. What did the waiter say?'

I ran through what he'd said, and the places where he had faltered.

'No one remembers every detail of everything. I suppose it's better that he didn't try to lie about it. But why does it matter what she was wearing?'

'I don't know if it does matter. I wanted to know if she was dressed or not, because not long after that she was naked in the bath.'

'Maybe he confused the dress with a robe.'

'Both white.' I rubbed my eyes. 'Men.'

Liv sat down. 'On the other hand, why did he lie about the tip?'

'In case we confiscated it, I imagine.' I was frowning. 'On the CCTV, when she was walking into the hotel, she behaved as if anyone working there was beneath her notice. She didn't seem like the type to bother with a tip, which makes me think she might have taken something to make her more cheerful and generous.'

'If she was high, she might not have thought about getting her hair wet. She might have prioritised a bath over showing off the sexy underwear. She might even have spilled her glass of champagne before she got to drink it. She might have passed out in the bath and drowned.'

'All right,' I said. 'I take your point. I'm sure the pathologist will be taking samples for drugs testing anyway, but I'll mention it to him at the post-mortem.'

'He seemed nice.'

'That's not why I'm going,' I said. 'It's my job to be there.'

'I know.' She pulled a face. 'I think it would do you good to meet someone, that's all.'

'But I have met someone.'

'You have?' She folded her arms. 'Why haven't I heard about this?'

'It's at an early stage.' I relented. 'We haven't even gone out yet. We're building up to it.'

'Who is he?'

'Look, I'll give you all the details another time. He's nice and he's a bit older than me and I like him.'

'You sound as if he's bowled you off your feet, all right.'

'Oh, come on. You told me to meet someone, and I've met someone.'

'So I can't nag you about it anymore. I see what you've done there.'

I held her gaze, trying not to blush. There was a little too much truth in what she'd said. It was convenient to me to have someone in my life, to ward off helpful advice from my friends. Even more convenient was the fact that he was busy a lot of the time, so our relationship so far had been conducted by text.

'I don't know if he's the love of my life yet but I will tell you about him if it turns into something serious, OK?'

'I suppose.' Liv was looking at me with that combination of sympathy and shrewdness that made her such an annoyingly insightful friend. 'You need to move on.'

I looked down, busying myself with my bag. 'What I need is to leave now if I'm going to get to the mortuary on time.'

'Maeve . . .'

'I'll see you tomorrow,' I said, and slid out of the head of security's bleak office before Liv could say anything else.

5

'You're late.' Dr Brown looked up from the body as the newcomer closed the door behind him, and I couldn't tell if he really minded or not. As I'd discovered over the previous hour, the pathologist had a nice line in dry humour.

'Apologies. I got held up.' Derwent came to stand near the table, opposite me. 'What did I miss?'

'The worst parts.' I said it with feeling, and Dr Brown chuckled.

'She means the most interesting parts.'

'I know what you people call interesting and I'm glad I was late.' Derwent looked down at the body. Dr Brown had stitched Ilaria Cavendish up himself instead of leaving it to his assistant, talking to me as he pulled the parts of her body together and made her presentable for her family. Even with all his care, the Y incision in her chest and stomach was grotesquely disfiguring and her face was misshapen. The areas of skin damage were more noticeable now that the skin itself had dried out, curling away from her body. The beautiful woman who had marched into the Governor Hotel was utterly lost.

'You know what I want to know,' Derwent said. 'Accident, misadventure, or murder?'

'What are you hoping for?' Dr Brown asked.

'Anything but murder.'

'Bad luck.' The pathologist brushed a hair from Ilaria's forehead with gentle consideration, as if she could still feel it. 'Definitely a murder.'

'So you were right,' Derwent said to me.

'I generally am.'

'That's debatable.' He switched his attention to Dr Brown. 'What happened to her? Talk me through it.'

'My first thought when I came to the scene was that this could be natural causes, which I know you also had in mind as a possibility. The most likely scenario when a relatively young person dies in a bath is drowning, which is usually precipitated by some sort of cardiac event or epilepsy. The heat of the water, especially if it's over 40 degrees, can actually trigger arrhythmia in susceptible people. The Japanese noticed a trend of otherwise healthy elderly people dying in hot baths in winter and did a study on it.'

'Did she have any heart issues?' Derwent asked.

'None that I observed. Her heart looks normal for her age and weight. As for epilepsy, she had no history of it and there's no sign of a fit but it's very difficult to pick up on it during a post-mortem unless the person has bitten their tongue. Let's just say I think it's unlikely. More importantly, we know she didn't suffer an incapacitating incident and drown. Looking at her lungs, she was dead before she was submerged.'

'So what killed her?' Derwent seemed less thanced by the excluded possibilities, and I sensed his mood was about to get worse.

'These marks on her neck were barely visible when she was in the water, but now that she's dried out and we've got better lighting, you can see bruising – here.' He pointed at the ring of damage around her throat. 'She also has a fractured hyoid bone in her neck, and she had broken fingernails on both hands.'

'She was strangled?'

'That seems very likely, but I can't tell you much about the instrument that was used. Not manual strangulation, though – ligature strangulation. Some kind of material that didn't abrade the skin, but the hot water hasn't helped with preserving the mark it would have left. She had bruising to her arms that was perimortem and might have been caused by someone dragging her into the bath, and a further set of bruises on her back and thighs.'

'Dropping someone into a dry bath causes damage,' I said, and Derwent nodded.

'So the boyfriend did it during the ten minutes before he called for help.'

'Nine minutes before he called for help. Only eight minutes before he came out of the room,' I reminded him. 'That doesn't give him a lot of time to kill her, strip her, put her in the bath and run the water, let alone scald himself.'

'Dead bodies are hard to handle,' Dr Brown said. 'Awkward, heavy. He'd have been out of breath.'

'We'll look at the CCTV again. If he went in planning to kill her, he might have been able to speed things up, but it would have been tight.' Derwent considered it. 'He could have told her to take off her clothes – we can check her phone to see whether they were messaging one another.'

'I still don't think he'd have time to strangle her and submerge her in hot water,' I said diffidently, 'but I can't come up with an alternative scenario. It feels impossible but there's no doubt about the timings – we have her on CCTV all the way through the hotel, as far as her room. I checked with the hotel, and after the chambermaid left the room this morning they have no record of anyone going into that room until Ilaria let herself in at 2.13 p.m. The room has an electronic lock that records every single time it's opened, and it was securely closed all day. The waiter couldn't have killed her in a couple of minutes, which is roughly how much time he spent in the room – he was pretty efficient. Apart from him, Sam Blundell is the only person who was in there, so logically it must be him, and he must have managed to do everything in a very short space of time somehow, but I can't make it work. Strangling Ilaria would have taken time. Putting her in the bath – well, if he had to strip her, that could have taken ten minutes on its own. Her underwear wasn't ripped or cut. It was carefully removed. And the bath was full to the brim when the paramedics got there.'

'A diagnosis based on the elimination of other causes is still a diagnosis,' Dr Brown said.

'That might work in your game,' Derwent said grimly, 'but we'll need more than that to convince the CPS to charge him.'

I walked out of the mortuary with Derwent, glad to be back on the very ordinary central London street where the anonymous brick building stood behind high, uninformative gates. I wondered if the neighbours noticed the hearses driving in and out, or if they chose not to wonder about what went on there. It was after eight and there were very few people around. A car passed us and then the street fell silent. We walked down the street a little way before Derwent slowed, and stopped. I had gone a couple of paces before I realised he wasn't beside me. I turned and for a moment we were face to face. He stared at me with a kind of hunger, as if he needed to, as if it was all he had wanted.

Which wasn't right.

'What do you think?' I said, almost at random. 'The timings are baffling.'

A flicker of his eyelids and he was focused on the case again. 'We need Kev to find out how long it would take to run the bath that hot and that high.'

'He's all over it. I've got to let him know what height and weight Ilaria was so he can allow for that volume of water, but he's planning to go and test it out tonight while we still have access to the room. I'm stalling the manager until we're absolutely sure we've got everything.'

'Good. Thanks.' A pause. 'Are you heading home now?'

'I'm going to the hotel. Room 412 is calling me. I want to see if I can help Kev, and I want to run through my timeline again.'

'Sounds like a good idea. Shame I can't come with you.' He said it briskly, not wistfully. All work, no emotion. Which was what I wanted.

'I didn't expect you to come to the PM.'

'It's not far from the office. I thought I should drop by before I went home.'

'Is everything all right?'

'Yeah.' He took a deep breath. 'No. I wanted to talk to you about what happened earlier. The lift.'

'No need,' I said. 'Forget it.'

'Forget it,' he repeated. 'I see.'

'Yes.' I felt a flush of anger warm my cheeks. 'What's the alternative, exactly? Making a formal complaint about your lack of professionalism?'

He went still. 'Oh, that's where we are, is it?'

'I'm trying to do my job, and I'm trying to avoid causing you any trouble. That's all.' I tried to guess what he was thinking from his expression, and failed.

'I thought I might have been in the way.'

'At the hotel?'

'And at the morgue.'

'At the—' I shook my head, realising what he meant. 'Get a grip, Josh. You're barking up the wrong tree. Dr Brown's wife is a doctor too, and he's obviously mad about her. She specialised in paediatric emergency medicine. They've been living in Cape Town for the last five years and recently moved back to London.'

'He told you all that?'

'We talked while he was sewing Ilaria up, afterwards.'

'People always tell you things, don't they?'

'I can't help being curious.' I folded my arms. 'But all of that is beside the point, which is that you shouldn't have assumed he was flirting with me at the hotel.'

'I know. I shouldn't have said anything.' He didn't sound particularly sorry about it, though, and there was a warmth to his manner that had been missing before. I recognised it as relief, which was absolutely not what he should have been feeling. That was enough to give me the courage to go on.

'I thought I should tell you I'm going on a date tomorrow night.'

A muscle in his jaw tightened. 'Right.'

'With Luke's boss.'

Derwent's eyebrows shot up. '*My* Luke?'

'That's the one.' *Your adult son who you only met for the first time two years ago, the one who is you but fifteen years younger, without the dark cloud over your head and the burning anger that keeps you going when you're close to being totally exhausted, like now.* That *Luke*.

'How did that come about?' His voice was cold.

'I met him a couple of weeks ago at Luke's birthday drinks.'

'I didn't know you were planning on going to that.'

'Luke asked me to and I didn't want to let him down. I was only there for an hour.' The drinks had been in a swanky bar near Luke's office in the City. I'd felt out of place when I got there.

'I'd intended to go but . . .' he trailed off. 'So you met this guy there, did you?'

'Owen came over and introduced himself. I didn't know anyone apart from Luke so he took me around the party and made sure I got to meet interesting people.'

'I bet he did.' His expression was unreadable.

'He was kind. I liked him.'

'And he asked you out?'

'He didn't ask for my number while I was there but Luke got in touch a few days later and gave me his contact details in case I might be interested.'

Derwent's lip curled. 'So he didn't even ask you out himself? He made you ask him?'

'It was all very grown-up and respectful,' I insisted, embarrassed in spite of myself. 'No one put me under any pressure.'

'What's his full name?'

'Owen Lord. Please don't do anything stupid like a PNC check.'

'Age?'

I shrugged. 'Older than me? I don't know his shoe size or where he went to school either.' I was trying to give the impression I found the interrogation amusing, when I did not.

'Divorced?'

'Again, I don't see how it's your business, but he's single. He came out of a long-term relationship last year, by mutual consent.'

Derwent smiled, as if he'd found the weakness he was probing for. 'That sounds like bullshit to me.'

'It's what Luke said.' I hesitated. 'I did check up on him before I said yes.'

'I'm going to have a word with Luke.' A mutter, under his breath.

'I happened to meet him at Luke's party,' I said quietly. 'Luke didn't set us up. And even if he had, why would you care?'

He made a move towards me, but stopped himself. 'You know why.'

'Well, you shouldn't.'

'I know.' He looked down at the pavement, brooding. 'I'm glad he's nice.'

'You certainly seem to be happy about it.' I glared at him. 'Why did you come here tonight?'

He looked up and I almost flinched at what I saw in his eyes. 'Because I wanted to see you.'

The truth, at last, and now I wished he hadn't said it. 'You know better than I do that this can't happen. You need to stop behaving like this. I'll work with you, and I'll be there for you as a friend, but I can't be anything else to you.' I was, suddenly, terrified that I would cry. I swallowed and focused on getting to the end of what I needed to say. 'Go home, Josh. It's where you need to be.'

He let me walk away, and I didn't look back.

6

I was tired the next day, my eyes dry and gritty. I had stayed at the Governor Hotel until close to midnight, watching Kev and his team gather every scrap of evidence that we might need, checking the timings to see how long it would take to run a bath so hot that the water was scalding, to the height of the overflow pipe. Even allowing for the volume of water displaced by Ilaria's body, it took longer than I had hoped to get the water hot enough and high enough.

'No way there was any cold water in there,' Kev said, referring to his notes. 'It was still hotter than a normal bath when we got here. Using the hot water only immediately limits your flow of water, so to fill the bath would take longer than normal. And it's a big bath – eighteen hundred millimetres in length.'

'He couldn't have done it in the time,' I concluded.

'I can't see how it was possible. Unless the victim had started running the bath already.'

'But then she wouldn't have had bruises on her back from falling into the bath. The water would have cushioned her.'

'What if the bruises came from something else? A lot of hard flooring in here, for example.'

I had struggled to imagine it, moving through the bedroom and bathroom, visualising a struggle that left no trace of violence in the room as the water thundered into the bath, drowning out the sounds of a fight there hadn't been time to have. It didn't make sense, and still I would have preferred to stay there, thinking about that, than go home and lie awake thinking about Josh Derwent. I tried to wait until I was truly exhausted before I left, but even then I found sleep wouldn't come.

All in all, it wasn't surprising that I was low on energy the following morning as I dragged myself into the narrow mews where Angus Cavendish lived in the heart of Knightsbridge. I'd had more fun prospects than interviewing a grieving widower about his unfaithful dead wife.

He answered the door and I assessed him: a thin, tall man who was maybe fifty, with a receding hairline and sloping shoulders and triple bags slung under bloodshot eyes. None of that should have made him attractive but he was, in a louche and dishevelled way. He was dressed in suit trousers, with bare feet and an untucked, half-buttoned striped shirt that was not on its first day of wear. One hand hung down by his side, holding a glass tumbler. He had his thumb inside the glass and his fingers curled under the base negligently, and I stared at it with absolute dismay as I introduced myself.

'Is that alcohol?'

'This?' He lifted the glass and looked at it in puzzlement as if he hadn't realised he was carrying it. 'No. Water.'

'OK. Have you been drinking this morning?'

He raised a hand and rubbed his eyes, grimacing. 'Do I look that bad? Don't answer that.'

'I need to interview you,' I said gently. 'And I don't want to do that if you're not in the best shape.'

'I haven't been drinking. I can talk to you. I don't want to, obviously, but I don't think that's going to change even if we wait another day, or five.'

'I understand. I'll try to make it brief.'

He sighed and stepped aside to let me enter. I stared around with frank curiosity; I had looked it up and knew they'd bought it three years earlier, for an eye-watering five million pounds according to the Land Registry. Living in a mews house in Kensington was a statement about wealth and lifestyle; you could spend less to live in a genuine mansion if you were prepared to settle for somewhere further out and not as fashionable. This house was tiny from front to back. There was no hallway: I walked straight into a small dining room and beyond it there was a microscopic galley kitchen. The dining room felt as if it had borrowed ideas from a private room in a Michelin-starred restaurant, though here there was only room for six chairs around the table. The walls were lined with wood panelling and a brass light fitting over the table was a work of art; I assumed it had cost a fortune. I remembered Ilaria's job had been interior design. She had certainly lived the part. The air smelled of expensive room scent overlaid with the brackish tang of cigarette smoke, a discordant note like the dishevelled clothing Angus wore.

'The stairs are at the back,' he said, pointing. 'We'll go up.'

There were two floors beneath us, I knew from my online snooping, and two more above: they had a small share of this crowded part of London to work with but they had gone as deep and as high as they could. I was glad I wasn't expected to descend to the windowless basement. The sitting room upstairs was pleasant, with a rose-pink velvet sofa and an abstract painting above the fireplace that I wanted to stare at for hours. An Eames chair by the window was clearly where Angus had been sitting. It was a survivor from a previous home, I guessed, maybe before they were married, because its masculine style clashed with the overall femininity of the room. A small brass table beside it held a full ashtray along with a packet of Marlboro Reds and a gold lighter. He threw himself into the chair, gesturing at the sofa as he shook a cigarette out and lit it with practised ease.

'Sit there. Ask your questions.' He had a deep, gritty voice, at least today, but I was inclined to put that down to the smoking. His accent was a drawl, money in every syllable of it, and even though his clothes were untidy he wore an expensive watch and a gold signet ring that had the soft, worn quality of a family heirloom. From money, then, and comfortable with it, and good at making more. Also, he had good manners, which he remembered after the first long inhalation of smoke.

'Do you want anything? A drink? A cigarette?' He held the packet out towards me.

'No, thanks.'

'You probably don't smoke, do you?'

'No.'

He stared down at the cigarette packet before reading out the warning. 'Smoking clogs your arteries. And there's a picture, look. Disgusting.'

The clogged artery – a scarlet tube oozing white sludge – reminded me all too much of the post-mortem I'd attended the night before. I dragged my eyes away from it.

'They're not messing around with how they describe the risks these days, are they?'

'I suppose it works for some people.' He took a deep drag on the cigarette and blew three perfect rings. 'I don't happen to care what happens to me. If these clog my arteries, so much the better.'

'Mr Cavendish, I'm so sorry about what happened to your wife. It must be very upsetting for you.'

'It's devastating. I'm devastated.' A thread of blue smoke swirled up and disappeared into the air. His hands were shaking. 'There aren't really the words to explain how utterly awful it is – everything I say falls short. I feel like an axe has split me in two, and I will never be whole again. I spent last night holding a shirt that smelled of her, and when I woke up I thought she was there, but she'll never be there again. Never. I'll never see her face again.'

'Mr Cavendish—'

'Wait.' He held up a finger. 'Let me say this. I need to say it to someone. She had the most beautiful smile, Ilaria, but what I loved was the way she turned her mouth down when she was upset about something. Her whole face would change. Like the mask of tragedy. And then when I fixed whatever was wrong, or told her she was beautiful – whatever she needed – her eyes would light up and her mouth would curve the other way. I have pictures of her smiling but I don't have a picture of her looking sad. All I can do is remember it – and one day, that memory will fade. People forget, even if they don't want to. You can't help it. I'll forget the way her mouth turned down. Damn it.'

He began to cry, quite openly and helplessly. I put my notebook down and waited, looking at the photographs on a table by the window: a wedding picture in pride of place. It had been taken somewhere abroad, Italy perhaps, with a crumbling castello in the background and fairy lights strung overhead. The bride was radiant even in black and white, smiling in triumph at the camera, while Angus stared at her with total devotion. They had been a handsome couple. He had less hair now, and his face had hollowed. Even allowing for the effects of his grief, he had aged. I thought of the way Ilaria had stalked into the Governor Hotel – the confidence of her, the head-turning beauty – and I wished I could avoid asking Angus the questions on my list.

He sniffed and wiped his eyes with the heel of his hand, pulling himself together. 'Sorry. That keeps happening.'

'Of course. It's only natural,' I said softly. 'Do you have anyone with you here?'

'My lawyer tried to sit in on this but that wasn't necessary, and my PA was here this morning.' I must have been looking taken aback because he added, 'Aside from people I pay, a couple of friends came round. I sent them away. I didn't want anyone else. I only want *her*.' He hugged himself, shivering.

The best thing I could do was to get this interview over so I could leave him alone. I steeled myself.

'Did you know she was at the Governor Hotel yesterday afternoon?'

A frown as he stubbed out his cigarette. 'She went to work yesterday. Wednesday was one of her days to be in the office.'

'Every Wednesday?'

'Yes. It's a small business – just four of them – and she and her partner come and go a lot, seeing clients, travelling so they can source pieces. They had a rule that everyone had to be at work on Wednesdays unless they were on annual leave.'

Which explained why she had booked the hotel for every Wednesday afternoon, I thought.

'Did you know she went to that hotel regularly?'

'No.'

'Did you know – I'm sorry, I have to ask this – that she was having an affair?'

There was a long silence. He occupied himself with lighting another cigarette, taking his time. I yearned to open a window.

Eventually he looked straight at me. 'Yes. I did. I turned a blind eye to it. I wanted her to be happy.'

'Do you know the man in question?'

'Sam. Yes, I do. I sat them next to one another at a work dinner. He was working with my company on some marketing ideas. I thought she'd like him.' He grimaced. 'I didn't realise how much, obviously.'

'When was this?'

'A year ago. It was instant. I watched them that night and I knew what was happening. There was nothing I could do. There was nothing they could do either. A *coup de foudre* is what the French say for love at first sight. It literally means a bolt of lightning and that's what it was like. Unstoppable.' He looked at me. 'Have you ever had that experience? Meeting someone and falling for them straight away?'

'No.'

'Me neither, but I knew it when I saw it. I couldn't miss it. Have you met Sam?'

'Not yet.' I was saving that up. I wanted to know all I could before I walked into a room with my chief – and so far only – suspect.

'He's – he's likeable. I didn't blame her for being attracted to him.'

'Did the affair start then?'

'Emotionally, yes. Physically a little while later.'

'And when did you find out about it?'

'When Ilaria told me.' He frowned, concentrating on stubbing out the cigarette. 'You might find this hard to believe, but she wanted to be honest. It was respectful, not a betrayal. She told me she thought it would happen, and she told me when it had happened.'

'That must have been hurtful.'

He smiled. 'It was difficult, but it would have been worse to lose her trust by reacting in a hostile way. I didn't tell her it was hard. I let her think I didn't mind. It was something she needed so that she could be happy, the same way that she sometimes longed for a particular piece of jewellery or to visit a particular country. She had passions. It was my job to indulge them however I could.'

'You sound like a very loving husband.'

'I didn't want to lose her,' Angus Cavendish said quietly. 'I would have done anything she wanted if it meant I got to keep her.'

7

'We all knew she wouldn't be here on a Wednesday afternoon. That was completely normal.' Dally Field sat in Ilaria Cavendish's office, one leg tucked under her. She was twenty-three and impeccably turned out, her complexion like glass, her eyeliner perfect. Her outfit was conservative – a black shift dress with a white shirt underneath, and she had pulled her hair into a high, messy bun – but there were tiny tattoos scattered all over her arms and legs like doodles. A constellation of jewellery studded her ears, inside and out – stars, flowers, a minute enamel eye and slender diamond hoops that hugged the curve of her ears, high up. A narrow hoop pierced her septum too. I felt impossibly boring in comparison.

Dally was Ilaria's assistant and, currently, the only member of staff in the Cavendish Hickey office. I had expected something more glamorous than the three slightly dingy rooms on a single floor of an office building, but it was a working space, Dally had explained, where they called in samples and drew up technical plans and handled admin. Clients didn't come to the offices. Ilaria and her partner, Jennifer Hickey, met them in bars and restaurants or at their homes. The fourth member of staff was part-time ('because she's got, like, kids?') and did the tedious but essential jobs like invoicing and bookkeeping and VAT.

'And what's her name?'

'Anne Pusey.'

I stopped. 'That's the name Ilaria used at the hotel.'

'Is it?' Dally sounded bored, but then a lot of things seemed to bore her. If the death of her employer had been a shock, she seemed to have assimilated it completely by the time I spoke to her, less than twenty-four hours later. She spoke in a low voice that had a slight mid-Atlantic inflection, a way of speaking that I associated with influencers on social media.

'Did she tell you where she went on a Wednesday?'

'No. She told me she was contactable by phone in an emergency but I knew that meant not to call her. I didn't want to interrupt.'

'Interrupt what? She hadn't told you where she was going.'

Dally smiled. 'I worked it out. She would come in wearing beautiful clothes on a Wednesday – like, she always dressed well but on Wednesdays she was in sexy dresses and heels. You could tell she was wearing expensive lingerie and she'd drench herself in perfume. She was excited on Wednesdays, at least in the last few months. Happy. It didn't take a huge amount of insight to guess that she was seeing someone. And when it was time for her to go, she was out of here. She was really particular about being on time for whoever she was meeting. She would literally run out the door, and I know it's ironic but I used to think she'd be hit by a car or a bus or something because she was so fixated on getting to wherever they were meeting, so when I heard she'd died, I assumed it was an accident. I wasn't expecting murder but I wasn't surprised she was dead, if that makes sense.'

'Sometimes it takes a while for that kind of news to sink in.'

'I'm not in denial or anything.' She shrugged. 'I suppose I was just expecting things to go wrong. That's sort of how life goes for people my age. You lose your job or you have to move house unexpectedly or someone starts a random war somewhere so everything suddenly costs twice as much. Murder is extreme, for sure. It's like a true-crime podcast but I'm in it? Even this conversation feels kind of surreal but weirdly familiar, like I'm listening to it rather than part of it.'

'That can happen when you experience something traumatic.'

'Really?' She looked interested for the first time. 'I suppose it is a shock. I hadn't really thought about it that way.'

I tried to steer the conversation back to what I wanted to know. 'And Wednesday was the day everyone was supposed to be in the office?'

'Yes. Literally the only day I ever have any company.' Dally picked at her cuticle. 'When I got this job I didn't think I was going to be working alone. They need someone to let in couriers and answer the phone and that's me. It's not as creative as I was hoping.'

'Do you mind being here on your own?'

'I'm an introvert, so.' She shrugged. 'I do a lot of reading. Drawing. I can call my boyfriend if I want and no one cares.'

There was a photograph on the windowsill behind her desk, buried in a collection of potted plants in various vintage containers: Dally with a large man standing behind her, one arm hooked possessively around her throat. He had full-sleeve tattoos and a shaved head with multiple piercings in both ears, but he had a sweet smile. It was nice that they had a shared hobby, even if that hobby was body modification.

'I sometimes come up with ideas for Jen and Ilaria, if they're struggling with pitches. It's a bit of a nothing job but it's good experience to have on my CV. I've only been here for a year and a bit, and I need to stay for long enough to make it look good but, you know, this could be a reason to move on. I was hoping for a solid reference from Ilaria but now I'm going to have to depend on Jen and she's not as well known in the business.'

'I noticed that – Ilaria was the one featured in all the magazine articles I read about the company.'

'Yeah, Jen doesn't really like the limelight but Ilaria loved it. Not speaking ill of the dead or anything, but she was the one who hired a PR agency and she used to talk up what they were doing like she was some sort of cutting-edge designer. It was mainly, like, their friends' apartments? She redecorated her own house and put it all through the business. That took up a whole year. But then she used to have people round to her house to show them what she'd done and she did book jobs as a result so I suppose that's the game. She had social media for a while, sharing pictures of her house and her holidays, but her husband didn't like having his private life all over the internet so she took it down in the end – but, like, she cried over it. She loved having followers and getting compliments on what she was wearing or a new piece of furniture in her home. I guess it was validation.'

'What was she like to work for?'

Dally leaned forward and mouthed, 'A total bitch.'

'Really?'

'Yeah. She started off being so shitty I almost left after a month. Then I got used to her. She never said please or thank you for anything. She was massively spoilt. She was always on some fast or diet or something and that made her snappy. Like, awful. But she could be charming when she wanted to be and after a while she started being slightly nicer to me? Basically when she found out I could be helpful. But we were never friends or anything. She would never have confided in me about anything personal.'

All I was going to get from Dally was what she had noticed, I thought, but that was far better than nothing, especially when she was being so free with her opinions. 'When did she start leaving the office on Wednesday afternoons?'

'February, maybe?' Dally frowned. 'She went through a really rough patch before that. She lost loads of weight, she kept throwing up and she kept complaining about being tired. I thought she was pregnant, but Jen told me she didn't want to have kids and she was having a relapse with her bulimia. She went on antidepressants, like most of the rest of the world. She would come in and sit in her office and cry. She was here, but she wasn't doing any work. She was just . . . hiding.'

I made a note of it. This would have been the time she was fighting her attraction to Sam Blundell, from what Angus had said, but it was still out of character. And what if it was nothing to do with Sam? What if something else had been going on?

'When you say she was hiding, what was she hiding from?'

'I don't know.'

'Did she seem scared?'

Dally thought for a second. 'I mean, maybe. She was here when I got in sometimes, like she'd slept in the office. I thought she was going through some shit with her husband, to be honest with you. He would call her a lot. He sent presents – amazing things, like Hermès bags and jewellery and meals from her favourite restaurants and even a couple of paintings. He was so attentive and it seemed to make her *more* upset, if anything.'

That fitted with her failing to resist her feelings for Sam, I thought, and still felt uneasy about it.

'So what changed?'

'She cheered up. Eventually. It took a few months – she was actually worse on Wednesdays than any other day. We were all walking on eggshells. Then she seemed to get over whatever it was. She went back to being herself again – a stroppy cow but kind of fun at the same time.' Dally folded her arms. 'It might not sound like I liked her, but I did. I enjoyed the challenge of making her happy. It added interest to my day, you know?'

'Did she have any enemies that you're aware of? Anyone who was unhappy with her?'

'Someone who would have wanted to kill her? Not to my knowledge. People who weren't happy with the work she did? A few. And there were a couple of designers who were angry with her for ripping off their ideas, but we all get inspired by everyone else, you know? She actually didn't do anything wrong. She was just mid.'

'Mid?'

'Average. Not the best, not the worst. What she was really good at was making clients feel special. This job was always a bit of a hobby for Ilaria so she could be flaky and Jen had to pick up the slack with clients a few times when Ilaria had fucked up or lost interest. Jen is actually the one who's a proper designer.'

'Where is Jen?'

'She's on her way back from Bali at the moment? She's been there for ten days. Getting inspired. I rang her and told her the news about Ilaria so she knows. She keeps messaging me with questions that I simply cannot answer.' Dally looked around. 'I don't know what's going to happen now, with this place. Ilaria's husband was the one who paid the bills. There's no way we can afford to keep the office open if he's not paying the rent and the overheads. Jen put up with a lot from Ilaria because she depended on her for financial stability. I asked her about it once and she admitted that if Angus wasn't funding the company they'd have gone bust a long time ago.'

'Angus seemed devoted to Ilaria,' I said.

'Oh my God, completely. And the other way round too. It wasn't that he had money. Whenever I saw them together, she was like a different person, worried about his opinion and kind of eager to please. It was a power thing. No question of who was in charge. He was the only person who could make her behave.' Dally looked wistful for a moment. 'It's not that I have a thing for older men but there was something really attractive about him and I used to look forward to him coming in – not that it mattered. He never noticed me because he never took his eyes off her. I have no idea how he's going to cope now she's gone.'

8

I was walking out of the office after lunch, still feeling tired and out of sorts, when Derwent followed me into the hall.

'Where are you going?'

'I'm on my way to interview Sam Blundell, remember?'

He had already been looking disapproving but now the glowering intensified. 'On your own? Absolutely not. You need to take someone with you.'

'Why?'

'Because he's the main suspect in this case and it's potentially a dangerous place for you to be on your own.'

'Dangerous,' I repeated. 'Seriously?'

'You don't agree? Christ, Maeve, you walk through the world like nothing bad ever happens and no harm could ever come to you. I don't want you going into a suspect's house on your own if there's no reason for you to take that risk.'

'So what do you want to do? Were you planning to come with me?'

'I can't.'

I told myself to be glad. When he wasn't even capable of looking me straight in the eye I knew spending time alone with him was a bad idea. I didn't want another awkward conversation, or worse.

And I wasn't certain I'd be able to bear it if I had to stop him from touching me again.

'All right. Who should I take with me?'

'I'll see who's free. Wait there.' He went back into the office. I occupied myself by checking my messages on my phone, telling myself that yes, he was being overprotective but it was just him trying to do a good job as my boss, so I didn't need to worry about it.

Derwent was on the phone when he returned, looking like death. He had been irritable before, but this was different.

'Yeah, I'll see – hang on.' He moved the phone away but didn't cover it, as if he wanted the person at the other end to be able to hear our conversation. 'Maeve, do you think your parents would be able to collect Thomas from school for us? Melissa has a client coming to the house for counselling and she doesn't want to put him off.'

There was a tinny burst of words from the phone and he listened briefly.

'Right.' To me, he said, 'She can't put him off, I mean.'

'Yes, I'm sure they'd be happy to pick him up.' I had said they wanted to see him – and it wasn't the first time they'd stepped in to collect him, when Josh and Melissa were both busy.

'Is that all right?' He was talking to Melissa again. He closed his eyes and pinched the bridge of his nose, listening to her, waiting for a chance to speak. Eventually, he said, 'As I told you, I have a meeting at three thirty. I can't miss it. I'll leave as soon as possible after that and come home. I'll ask the Kerrigans to drop him at the house when I'm on my way home.'

Another burst of words.

'Yeah. Yeah, I know. I won't be long. Around five thirty.'

He went silent again, chewing his lower lip.

'I'll do my best.'

When he had hung up, he stared at the phone for a second, then looked at me, hollow-eyed.

'Are you sure she's all right with my parents picking him up?'

'No, but she couldn't think of any better options.'

'I don't want to cause you any trouble,' I said, uncertain.

'You aren't. It's not as if I can do anything right anyway. At least Thomas will be happy.'

'Josh.' I was horrified by the bitterness in his voice, and he shook his head.

'Leave it, Maeve. Just let it go, for once. You're helping me out and I appreciate it.'

All right. I'd been told; all I could do was go along with it. 'Do you want me to call my folks?'

'I can do it. It's my responsibility.'

I sighed. 'That means I'll need to call my mother later. I get in trouble if I don't check in with her every couple of days. Ideally she'd like me to call every night.' I hesitated. 'How's Melissa? She sounded stressed.'

He shook his head again, a brief movement that seemed almost instinctive. *No, I don't want to talk to you about her* more than *no, she's fine.* Before he could say anything, Georgia Shaw came out of the office behind him, pulling on her coat. My heart sank at the sight of the most glamorous detective constable in the Met. I'd expected Liv; I hadn't thought Georgia was available.

On the whole, I'd come to enjoy working with Georgia, even though she was almost completely lacking in the kind of instincts that made someone a good police officer. She also specialised in blurting out exactly what you didn't want her to say. However, she was fun to be around, she was loyal and she was hard-working. Derwent saw her as a liability, and occasionally a danger to her colleagues. If he'd asked Georgia to go with me, he'd been desperate. Georgia was never going to be top of his list.

'I'm here! I'm sorry. It took ages but I'm finished.' She flashed him a bright smile and trilled, 'See you later.'

'I'll be gone when you get back.' Derwent never bothered to waste any charm on her.

'Oh. Well then, see you tomorrow.' She was just as perky as before, focused on flicking her fair hair into the ideal bouncy waves rather than on what he said or how he said it. She was used to Derwent, or she didn't care, or she simply didn't notice when he was rude to her. I wished I knew how to pull that trick off.

'Call me if you find out anything helpful from Sam Blundell,' Derwent said to me. 'Try not to arrest him unless there's some very urgent reason to take him into custody. We are nowhere near ready for charges and at the moment he's cooperative so let's take advantage of that. I don't want to arrest him and have to let him go because we've rushed it.'

'Fine.' It was what I had thought myself.

'OK. And Maeve? Thanks.' He sounded gruff, and he flicked a warning look at Georgia, who was suddenly looking highly interested.

'For nothing.' I pressed the button for the lift and the doors slid open immediately, so Georgia and I were able to step inside and disappear. He watched us go, his face grim. I leaned against the wall and inhaled deeply as the lift shuttled down. It felt easier to breathe somehow now that I was safely out of Josh Derwent's presence.

9

Sam Blundell lived on the second floor of a red-brick mansion block in West Kensington, in a two-bedroom flat that had high ceilings and acres of floorspace and not very much furniture. It was modern and understated. There was a total lack of clutter and an absence of framed photographs, which meant I had no clues about the man in front of us who was sitting upright on a single armchair, trying not to fidget. Even the kitchen was the kind where every small appliance was hidden – no toaster, no kettle, nothing but a fruit bowl on the work surface. The space was bland, artfully so. It reminded me of something and I couldn't think what it was.

Sam was wearing a white T-shirt with black jogging bottoms and thick white sports socks that drew attention to the way he was compulsively tapping his toes. He looked unhappy, but less shell-shocked than Angus Cavendish had been. I thought all of his concern was for himself, not Ilaria, and that interested me.

'Obviously, I'm the main suspect. I know that.' He swallowed, his throat bobbing nervously. In real life the square jaw and high cheekbones were just as striking as they had been on the CCTV, but he looked more interesting than I'd anticipated when his face was animated – charming, in fact, with a direct gaze and expressive eyebrows. He was younger than I'd thought too – thirty, he told me. Georgia had pulled a face behind his back when he let us in, wide-eyed and giddy, and I'd frowned at her with as much professional gravitas as I could manage. 'All I can say is that, if I'd planned it, I wouldn't have scalded my hands like this.'

They were heavily bandaged and lay in his lap like shot doves. Because I had a suspicious mind I'd spoken to a yawning doctor at the hospital who confirmed he had serious injuries to both hands and would possibly need skin grafts; whatever else he was lying about, he wasn't pretending about his injuries.

'How did you do that to yourself?' I asked now.

He looked at me as if I was insane. 'Trying to lift her out of the bath, of course.'

'Did you know she was dead?'

'Not then.'

'Tell me everything that happened after you walked into the room.'

Sam had already described his day, and agreed that it followed the pattern of every Wednesday – leaving work early, going to the hotel, getting the key, going to the usual room. He raised a shoulder and grimaced. 'I walked in and called her name because I couldn't see her anywhere. The bathroom door was closed. I saw her clothes on the floor and realised she was probably in the bathroom, so I took off my coat and jacket and threw them on the bed.'

I had seen them there, rumpled, lying where they'd fallen.

'I knocked on the bathroom door,' Sam went on, 'and I could hear the water running but I couldn't hear her. I tried the door and it opened and I saw her – she was under the water, naked. I thought she'd fainted or something and was drowning. I turned off the tap and tried to pull the bath plug but I couldn't work out how to do it – there's a lever and I – well, we never used the bath so I wasn't familiar with it.'

The way he told the story was flat and felt rehearsed. I wondered if he had practised the wide-eyed stare in the mirror, or if it was shock that made him sound robotic as he described what he'd done.

'I knew it was hot water but I didn't realise how hot until I reached into it. I couldn't get a grip on her. Eventually I got hold of her head and when it broke the surface of the water I realised that I was pulling her scalp away from her head, and I dropped her into the bath again. It was *disgusting*. Like a nightmare. I hadn't been rough, I swear, but her skin just disintegrated.' He shuddered. 'And then I tried to lift her by the shoulders but my fingers were hurting so badly I couldn't grip her, and I realised my hands were burning. I didn't feel it at first because I was so focused on Illy, but then I couldn't stand it anymore. I looked around for something to use to lift her but there was nothing. Then I ran into the hall and called for help. No one answered, so I went back and called down to reception from the room.'

'Not 999?'

'No.' He looked surprised. 'Should I have? I wasn't sure. And the receptionist did it anyway.'

'Did you do anything else before you went into the bathroom?'

'No.'

'So there wasn't much time between you entering the room and finding her.'

'It's hard to say – a couple of minutes, maybe?' His forehead was creased with earnest effort.

'And did you notice anything out of place? Anything unusual, apart from Ilaria being in the bathroom?'

'I wasn't paying much attention. It didn't seem all that strange that she was in the bathroom, either. Why not, you know? I was running late. I thought she'd wanted a soak before we—' He cut himself off and looked pained. 'Do I have to say it?'

'Before you had sex with her.' I felt Georgia react beside me: a tiny quiver that might have been a giggle. I would have been the one listening to Derwent say it if he'd been there, I reflected, and pushed him out of my mind.

Sam ducked his head, his face reddening. 'I suppose.'

'You were having an affair with Ilaria Cavendish.'

'Yeah.'

'Since when?'

'Um.' His voice had got very quiet. He stared down at his hands. 'February.'

'When did you meet?' Georgia was leaning her chin on her hand, enthralled. She loved a love story.

'Before Christmas last year. We sat together at a dinner.' He looked uncomfortable. 'I was trying to get some work with her husband's company so I managed to get myself invited.'

'And what happened?'

'There was . . . an attraction. Mutual. But I knew she was married, obviously, and she shut down any flirting pretty early on. We had a nice evening together. That was all.'

'And then?'

'Then . . . I don't know. I bumped into her a couple of times, on the street near my office. We worked close to one another so I suppose it wasn't all that surprising. We went for a drink one evening when we both had somewhere else to go and time to kill.' He made a helpless gesture with one of the bandaged hands. 'It sort of went from there.'

'And you started meeting every Wednesday.'

'It was her idea. She arranged it. She booked the hotel.' He looked ill at ease. 'I went along with it, really. I mean, I liked her a lot. But it never felt completely real to me. It was like a fantasy.'

'Yours?' I asked.

'Hers.' He shrugged. 'I was a willing participant and we had a great time together, but I had the feeling sometimes that it wasn't about me at all. It probably sounds strange, but I didn't get to know her on any deeper level than what she liked in bed. We talked about when we were going to meet up again and what we wanted to do to each other, but beyond that? Nothing.'

'So it wasn't a real relationship,' Georgia said, and he nodded at her.

'Exactly. Any time I tried to talk to her about anything else – her marriage, her friends, her work, even – she shut me down. I felt like a personal trainer or a hairdresser or something. I was there to have sex with her and nothing more. I looked right and I could do the job but she didn't actually care about me.' He tried to smile. 'God, I sound pathetic, don't I? And I could have said no. I should have. I have a girlfriend who I really care about.'

'So why didn't you say no?' I asked.

'I don't know. I was flattered, I suppose. And I knew it would end at some stage. I didn't mind waiting until she was ready to stop. It felt easier than upsetting her.'

As he said it, I realised what his flat reminded me of: the backdrop on a reality TV show. It was a neutral space and Sam was the kind of person who could be whatever you needed him to be. *I looked right and I could do the job.* There was something grim and calculated about it – and somehow that was worse than the thunderclap attraction Angus had described.

'What kind of person was Ilaria?' I asked.

'She was a princess. She liked things to be a certain way,' he said slowly. 'High standards. I made sure I made her happy.'

'What kind of things made her happy?'

'In bed?' He flushed again. 'I don't know. The usual.'

'What about unusual things?'

'Like what?'

'Did you ever hit her?'

'No, I—' He broke off. 'Shit. A couple of times she asked me to be rough with her.'

'What did that involve?'

'I slapped her.'

'Where?'

'Across the face and – and on her body.' He folded his arms, awkwardly, hunching in the chair. 'It was only because she asked me to. That's not really me.'

'Did you hit her with anything else?'

'A belt.'

'Your belt?'

'No. She brought it with her. A man's belt.' He pulled a face. 'Do I really have to talk about this? I'm not proud of it.'

'I only have a few more questions,' I murmured, glad for once that I had Georgia with me, with her extensive knowledge of human relationships, instead of Josh Derwent and the way he raised his eyebrows at me. 'Did that happen often? Hitting her?'

'No. Not at all.' He thought briefly. 'I didn't think she liked it? I was glad she wasn't keen, to be completely honest. It wasn't doing anything for me.'

'Did you ever choke her?' I asked in the same coolly interested tone of voice, as if it wasn't particularly significant.

'No. It never came up and I didn't suggest it.' He shrugged. 'Look, it wasn't all that wild. We had sex. Sometimes she wanted to be spanked or punished – she made me call her names, pull her hair, that kind of thing. A bit kinky but the normal end of it. Mostly she just wanted to have fun. She was pretty clear on what she liked and what she didn't, so I went along with it.'

There was a clatter of footsteps on the stairs and Sam sprang up, instantly alarmed. 'Shit. Shit, she's back.'

'Who?' I was listening: a jangle of keys, someone singing. It was a fragment of *Les Misérables*.

'My girlfriend, Lora.' He looked around wildly, as if he could hide us. 'She's supposed to be at the theatre. She doesn't know about Ilaria.'

'That she's dead?' Georgia asked. 'Or that—'

The door was opening and, mercifully, Georgia cut herself off before Sam Blundell could lunge across and make her stop talking. Footsteps in the hall came closer and the girlfriend appeared in the doorway.

'Hi.' Lora looked at us with surprise and not a little suspicion. She was small, fair, very slim and seemed much younger than Sam Blundell. She was bundled up in a large scarf and a bulky fake fur coat that made her look as if she was playing dress-up in her mother's clothes.

'Darling.' Sam went over and kissed her. 'Did you lock up your bike?'

'Yes.' She looked at me. 'What's going on? Who are you?'

'We're police detectives,' I said, and stood. 'We were just finishing up here.'

'What's wrong? Has something happened?' Lora unwound the long scarf and slipped off her coat, staring at Sam instead of us, as if nothing else mattered. 'Are you all right?'

'I'm fine.'

'Did someone mug you? Did they get your phone?' She put a hand on his arm, looking up into his face with tragic, wide eyes. 'It doesn't matter as long as you're all right. My poor baby.'

Without her coat she looked less childlike: she was small but wiry with posture that was nothing short of perfect. She looked like a dancer, and she seemed totally in love with her cheating boyfriend. When she turned to me, I caught my breath at the small but unmistakable swell of her belly in her clinging dress. Sam's girlfriend was pregnant, which was one reason why he might be trying to avoid telling her what he'd been doing.

'No, it's not that. Look, we're almost finished.' Sam looked at the clock on the wall, as if it had betrayed him. 'I thought you had rehearsals all day. I didn't think you'd be home yet.'

'I wanted to see how you were.' Lora turned to me again. 'Is this about what happened at work? His hands?'

'It is about his hands.' That wasn't a total lie, I thought. I wasn't lying for Sam's sake, either. He might break Lora's heart but I wasn't going to be the one who wielded the hammer.

'It's been awful,' she said, tears welling along her lashes. 'You have no idea. He can barely cope. He's so brave and he doesn't complain but he's in agony.'

I nodded. 'Mr Blundell, we may need to talk to you again.'

'Anything. Any time. Happy to help.' He was gabbling, leading the way towards the door. It irritated me that he was looking pleased, as if I'd done him a favour.

'I don't understand. Why would you need to talk to him again?' Lora was frowning. I realised we hadn't the first idea of what he'd told her to account for his injuries.

'Sam can explain,' I said, and led Georgia out of the flat past him before she could blurt out the truth.

10

'That was nice of you,' Georgia said, skipping down the steps beside me. 'Did you like him?'

'No, not particularly.'

'So you're just in a good mood today.'

I eyed her, suspicious. 'What does that mean?'

'Well, Josh was thanking you for doing something for him, earlier.'

'That took a while to come back,' I observed.

She grinned. 'I was waiting for the right moment. What's going on? What have you done?'

'Nothing. My parents are helping out with Thomas. They've been missing him so when there was a chance to pick him up from school they were delighted.'

'They haven't been seeing him? I thought they babysat for Josh and Melissa a lot.'

'They used to.' *Please don't ask me for the details*, I thought. Even though Georgia was generally lacking in sensitivity, she took the hint, asking only, 'Is there any news about the diagnosis?'

'No.'

'Did you ask Josh?'

'Of course I did.'

'OK, *you* can say "of course" but I wouldn't have dared to ask him.' Georgia shook her head. 'He wouldn't tell me anything anyway.'

'He probably wouldn't,' I agreed. 'But don't take it personally. And it's not as if he shared anything with me.'

'No news is good news, I suppose. It's the worry, though. The not-knowing means you imagine the worst.'

She was often maddening but occasionally Georgia was exactly right. I felt my heart drop into the pit of my stomach, thinking about Thomas. I spent a lot of time not thinking about what might happen, and I certainly didn't want to discuss it with Georgia. I changed the subject.

'Thanks for coming with me to do that interview.'

'Not that I had much choice, but you're welcome. I didn't contribute a lot. I was more listening than talking.'

'That's important too. What did you make of him?'

'I only know what you told me about the case on the way over here but I thought he was telling the truth, assuming the timings match up. He included plenty of random details, as if he was remembering something that actually happened instead of trying to be convincing.'

I must have looked surprised because she laughed. 'That was something Josh told me to look out for when he was mentoring me – remember? It's a useful one. Sam sounded really sure of himself too.'

'What else?'

'Well, he definitely didn't love Ilaria. The sex sounded uninspiring and I wonder why he bothered.'

'He made it sound as if it was just good manners.'

Georgia pulled a face. 'I know sometimes you go along with things to be polite, but a ten-month affair is a big commitment, especially when you're in a relationship with someone you actually care about. He sounds so passive. And that doesn't fit in with the belt and the spanking, does it? He was submissive.'

'You think Ilaria was the dominant one? Maybe she used the belt on him and he didn't want to admit it to two female detectives.'

'Maybe.' Georgia was frowning. 'Did she seem keen on him? Had she made an effort?'

'Very much so.' I described the underwear and the way she had looked on her way to meet her death.

'You need to talk to someone who knows more about BDSM than I do.' She considered it. 'Hardy might be able to help.'

Hardy was Georgia's boyfriend, a psychologist. I gave her the raised-eyebrow look that Derwent would have given me and she blushed.

'He's not *into* it. But he knows all about things like that. He knows lots about everything.'

'Still going well?'

'Yes.' She grinned to herself, not giving me any details, which told me that it was really serious. She didn't talk about him much, whereas usually Georgia would have wanted to overshare. 'Anyway, what now? Are you going back to the office?'

I gave myself a mental shake. 'I think I'm going to head off. I'll just jump on the tube.'

She perked up, interested. 'Are you going out?'

'I have a date.'

'Do you?' Her voice was casual. 'Who is he?'

'No one you know.' I relented. 'His name is Owen Lord.'

'Solid name. How did you meet? Online dating?'

'No, actually. A friend of a friend. And that's all you're getting.'

She groaned, frustrated, but when I looked up her eyes were gleaming. 'Tell me everything tomorrow.'

'I might.' Even if it had gone badly, I thought, I might pretend it was amazing. That was a better story for everyone else. Anything to take some pressure off me.

'I miss this kind of thing,' Georgia said wistfully. 'Hardy and I are happy but I love the thrill of a new romance, you know?'

'What if I don't find it thrilling?'

Her face fell. 'Then you shouldn't be going on a date with him.'

'It's not that bad. I just . . .' I trailed off. 'He's nice.'

'That's a start.' The words were encouraging but her eyes were full of doubt, which probably reflected my own expression.

What was I doing?

I said goodbye and walked to the tube station feeling as if I was wearing lead-soled boots. Tiredness was hitting me hard. The last thing I wanted to do was get dressed up and go out on a date, of all the frivolous ways to occupy my time. And that was exactly why I needed to go, I told myself. Owen, who had made me laugh, who was shorter than me and didn't care, who had dark hair with a scattering of grey and a nice line in jokes. Owen, who dressed well and wore a watch that would get him mugged in about ten minutes in certain parts of London. Owen, who had found a way to ask me out without putting me in an awkward position. I had liked him when I met him, and Luke liked him, as a boss and as a friend. We would have fun.

I felt as if I was going to a funeral.

I hadn't really thought about the fact that it was rush hour, either, or factored in the serious delays that were afflicting the District line. I was going to be late, I thought, and felt myself tense up, as if it was a real problem and not something I could fix with a text message.

Catastrophe comes when you least expect it, and I should have known that, but I had no sense that anything at all was wrong when my phone rang. I was in the middle of the crowded platform, hoping against hope that the next train would be empty and going my way. The last three trains had been cancelled, and I was a long way from where I needed to be. The only positive was that West Kensington tube station was above ground, so I had both phone reception and fresh air while I waited in the swelling, jostling crowd. I had just been reminding myself that things could be worse when my phone hummed in my pocket. Out of habit I glanced at the screen before I answered it. When I saw it was my father, a tiny knot of worry drew itself tight inside my stomach. He never called me.

'Hello? Daddy?' The childish name for him came out of nowhere.

'Maeve.' His voice burst out of the phone, loud and panicked. 'Maeve?'

'Yes, it's me.' A train slid to a halt at the platform opposite, brakes squealing. I jammed my knuckle into my free ear and pressed the phone hard against the other one. 'Sorry, it's really loud here. Are you all right?'

'Maeve, I—' He broke off to hush someone who was making noise in the background.

'Daddy? Is everything all right?' I was cold all of a sudden. 'Is it Mummy?'

'No. No.'

'Is that Thomas?' I had forgotten for a moment that they were looking after him that afternoon. 'Is he *crying*?'

'It's Thomas.'

'What's wrong with him? Is he OK?'

'He's fine. You're fine, Thomas. Stop your whining, there's a good boy.' My father, infinitely patient, sounded almost irritable, and that made me more worried than anything else that had happened so far. I could hear a siren in the distance at his end of the call, and it was getting louder.

'Daddy, what's going on?'

'Maeve, my darling, I'm sorry . . .'

'What is it?'

The tone of his voice, his reluctance to get to the point. I knew what he was going to say, and I needed him to say it, but when he spoke I sank to my knees in the middle of the platform, careless of everything that was happening around me, forgetting about my date, my case, everything else. Two words only, but they brought my world crashing down around my ears.

'It's Josh.'

PART TWO

Interval

'I do perceive here a divided duty.'
Othello

11

'You are under arrest—' PC Anthony 'Gorgeous' Giorgios hooked one of the cuffs on and struggled to get the second into the correct position so he could lock it around the man's other wrist. It wasn't that he was fighting – not exactly – but he was fit and strong, and he had trouble written all over him, from the icy blue stare that suggested he was thinking of a hundred ways to rip Giorgios's head off to the way he moved. There was something about him that made the hair stand up on the back of Giorgios's neck, which was why Giorgios had taken the initiative and decided to arrest him.

'For *what*?' the man snapped.

'On suspicion of – of attempted murder—' He almost had the handcuffs on but at the last second the man made a small movement that could have been accidental, but wasn't, and Giorgios had to start again.

'Wait. You're jumping to conclusions here.'

'You do not have to say anything but it may harm your defence if you— Clarkey, a bit of help.' He shouldn't have to say it, he thought, feeling a droplet of sweat slide down his spine. Of course he was crewed with the laziest member of C team for this.

'I'm not resisting, for fuck's sake!'

Clarkey – PC Ben Clarke – grabbed the man's arm, at long last. 'I've got him.'

'No, you don't.' The man twisted in his grasp, a complicated shrug and twist, and somehow he was free again. 'You need to do your training again, mate. Also, why are you cuffing me in front? Asking for trouble. If you're going to cuff someone, do it behind their backs where they can't use the cuffs as a weapon. Not that I'm going to, because I'm not resisting arrest. You don't even need the cuffs.'

Gorgeous Giorgios wasn't falling for that, but he did take the man's point about cuffing him behind. He yanked the man's left arm behind his back and shoved him against the wall, holding him in place. 'Hand.'

'Yeah, you've trapped my arm in front of me, pal. Do you want to try that again?'

It was like being in training, Giorgios thought. That heavy sarcasm, the effortless wrong-footing. The one lesson he had absorbed fully was that it was essential to control the situation, and never lose face.

'Look, shut the fuck up.' He shoved him against the wall, hard, so he made a low sound through gritted teeth. Giorgios's body-worn camera would show that he had been firm but not rough, which was all right. They were allowed to use force when they needed to, even if members of the public didn't expect it. 'Hand. And no messing around this time.'

The man brought his right hand around and Giorgios snapped the second cuff onto his wrist. There was blood all over his fingers, smudged on his palms, streaked on his arms. The front of his shirt, as Giorgios had noted immediately when he arrived at the address, was saturated.

'Right. As I was saying, you are under arrest on suspicion of attempted murder. You do not have to say anything but it may harm your defence if you do not mention when questioned something which you later rely on in court. Anything you do say may be given in evidence.' He gabbled the caution, running the words together.

'Do you really think it's worth starting the clock when you don't know the first thing about what happened? You don't even have anyone from CID here yet and from when I walk into the nick they've only got twenty-four hours to charge me or let me go. You must know this stuff, mate, it's what you're supposed to learn on day one.'

'I can see you're covered in blood, *mate*, and I've seen the state of your wife. And you were trying to leave the premises.'

'Not my wife. And I was trying to go with her in the fucking ambulance,' he snarled. He was still facing the wall, which

Giorgios actually preferred. It was easier to deal with him when he wasn't giving them that straight-browed, hostile look. His jacket was on the floor by the front door and Clarkey picked it up, patting the pockets.

'Left trouser pocket,' the man said. 'My wallet's in there. And you should be searching me, right now, for anything I might have on me that could hurt you.'

'Is there anything I should know about? Anything that could cause me grief?'

'Only what's in the wallet.'

Giorgios wasn't an imaginative person but a couple of times in his life he had felt a faint shiver of doom pass over him when he realised that he had made a mistake, that his judgement had let him down. Once was in school, on a ledge on the third floor, climbing from one window to another to win a bet. Once was on holiday in Ibiza when he'd gone on a trip with an unlicensed speedboat operator and fallen overboard two miles offshore. He had the same feeling now as Clarkey took out the wallet and flipped it open, then showed it to him.

'You're Met,' Giorgios said.

'You couldn't tell?'

'A detective inspector. Inspector Josh Derwent.' Clarkey looked as if he was going to throw up, which was all they needed. 'Where do you work, sir?'

'Based in Westminster but I go anywhere the Met needs me to go. I'm on a murder squad.'

Giorgios swallowed. 'Well, in that case, you know why I've arrested you.'

'Oh, I know why you arrested me. Can I turn around?'

'Yeah.' Giorgios took a step back, still wary. 'Clarkey, can you give the guv a ring? Let him know where we are.' *And that we've arrested a fucking* DI *by accident.* 'Ask them to send a van too.'

Josh Derwent looked tired, when he faced him, rather than arrogant or angry. There was a red mark on his jaw, where he had collided with the wall.

Shit, Giorgios thought. *Shit.*

But when he spoke, he sounded entirely reasonable. 'Look, you got here five minutes ago. You haven't had a chance to work out what happened. Let me tell you what I know and then you can de-arrest me and call in the detectives and let them decide what to do from here. But if it could include getting me out of these cuffs so I can go to the hospital to be with Melissa, I'd be grateful.' He looked past Giorgios to the crowd of neighbours who had gathered on the opposite side of the road, and a muscle tightened in his cheek. 'And do we have to do this out here, in full view of everyone?'

Giorgios ignored that. It was a nice middle-class neighbourhood full of respectable 1930s terraced houses, including this one, and it would be big news that the man at number 23 had been arrested, but that wasn't his problem.

'Start at the beginning.'

He took a deep breath before he answered, and Giorgios wondered why it was more unsettling for him to be so outwardly calm instead of raging at them. 'OK. Well, I got here not long after five. I was in the office today but I was able to leave work early so I could get home. I'd arranged that my girlfriend's son would arrive here at half past five – which is in five minutes, so please, if you could uncuff me before he gets here—'

'Go on. You got here and what?'

He swallowed. 'Right. I parked the car on the drive, as you can see. I walked up to the door and let myself in. I didn't notice anything strange outside. The door was secure and closed but it opened with the Yale lock, as I'd expected. The second lock wasn't in use. My . . . Melissa, was supposed to be at home but she was working this afternoon, so I thought she'd be upstairs.'

'What does Melissa do?'

'She's a psychotherapist. She sees clients here. She has a room on the first floor for that, so I thought she'd be up there.' His face was pale and Giorgios thought of what had greeted him instead. In spite of himself, for a moment he felt sorry for the inspector.

'As soon as I opened the door, I saw her.' He paused, staring into the distance with eyes that saw nothing. 'She was lying at the bottom of the stairs and she was covered in blood. I went to see if she was breathing, first of all, and checked for a pulse, and I realised she was alive.' His voice broke a little and he cleared his throat. 'I had my phone on me so I called it in before I did anything else. She was lying on her back and she wasn't breathing too well, so I moved her into the recovery position. I was supporting her head. I got a lot of blood on my clothes doing that. The dispatcher can tell you – she probably heard me doing it. Then I stayed with Melissa while I was waiting for the paramedics to get here. I held her hand and talked to her. I didn't know if she could hear me but I wanted to reassure her.'

'What happened when the paramedics got here?'

'They treated her. I stayed out of the way. I was looking to see if there were any signs of a break-in at the rear of the house or upstairs.'

Giorgios had spoken to one of them before they'd left with Melissa, a woman who had described Josh Derwent as 'beside himself' which was quite the contrast with the slow, measured description he was giving of his actions.

'And did you find any signs of a break-in?'

His face darkened. 'No.'

'So she was just here, injured.'

'Yes. I thought at first she had fallen down the stairs, but someone did this to her. Someone beat her.' He stared at Giorgios, his eyes cold. 'I would like very much to find out who it was.'

'Right. Well I'm satisfied we need to take you to the nick so you can talk to our detectives. You've got a lot of blood on you and, as you said, there's no sign of a break-in so we have to assume your girlfriend was injured by someone she knew.'

He gritted his teeth. 'This is only going to waste time.'

'Let us worry about that. You worry about yourself.'

'I'm not worried about myself,' Josh Derwent said, his eyes tracking a car that was sliding to a stop on the road. 'Look, Melissa's son is here now. He's only eight. He's going to want to know where his mother is and what's happening here. Please, can I talk to him?'

'I don't think that's a good idea.'

'Why not?' His jaw was clenched now, his temper slipping. 'I want to reassure him. He won't know what's going on.'

'Stay there, please,' Giorgios called, and the elderly man who had got out of the car stopped at the end of the driveway, his face puckered with worry. The boy beside him was pale and thin, small for his age, and looked at Giorgios with wide, terrified eyes.

'Then take me inside. If I can't talk to him, I don't want him to see me like this.'

'All right,' Giorgios said, not finding a reason to say no. He took hold of the other man's arm and Derwent leaned past him.

'Seán, can you hang on to Thomas? Take him home to your house for now.'

'What – what happened?' He reached down and took the boy's hand.

'I'll try and get everything sorted out so I can come and get him. This officer will tell you what's happened.' He threw a look at Giorgios that was, for the first time, a plea. *Don't make me shout the information that Thomas's mother is in hospital.*

'Of course,' Giorgios said. 'When the boy is in the car.'

'Thank you.' He was still resisting the pressure that Giorgios was putting on his arm though, still lingering before he disappeared through the doorway.

'Everything is going to be all right, Thomas.'

The boy nodded, looking terrified. His lower lip quivered and the man with him squeezed his hand.

'Come on.' Giorgios was beginning to get annoyed. 'Are you going in or not?'

'One more thing. Seán, I need you to tell Maeve.' Josh Derwent paused for a second, his face white. He swallowed, and tried again. 'Just tell Maeve . . .'

12

I cancelled the date.

From the moment the phone call with my dad ended, once I'd pulled myself together, I was absolutely focused. I walked out of the tube station, cutting through the crowd, and found a quiet corner. Without even thinking, on autopilot, I made a call to Una Burt and told her what I knew: that something had happened to Melissa, that she was in hospital, that Derwent had been arrested.

'Christ,' Una said, which was not like her, and 'How do you know?' which was.

'My dad was there. He called me.' I heard an intake of breath from her end and ignored it. 'Look, I have to see if I can help. My dad has Thomas with him – I can't leave my parents to sort this out by themselves.'

'What about Ilaria Cavendish?'

'I've spoken to the main suspect.' I tried to think of anything to say about the case and came up with nothing. 'It's all fine. Progressing.'

'I understand that you're worried.' She sounded as if she was choosing her words carefully, which was unusual too. 'I can't let you lose yourself in Josh's problems when there's a murder investigation that is now missing its SIO, since I have to assume Josh is not going to be available for the foreseeable future. We're stretched so thin as it is. I don't have the staff to let you walk away from it too.'

I squeezed my eyes closed. 'I'm not. I'll be at work tomorrow morning, as scheduled.'

'And if something comes up in the meantime?'

'Um . . . Liv and Georgia are available. They can call me. I don't think there's anything urgent, though. We're nowhere near making an arrest.'

An arrest.

Josh.

They must be sure of themselves if they had arrested him.

I thought of his face when he was on the phone to Melissa and how he had seemed to me like someone reaching the end of their tether. But it had to be a mistake. It couldn't be anything else.

'It's about priorities, Maeve.' Burt's voice sounded as if it was coming from a long way off. Was I going to faint? I stood up straight and took a deep breath, trying to focus on her voice. Maybe it was my fault. I had wanted to sound calm when I spoke to her. Maybe she didn't understand how serious it was. Maybe she thought I didn't care.

'I imagine they'll be in touch with me to let me know he's been arrested,' Una went on, 'but if you hear anything – anything at all – I want to know it straight away. I don't like being out of the loop.'

'I know.'

'And Maeve – I'm sorry.'

Sorry this has happened; sorry you're involved; sorry I can't help.

Also, sorry you're upset, but what do you expect when you care about a man like that?

She was too much of a professional to assume that there was no good reason for Derwent to be arrested, and she was far from his biggest fan at the best of times. Better not to challenge her even though I longed to ask how she could believe he would ever do anything like that. My teeth were clenched so hard that my jaw ached as I said goodbye.

West Kensington to my parents' house in South London was a long way, no matter how you did it, but with the trains snarled it was impossible by public transport. I called Georgia, even though I knew she would be long gone.

Providentially, she was two streets away.

'What are you still doing here?' I asked, as if that mattered.

'I had to do some shopping before I went home.' She sounded wary. 'I'm not in trouble, am I? I didn't think anyone would mind.'

'Something's happened. Can I take the car?'

'Of course.'

I ended the call and ran all the way to where she was standing beside the car on the pavement, the wind blowing her hair across her face.

'Are you going to the office? I can come with you.'

'No. No – I have to see my parents.' I couldn't tell her what had happened, I discovered: the words were jammed in my throat, painfully, and wouldn't come out of my mouth. 'I can't talk about it now. The boss can fill you in.'

'OK.' Georgia's eyes were wide, as if it definitely wasn't OK from the look on my face, but there was nothing I could do about that. I took the keys, jumped into the car and raced down to Sutton through every shortcut I could find, like a minicab driver with something to prove.

They saw me parking outside the house and Mum waved from the window. Dad came out, all the way to the side of the road. He looked fragile, as if he had aged ten years in an afternoon.

'Maeve . . .' He put his arms around me for a moment and held me, and he wasn't generally demonstrative. It almost undid me.

'What happened?'

'It's bad.' He touched a hand to his forehead, looking shaken. 'We didn't see her. We got there after the ambulance had left. They said she was unconscious.'

'Does Thomas know?'

'He knows some of it. He's very quiet.'

'He is anyway,' I said, and Dad shook his head.

'Not like this.'

'Was there a break-in?'

'Apparently not.' He leaned on the car. 'The policeman who talked to me said Josh came home and found her in the hall.'

'And she'd been beaten.'

'That's what he said. They took her off to hospital awful quick, Maeve. I'd say she was in a bad way.'

I felt sick.

'Which hospital?'

'St Michael's.'

It was the nearest accident and emergency department. At least they hadn't taken her to one of the major trauma centres; there were bigger hospitals for more complicated cases.

'Is there any way you could find out how she is?' Dad asked, tentative.

'I'll try.' I imagined Melissa lying there, vulnerable, on her own. Melissa wasn't my favourite person, but I thought Derwent would want me to check on her. 'Did she have anyone with her?'

'Someone went in the ambulance, apparently. A friend.'

'That's something.' I dropped her down my mental list of things I needed to worry about, which pushed Thomas right back to the top. 'I just keep thinking about what Josh would do if he was here and I think he'd want to make sure Thomas was all right.'

'Of course.'

'Did the police take your contact details at the scene?'

'They said social services would be in touch.'

He sounded grim and I felt my stomach drop. 'We should try to avoid that if we can.'

'Understandably they didn't want to leave him with us when they found out we weren't family. And Josh isn't Thomas's legal guardian, so . . .' My father trailed off and lifted his hands in a helpless gesture that twisted my heart.

'Right. Well, I don't think he's going to need a foster placement. There's Thomas's grandmother, for starters . . . and his biological father,' I added, with some reluctance. 'He should probably know about Melissa.'

Mark Pell, Thomas's father, the man Melissa had fled in terror, which had brought her into Derwent's life. He had never been convicted of being violent towards her, so Melissa had had to fight through the family courts to keep Thomas away from him, with varying degrees of success.

'Would he be allowed to take him?'

'Mark has got unsupervised visits every other weekend now. He's been pushing for more time with Thomas.' I hesitated. 'Josh doesn't like him.'

'Not surprising,' Dad said, and didn't clarify whether he meant it was because Mark and Melissa had been married and Derwent was jealous, or because Mark had tried to take Thomas away from her and therefore Derwent, who adored him.

'Do you think the police know about Mark? He'd be my choice for an early interview. He and Melissa barely speak, unless it's through their lawyers, and I know he's been frustrated with her in the last few months. They were in court again not that long ago.'

'You could tell them about him.'

I chewed the edge of my thumb. 'Hopefully they'll get there on their own. Josh will tell them. He'll be drawing up a list of suspects now, if he has nothing better to do.'

'If they listen.'

'They will.' I said it without conviction, though. Diplomacy wasn't Derwent's strongest trait, particularly when he was under pressure. He would be *furious* about being arrested.

Dad touched my arm gently. 'We should go in. Your mother will be waiting. And Thomas.'

'And Thomas,' I repeated, and squared my shoulders. What was needed from me at this moment was confidence, and if I didn't feel it, I would just have to fake it.

Thomas was sitting beside my mother on the sofa, watching television. An untouched sandwich sat on a plate beside him.

'Eating on the sofa, Thomas? I was never allowed to get away with that.'

He looked up and gave me a quick, preoccupied smile, and my heart gave another, vicious twist.

'How are you feeling, pal?'

'Yeah. OK.' A small voice. He looked tiny for his age, thin and fragile, his legs like sticks in his school trousers.

'He's feeling a bit peaky,' my mother said, and brushed the hair out of his eyes. 'I made the sandwich, but he hasn't touched it.'

'I'm not hungry.'

'But you're not sick? You'll tell us if you feel worse, won't you, Thomas?'

'Yeah.' A thread of a sound.

'What about sausages for tea?' my mother suggested. 'And some beans? And a few chips? And ice cream afterwards?'

I thought about explaining to Thomas that food was my mother's way of showing love, but from the smile he gave her, he knew.

'Sausages.' My father rubbed his hands together, his eyes gleaming. 'And I thought I was getting bread and scrape for my dinner.'

Thomas giggled, and then ducked his head, as if he was ashamed.

'Tough day.' I moved the plate to sit down beside him and put my arm around his shoulders. He leaned into my side and gave a massive sigh.

'Is Mummy OK?'

'I don't know yet, but I'm going to find out.'

His hand was on mine and he squeezed it, urgently. 'And Josh.'

'He's a muppet for getting himself arrested, isn't he? If anyone should know better, he should.'

'Yeah, he should have told them not to arrest him.'

'I bet he did. But I also bet he wasn't very polite. He can be very rude.'

Thomas grinned. 'Sometimes he says rude things in the car, when he's driving.'

'He does that when I'm in the car too.'

'Mummy doesn't like it.' A husky little whisper. He looked down, his eyelashes fanned out over his cheeks.

'Well, she's right about that. We can't have you learning bad words.'

'People say them in school.' He looked up with a gleam of excitement. '*All* the bad words.'

'I'm shocked. Don't say them in front of these two.' I indicated my parents. 'They'd faint.'

'Sure I wouldn't even understand them,' my mother said, her face saintly, and I rolled my eyes at her over Thomas's head. I had learned all of my swearing from her: baking was one trigger and my brother was another.

'Thomas, I don't think your mum and Josh are going to be home for a few hours. Would you like your nana to come and collect you?'

'I want to stay here.' He thought about it. 'But I wish she was here too.'

'We'll see what we can do.' I looked at my mother again and she patted his knee.

'There's room for her to stay. How's that? She can have the guest room and you can be in Maeve's old room.'

'Yessss.' He bounced up and down.

'I'll go and call her.' Ellen Moore had moved from Lincolnshire to Ascot, I recalled. It would take her a while to get to my parents' house, but I knew she would come – for her daughter's sake, and for Thomas.

Phone call made, I was in the hall, pulling on my coat.

'Are you off, love?' My dad was still looking worried.

'Yes. Mrs Moore is on her way. I'm heading to the hospital but first I want to go to Josh's house and see what I can find out. With any luck I'll be able to speak to the detectives and find out what they're thinking.' I was glad I had a plan. It gave me something to do with the adrenaline that had been hanging around my system sourly since West Kensington. I needed to know what had happened so I could stop imagining scenarios where Derwent had come home and snapped, where he had lost his temper and lashed out at his tormentor – where he was so desperate to escape her that he had lost his grip on his self-control.

Then again, what self-control? He had been demonstrating all too clearly that it was shaky, that he was coming apart at the seams. I remembered him reaching for me in the lift, and snapping at me in the hotel, and following me to the post-mortem. I felt sick. But he couldn't have hurt her. I knew him well enough to be sure he wasn't capable of that.

I shook it off and smiled at my father.

'You know, you need to work on your phone manner. When you called me, I thought it was the end of the world.'

He looked more distressed, not less. 'It's serious, Maeve.'

'Yes, but Josh isn't dead, which is what I thought first.'

'He could lose his job over it and I know what that would do to you.'

I shook my head. 'He won't.'

'It's a possibility.'

'No. I can fix this.'

'Maeve . . .' My father ground to a halt, grasping for words. 'I should tell you what Josh said – before they took him away from us. The last thing he said.'

I stopped. 'Go on.'

Something about the way he was speaking – as if it was difficult, as if he wished he didn't have to say it . . .

'He said to tell you.'

I went on with buttoning my coat, the rush of relief making me feel slightly giddy. 'Well, of course. He'd know I'd want to know. And anyway, he needs me to sort it out for him.'

'No, love. He said to tell you . . . not to get involved.'

The smile died on my face. 'What did he say? The exact words.'

'"Tell Maeve not to come here. Tell her to stay out of it,"' Dad quoted, shamefaced. He knew how it sounded. He knew how it would make me feel. And he also knew that he had to finish saying it, and of course the last words were the worst part.

'He said, "I don't want her here."'

13

I went to the house in Jena Road anyway, whether Derwent would have wanted me there or not. I wasn't sure anymore whether I was more anxious about him or furious with him, but either way, I couldn't stay at home and let his life fall apart without at least trying to help him. It wasn't the first time I'd gone to his rescue, but he would have done the same for me, and had, and more. Why he didn't want me to be involved – why he had specifically said as much to my father – I couldn't understand. Unless, of course, it was because he didn't want me to know what he had done.

Impossible, I told myself, as I parked behind a silver Nissan Micra that was just about not blocking number 45's drive, then walked back to Derwent's house, number 23, trying to keep a low profile. A forensic van was parked outside it, which gave me a frisson of unease: there was nothing as unsettling as seeing somewhere you knew treated like a crime scene. Someone had slung police tape across the driveway and I ducked under it, glad that the local rubberneckers seemed to have found somewhere better to be. It would have been big news that something terrible had happened, even if they liked Melissa and Josh – even if they were shocked to see him marched away in handcuffs.

The front door was open and I slipped inside, hearing voices from the kitchen. I paused for a moment in the hall, looking at the horror story told in swirls of blood on the wooden floor at the base of the stairs. There was a dent in the plaster halfway down the stairs. Maybe Melissa had tripped. Maybe this was all a terrible accident.

'Can I help you?'

I turned with my warrant card in my hand and saw a tall Black man in an elegant suit. His face was unwelcoming, which was understandable since I was standing in the middle of his crime scene. 'Sorry, there was no scene guard outside.'

'We let them go. We're pretty much done here. The forensics guys are finishing up.' At the sight of the warrant card, he had relaxed. He was strikingly handsome, and somehow familiar. 'Are you local CID? I thought you were a journalist.'

'No, not a journalist.' I hesitated. 'And not local CID either. I work with Josh Derwent. I'm a DS on the same team.'

If he had been local CID himself, he'd have known I wasn't, which meant that the Department of Professional Standards had already arrived. If I was ever going to lie to anyone about who I was and what I did, I wasn't going to start with a detective from the DPS, but part of me wished I'd taken the chance.

He frowned again, and something clicked in my mind.

'I know you.'

'What?' He was genuinely surprised.

I was chasing down the memory. 'I met you, years ago. You might not remember – it was a strange one. A computer geek who was tortured to death above a laundrette.' The detective's name was hovering on the edge of my memory. 'You were Brixton CID.'

'That's right.' He shook my hand, his manner noticeably warmer. 'Henry Cowell. I'm sorry I didn't remember you.'

'Don't worry – I just have that kind of mind. I'm Maeve Kerrigan. I was a DC then.'

'Yeah, it's coming back to me.' His smile faded. 'That case was really unpleasant. It put me off murders.'

'Whereas I've never moved on,' I said. 'And now you're DPS.'

'Yeah.' He sounded wary. Most police officers regarded the DPS as a necessary evil, but that didn't mean they liked the cops who chose to work in that area, investigating their colleagues. 'It was an opportunity. I needed to go somewhere after I passed the sergeants' exam.'

It was common for people to change jobs to find a sergeant's position. I had been able to stay where I was because my then boss Superintendent Godley wouldn't let me go anywhere else. If it hadn't been for him, I would have struggled. I hadn't been a good fit with the other members of the team when I'd met Henry Cowell – the only woman, and young, and too inexperienced to be diplomatic in telling other detectives they'd made mistakes. I had been lucky, and Henry Cowell had not.

'I bet it's interesting,' I said, keeping things neutral, and he nodded.

'It has its moments.' A beat. 'What are you doing here? You said you work with Josh Derwent?'

'Yes.' I wondered if I should remind Cowell that he'd met Derwent too, on that day so long ago. It was during the time when he'd made the opposite of a good impression on most people, including me. 'Look, it's a weird coincidence but the boy – Melissa's son – he was spending the afternoon with my parents.'

'And you came to get something for the son?'

I could have said yes and left it at that. 'I came to get him some clothes and a toothbrush, but I also wanted to find out how Melissa is.'

'She's being assessed.'

'No update from the hospital?'

'Not yet.'

'Look, I also wanted to see what happened here for myself because I can't believe that Josh had anything to do with it.'

'Because he's such a good person?' The question came from a woman who had come to the kitchen door to see who Cowell was talking to, and it was edged so sharply with sarcasm that I physically flinched. The new arrival had the light behind her, and the advantage of me.

'Because it would be out of character,' I said. 'I've known him for years and this surprises me.'

'That happens. Sorry, who are you?'

'I'm Maeve Kerrigan – I work with Josh. I'm a DS on his team.'

'She's here to pick up some stuff for the kid,' Henry Cowell explained. 'He's with her parents.'

'You can take her upstairs. Watch her pack.' She checked her watch. 'We need to get a move on.'

'Yes, the clock is ticking,' I said, irritated by her manner. 'It almost makes you wonder if someone jumped the gun by arresting him.'

'I think it was a good call,' she flashed back, stepping into the light so I could see her clearly. She was a couple of inches shorter than me, with wide cheekbones and a triangular bob of fluffy light-brown hair, wavy rather than curly. She had brown eyes and a small round mouth that gave her the pretty-doll look of a silent film star. She stood without fidgeting, assessing me in the same way I was eyeing her, as I ticked off the similarities between us: neutral clothing, practical boots, discreet jewellery, minimal make-up. The uniform of the professional woman who wants to be taken seriously.

'I didn't get your name.'

'Roz Fuller.' There was no hint of friendliness in her face. And I needed her to like me, for Derwent's sake. I tried a smile.

'Look, you've just come into this. I don't want to get in your way. You have to draw your own conclusions from the evidence, and I understand that. But I think that when you speak to Josh, you'll see he's not that kind of person.'

'What kind?'

'The kind to lash out.'

She raised her eyebrows, amused. 'This is the same Josh Derwent who was in the army and left because he couldn't hack the discipline.'

'He told me he left because he realised there was more to life than the army,' I said levelly. 'He hadn't taken his A levels so he went back and did that, and then he joined the Met.'

'Does he seem to you like the kind of person who's good at following orders?'

If he thinks they're a good idea, then yes.

'He's never going to be someone who goes into a situation without thinking about it,' I said. 'And sometimes he challenges people who want him to do something that he disagrees with.

He still understands how to play his part in a hierarchical organisation like the Met.'

She exchanged a meaningful look with Cowell. 'That's a very diplomatic way of confirming what we've heard from his boss.'

'Superintendent Burt?' Una and Derwent had clashed from day one. I quailed internally. 'They have a very different approach to the job, but ultimately that means they get results.'

'Again, diplomatic.' She smiled. 'Luckily I can read between the lines.'

'You know, you should ask Charles Godley what he thinks of Josh. He brought him onto my team. He'll give you a very clear idea of what he's like and why he couldn't have done anything to Melissa.' Godley, an old friend of Derwent's, was now Assistant Commissioner. It was a hell of a name to drop, and I did it with my fingers crossed that it would help instead of putting Roz Fuller's back up.

She lowered her eyelids, hiding whatever she was thinking, then retorted, 'Josh Derwent has a history of complaints – did you know that? From members of the public and from colleagues.'

'They can't have been that serious if he's still an inspector,' I pointed out. 'He's the kind of person who likes to provoke a reaction from people. It's one of the things that makes him good at the job.'

'There are ways of getting results and some of them belong in the dark ages. Does he ever cross the line?'

'No.' Not *exactly*, I thought. 'If you're doing the job properly, you're going to clash with people. Vexatious complaints are part of life.'

'Have you had many? I haven't.'

'Well, you're not really public-facing. You're not going to come across the kind of people who don't like the police. They'll take any opportunity to complain about us and what we do.' I could hear the stress in my voice and I stopped to gather myself together. Roz Fuller was watching me. She reminded me of someone but I didn't dare distract myself by working out who.

'Josh is good at what he does. He gets results. He keeps to the rules.' At least, now he does, I thought, mentally discarding the many occasions when he had done nothing of the kind. 'I've worked with him for a long time and I know he's a good police officer. And if he's the kind of person who gets complaints made against him, isn't it possible that he's annoyed someone? Maybe one of them found out where he lives and wanted to hurt him, but settled for attacking Melissa.'

She didn't nod in agreement, but she didn't turn away either. 'We have to think about how he is when he's not at work.'

'I sort of know that too.'

Her eyebrows slid up. 'Oh?'

'We were undercover together in the summer, last year. We were pretending to be a couple. We lived together for a few weeks.'

'It's hardly the same as being in a relationship with someone.'

It's as close as we got, I thought and didn't say.

'It gives me a little more insight than I'd have otherwise. That and the fact that we're friends. I probably know him better than anyone.' I braced myself, not wanting to give her the next piece of the picture, knowing that it had to be said. 'When my ex beat me up, Josh came and found me. He saved me from whatever else my ex had planned to do to me. He saw how much it affected me, and he was upset by it. He's the last person who would want to harm someone weaker than him. I've heard him talk to Melissa when he didn't know I was listening, and he was patient and kind. I've seen them together, many times. I don't know everything about their relationship, but I know she loves him. If it's true that he hurt her, then I don't know him and if I don't know him, I don't know anyone.'

After I finished speaking the silence felt dense.

'That's interesting. Thank you.' She said it very much as if it was me she found to be of interest, and not anything that I'd said to her. 'I'm glad I got to talk to you. You would have been on my list.'

I wasn't sure I'd done any good. 'You've made up your mind already.'

'No. But I will tell you this. From what I've heard so far – from his background, the history of complaints against him, from what I've been told by people who work with him – I think Josh Derwent is exactly the kind of police officer who can snap without warning. They keep a lid on their feelings for years and once that comes off, they can't control themselves.'

I thought of what had happened in the lift and felt a wave of fear roll through me. I hoped I'd hidden it from Roz Fuller.

'He sounds like someone you care about very much,' she went on, not unkindly, 'but he also sounds like someone who has always got away with bad behaviour because people like you cover for him. Unfortunately for him, you can't do anything to help him now. He's on his own.' She turned to Henry Cowell. 'I'm going to make a phone call. Can you help – Maeve? – to get what she needs for the boy and then lock up here? I'll see you at the car.'

I followed Henry Cowell upstairs, not touching anything, trying to take in every detail I could of the house as I passed through it, but my mind was hazy with fear and uncertainty. I had realised something while Roz Fuller was laying out the reasons Derwent was a credible suspect.

The person she reminded me of was me.

14

Henry Cowell stood in the hallway outside Thomas's bedroom, looking everywhere except at me.

'Aren't you supposed to be watching me in case I pocket some vital evidence?'

'Yeah. Sorry about that.' He dragged his eyes to mine, reluctance visible. 'You know we have to be careful.'

'You can't trust anyone these days,' I said, trying to keep my tone light. 'Which you would know, of course.'

'She's good at what she does,' he said abruptly. 'In case you were wondering.'

I knew he meant Roz Fuller. She was outside in their car, on the phone, and safely out of earshot.

'She's terrifying,' I said frankly, folding a T-shirt. 'And she didn't listen to a word I said.'

'No, she did. But she won't take it at face value. She'll follow up on everything and then form her own judgement.' He shrugged. 'It's one of the things that I like about working with her. She goes the extra mile.'

'In other circumstances, I'd be delighted she's so dedicated,' I said dryly. 'As it is, I hate to see her wasting time on Josh for this when he couldn't have done it.'

'Couldn't?'

'Wouldn't.' I hesitated. 'Downstairs . . . there was a lot of blood.'

'A head injury. The victim bled a lot.'

'Could it have been an accident? If Melissa fell and banged her head?'

'I haven't seen her yet,' Cowell said. 'But I have to tell you, what we were told was multiple injuries. Contusions. What the paramedics said was that she'd been beaten up.'

'Poor Melissa.' I sat down on the edge of Thomas's bed and stared unseeingly at the sweatshirt I was holding.

'Do you like her?'

'I don't know her very well,' I hedged.

'From what you know of her.'

There was absolutely no point in pretending; all I could do by lying was shatter the fragile trust I was building with Henry Cowell. I sighed. 'Look, it's difficult. You'll find this out from someone else anyway, and I want to be honest with you, so I'll tell you the truth. She was convinced that Josh and I were having an affair.'

He didn't react in any way that I could see, so maybe he had known all along. 'And were you?'

'No. Absolutely not. Josh wouldn't have considered it. Neither would I.'

'Sure about that?'

'Nothing ever happened.'

He raised his eyebrows. 'Nothing?'

'Basically nothing.' I knew my face was hot. 'I really care about him though, as a friend.' Emphasis on *friend*. 'He's a good man.'

'Melissa didn't seem to think that. She called 999 on him a few months ago.'

'Oh, I remember that.' I frowned. 'They had disagreed about something, and she locked him out of the house.'

I had a fairly good idea of what they had disagreed about but I wasn't prepared to hand that kind of information to Cowell for no reason when it could turn into a motive. She had told Derwent that if he ended their relationship, she wouldn't let him see Thomas again, something that still made my hackles rise.

'And called the police?'

'I don't know why she did that. They didn't have a fight, because she wouldn't talk to him. He gave up. He was leaving when the officers turned up.'

'Is that what he told you?'

I remembered exactly what he'd told me.

Did Melissa think you were going to hurt her?

I can't tell you what she thought. I would never hurt her. She knows that. And so should you.

'That's not what happened?'

Cowell kept me waiting for a long minute before he replied. 'More or less my understanding. We're looking into it. Obviously it's of interest.'

'Obviously,' I agreed, because it would be. 'I'd look at that too.'

'You should be aware that if the media find out there was police contact because of a domestic argument at this address, he'll be burned at the stake no matter what happens with our investigation.' And rightly, his tone seemed to suggest.

'Melissa was hurt by her ex-husband. Mark Pell. She ran away from him. He was violent and abusive. I've had . . . bad experiences myself so I know how you can see a threat in a situation where you're perfectly safe.'

'You think she overreacted.'

'You're putting words in my mouth. I think it's natural that she would be fearful of the same thing happening again. And you shouldn't discount the possibility that someone had a grudge against Josh. Or Melissa.' I snapped my fingers. 'I mean, there is her ex-husband. They've been at each other's throats over custody of Thomas. He's a good place to start.'

'I promise we'll keep an open mind.'

'Will you?' I bit my lip. 'It's only that he's an inspector. You'd get a lot of positive attention for getting rid of him. It's human nature to think about how something like this might advance your careers.'

'That's not how we work. We go on the evidence, same as you.' Cowell leaned against the doorframe. 'I remember him, you know. As soon as you said it, I remembered that day and that place. I have a clearer memory of him than of you.'

'Well, he probably did more of the talking. I presume you remember him in a good way?' I was hoping against hope with that one.

'He was clearly an arrogant bastard, but there was something about him. He was quick to get his head around what had happened there, and he was good at talking to the victim's wife when she turned up. I envied you that you got to work with him. I thought it would be hard going, but you'd learn a lot.'

I nodded.

'And he listened when you talked.' Cowell gave me a lopsided smile. 'One of the reasons I moved on was because no one in my old job ever paid any attention to anything I said. He might have given you a hard time, but he cared about what you thought.'

The lump in my throat made it hard to speak. 'That was the first time we ever worked together.'

'Really? You seemed like you were a good team already.' He shrugged. 'Goes to show you can't always tell.'

'No, I think you were right. We were good at working together from the very start.' I tried to smile. 'It just took me a while to appreciate his qualities.'

I called Una Burt myself, once I'd left the house. Cowell had shadowed me to my car so there was no opportunity to look around. Everything seemed normal, though, apart from the blood in the hall. Melissa had let someone in and they attacked her, I thought. She must have. Someone she knew, or someone who talked their way in.

It couldn't have been Derwent.

'Well?'

'I don't have a lot to report,' I said carefully.

'Forget my rank and tell me what really happened.' Una sounded almost human.

'I spoke to the DPS officers who are investigating the attack on Melissa.'

'That was not what I wanted to hear.'

'I didn't mean to. They were at Derwent's house when I got there.'

'Why were you even there?'

'Picking up some clothes and books for Thomas. He didn't have anything with him.' Thank God for Thomas. 'Did you talk to the officers about Josh?'

'I spoke to Roz Fuller.'

'What did you say to her? She sort of implied you'd said he was unreliable and undisciplined.' I watched through the windscreen as Cowell joined Roz in their car and they drove away. They would be going to talk to Derwent, I thought, with a pang of longing that left me dry-mouthed.

'I gave her my views on him as a member of the team. I told her he could be argumentative and sulky when he didn't get his own way. I told her I found him challenging when I first took over from Charlie and started running the team, but you knew that.'

I did. He had been a nightmare for her. I gave a small, unhappy sigh.

'But Maeve, I also told her that I'd come to realise he saved me from making some big mistakes when I first took over, and that what I'd seen as him being obstructive was actually helpful in the long run.'

I blinked. 'I never thought I'd hear you say anything nice about him.'

'I do try to be fair.'

'I think you make him better at doing his job too,' I offered, knowing that Derwent would be furious at the very suggestion. There was something to be said for him being safely tucked away in a custody suite.

'I'd like to think so. I try to rein him in. When I took over, Charlie told me he would be my biggest asset and my greatest problem, and so it's turned out.'

'What did the boss tell you about me?'

I could hear the smile in her voice. 'I thought you might ask that. I can't tell you, I'm afraid.' She paused. 'But he did say something that feels relevant. He said you never held back and you were prepared to sacrifice yourself for what was right. He told me my job was to keep you from getting yourself into a bad situation for a good reason, and this certainly counts. You are not to get involved in this when it's not your fight.'

'I'm already involved. I can't just walk away and pretend nothing is happening.'

'I won't be able to protect you if you get yourself in trouble over this.' She sounded serious and slightly irritated, which was the Una I knew best. 'Pushing yourself forward so you attract the attention of the DPS is not a good idea. Making your future depend on the outcome of this investigation into Josh Derwent is madness. Besides, he wouldn't want you to sacrifice your career for him.'

'If anything happens to Josh, I don't think I want to do this job anymore.' The truth. It surprised even me to hear it come out of my mouth.

Una made a noise that was halfway between a whinny and a snort. 'That's ridiculous.'

'I've always believed in justice, even if the outcome of an investigation was disappointing – even if a jury didn't see things my way. It will hurt him unbelievably if he's charged with hurting Melissa, and if he's convicted, he'll never recover. It shouldn't happen to him, and it won't if I have anything to do with it. But if it does, I don't see how I can continue to be part of the system.'

'Ilaria Cavendish's murder should be your priority, not this.' Una sounded deeply frustrated. 'I expected better from you. I thought you were able to separate your private life from your professional obligations.'

'I am. I do.'

'I've spoken to Liv and Georgia. *They* are focused on the investigation.'

Even if you're not, I filled in for myself. 'That's good. If they need to talk to me, they can.'

'I want you working on it.'

I closed my eyes, frustrated. 'She died two days ago. We don't have anyone in custody. We're waiting for the result of forensic tests and reviewing CCTV and conducting interviews. I don't know what you want me to do that I'm not doing. I was supposed to be off-duty now anyway. If there was something that needed a fast-time response I would be fully focused on that, but there isn't at the moment.'

Silence from the other end of the line. Slowly, sluggishly, a thought started to form.

'Are you trying to distract me from Josh? Is that it?'

'He doesn't want you to be involved.'

'Did he tell you that?'

A silence fell at the other end of the phone. Una didn't want to say yes, but she couldn't lie either. In the end, she settled for, 'He wants you to stay away from this, Maeve. And it's what I want. I don't want to give you a direct order to stay out of it—'

'There's no need for that,' I said quickly. 'I know what I have to do.'

'Good. I'm glad.' She genuinely sounded it too. 'Because I don't want to lose both of you.'

15

One of the things that Roz Fuller liked about interviewing police officers who had been arrested was that they started off at a serious disadvantage. They weren't used to being on the wrong side of the table, sitting next to a solicitor. They always had a solicitor, though, because they all knew better than to try and go it alone. So much the better if their clothes were taken for forensic examination and they were forced to wear the cheap tracksuit that made everyone look like a criminal. It cut them all down to size and reminded them why they were there, facing her – they'd done wrong, like the people they locked up, and now there were going to be consequences. They weren't accustomed to being the person in the room who had to decide whether it was riskier to answer her questions or opt for a 'no comment' reply.

She didn't worry about whether they talked or not. Interview was not where you broke a case, in her experience. Interview was where you got to know the person you were investigating, and that was as important as the physical evidence. Interview was where the job she was doing became personal, and she loved that.

This one was different.

She had picked up on it straight away when Josh Derwent walked into the room behind his solicitor, escorted by Cowell. It was Roz's preference to be in the room first, to set everything up the way she wanted it, so the moment they laid eyes on her they knew she was competent, motivated, highly professional – better than them.

But this time there was Lesley Mackenzie, the solicitor that Josh Derwent had requested. She had salt-coloured shoulder-length hair, a slim dress, flat shoes and an aura of easy confidence. She had earned her reputation over forty years and it was a very brave or foolish police officer who underestimated her. More than that, there was the very fact that she'd turned up at the police station when Josh Derwent asked her to. It meant that she respected him, because Lesley Mackenzie was certainly important enough to send a junior member of staff in her place. It was enough to make Roz fumble with the recording equipment.

Then there was Josh Derwent himself, who to Roz's tremendous annoyance was looking as if the custody tracksuit was made for him, as if it was the kind of thing he'd choose to wear to be comfortable. Roz had learned to depend on her own opinions of people rather than taking their friends and colleagues as reliable sources, but she had formed a picture of him nonetheless from what they had said. She had stared at the photographs that were in his file until she could see his direct blue stare and square jaw when she closed her eyes. She was used to seeing people soften over time, from their first picture to reality, weight creeping on and blurring their features, gravity pulling on bags under eyes, swinging jowls from jawlines. The man in front of her had progressed from taut, over-muscled army fitness through a battered, broken-nosed, devil-may-care arrogance that Roz recognised and despised as she flicked through the pictures. Here, now, in person, he was different: still lean and fit but less showy about it, still a head-turner, looks wise, but more sensitive and intelligent than she had anticipated: it was there in the set of his mouth, the minute narrowing of his eyes as he considered, in turn, his situation, and Cowell, and Roz herself. The force of his personality tripped her up. In the pictures he had given the impression of being the kind of person who would get into a physical fight at the first opportunity. Now she thought he could probably stop any fight before it started, assuming he wanted to.

He nodded to her, for all the world as if this was his interview, not hers. Roz felt herself bristle and tried to hide it. He was supposed to be charming – that DS who'd turned up in his house was certainly wound around his little finger – but Roz wasn't planning to allow herself to be influenced by that. On the other hand, he didn't seem to be interested in wasting any charm on her. There were no lingering looks, no wide-eyed innocence, no attempt to make an emotional connection or bargain with her. He sat on the other side of the table and leaned his forearms on it, his hands lightly clasped, his expression serious, while Cowell ran through the pre-interview formalities for the benefit of the tape.

'You two had a chance to have a chat, I take it?' Roz said.

'Yes, I'm up to speed.' Lesley Mackenzie had a lovely voice, clear and carrying.

'Do you know each other already?' Cowell asked, making conversation while Roz made a mental note to tell him not to, next time.

'Josh has locked up some of my clients over the years,' Lesley said, giving him a warm glance.

'They all deserved it.'

Oh, I see, we're meant to be impressed that he picked someone who's seen him on this side of the table. Roz gritted her teeth through the routine introductions and caution before they got on with the interview itself, when she was back in charge, and could relax.

Except that here, too, Josh Derwent seemed determined to run things his way.

'Before we begin, have you heard anything about Melissa? How is she?'

'I haven't heard anything new,' Roz began, but Cowell cut across her.

'I've been on to the hospital and they're happy with how she's getting on.'

Derwent's head dipped: unfeigned relief. The solicitor put a supportive hand on his arm.

Of course you're pleased she's not dying, Roz thought. It wasn't that she wanted Melissa to be seriously hurt or to die – but there was a big difference between a minor assault and murder. She wanted Josh Derwent under pressure, panicked, uncertain, not waiting for the clock to come to his rescue and put him back on the street.

'You haven't been able to speak to her yet, obviously,' Derwent said, as if he was confident that would be the end of their interest in him.

'Not yet. As soon as they tell us she's able for it.' *Before you can terrify her into lying to us*, Roz added silently. She believed wholeheartedly in believing women but sometimes they were afraid to tell the truth, which was where she came in.

'If you hear anything about how she is, can you let me know? Please?'

'Aren't you more concerned about the fact you've been arrested?'

'Not really.' He stared at her across the table, a level gaze that made her want to fidget, which was usually the effect she had on other people. 'I understand why I was arrested but it was a mistake and I have no doubt you'll discover that for yourself sooner rather than later. I'd rather be with her in the hospital than wasting your time. This feels like a needless delay. The sooner we get through this interview, the better.'

'Well, let's not hang around then,' Roz said brightly. 'Tell us about how you and Melissa met.'

For a moment, the muscles in his forearms flickered as his hands tightened on one another, involuntarily. Then he relaxed, with an obvious effort.

'I met her while I was investigating a fatal tower block fire in North London, on the Maudling Estate.'

Roz nodded. She remembered it.

'Melissa was living on the floor where the fire started. She was injured during the evacuation. I came across her little boy, Thomas, in the car park. He was lost, on his own.' He gave a small, weary shrug. 'Nothing happened between me and Melissa during the investigation. We got together afterwards.'

'Why was she living there?'

'She was hiding from her husband, Thomas's father. He's now her ex-husband, Mark Pell.'

'Why did she need to hide from him?'

'She was scared of him. He had been abusive.' Derwent's voice was low but there was an edge to it, as if it still made him angry.

'Was that something that appealed to you about her?'

He tilted his head an inch to the left and she had the sense he was considering her, rather than the question, before he answered.

'No.'

'You didn't want to rescue her.'

'No.'

'Some women end up in one violent relationship after another, don't they?'

'Do they?'

'They're easy targets for abusers. Low self-esteem.'

The room seemed to get a degree or two colder. It was Roz's turn to tilt her head an inch to the left, and she enjoyed watching him notice the way she'd mirrored him. 'Aren't you going to answer that?'

'It wasn't a question.'

Shit. She looked down at her notes, thrown. She had just been hitting a sweet rhythm and now she was stalled.

'You must have investigated domestic murders.' She made herself slow down, lowering her voice so she sounded calm and in control. 'Two women a week are murdered by their partner or ex-partner in the UK. You've been a murder detective for years.'

'I've investigated domestic murders.'

'So do you have any opinion on them?'

'They're tragic.' He looked at his lawyer, who blinked at him, a silent communication that Roz couldn't interpret. Beside her, Cowell was shifting on his chair.

'When did you get your nose fixed?'

The question was the one that had been uppermost in Roz's mind but she hadn't intended to ask it, and wouldn't have asked it if she hadn't been off balance. Bemusement spangled the air over the table: she could feel Cowell staring at the side of her face. *Roz, what are you doing?* Composure was a habit for the solicitor but her pen had lifted from her notebook and hovered above the page, uncertainly. And Josh Derwent . . . his eyebrows had drawn together a fraction, and he was looking at Roz as if he was curious about her for the first time, but he answered her nonetheless.

'A couple of years ago.'

'Vanity?' Roz asked bitchily, aware that she was still digging in this particular conversational hole but unable to stop herself.

For a second amusement changed Derwent's features, the beginnings of a smile drawing the corners of his mouth up.

'I couldn't breathe properly. I was running a lot of marathons at the time and I needed all the air I could get.'

'Running away from something?'

'Trying to find something.'

'And did you?' Roz persisted, feeling it was important, not knowing why.

'Yes and no,' Derwent said, and the warmth was wiped from his face, replaced with a bleak kind of acceptance.

Move on.

'Tell us about today. What happened?'

He looked bored, irritated. 'Where do you want me to start?'

'When you woke up this morning.'

'All right.' Quiet but lethal. The transcript wouldn't convey the look in his eyes, Roz thought, but she wouldn't forget it. 'I woke up before five. I went for a run. I got home at half past six.'

'Long run,' Cowell observed and Derwent nodded.

'I got ready for work, got Thomas up, gave him his breakfast. I woke Melissa up a few minutes before I had to leave.'

'Did you talk about anything?'

He frowned. 'Nothing major. She had a busy day. She was seeing clients this afternoon – she's a psychotherapist. Did you know that already?'

'Yes,' Roz said. 'Go on.'

'She asked me if I'd pick Thomas up from school but I couldn't, so she said she'd try to organise a playdate for him. Then I went to work. I'm running the investigation into a murder that happened yesterday at the Governor Hotel in Mayfair.' He paused and grimaced.

Not any more, you're not, Roz thought.

'After lunch Melissa rang me to say the playdate had fallen through and she had to see a client who she couldn't put off.'

'Who was this client?' Henry Cowell asked.

'I don't know. It's confidential. And I don't know why she said it was so urgent.' Derwent leaned forward, his eyes fixed on Cowell. 'You could find out who it was. She'd have a record on her computer – her phone . . . It's been driving me mad that I don't know and I can't find out myself, but you can.'

'Leave that to us,' Roz said. 'You need to concern yourself with explaining your own actions. You say Melissa rang you because she couldn't collect Thomas.'

'Yeah. Neither could I. I had a meeting that I couldn't miss. I managed to get hold of a couple who sometimes babysit for Thomas. He knows them and he likes them. They were happy to pick him up and take him to their house until I was due to be home. I rang the school and let them know.'

'And can you give me their names?'

'Seán and Aileen Kerrigan. If Melissa hadn't been working at home they'd have taken him back to Jena Road – they have keys – but she needed to have the house to herself.'

She was halfway through writing the surname down when she stopped, but Derwent was still talking and she let him. He was talking more quickly, with more detail than before. It was supposed to distract her from what he'd just said, Roz thought with a tiny thrill of satisfaction.

'I got a phone call from Seán at half past four. He said he had Thomas but Melissa wasn't answering her phone and he didn't know what time to drop him off. I tried to get hold of her myself and she didn't pick up. I assumed she was busy – I thought that maybe she expected me to be there to handle

Thomas. I had said I'd try to be home early. I checked with my boss – Superintendent Burt – and she was happy to let me go. I'd tasked the team with various lines of enquiry and there was nothing requiring a fast-time response from me at that point. I got back around five, I think. You can check that with the 999 call, because that was the first thing I did. That'll give you the exact time.'

If we believe your version of events, Roz thought.

'I saw her the second I opened the door and I thought she was dead.' He swallowed. 'I checked her pulse and I couldn't find it at first. Panic, I suppose. Then I called it in and started trying to help her. I got covered in blood – you'll have seen my clothes. I told the response officers who arrested me all of this. You can check their bodyworn. I know they were only doing their job but it wasn't how it looked, and you're wasting everyone's time by focusing on me when you should be trying to find the person who did this to Melissa.'

'Go back for a minute. Tell me about the babysitters.'

He paused for a moment before answering. 'What do you want to know?'

'How did you meet them?'

'How is that relevant?' he countered, staring her down. Beside him, his solicitor maintained a perfect poker face but Roz was aware of her brain racing as she tried to work out what was going on.

'It's not a difficult question, is it?'

He didn't answer, but his expression darkened.

'It's an unusual name, Kerrigan. I don't think I'd ever met anyone called that until today.'

His face cleared. 'Did you meet them? Did you see Thomas?'

'No. No, I didn't. I met someone else.'

'I see.' It was all he said but she felt a chill race over her skin at his tone.

'Tell me about Maeve Kerrigan.'

'There's nothing to tell. She's a colleague.' Stony-faced now.

'Whose parents look after your stepson.'

'He's not my stepson. Melissa and I aren't married.' He was frowning, looking down at the table instead of at her. 'The Kerrigans live near my house. They like kids.'

'What about Maeve?'

He pressed his hands flat on the table. 'This has nothing to do with her.'

'She was in your house when I met her.'

'Of course she was.' He said it under his breath and paused for a second to regain his composure. 'Look, she's a friend and a colleague. That's all. If she heard I was in trouble, nothing would stop her from trying to help. It's how she was brought up. As you can see, her parents are the same – they knew we needed help with Thomas and they stepped in. Now can we move on?'

'Why don't you like talking about her?' Roz asked, interested.

'Because I don't want her to be involved in this.' He stared at Roz and she realised with a spark of interest that there was something he would bargain with her for, after all. 'There's nothing I won't tell you, I swear. Just leave her alone.'

16

Derwent's house was five minutes from the house where I'd grown up, or three if you put your foot down and got lucky with the lights, which I found out by doing exactly that. I had been sitting staring into space outside 23 Jena Road, wondering what to do after my phone call with Una. There was no way I was going to stay out of it, no matter what Una said – or Derwent, for that matter. Of course he would want me a million miles away from his domestic problems, for all kinds of reasons. Even being in his house had felt like crossing a line into a world that he kept strictly private. I had seen and heard enough to know that his relationship with Melissa was miserable, but he didn't go into the details and I had never asked. I hadn't wanted to know what it was like for him when he went home to her – not after he had made his choice between us and picked her.

The phone was on the passenger seat where I'd flung it at the end of my conversation with Una. It started humming and my heart sank when I saw my mother was calling.

'What's wrong?'

'Are you nearby? Can you come home?' She sounded upset and I was already starting the car and putting the phone on speaker mode, in hyper-efficient crisis mode again.

'I'm on my way. What's up?'

'It's Thomas's dad.' She whispered it, her hand cupped over her own phone to muffle her words.

'Mark Pell?' I felt a jolt of cold horror. I had met him once, in a hospital corridor, and formed no good impression of him. Melissa had been terrified of him, and probably still was.

'I don't want Thomas to know he's here. Your dad is talking to him outside.'

'What's he doing at your house? What does he want?'

'He says he wants to see Thomas.'

'Who told him he was staying with you?' Even as I asked the question I realised I knew the answer. 'Was it Ellen Moore?'

'That's what he said. Why would she call him?'

Because Melissa's mother had always had a soft spot for her ex-son-in-law, if not an actual blind spot. My hands tightened on the wheel and I forced myself to concentrate as I pulled out onto a busy road.

'I'm almost there.'

'Should I call the police?'

'No, I'll handle it,' I said, sounding considerably more confident than I actually felt.

I parked two houses down, pulling in unobtrusively so I could get a look at Mark before he knew I was there. He was standing in the front garden of my parents' house, well back from the door, and his demeanour was the opposite of what I had expected. His hands were in the pockets of his long dark coat, and he had left a respectful gap between himself and my dad. They were having what seemed to be a pleasant conversation, but that only reassured me very slightly. Mark had a temper, I remembered, and was the sort of man who could explode into violence without warning. He was a handsome man, with close-cropped dark hair and regular features. He had a wiry athletic build and he held himself very straight.

My father saw me first and reacted with a widening of his eyes, which was enough to make Mark look around. I walked up to him, stopping a few paces away, and showed him my warrant card to establish immediately that this wasn't a friendly chat.

'Why are you here?'

He blinked. 'Sorry, who are you?'

'This is my daughter, Maeve,' my father said, and I ignored him because I wasn't there as his daughter.

'Detective Sergeant Maeve Kerrigan. We've met before, Mr Pell,' I said. 'In the hospital, when Melissa was there after the fire. You were there to threaten her.'

'I was there to *see* her,' he said. 'I had been looking for her and Thomas for months. I was desperate to find them.'

'I remember. She was hiding from you.'

'Oh, you remember that.' His face had changed from open friendliness to a kind of wary hostility. 'It was a difficult time.'

'Difficult for you?' All the anger that I felt, all the frustration and worry seeped into my voice and I was aware of my father stiffening, shocked at my tone.

'I can tell you don't think it should have been hard for me,' Mark Pell said levelly. 'I don't expect you to understand. Generally speaking, people take Melissa's side.'

'Do you blame them?'

'Sometimes.' His expression left me in no doubt how he felt about me.

'But not always. Because you feel guilty about what you did to her?'

'No, I didn't say that. I don't blame them because her story is very convincing. But I would remind you that I was never convicted of anything.'

'Sorry if I'm not impressed. You should know better than to think I'd give that a lot of weight, given my job.'

'Police make mistakes too.'

'Yes, sometimes they trust the wrong people.'

'Look, Sergeant, I've gone through hell in the family courts to get access to my son. I've proved myself to be reliable, cooperative, trustworthy and a safe person for him to be around. I've never laid a finger on him – or on Melissa either, but I'm probably not going to be able to change your mind about me and, honestly, I don't care enough to try.'

'OK. Let's skip that part.' I folded my arms. 'Why are you here now?'

'To see my son. I'm sure you'll agree with me that he's had a hell of a day. His mother's in hospital and I might not like Josh

Derwent but Thomas does. He'll be worried, and he's eight, and he needs someone to reassure him that everything is going to be all right.'

'We're here for that.'

'*Christ*, I'm his—' He stopped and clenched his jaw, controlling his temper with a visible effort. 'I'm his father. I just want to give him a hug. Is that really too much to ask?'

'Maeve.' My dad came a step closer and I wished he hadn't. 'If Mark comes into the house and has a cup of tea we could handle this like civilised humans. He can see Thomas while we're there. No need for this to become a fight.'

'I'm not going to try to run off with him or whatever it is you're afraid I might do.'

'I'm more afraid of what you might have done already,' I said tightly. 'Where were you this afternoon, Mr Pell?'

He blinked, surprised or good enough at acting to fake it. 'At work in Slough.'

'All afternoon?'

'Yeah. My team can vouch for me. You can call them if you want – I can give you their numbers.' He was reaching into his coat for his mobile phone and I held up a hand to stop him. It wasn't my investigation and I wasn't going to be calling anyone to check his alibi, but I hoped someone else would. Henry Cowell might listen, if I could get hold of him . . . and in the meantime I was wondering why Mark had been so careful to keep his fists balled up in his pockets.

'Let me see your hands.' I took out my phone and switched on the torch. 'Hold them out.'

He held them in front of him, palms up, and turned them over so I could see his knuckles in the bright white light from my phone. Unblemished skin, without a trace of a bruise. I switched off the torch. Disappointment was a lead weight in my gut. It would have been so easy if it had been Mark Pell who punched Melissa unconscious. But that didn't mean he hadn't hurt her. He could have used a weapon, or his feet, or he could have worn gloves.

'When was the last time you saw Melissa?'

'Last weekend when I dropped Thomas off at her house.'

'And how did she seem?'

'Normal. She seemed normal.' He shrugged. 'She was never very keen to chat on the doorstep when I was picking him up or bringing him home. I told her how the weekend had gone and that he'd done his homework. We agreed I'd see him in two weeks. Nothing strange about it.'

'No argument?'

'We do our arguing through our lawyers these days. It's more expensive but it's a lot less wearing.'

I looked at him for a long moment, trying to imagine what I would make of him if I hadn't known about his history with Melissa, who had been so scared of him she had run away from him with little more than the clothes she wore and her precious son. I couldn't separate that knowledge from what I thought of him now. I didn't trust him, and neither did Derwent, and he knew him better than I did. I'd been fooled before by someone who was smooth and plausible.

On the other hand, Pell had turned up at my parents' house because he thought his son needed him, and he might have been right about that. Also, he had shared custody of his son. I wasn't sure I had the right to stop him from seeing Thomas, even if he made my skin crawl.

Something of what I was thinking must have shown in my expression.

'It's not about me. This is about Thomas. For his sake. Please.'

I nodded reluctantly. 'But you're not to be alone with him. We can go in together.' He made a move towards the door. 'Wait. First I want your phone number and your address. I want to know where I can find you.'

'My home address or where I'm staying? I've booked into a hotel down the road from the hospital. I want to be nearby.'

'Both,' I said, and watched him write them down in my notebook. When he handed it to me, I asked, 'Are you worried about Melissa?'

He looked taken aback. 'Of course.'

'She's made your life a misery.'

'Yes, she did, but she's Thomas's mother, and she's always been incredible with him. She always put him first.'

'I'm fairly sure Ellen was hoping you two would get back together.' I said it to see how he would react, and was rewarded with instant horror.

'That's not what I want. Not at all.'

I admired his judgement; it was a lot better than Derwent's. 'You said she was never keen to chat on the doorstep. What about at other times? Did she meet up with you? Or call you?'

He looked as if he wanted to say no, but he must have known her phone records would give the game away if I was in any position to check. 'She rang me. A few times.'

'Recently?'

'No. Several times over the last year and a half. Not very often. It was usually when she was upset about something.'

'Something to do with Thomas?' It made sense, after all – they were his parents.

'Sometimes.' He hesitated, then added, 'More often it was because of Josh. They weren't happy, you know.'

I did know.

'What did she say to you?' I was trying to sound normal and casual. To my ears I was failing miserably.

'That she missed me.' He looked uncomfortable. 'She said Josh was cold with her. Withdrawn. She said he was sleeping in a different room.'

Don't think about that now. 'Were they arguing?'

'No. That was what bothered her most. He wouldn't fight with her. She wanted to get a reaction from him and he wouldn't play the game. He'd walk away whenever she tried to provoke him.'

'Can you tell the police that when they interview you?'

He snorted. 'Are you asking me to do him a favour?'

'I'm asking you to be honest.'

'Why do you care?'

'Because it's the truth, for one thing. And I don't want to see Josh on trial for something he didn't do. It would ruin his life.'

'But you don't have any sympathy for me even though I was in the same position as him.'

'The same? Really?' I folded my arms. 'Because I know he's innocent.'

Something that might almost have been pity swept over Mark Pell's face. 'Yeah, well, you're about to find out that innocence is no defence against scandal. Even if the accusations don't stick, they'll follow him around for the rest of his life. Something like this happens – you're never the same afterwards.'

17

What Roz Fuller wanted more than anything in life – what she needed – was a statement from Melissa Moore describing, in great detail, how and when Josh Derwent had brutalised her. But the doctors were frustratingly unhelpful, despite her reminder that it was a serious investigation and Ms Moore was a vital witness and that she, Roz, didn't have unlimited time until her main suspect had to be charged or released.

'She's not well enough to speak to you,' the consultant said, signing something that a nurse had handed to her. 'You won't get anything out of her for a couple of hours.'

'If I could see her . . .'

'There's no point. She's not in a position to talk.' The consultant was small and moved at speed so Roz had to run to keep up. 'I've got to look after my patient and what she needs is to be able to recover.'

'How bad are her injuries?'

'No broken bones. She probably has concussion. She certainly has a lot of bruising, which is very uncomfortable, so we've given her pain relief. She isn't particularly alert at the moment.' She stopped for a second, turning to face Roz. 'She was lucky. Her arms and legs and back are black and blue but her major organs are OK. We want to keep a close eye on her in case there's internal bleeding or some other damage that we haven't spotted yet, but at the moment it looks as if all she needs is time to heal.'

That in itself was interesting, Roz thought. Someone who knew about causing harm might know to avoid major organs. Someone who had been at more than a few post-mortems in his time would have a decent knowledge of anatomy. He would have known how to hurt her.

'Did it seem deliberate to you that the damage was fairly superficial?'

The doctor blinked. 'I couldn't say.'

'Because the man we have in custody would know there's a big difference between a charge of actual bodily harm or grievous bodily harm.'

'It's outside my area of expertise.'

Roz changed tack. 'Look, I've only got twenty-four hours to hold on to my suspect. After that I have to charge him or let him go. At the moment I don't have enough to get the CPS to agree there's a case against him. I desperately need to talk to Melissa.'

'I understand that, but she's resting. She barely knows she's in hospital, let alone what happened to her.'

'So when can I talk to her?'

'Maybe you haven't noticed, but this department is on the brink of complete chaos,' the consultant snapped. She pointed at each cubicle in turn. 'There's a cyclist with a fractured pelvis who needs my attention, and an elderly man who had a fall at home, and a footballer who took an elbow to the face, and a suspected heart attack in the cubicle at the end, and a chronic alcoholic whose liver is about to give up completely. The waiting room is full of potential patients and ambulances keep coming all the time. Melissa is on my list of things to think about, but not very high up. I understand that, for you, Melissa is the only thing that matters, but I can't think that way. Everyone has different priorities.'

'Yes, but my priority is a woman's safety,' Roz said, apologetic now but not backing down. The consultant sighed.

'I can't tell you when she'll be able to talk. Hours. Probably tomorrow morning, by which time she should be on a ward, which would be a better environment for a quiet conversation anyway. This place is a madhouse.' She leaned sideways to see past Roz. 'I've got to go, I'm afraid. There's always the friend, if you want someone to interview.'

'Friend?'

'She came in with her. She was in one of the relatives' rooms. Ask one of the nurses to help you.'

The consultant was gone before Roz could get anything useful like a description, but that didn't matter. A friend would do, in the absence of the victim's own testimony. A friend could be very useful indeed.

Clara Porter was in the hospital café near the entrance when Roz finally tracked her down, huddled in her coat, her hands wrapped around a cup of coffee. Every time the nearby doors slid open, an icy gust of wind tore a pale streamer of steam from the liquid and blew her fine, mouse-brown hair across her face. She was solid, stocky, her skin clear and free of make-up, her hair showing a couple of silver threads. Roz was conscious that Clara looked terrified while she was introducing herself, and she set out to build a rapport with a woman who seemed more shy and withdrawn than the avenging angel Roz had envisaged.

'What can I do to help? Have you spoken to Mel yet?'

'The doctor won't let me talk to her until the pain medication wears off a bit.'

'She was completely out of it the last time I saw her. She didn't even know I was with her in the ambulance.' Tears brimmed in the woman's eyes and she sniffed. 'I hate seeing her like this.'

'It must be very upsetting. Are you good friends?'

'Very close for the last couple of years. I met her at her son's school.'

'Are you one of the other parents?' Roz had already noted that the other woman's hands were bare of rings, not that that meant anything necessarily.

'I'm a classroom assistant. I did some babysitting for her, now and then.' There was a faint flush of colour in Clara's cheeks. 'I mentioned that my back was bothering me and she invited me to join the Pilates class she went to. It was on Sunday evenings so we would meet there and go for a drink afterwards – a smoothie or something in the gym café. We became friends.'

'Is that usual? For you to be friends with the school mums?'

'They're quite cliquey. Mel is different. She really sees people – I think because she's suffered herself.' Clara's hands tightened on the cup. 'You know about her ex-husband.'

'Tell me about him,' Roz said.

The story was confusing, as Clara told it, but Roz got the gist: Melissa had fled for her life after her ex-husband threatened her and she had crossed the path of Detective Inspector Josh Derwent when she was at her most vulnerable.

'And where is the ex-husband now?'

'Still around. He has Thomas every other weekend.'

'That can't be easy for Melissa.'

'It's not but she gets on with it.' Clara dredged up a watery smile. 'She's very brave. She told me she has to go along with the courts and what they decide, but it kills her to see Thomas going off with him.'

'Clara, I really need to talk to Melissa about her current relationship but she's not well enough at the moment. Can you tell me anything about it? Did she ever confide in you about any problems she was having – anything that was worrying her?'

Clara gave a little gasp. 'I don't know.'

'I think you do.'

'I'm not sure if she would want – if I should say . . .' Her breathing was faster, her skin pale.

Roz reached across the table and put her hand on Clara's arm. 'Look, this is off the record at the moment. Just talk to me. Tell me what you know and what you think. I really want to understand the dynamic between her and Josh. What's he like?'

'He's awful.' Clara said it with suppressed violence.

There it was. Roz was pleased; the right man was in custody, she told herself. She was doing the right thing.

She had, she discovered, wanted to be wrong, if only because Josh Derwent seemed to inspire such loyalty from the people he worked with.

'In what way is he awful?'

'He's horrible to her. He hit her.'

'When?' Roz made a conscious effort to speak softly. 'Was it a one-off?'

'It happened lots of times. She had bruises on her arms and legs. She only told me because she was limping, and I asked.' A tear slipped down Clara's cheek. 'I wanted her to leave him, but she was terrified of him. She was afraid to report him because he's a police officer. He told her no one would believe her.'

'Well, he was wrong about that. I believe her. And I believe you.' Roz paused. 'But the other thing that would really help is evidence. Do you have any messages she might have sent you at the time? Pictures, that kind of thing?'

'Yes, I have. I've been saving it for Mel, in case she changed her mind about reporting him.' Clara dug in her bag and produced a phone in a pink sparkly case. 'It's all on here.'

Roz flicked through the pictures that the woman kept in a separate file on the phone, impeccably organised: close-ups of bruises in various stages of healing, a rainbow of damage, all catalogued and dated. With every image, her sympathy for DI Josh Derwent diminished a fraction more.

'Clara, I could kiss you. This is amazingly helpful.'

The woman's eyes lit up. 'Is it? Really? I always hoped it might be.'

'It will make all the difference.'

'Good. He shouldn't get away with it.'

Roz reflected that her career should have taught her avenging angels could come in all shapes and sizes. She beamed at Clara. 'I absolutely agree.'

'I do have one other thing that might help to prove what he did.'

Roz leaned forward, intent now. 'Tell me more.'

18

When Ellen Moore arrived at my parents' house, she didn't seem remotely surprised to find her ex-son-in-law there, and she wasn't inclined to apologise for his presence either. Melissa's mother looked similar enough to her that I felt jolted as she walked up the path to the front door: the same colour eyes, the same shape of face, the same slight build. I had expected her to be anxious about Melissa but she wore her habitual tight-lipped frown as she nodded to me. Unlike her daughter, who had long, glossy hair, she had a neat hairdo with a fringe. She wore a navy blazer, a striped top and navy trousers, which was very much her style. Unbidden, a memory swam up from the recesses of my mind: Derwent saying darkly, *The thing about Ellen is that she always looks as if she's parked her yacht on a double-yellow.* I suppressed a very inappropriate bubble of hysteria and concentrated on taking her coat and overnight bag.

'This is a terrible situation.' Ellen Moore spoke in an accusing tone, as if it was somehow my fault.

'Thank you for coming so quickly. Did you go to the hospital first?'

'I rang them. They said she wasn't on a ward yet so there was no point in visiting, and she wasn't able to talk to me on the phone. But they said she was stable and doing well. I can't understand how this can have happened to her. It's *appalling*.' She tilted her head to one side, listening to the voices from the sitting room: one high-pitched, two deep. 'Is Mark here?'

'You told him to come.'

'He's the boy's father.' She brushed an imaginary piece of fluff off the lapel of her blazer. 'He should be here.'

'Well, he's not staying,' I said, stony-faced.

'I must have a word with him before he goes.' Ellen turned and checked her reflection in the hall mirror, touching her hair with her fingertips. It was possible, I reflected, that Ellen had something of a crush on her son-in-law.

'I'd like to talk to you about him, later.'

Her eyes met mine in the mirror. 'He was terribly misjudged.'

'That's why I'd like to hear what you think about him.' I said it as neutrally as I could but she still looked suspicious, so I dropped it and let her go into the sitting room to see her grandson.

Not long afterwards, Mark Pell came out carrying Thomas, who had wrapped his legs around his father.

'You're getting to be too big to pick up, buddy.' Pell hefted him with a jerk that made Thomas squeak in surprise.

'I'm not too heavy.'

'No.' He kissed the side of Thomas's head and let him slide down to the ground. To me, he said, 'I don't want to outstay my welcome. Now that Ellen is here, I'd better head off.'

I would have wanted to escape from Ellen too. Getting rid of Mark was a positive, but having Ellen in exchange felt a little unfair. Thomas, though, was clinging to Mark as if he couldn't bear to let him go.

'You can stay longer if you like.'

'Not this time.' He brushed the hair from his son's forehead and smiled down at him. 'If it's all right I'll come back tomorrow.'

'Yes!' Thomas tightened his grip on him.

I couldn't really say no when Thomas was there, listening, but I felt out of my depth. I didn't know what Melissa would have wanted, and I suspected Derwent would be furious if he found out Mark Pell was hanging around.

'Let's see how things are,' I said, in the end, and Mark's mouth tightened: temper, as if I had needed a reminder of it.

'Can you let me know if there are any developments?'

I nodded and he thanked me, dropped a kiss on Thomas's head, and left on a gust of icy wind that seemed to contain all the bleakness of the November night.

* * *

I stayed in the kitchen, out of the way, while Ellen got settled in and put Thomas to bed. He was upstairs with her and his voice carried through the house, high-pitched and excited.

'He's tired,' Mum said quietly. 'He needs to get to sleep.'

'Good luck with that. She'll have to scrape him off the ceiling first. He must be so worried about Melissa and Josh.' There was a delighted shriek from upstairs. 'Still, he seems thrilled to see his dad and his grandmother.'

'It won't last. He'll be in tears soon if he doesn't get his head down.' She was loading the dishwasher methodically, the way she always did it, which was subtly different from the way my dad preferred to load it, which led to the occasional spat. The dishwasher was more or less the only thing they ever argued about. Maybe their marriage had given me unrealistic expectations of relationships, and that was why I struggled to find the right person. Did I really think Derwent and I would have kept our fights to how the dishwasher was loaded? A constant challenge was no basis for a relationship, even if it was exciting. I sighed, and emerged from my thoughts to see Mum eyeing me.

'Are you all right, Maeve?'

'I just want to get this sorted out.'

'Of course you do.'

'It's absolutely ridiculous that he's been arrested, Mum. There's no way he would have harmed her.' I folded a clean tea towel, concentrating on lining up the pattern before I hung it on the cooker.

'Mm.'

My head snapped up. 'What does that mean?'

'Nothing.' She wasn't looking at me. 'Only that your father and I – we know you want to fix this.'

'Of course I do. It's not fair and it's not right.'

'And presumably he'll be grateful if you're the one who solves his problems.' There was an edge to her words and I flinched.

'That's not why I want him to be released – for him to be *grateful*. That's not it at all.'

'Then why?'

'Because – because he would do the same for me. He would go to the ends of the earth to help me, you know that. I owe him this.'

'You don't owe him anything.'

'Mum!'

'You've been doing so well. Looking after yourself. Getting on with your life. To see you ruining it all for him again – I can't say I'm pleased about it.'

I folded my arms. 'I'm not ruining my life. And anyway, it's my choice, not yours.'

'Oh, I know. You've made that very clear. It's your life and we're the ones watching you make a mess of it.'

'*Mum.*'

'And if you think this is what he wants, you're wrong.'

I went still. 'What makes you say that?'

'Do you think I haven't spoken to him, Maeve? Do you think he didn't talk to your dad about this whole mess? That he didn't sit inside there with us and we could see he was tormented over the whole situation?'

'But he didn't even talk to me about it,' I protested, and heard too late how pathetic I sounded. Her face twisted in sudden sympathy and I turned away, fighting for control.

'You poor pet. Don't be so hard on yourself.' Her hand was on my back, between my shoulder blades. The classic Irish mother. She was allowed to be mean to me, but I wasn't supposed to join in.

When I could, I said, 'What did he say when he talked to you?'

She shook her head. 'Ah, you know how it was. He wasn't making easy decisions. He wanted to do the right thing by everyone.'

'Well, that's not always possible.'

'Did he not do the right thing by leaving you to get on with your life?'

I went cold. 'Did you tell him to do that?'

She raised her eyebrows. 'Since when was anyone able to tell him anything? It was his idea. But we didn't discourage him.'

'You sent him after me when I went away . . . in the spring . . . you told him to come and find me.' My throat was tight.

She had the grace to look guilty. 'That was before. And we were worried about you then too. You were upset. You were hiding away from your feelings.'

'I was putting myself back together and then he turned up and told me everything was going to work out, which was not in fact the case.'

'Well, he couldn't know that then.'

'No.'

'He had to make the best of a bad situation. You both did.' She sighed. 'Maeve, we like Josh. Of course we do. But the reason we like him is because he tries to do the right thing by you, and in this case the right thing was leaving you alone.'

I felt my bottom lip quiver, no matter how I tried to stop it. 'If what he did was the right thing, why does it hurt so much?'

She put her arms around me and held me and I inhaled that mother-smell of cooking and familiar perfume and love, and it was something to know she was on my side, even if she disagreed with every decision I made and every feeling I had.

Derwent didn't have anyone like that, I remembered. He wasn't in touch with his family. He only had me.

I detached myself gently. 'I'm fine, Mum. I'm not the one in trouble.'

'But you could be, Maeve. If this goes wrong. You have to think about the consequences for you too.'

I shook my head, impatient. 'I don't care about that.'

'No. I know. And that's not like you. This job – you've given it everything. Too much, if you ask me.'

'I didn't.'

'I know.'

'There's nothing wrong with wanting to be happy, Maeve.'

Footsteps were coming down the stairs and Mum cocked her head to listen.

'You'll get more out of Ellen if you're nice to her. Pour her a glass of wine and let her talk. You can see she's dying to tell you everything.'

Not for the first time I reflected that everything I'd ever known about handling people, I'd learned from my mother, and that if she'd been a police officer there wouldn't have been an unsolved crime in a twenty-mile radius.

Mum went out to intercept Ellen and I got three glasses out of the cupboard while I listened to them talking in the hall. Ellen was a red-wine drinker so I opened a bottle of Australian Cabernet Sauvignon and poured with a generous hand. I wasn't going to drink the wine in my glass. I wanted a clear head. However, I also wanted Ellen to feel we were bonding, and I wanted her to relax. I needed to build trust with a woman who had never been anything other than cool with me, and I didn't have time to waste.

My phone rang and I snatched it up to silence it. Georgia, I saw from the screen, and my heart sank.

'Sorry, Georgia, it's not a good time. Can this wait?'

'Maeve?' She sounded panicky, which was not actually all that usual for her and I leaned against the kitchen counter.

'What's wrong? Are you OK?'

'No.' Her voice wavered. 'I think I've done something really stupid.'

19

It took precisely one half-glass for Ellen to start talking, but once she did, I couldn't stop her. We were sitting at the kitchen table, Mum beside Ellen, me lounging in my chair as if I was relaxed but really so I could keep an eye on the clock on the wall. The minute hand seemed to have moved forward in leaps every time I looked up at it.

If they charge him, this gets a lot more complicated . . .
You must *stop them from charging him . . .*
Roz Fuller will definitely want to charge him with something . . .
So you don't have long.

And when I wasn't thinking about that, I was worrying about Georgia, who had realised she'd left her blue book in Sam Blundell's flat. Her blue book – the A4 notebook that detectives carried, with every single note she had made about Ilaria Cavendish's murder. With a sinking feeling I remembered the drive over to interview Sam, when I had told her everything I knew about Ilaria and what had happened to her, as Georgia took it all down in her clear, rounded handwriting. The entire case, laid out in detail.

'How did you manage to leave it behind?'

'I put it down on my chair and then the girlfriend came in and I got distracted.' She sounded on the verge of tears.

'Well, go there and get it.'

'No, I did.'

'And?'

'Sam wasn't there. He'd gone to the pub with a friend. But Lora was there. She – she'd been reading it.'

'*Shit.*'

'She was so upset, Maeve. Hysterical. I tried to calm her down – she's pregnant and I kept telling her to think of her baby, but that made her worse.'

It would, I thought, biting my lip so I didn't snap at Georgia. 'Did she say anything interesting?'

'She'd never met Ilaria. She knew Sam was meeting with her every week but she thought it was at work. He told her they were working on a project together.'

'Anything else?'

'She's four months pregnant. The bump started showing a week ago, she said, but only in some outfits so mainly she feels fat. She kept saying, "He lied to me!" and "How can he have done this" – stuff like that. She was shaking. She told me he couldn't have hurt Ilaria, but, you know, maybe she didn't know him as well as she thought she did, given that he was having an affair under her nose.'

'Maybe we don't ever know the people we love.'

'Wow. That's bleak.' Georgia was sounding better now that she'd confessed. 'But it's interesting that her reaction was so definite. It could be a good thing I left my book behind and got to talk to her alone.'

'Don't push it, Georgia. It was pretty far from ideal. How was she when you left?'

'Calmer, I think. I've only just come out. Her sister had arrived to look after her so I left.' A pause. 'Am I in trouble?'

'There's nothing we can do about it now. But don't ever leave your book behind again,' I said.

'I won't.'

'I've got to go.'

'Is everything all right?'

'Not really,' I had said, and ended the call. What else could I say?

I would have to tell Una Burt about Georgia's mistake when I saw her next, and she would be furious, and that would be justified. If I hadn't been so absorbed in worrying about Derwent, I might have reacted differently myself.

I made myself focus on Ellen, who was winding up a long anecdote about the young Melissa. 'Really it was always a battle with her. She was never a very joyful child. Always anxious. Dissatisfied.'

'We all know people like that,' Mum said with a supportive look.

'Yes, but Melissa was different. She wanted something that I couldn't give her.' Ellen tipped back the last mouthful, not demurring when I picked up the bottle to refill her glass. 'Of course it was because my husband died when she was six. She never got over that sense of shock. Abandonment, you know. She had issues. She had counselling – that's why she became a therapist herself, I think.'

'Because it helped her?' I asked.

'No, because she loved it. The attention and the intensity and the close relationships she built with her counsellors. They were quite indulgent and I suppose I was less patient with her. It wasn't my job to watch her play house and tell her she was wonderful.' She seemed to hear the bitterness in her voice and flicked an anxious look from me to Mum to see how we were reacting. 'I was busy trying to keep things going on my own. It was hard, after Philip died.'

'How did he die?' I asked.

'Pancreatic cancer. It was awful.' She stared down into her glass, remembering. 'He was in hospital for a while after he was diagnosed and then a hospice. He was never well enough to come home so from one day to the next he disappeared from her life. She was so young – I kept her away from the hospital and she only saw him right at the end, when he was about to die, and he wasn't the father she had known. She found it terrifying. I think that was a dreadful mistake on my part.'

'Very hard to know what to do when they're so small.' Mum sounded as if she had confronted the same issue, which she had not, but Ellen didn't stop to consider whether she was speaking from experience.

'Yes, it is hard, isn't it? And it was hard when I was trying to come to terms with what had happened. My life had fallen apart, you see. Everything that we'd intended – all our plans – gone. I had to make a new life for myself as well as looking after her. I probably leaned on her too much, given that she was so young, but I was young too, and lonely.' Her voice broke on the word: the pain was still raw, I thought. 'When your husband dies, you become something that no one wants to be. There's no glamour in being thirty and a widow. There was no online dating then. No way to meet anyone else. It was me and Melissa on our own.' Another gulp of wine.

'But then she got older and went to secondary school and her behaviour wasn't so sweet anymore. She was a *nightmare* of a teenager. She was argumentative and demanding. If a teacher told her off it was the end of the world. If I said no to something she wanted, she would refuse to talk to me. You couldn't reason with her – you could only give in.' She looked at me. 'I know you think I'm unsympathetic to her when she complains but this is something I've lived with for years. That and the way she exaggerated everything. If one of her friends disagreed with her about something, that was bullying. I used to tell her she was like the boy who cried wolf. The *arguments* we had.'

'Ah, teenage girls.' Mum rolled her eyes and I glared at her.

'I was a delight.'

'You had your moments.'

I was thinking about how Melissa had talked to Derwent, though, when I'd heard her on the phone, and the way she had laid into him over what seemed to me to be nothing much. Her own mother had lost patience with her – and she loved her. How much worse had it been for him when he was trapped in a relationship with her, despite wanting it to end?

Was there the slightest possibility that it could have driven him to do something insane?

No, came the answer, instant and definite. And it wasn't just that I had awkward and unhelpful feelings for him. There was no world in which Josh Derwent lost his temper and lashed out at someone weaker than him and lied about it. I couldn't be wrong about that.

Mum turned to Ellen. 'I think it would be harder with only the two of you. I'm not surprised you found it difficult when she was a teenager. But presumably that passed.'

Ellen ran a knuckle under each eye, swiping away the tears that were threatening to fall. 'Sort of. What happened was that she went away to university and then she met Mark. Suddenly he became the person she talked to about everything. I was forgotten about.'

'Was he a student as well?' I asked.

'No. He's five years older than her. She met him at a job fair in her third year and I suppose he seemed very glamorous and grown up compared to the boys at university. He already had plans to start his own business. He was a lovely person – I liked him immediately when I met him – and he suited Melissa.'

'What was their relationship like?'

'They were very happy. They had a wobble after Thomas was born – but then it's hard when you're used to having all the attention and suddenly you have to share it.'

'Babies take up all your time and energy,' Mum said wisely.

'That was how they found it. I tried to help as much as I could, taking him for evenings and weekends so they could spend time alone together. Thomas was a delightful baby, too – he was no trouble apart from the usual teething and childhood ailments, but there again Melissa was an anxious mother. If he cried, it was meningitis. If he bumped his head, it was brain damage.'

'So when did Mark start hitting her?' I couldn't wait any longer: the clock was staring at me.

Ellen's mouth drew tight. 'Well, I don't know exactly because she didn't tell me. I didn't know anything was going on until he was arrested for it. The shock of that – I don't think I'll ever get over it.'

'There was no warning?'

'She kept it to herself.' Ellen blinked. 'At least, that's what she said.'

'People do,' I said simply.

'Yes, but Melissa? And Mark, of all people? The most reasonable man – the kindest, the most generous soul.'

'Sometimes they seem like an ideal partner to outsiders, but behind closed doors it's a different story.'

Mum looked at me quickly, knowing that I had personal experience of someone who behaved exactly like that.

'I know it makes me sound awful, but I can only tell you what I knew of her, and of him, and I didn't think she was telling the truth.' Ellen looked guilty. 'When she left him, I suppose I started to think I'd been mistaken. For her to leave like that . . . with Thomas . . . it made me think again, put it that way.'

'Did you think she would have come to you if you'd been more sympathetic?' Mum leaned her chin on her hand. 'Because I can tell you, we were the last to know when something similar happened to Maeve.'

'It's hard to be honest with people who love you, sometimes,' I said to Ellen, but really so my mother heard it. 'You don't want to upset them.'

'Well, I was upset. I loved Mark. And I still do.' Ellen looked defiant. 'He told me he never touched her and I found that easier to believe than my own daughter's story, which probably makes me a terrible mother.'

'No.' I got up and ripped a piece of kitchen paper off the roll, handing it to her so she could mop her watering eyes. 'It really doesn't.'

She sniffed. 'At least this time there's no doubt in my mind. She's in hospital, injured, and we know who put her there.'

'Do we?' There was a limit to how kind and understanding I could be, I discovered.

'He lost his temper with her.' Ellen shrugged. 'He's exactly that kind of man. Always so surly.'

Mum put her hand on my arm with a warning look and I wondered what exactly she had seen on my face. She said, 'He's very patient with her, Ellen, from what I've seen of them together.'

'We don't know who hurt Melissa,' I managed. 'Josh has been arrested, but that doesn't mean he did it. They've jumped to conclusions the way you think they did with Mark.'

'I don't know about that. I do know that I let her down once before by not taking her side,' Ellen said, her expression mulish. 'I'm not going to make the same mistake again.'

20

This time, after the usual interview preamble, Roz went straight to the point.

'Tell me about Melissa.'

Derwent had barely settled into his seat across the table from her. He looked up, frowning. 'That's what I was going to say to you. Have you spoken to her?'

'I haven't been able to interview her yet, no.'

'Then what are we doing here?' He glanced at his solicitor, who was making a note. 'This is futile.'

'I have questions that I'd like you to answer,' Roz said, unfazed.

'Pointless questions.' He ran a hand over his head, irritated. He was looking tired, Roz thought, and strained, which was exactly how she wanted him.

'They're not pointless for me.'

'You're wasting your time on me when you could be finding out who hurt her. It wasn't me, and she'll tell you it wasn't me when you finally get around to speaking to her. I can't believe that's not a priority.'

'Of course I want to talk to her. I can't at present. Her doctor wants me to wait.'

'So she's not doing well.' He leaned his elbows on the table and put his face in his hands.

Roz watched him for a moment. 'That upsets you.'

'Of course.' When he straightened up he folded his arms, hugging himself. It wasn't warm in the interview room – Roz had turned the air conditioning up – and the custody tracksuit was cheap, thin cotton. Still, she had the impression it wasn't physical discomfort that was bothering him. 'Of course it does.

Thomas will be so worried. And whoever did this to her is probably laughing to himself, wherever he is. He probably can't believe his luck.'

'Who else do you think might have wanted to harm Melissa?'

His eyebrows shot up. 'Who *else*? I take it you mean in addition to me? I didn't want to harm her, Roz. Can I call you Roz?'

'You can call me whatever you like.' *As long as you keep talking*, Roz added silently.

He stared at her, those blue eyes missing nothing. She thought he was going to lose his temper, but instead he smiled, a slow, lazy smile. 'Well, *Roz*, you can leave me off the list. That's presuming you do have a list of suspects. You seem to have focused on me from the very start but that would be unwise, wouldn't it? An experienced investigator such as you would know you need to keep an open mind at this point.'

'Of course.' Roz looked down at her list of questions, wondering how he had managed to divert her once again from where she had wanted to start.

'Would you like to know who's on my list? I've written it out for you.' He slid a piece of paper across the table. 'Those are criminals who have a specific grudge against me and might have wanted to target someone close to me. There's Melissa's ex-husband, too – Mark Pell. You should talk to him. And this guy may have been released early from his sentence. He's the sort who would get preferential treatment – he won't have put a foot wrong inside. I gave evidence against him and he's the type to have taken it personally. If I wasn't locked up, I'd check whether he's out or not. Aside from that I can't think of anyone who might have hurt her, unless it was a burglary gone wrong or some sort of psycho. Attacks like that do happen – rarely, but they do.'

'But more commonly, it's partners and ex-partners, isn't it?'

'That's what the statistics say.' He watched her draw the list towards her, glance at it, and then slide it away again. 'You're not going to look at it?'

'I've looked at it.'

'Not properly.'

'I think I've got the gist.' She smiled at him (*two can play that particular game, Inspector*) and he swallowed, a muscle tightening in his jaw.

Beside her, Henry Cowell stirred, and reached out for the paper. Before she could stop him, he had picked it up and tucked it into his notebook.

'Thanks.'

'You're welcome,' Josh Derwent said to him, and to him alone. Roz got another glower.

She felt like glowering herself. She had wanted to leave the page on the table while she questioned Josh Derwent, so she could ignore it. Then he would know his attempt at distraction had failed. Instead she made an actual physical note to speak to Cowell about initiative, and why he shouldn't assume she wanted him to have any.

'Right, as I was saying, I wanted to talk to you about Melissa, and you, and your relationship.'

'Again?' He sighed. 'If it's the wrong tree, Roz, you're not going to get anything out of it by coming back to bark up it again and again.'

'It's one specific question, really. Why are you two together?'

To her satisfaction, it was clear the question wasn't what he had been expecting, and he couldn't immediately see where she was going with it. He frowned. 'What?'

'You and Melissa. Are you a happy couple?'

He shifted in his seat. 'What does that mean?'

'Do you argue?'

'Argue? No. Sometimes we disagree about things. Sometimes she loses her temper with me, which is completely understandable. I can be annoying.'

No shit, Roz thought.

'Also, my job takes up a lot of time – time that she would prefer me to spend with her and with Thomas.'

'So there are tensions in the relationship – you admit that.'

'Is that unusual? Really? Are there relationships where two people agree on absolutely everything?' He leaned back. 'I'm not going to lie to you, Roz. I'm being honest. I spend a lot of time trying to be a good partner to Melissa. I try to look after her and Thomas to the best of my abilities. It isn't always easy. Sometimes I have competing obligations and Melissa has to come second to the job. I can understand it's frustrating for her. She gets angry with me. I'm the one who walks away. So we don't *argue*, but that's because you can't have an argument with someone who isn't there.'

'Would you say you love her?'

'Fucking hell,' Derwent exploded, losing his patience at last. 'What sort of question is that?'

The right one to ask. Roz raised her eyebrows. 'It's a very straightforward question.'

'If you think that,' he began with heat, and then stopped abruptly, much to Roz's disappointment. He took a moment to get his feelings under control, and when he went on, his voice was quieter. 'I loved her when I met her first. We moved in together very shortly after that. My feelings for her changed over time, but I've only ever wanted what was best for her. I care about her.'

'So you don't love her.'

He sighed. 'Is this going anywhere?'

'Bear with me.'

'I have little choice.' His eyes were hard.

'It's just that someone told me Thomas was the reason you and Melissa stayed together.'

'Someone?' he repeated, and if the room had seemed cold before, it was downright arctic now. 'Who was that?'

'Why does it matter who said it? Is it true?'

For the first time he dropped his head, genuinely uncomfortable, frowning. 'To be honest with you, yes. Thomas kept us together. We almost split up in April of this year – we got as close to it as you can. It was all decided. But then, there was Thomas.'

'Explain that to me. Surely Thomas was a factor already in your relationship.'

'Not like this.' He closed his eyes, summoning the strength to go on. 'At first it didn't seem like anything important. He had a stomach bug – norovirus, something like that. The kind of thing you forget about two days later. But he didn't shake it off. He got sicker and sicker. He started losing weight, which wasn't all that surprising because the poor kid couldn't keep anything down. We took him to the GP two or three times – Melissa was worried about him from the start but I thought she was overreacting. Then eventually she called 111 at about four in the morning when he was in misery, and they told her to take him to hospital, so she did.'

'Where were you?"

'Working.' His face was bleak. 'She rang me and told me she was sitting with him in A and E. I got there as soon as I could. At first, it's a relief to be in hospital because at least someone is trying to fix whatever's wrong and give you some answers, but once you get drawn into the hospital system it's impossible to get out again. They kept him in for a night, and then extended it to two, and they kept running more tests and more tests. No one seemed to know what was causing the stomach issues and that made me really worried because you don't want it to be something rare and unusual, do you? You want something that responds to antibiotics, or something the kid will grow out of. Harmless stuff that won't affect him going forward. But that wasn't what the doctors said.'

'What did they say?'

'Not a lot. They didn't have answers for us. They still don't. They kept putting him through more procedures – and he's a brave kid, but he started to get upset when they came to get blood or took him away for a scan. He would cling to me – he always wanted me to go with him when he was taken to a different part of the hospital, and I wasn't going to say no.' Derwent's voice was rough, emotion choking him. 'I couldn't leave him when he was sick. I couldn't leave Melissa to deal with it on her own, either –

that wouldn't have felt right. She and I talked and we decided it was worth leaving things as they were for the time being.'

'Continuing in the relationship, even though you'd nearly split up.'

'To some extent.'

'What does that mean?'

Derwent's jaw was clenched so tightly it was remarkable he was able to speak. 'We weren't sleeping together anymore.'

'And you were all right with that?'

He smiled. 'It was my choice.'

'And was she all right with that?'

'No, I don't think she was, but there was nothing I could do about that.'

Roz frowned. 'You could have ended it and still been supportive to her and Thomas.'

'Melissa didn't think that was possible,' Derwent said slowly, reluctantly. 'If I was with her, I could be with Thomas when he needed me. If I wasn't, I couldn't. It was all or nothing.'

'Not quite all, according to you.'

'I had my limits.' He said it quietly but Roz had the impression that his mind, once made up, was not to be changed, and she felt sorry for Melissa all over again.

'Were you unfaithful to her?'

'Why is that relevant?' Lesley Mackenzie asked, the question sliding in before Derwent could answer.

'I'm trying to get a picture of the relationship. I want to know what might have made them argue.'

'It's all right,' Derwent said to his solicitor, and to Roz, 'No. That's not something I would do.'

Roz let the silence lengthen before she asked her next question, so he knew she didn't believe him.

'I want to ask you about Clara Porter.'

It wasn't easy to surprise Josh Derwent but for the second time he looked genuinely bewildered at Roz's line of questioning. 'What about her? She's one of the TAs at Thomas's school. A teaching assistant,' he clarified for Lesley's benefit.

'Do you know her outside of school?'

'Barely. She did a bit of babysitting for us, once or twice.'

'She's friends with Melissa.'

'Is she?' He shrugged. 'I didn't know that.'

'She went in the ambulance with her, when they took Melissa to the hospital.'

'I was a bit busy being arrested at that stage,' Derwent said, frowning. 'But I'm glad Melissa had someone with her.'

'You didn't know Melissa and Clara go to the same exercise class on Sundays.'

'No. I didn't. Melissa doesn't have to get permission from me to go out. If she wants to see friends or go to a class, she goes. I never asked her who she was with or what she was doing.'

'It's normal, isn't it, to ask someone where they're going?'

'Yeah, it is, and I'm sure we talked about the basic logistics, like when she'd be home, but she never mentioned Clara to me.'

'She mentioned you to Clara.'

He raised his eyebrows. 'What does that mean?'

Roz opened her folder and took out a sheaf of printouts from Clara's phone. 'We haven't downloaded everything yet. This is a selection of messages from Melissa to Clara. As you can see, there are pictures. Clara kept everything.'

'What . . . what are these?' He was staring down at them, so pale that his complexion looked like wax. The pages fanned out on the table, close-ups of blue bruises and red marks on smooth skin.

'It's a very detailed record of ongoing abuse, Josh.' Roz waited a beat. 'Can I call you Josh?'

He didn't seem to hear her. Lesley accepted a copy of the printouts from a grim-faced Henry Cowell.

'We're going to need some time to look at these and anything else you've got,' she said, with impeccable composure.

Roz smiled. 'I'd expect nothing less.'

21

I couldn't settle in the house after my conversation with Ellen. My stomach was a knot of tension and I was restless, feeling I should be taking action, not sure where to start. I was looking for something as I drove around, past Thomas's school, past the darkened, empty house in Jena Road – I just wasn't sure what it was. My phone rang and I pulled in, heart thumping, to discover it was Liv.

'We've got preliminary lab results for Ilaria Cavendish.' She sounded diffident. 'I didn't want to wait.'

'Don't worry, I told Una I was available if you needed me. Go ahead.'

'She tested negative for cocaine and alcohol.'

'So she didn't drink the champagne.'

'Nope. And she hadn't been taking anything else, apart from an antidepressant.'

'Not unusual.'

'Yeah. She was on quite a high dose, according to the pathologist.'

'Well, she was rich and beautiful. Of course she was miserable.'

Liv chuckled.

'Was that it?' I said. 'Is that the only reason you rang?'

'I wanted to know if you were OK.'

I closed my eyes for a second. 'You talked to Georgia.'

'She rang me.'

'Did she tell you about her blue book?'

'Yes. And about you running off with the car looking like it was the end of the world. And Una told me you were contactable by phone for the next few hours but you were tied up with something else. What's going on?' Liv's voice was full of concern. 'What happened? It's not your parents, is it?'

'No. Well, not exactly.' I hesitated, weighing it up. Derwent wouldn't want to be gossiped about, and Una Burt had been discreet even though she knew he had been arrested, and why. On the other hand it was bound to get out if he was charged. All I was doing was getting in a few hours ahead of the news. 'Josh has been arrested.'

'What! Why? What did he do?'

'Nothing. It's a mistake.' Saying it out loud made my throat tighten. 'I'm trying to help.'

Liv listened as I told her what I knew, which wasn't all that much.

'For what it's worth, I agree that it's hard to imagine him hurting her.'

Hard, but not impossible. I tried not to bristle. 'The angriest I've ever seen him was when I was hurt. If anything, Melissa's history of being a victim of domestic violence was one of the things that made him want to be with her. He wants to protect people, not bully them.'

Liv sighed. 'What are you going to do?'

'Whatever I can.'

'Maeve . . .'

'Don't.'

'I don't want to see you get hurt.'

'How would that happen? This isn't about me.'

'You shouldn't get involved.' Her unhappiness was unmistakable. 'Every time I think you're getting over him, something like this drags you back. You need to let go of him or you'll never be happy. There'll always be some disaster, some life-or-death situation, just when you're starting to get your life together.'

I had done a better job than I'd thought of presenting a composed, contented face to the world if I'd even fooled Liv.

'He needs me. And I want to be there for him. It sometimes feels like I'm the only person who's on his side.'

'Yeah, and why is that? He doesn't deserve you.'

'I think he does,' I said quietly, and Liv sighed.

'There has to be someone else out there for you. I refuse to believe he's the only attractive man you can find to be rude to you, which is apparently the thing that hooks you like a fish.'

I managed a shaky laugh. 'I'd better go.'

'Keep in touch,' Liv said. 'Even if I don't agree with what you're doing, I'll help if I can. But for your sake, not his.'

I hadn't intended to go to the police station, but I found myself drawn there. I parked opposite it and stared at the building, an architecturally disastrous 1970s block with mirrored glass in the windows. An elderly man in a navy anorak sat outside it, huddled on a bench, his breath clouding the air around him. Otherwise there was no sign of life. Police stations were usually places of refuge for me, where I was welcome, where I could find people like myself, engaged in work I respected. For the first time I saw the police station as an unfeeling institution designed to hurt. It was less of a building than a threat. He was in there somewhere, sitting opposite Roz Fuller and Henry Cowell in an interview room, trying to talk his way out of custody, or lying down in a cell getting some rest. He wouldn't be in a good mood, wherever he was.

I wasn't either. After I talked to Ellen Moore I wasn't sure what to think, and I didn't like it. With my view of Mark Pell refracted through Derwent's unforgiving lens I had always been completely satisfied that Mark had been violent towards Melissa and that she had fled in total fear, and I'd decided Ellen was deluded if she didn't back her daughter up. Now I was having doubts, which I didn't want. If Mark was responsible for Melissa's current injuries, Derwent could be exonerated.

It would all be so simple if it was Mark's fault.

Movement across the road caught my attention: a woman coming out of the police station with a folder under her arm. She stopped to make a call, her hair white in the bright streetlights. Her face was grim and as she talked she chopped the air with one slim hand: things were not going her way, evidently. I must have looked at her for a full minute before my brain kicked in and I recognised her: Lesley Mackenzie, a criminal defence solicitor that I knew well from sitting opposite her, interviewing clients. I liked her, respected her and feared her in equal measure, and if I was in trouble I would want her on my side.

And Josh knew her too.

I was out of the car and crossing the road before I thought about whether it was wise or not, wrapping my coat around me against the chill of the night.

'Lesley?'

She had been about to go inside again but she stopped, surprised.

'Maeve Kerrigan – I work with Josh . . .'

'Maeve! What are you doing here?' She looked behind her, checking we were unobserved. The man in the anorak was reading a pamphlet of some kind, oblivious to our presence. She took my arm. 'Where's your car?'

'Across the road.' I pointed. 'But—'

'Not here.' She said it with total authority and I went silent, allowing her to steer me across to the car. Once we were inside with the doors closed, she seemed to relax.

'Why are you here?'

'I wanted to see if I could help – if there was anything he needed . . . I don't know.' I felt embarrassed at the way her face had softened as I spoke. 'You are here with Josh, aren't you?'

'Yes.'

'And it's not going well.'

'No.'

I'd expected it – I'd been braced for it – but it still hit me like a punch in the gut. 'What – what's happened? Is it Melissa? Is she—'

'She's recovering. She's doing well.'

'So what's wrong?'

Lesley hesitated, drumming her fingers on the folder on her lap. 'I know he wouldn't want me to show you this. He doesn't want you to be involved.'

'Of course he doesn't. He likes to keep his problems to himself.' If she didn't give me the folder I was seriously considering grabbing it. 'And he's overprotective when it comes to me. But this is too important to leave me out in case it affects my career. It is *my* career, after all. I get to decide what happens with it, not him.'

'That's not the whole story,' Lesley said, and something in her tone rang a warning bell for me. 'I don't think he would want you to know this.' Another nervous tap of her fingers on the cardboard folder. 'I think he'd be devastated if it changed your opinion of him.'

'Nothing could change my opinion of him,' I said steadily. 'I *know* him. If there's something bad in that folder, there'll be an explanation for it.'

Lesley didn't look convinced. If anything, she looked more worried – this time for me.

'I don't know what else to do.' It was a mutter, part of a dialogue with herself. I waited, knowing that pushing her was going to be counterproductive, ready to snap. My nails were digging into my palms.

'OK. Here's what I have.' She handed me the file. 'These are printouts of picture and text files downloaded from a phone owned by Melissa's friend, Clara Porter. We don't have all the material yet but Roz Fuller – you know her?'

'I've met her,' I said.

'She was in a hurry. She wanted to show us what they had so she can rush Josh into a confession. If he admits it in interview he'll get the most credit for it. With his job, with the circumstances, he'll be looking at a hefty sentence anyway. We can talk about stress – he's a prime candidate for PTSD with his army experience and the job you do, plus there was the extra burden more recently with Thomas's illness—'

'Wait,' I said. 'Why are you talking about mitigation? He's not pleading guilty to anything.'

'That's what he says too, but you haven't looked at what they have.' Lesley sighed. 'I wish it wasn't so convincing, really I do, but it's detailed and damning.'

I had been desperate to see what was in the file. Now I had to fight the urge to hand it back to her unopened. I put the interior light on in the car and flipped the folder open.

My first thought, as I turned over the pages with numb fingers, was that it looked bad – as bad as Lesley had said, if not worse. It wasn't that the injuries in the photographs were severe, it was more that there were so many of them: misshapen bruises along an arm, a ring of fingermarks around a wrist, a graze on Melissa's jaw near her mouth, a circle of raw skin on her scalp where hair was missing. I made myself read the messages that went along with the images, blinking hard.

I said the wrong thing again . . .
Do you think anyone will notice this if I wear my hair down?
I can't go on like this. I'm so scared.
It's happened again and I don't know what to do.
I feel so trapped.
This isn't how you treat someone you love, is it?

I thought for one awful moment that I was going to be sick. I closed my eyes, breathing deeply, until I was sure I had myself under control.

'This is impossible.'

'It's all there. The messages start over a year ago. There's one every two or three months. And when you get to the end, there's a sort of timeline that Clara Porter kept with a list of incidents and dates and what provoked them and what injuries Melissa had, where they'd talked about what happened. It's incredibly damaging to him. I don't see any way around a guilty plea. Juries are receptive to this kind of ongoing record-keeping and it helps with the witnesses being able to remember what happened and when.' She paused for a beat. 'And I think he should plead guilty, if I'm being honest, but keep it to yourself. He may have been struggling with his mental health but look how this poor woman has suffered.'

I had stopped on a picture of Melissa where she had photographed herself in the mirror, staring into the lens, her eyes dead. A red welt circled her upper arm. It was a dreadful image, upsetting on every level.

'You'd better give it back to me.' Lesley held out her hand for the folder. 'I need to go in there and convince him to make the best of this, but he'll probably sack me instead.'

'He mustn't do that.' I looked at her. 'Please – can I go through it one more time?'

'I'm surprised you can bear to.' Her mouth tightened. 'He couldn't look at them.'

I nodded, my attention already on the file. I looked at each image with the kind of focus I brought to my work, detached from the significance, concentrating only on what it showed me and how that matched up with the story in the timeline that Clara Porter had so carefully and laboriously kept. I took out my phone and checked a few details, my hands trembling, and then I went back to the start again.

'I really think—' Lesley began as I reached the end for the second time and I shook my head.

'No. This is impossible.'

'I know.' She sighed. 'It must be even worse for you, knowing him so well.'

My heart was singing. 'That's not what I mean. I'm not worried at all, because it's *impossible* for him to have done what he's supposed to have done. This file – it's clear and rigorous and organised and it doesn't do anything but help him. You can use it to get him out of this mess.'

She was looking at me as if I was insane. 'What do you mean?'

'There's a perfect record here, isn't there? A detailed account with everything listed by date, in a document kept by a third party. No room for any argument about when something happened.'

'Exactly. I don't see how that's helpful.'

'Because it started seventeen months ago,' I said, pointing at the first date. 'And I happen to know exactly where Josh Derwent was that day, and before it, and afterwards. He was nowhere near home. When Clara describes him holding Melissa down and choking her until she blacked out, he was sitting with me in a town called West Idleford, watching *A Midsummer Night's Dream* at an open-air performance in front of many, many witnesses. We were working there for weeks. He returned to London for a few days during this period but the dates don't match up with the dates Melissa was alleging she was injured. And here – this picture of her from March – he was in the Lake District that night, for work.'

'You remember that without checking?' It was a polite enquiry, not a challenge, but I flushed.

'I remember.' Then, with more focus, I added, 'If you match up the incidents in the record with his work diary, you'll find that she only had time to create these injuries, or the appearance of them, when he wasn't around to see them. She faked it.'

'Why would she do that?'

'Because she was angry with him. Because he started to pull away from her seventeen months ago. She knew she was losing him and she wanted to punish him by taking away his job. She always said he loved it more than her.'

'That's evil,' Lesley said faintly. 'What if you hadn't noticed the dates?'

'Josh should have noticed them himself.'

'He wasn't in a condition to notice anything, believe me.' She was frowning. 'Our trouble is Roz Fuller. Even if we can prove the dates are wrong, I don't think it will be enough to convince her he didn't hurt Melissa. She'll come up with some reason why it doesn't matter.'

'This picture, with the injury on her arm.' I showed it to her. 'Look at what's on the bed behind her.'

'It's hard to see . . . Rubber bands?'

'They leave a nasty mark if you twist them tight enough. A mark that fades so no one asks you about it later.'

'But we can't prove that's what she did.'

'We don't need to. We just need to make it clear they can't rely on this evidence to prove Josh hurt her.'

Lesley pulled a face. 'Josh thinks his way out is Melissa. He's expecting her to tell the police he didn't attack her when they talk to her, but you're suggesting she set him up. She's going to tell them he was the one who put her in hospital, isn't she?'

'Very possibly.' I was feeling sick again. If she said he had done it, then it was game over. Mark Pell had said it himself.

Even if these accusations don't stick, they'll follow him around for the rest of his life. Something like this happens – you're never the same afterwards...

'So what do we do?' Lesley had clearly decided I was part of the team now, and I wasn't going to demur. 'How do we get ahead of her?'

'I have one idea. I think there's someone who might be able to help us.' I held up the file. 'Can I keep this?'

'Yes, of course . . . but why?'

'I want to show it to someone. I think Melissa has done this before.'

22

Mark Pell was waiting for me outside his hotel, pacing up and down while I parked.

'You could have stayed inside,' I said.

'I couldn't. Anyway, the door is locked for non-residents after ten.' He pressed the intercom buzzer and then held the door open for me when it came open, the habit of politeness stronger than whatever reservations he might have about me personally.

'I forgot it was so late.' I checked the time: hurrying on. 'Thanks for seeing me.'

'Do you want to talk here or in my room?' He looked around the bleak reception area, where there was a single bench seat. 'I didn't think I'd need to entertain anyone at my hotel so I went for a budget option.'

I wasn't altogether keen to shut myself away with Mark, but the alternative wasn't appealing. The night manager was shuffling papers behind the desk, barely disguising her interest in our conversation. She had long acrylic nails that she flicked against the desk with a rattle that reminded me of scurrying insects. I thought of the groomed, elegant lovelies at the Governor Hotel and their impeccable discretion. The Albion Hotel was a different story.

'I think it'll have to be your room.'

He nodded, frowning, and let me go ahead of him down the long corridor. 'Right at the end. Room 109.'

'I never stay on the ground floor in case someone breaks into my room.'

He gave me a wry look. 'I weighed up whether I was more worried about being burgled or dying in a fire and burglary won.'

'Was this really the best hotel you could find?'

'I just wanted to be close to Thomas,' Mark said quietly.

He reached past me to open the door and stepped back again, careful to leave plenty of space between us. It had to be awkward for him, especially given the way I'd spoken to him earlier. I went in, scanning the room: basic but clean, and it was as tidy as Derwent himself would have left it. There were faded short curtains at the window and a thin coverlet on the bed had seen better days. It was the sort of room I'd been in many times when I was in uniform, for sudden deaths that had almost always been a suicide.

I took the lone armchair and waited while Mark wavered between sitting on the edge of the bed and remaining on his feet. The bed won, but he stayed as far away from me as he could.

'There isn't a minibar but I can offer you a tea or a coffee. Don't get excited, it's UHT milk.'

'That is the smallest kettle I've ever seen,' I said, distracted by the tray he was indicating. 'But no. I'm fine.'

He looked relieved; the offer had been a reflex, like holding the door open. 'You said on the phone it was important and you obviously wanted privacy to talk about it. What is it?'

'Before I rang you, I called Karen Samuels.'

His wariness increased by a notch. 'PC Samuels. I haven't heard that name for a while.'

'She sends her best.'

He laughed, without humour. 'I doubt that. She took great pleasure in arresting me. If she'd had her way I would have been locked up for some of the last few years. She was very much convinced that Mel was telling the truth.'

'Mel can be convincing.' I sat up straight, lacing my fingers around my upper knee. 'I wanted to talk to you in more detail about the first time we met, in the hospital when she was recovering after the fire. You said earlier you'd been looking for her after she ran away from you.'

'I'd hired private detectives to try to trace her and come up with nothing. I was desperate to see Thomas. I understood she wanted to leave me and that was something I had to accept, but I wanted to check that he was all right and I wanted to know that she was safe too. I was still very much in love with her and I was . . . desperate.'

'You said to me then that Melissa was paranoid. You described her as a fantasist, which annoyed me.'

'I remember.'

'I spoke to Karen after that,' I continued, 'and she convinced me that Melissa was telling the truth.'

'They arrested me three times and never charged me.' Mark frowned. 'If Karen could have locked me up, she would have.'

'She said you knew her boss – he was a friend of yours.'

'He was. But he would have locked me up too if there'd been any evidence.'

'Melissa was vulnerable. She'd tried to kill herself, hadn't she?'

He looked irritable. 'She stood on a bridge for a couple of hours. It was her hormones, the doctors said, because she was pregnant and it affected her mental health. She was diagnosed with temporary psychosis. She wound up in hospital for a few weeks and then we watched her incredibly closely, night and day, until Thomas was born. It was gruelling.'

'Ellen told me that after Thomas arrived you started having trouble in your marriage. It must have been difficult for you if Melissa was focused on Thomas all the time.'

He looked taken aback. 'What did Ellen say exactly?'

'Um . . .' I tried to remember the precise words. 'That it's hard when you're used to having all the attention and you have to share it, so Ellen helped out as much as she could.'

'I wasn't the one who struggled. Mel resented Thomas. But he must never know that – promise me you won't tell him.'

'I won't,' I said, although I was cold with shock. 'Did she feel neglected?'

'Thomas had to come first.' Mark shrugged. 'I think, looking back on it, that was the turning point. She kept looking for ways to get attention.'

'So she made false allegations against you.'

'Yeah.' He squeezed his hands between his knees, looking exhausted. 'All kinds of things.'

'Can I read you something?'

'Go on.'

I opened the folder and read out, '"He dragged me into the hall by the hair and held me up against the wall. He had a knife in his pocket and he showed it to me and threatened me. He told me no one would believe me if I said he'd hurt me. He pushed me down the stairs and stamped on my back. I curled into a ball and he kicked me in the ribs and thighs where no one would see the bruises. He told me I was lucky to have him, and most men wouldn't put up with me."'

Mark had jumped up, stumbling backwards until he collided with the door. 'Stop.'

'Do you recognise that?'

'It's from Melissa's statement that she made the first time I was arrested.' He swallowed convulsively. 'And none of it happened.'

'It's not, actually. But you're right, none of it happened. Those sentences are taken from messages that Melissa sent to a friend of hers over the last seventeen or eighteen months, around the time she started complaining to you about Josh Derwent and saying she missed you.'

'But that's what she said about me.' He shook his head. 'I never hurt her physically. I never told her she was lucky or that no one would put up with her.'

'Either she's repeating what happened with you, or she lied about you too, because there's no way Josh did or said any of those things.'

'She's lying. I've said it all along.'

I closed the folder. 'It goes against everything I believe to question her version of events, but I have to admit it doesn't hang together. Even so, she got the police involved. She had social services helping her. She got support from the organisation that arranged for her to stay on the Maudling Estate after she left you.'

'That was part of the scenario she was acting out. She knew she could come home anytime if she wanted. She knew her mother would have taken her in even if she didn't come home to me.' He looked down. 'I don't expect you to understand it, but I wanted her back. I loved her so much.'

'And then she met Josh.' I tried very hard to keep my voice neutral.

'He was everything she'd ever wanted. A real hero, and tough. Someone who would look after her and Thomas and put me in my place.' Mark spread his hands. 'How could I compete with that?'

Everything that had made Derwent attractive to her had ended up annoying her, I thought. 'Being a police officer – she didn't like the reality of the job, but she's not the only partner who has issues with it.'

'She didn't like you. She was jealous.'

'I assure you, she had no reason to be.'

'No?'

I felt the heat rise in my face.

'Maybe he was too decent to act on his feelings,' Mark said slowly, 'but she could still be jealous that he had them.'

'I don't know. He didn't talk to me about that. He tried to keep it to himself.' I cleared my throat, determined to keep my composure. 'Anyway, I think she learned a lot from what happened with you. She realised that there had to be evidence over a long period. She understood that she needed third parties to act as witnesses.'

Mark grabbed the folder and leafed through the contents, his face grim. 'This is a step up, isn't it? But it's all the same situations. The same confrontations. The same language. And none of it happened in my case. I suppose it's even more unlikely that it *did* happen with Josh. I'm not particularly motivated to help him – he hates my guts, after all – but I know I didn't hurt her and that makes me think he didn't either.'

'Karen Samuels is sending me the statements that she took from Melissa, so I can match up the places where they overlap with these messages, but I wanted you to see them too.' I hesitated, then steeled myself. 'Karen suggested she was using her experiences with you to come up with the scenarios involving Josh.'

'No. Really, no. I never hurt her. Not even once. But I do recognise so much of this.' He shook his head. 'Obviously I was unfinished business for her. She was still thinking about it. When the time came, she told the same story with better visuals.'

I wasn't sure if he was lying to me or not, but I needed to believe him. It made me feel sick to think of how much time and care Melissa had taken to build a trap for Derwent. And if I couldn't get him out of it, the consequences would be appalling. I allowed myself to imagine it for a moment: losing his job, his pension, prison, disgrace, losing Thomas, ending up in a small, cheap hotel like this one thinking about the probationer who'd soon be able to tick off 'suicide' in their workbook . . .

'I want to put together something that convinces the investigators that Josh couldn't have been involved in hurting Melissa. I need something to counter the evidence she's invented. Will you make a statement?'

'You're asking a lot.' He threw the folder onto the bed. 'If you believe she's lying about Josh, why didn't you believe me?'

'I don't know you the way I know him.'

'With respect, you haven't tried to know me. You've bought into the idea that I'm a monster. And I don't think you fully trust me, even now.'

'I have my issues,' I said, with difficulty. 'But I'm trying. And I think you could make a big difference here, if you speak up.'

'I'll think about it.'

'Please,' I said. I wished I'd been nicer to Mark Pell – a little less spiky, a little more gentle. 'Look, I don't have time to waste. I'm not asking for my own sake. I'm trying to help Josh, and I know you don't care about him but Thomas does. I really need you to speak up and tell Roz Fuller about Melissa, and I need you to do it now.'

'Why should I?'

'Because it's the right thing to do, and if you are all the things you say you are, you wouldn't hesitate to do the right thing.' I swallowed. 'I need your help, Mark. She's had seventeen months to put this together, and I've got seventeen hours to pull it apart.'

'She may have had longer to plan this,' Mark Pell said slowly, 'but I'm still betting on you.'

23

It was close to one in the morning when I left the Albion Hotel. I sat in the car and called Lesley Mackenzie, to update her about Mark, and Melissa's original statements to the police.

'I don't know if he'll help.'

'I hope he does. We need it.' She sounded exhausted.

'What's happening now?'

'Officially they've given us a break between interviews. Unofficially, if I had to guess, Roz Fuller is trying to decide if it's worth asking the CPS for permission to charge him.'

'Already?' I couldn't keep the panic from my voice. 'Have they even spoken to Melissa yet?'

'No. They're still here at the police station.'

'Then there's no way the CPS will charge him tonight. They'll bail him until they've spoken to Melissa. What if she doesn't support the prosecution?'

'You know they can go ahead without her cooperation. It wouldn't be the first time a victim of domestic violence chose not to give evidence in a trial.'

Oh God... I did know that. Even if Melissa changed her mind this nightmare might not end. I could imagine Roz insisting on a prosecution, using the rules that had been introduced to help terrified, vulnerable people who were too scared or too defeated to speak up about what had happened to them.

'What are you doing now?' I asked.

'They want to interview him again at 9 a.m. once he's had some sleep.'

'They won't be sleeping.'

'Probably not. But he needs a clear head to answer the allegations. And so do I.'

'Absolutely,' I said with feeling. 'Get some rest.'

'What about you?'

'There isn't much I can do at this time of night.'

'So go home.'

'Yes.' I was thinking *no*, though. It didn't sit well with me that Roz Fuller and Henry Cowell were fired up, hunting for the evidence that would destroy Derwent's life while I sat around doing nothing about it. I wanted to be ahead of them in the morning, not trying to catch up. And if there was a development in the Ilaria Cavendish case I would need to know about that too.

In an alternate universe I had gone out for dinner with a pleasant, charming man and had returned home thinking about whether a second date was a good idea, and what I should wear the following day, and how Ilaria had died, and whether I would see Derwent tomorrow or not, and whether that would make me happy or not. I longed, quite fiercely, for that world where the problems were at least familiar, instead of this remorseless spiral of events that I couldn't control.

'Thanks, Lesley. I'll speak to you before eight if I've got anything useful to tell you.'

Where I went, in the end, was the hospital. It never closed, and, like an airport, it didn't seem to obey the same temporal logic as the outside world. The area around A&E was as busy at midnight as it had been at midday. I was hoping to see Melissa, but failing that there was Clara Porter who had assumed unexpected importance in my life, considering I'd never heard of her a few hours earlier. Through a combination of charm and badge-waving I managed to track Melissa from the accident and emergency department to the ward where she was resting. I didn't say I was on official business, but I didn't say I wasn't either.

'You can go up with her friend, if you like.' The nurse who told me where to find Melissa nodded at a figure who was disappearing down the hall. 'That lady there. She's got her belongings.'

I thanked her and ran, catching up with Clara Porter by the lifts. She was tall and bulky and utterly unremarkable, the sort of person who was easy to overlook. She wore a long padded coat in a shade of beige that I actively disliked, pale jeans and a pair of trainers that had once been white but now had a grey tinge. She was in her early thirties, at a guess, but she looked older, her face naturally tending towards glumness in the set of her mouth and eyes, her posture terrible. She was carrying a second coat and had an overnight bag slung over one shoulder.

'Clara!'

'Yes?' She looked wary.

'I'm a police officer,' I said. 'Are you going to see Melissa?'

'I have her things.' She gestured at the bag. 'I'm dropping them off for her before I go home. I didn't think I'd be here so long but they've only just moved her to a ward.'

'It was kind of you to wait.'

'I don't mind.' She had gone slightly pink. 'I'd do anything for her.'

I followed her into the lift and pressed the button for the third floor. 'It's late. Do you have a way to get home?'

'My dad is picking me up.'

So I couldn't offer her a lift to gain her trust. Plan B.

'How did you meet Melissa?'

'I work in the school – I'm Thomas's TA.'

'Oh, I see.' The lift doors opened and we moved into the corridor. I stopped walking and she did the same, politely. Easy to influence, easy to control, I thought. 'Is that usual? Making friends with the parents?'

She bit her lip. 'I'm not good at getting to know people. I'm shy. Melissa was always nice. She made the effort to get to know me.' Her hand went to the small pendant that hung over the collar of her sweatshirt, a silver butterfly.

'Did she give you that necklace?'

'How did you know?' Her mouth curved into a small, private smile. 'Yes, she did. For my birthday. I didn't even remind her. She remembered it.'

'Lovely,' I said.

'My parents gave me money but Melissa was the only person who gave me a present.'

Which meant Clara was lonely as well as biddable. I was more and more certain that Melissa had singled her out because she suited her purposes.

'That's Melissa for you. She's very thoughtful.'

Clara's eyes lit up. 'Oh, you know her too?'

I wasn't going to lie to Clara, but I steeled myself for a reaction. 'I work with Josh.'

Instant, total shutdown as soon as I said his name. She took a step away from me, the smile disappearing, her eyes trained on the floor.

'I've got to go.'

'Wait, Clara, please!' I managed to get in front of her. 'I'd like to ask you a couple of questions. Please. It won't take a minute.'

'I don't want to talk to you. It's late and I want to go home.' She was looking past me, her face strained. 'My parents will be worried about me. I was only here in case Melissa needed me.'

'I'm sure Melissa will be very grateful to you for coming and waiting around for so long.'

'I'd stay for longer if it helped.' She was still refusing to look at me, her expression stubborn.

'I know you don't like Josh, Clara,' I said gently. 'I understand.'

That brought her eyes up to mine. 'Really? Do you? I'm not sure you do.'

'I've seen the record you kept of . . . incidents between him and Melissa.'

'Then you know he was hitting her. Terrifying her. You know he kicked her and pulled her hair out.'

I kept my voice quiet so it didn't seem as if I was challenging her. 'I know she *told* you that was happening.'

She stiffened. Clara might be quiet and docile but she was clever enough to spot what I was getting at. 'I saw the bruises. I saw the places where he ripped her hair out. I saw her lying unconscious in an ambulance a few hours ago, covered in blood. Did you see any of that?'

'No, but—'

'No. That's all you have to say. No. I saw it. I hugged her while she cried. I sat with her at the gym when she was too stiff and sore to go through a Pilates class but she needed to get out of the house anyway. I couldn't even bear to look at him once I knew what he was doing to her and you should be ashamed of yourself if you think anything he did is excusable or acceptable.'

'I don't think any of that is excusable. I'm just trying to understand what you saw as opposed to what you were told.' I was trying to keep a grip on my temper – snapping at her would be counterproductive, to say the least – but I wished I could describe, in detail, my own personal experience of domestic violence so she understood I didn't need a lecture. 'Did you ever see them arguing? Did you ever actually see him raise a hand to her?'

'No, but I wasn't there all the time.'

'You were there some of the time. You were in the house when they were there, and when they were out, and you saw Thomas on his own at school. Did he ever mention anything about it?'

'No. He was probably too scared to say that Josh was hurting his mum,' she said sulkily.

'Did he seem scared?'

'I don't know. I thought he probably was even if he hid it. I didn't want to upset him by asking about it.'

That was convenient.

'You know he adores Josh, don't you? He wouldn't feel that way about someone who hurt Melissa.'

'Maybe he didn't know.'

'But you knew.'

'Yes.'

'Because Melissa told you it was happening.'

'Exactly. And showed me.'

'She showed you what she wanted you to see.'

'She showed me what was happening,' Clara countered.

I took a moment. It was infuriating to hear her recite Melissa's version of events, but it was also instructive. 'Before you heard that Josh was violent, what did you make of him?'

'I never liked him. All the mums used to get excited when he was at pick-up or drop-off. They'd giggle and flirt. He enjoyed it.'

'He would,' I admitted. I would defend Derwent to the death on many counts but I couldn't argue about that.

'He should have been thinking about Melissa.' She sniffed. 'And he was so arrogant.'

'It's just his manner,' I said lamely. *And his personality . . .*

'He would look at me and then. . . look away. Like I wasn't important enough for him to notice me.' She was red now.

'I've seen him behave that way, but it's not because he didn't notice you. He notices far too much, believe me. It's usually when he feels someone isn't at ease around him. He wouldn't want to make you uncomfortable.'

'I never knew what to say, when he talked to me, when he was driving me home after babysitting.' She looked down, furious. 'I wanted him to leave me alone.'

'It sounds to me as if he did, though, if you thought he didn't notice you.'

She blinked, on the edge of tears. 'I'm always on edge around him. I can't relax.'

'I know that feeling.'

The wry amusement in my voice made her look up. 'Do you?'

'Very much so.' I hesitated. 'Did you say this to Melissa?'

'Once. When we were starting to be friends.' She wriggled. 'I told her he scared me.'

Bingo. Melissa had spotted that Clara was primed to believe the worst of Josh. She was the ideal witness: credulous and painstaking and eager to please.

'Look, Clara, I know you only wanted to help. I have one more question. The dates you listed in your record – are you sure they were accurate?'

'They were. I'm careful about that kind of thing.'

'That's what I wanted to hear.' It was truer than she knew. 'Did Melissa know about the record?'

'No. I never showed it to her. But I kept it, like a diary, in case she ever needed it.' Clara shrugged. 'I tried to persuade her to go to the police but she said she didn't trust them – you. I hoped she would change her mind one day, or that I'd get the opportunity to show someone.'

'And now you have. How fortunate.' I couldn't quite keep the sardonic edge out of my voice.

'He did hurt her.' She sounded breathless. 'He did all those things.'

'I know you believe that.'

'I believe it because it's true. And one day you'll have to admit it.' She slipped past me and hurried down the corridor, and this time I let her go.

24

A sensible person would have left the hospital after talking to Clara; I had pretty much got what I came for. I understood how Melissa had set her trap, and the mistake she had made by choosing Clara as her confidante, not realising she would go above and beyond her role by creating the dossier.

It was something else that made me stay, something stronger than curiosity.

I needed to see Melissa, face to face.

I slid into a dark waiting room dedicated to a clinic that wouldn't be open for another seven hours, and waited, fiddling with one of my earrings which kept coming loose. At last I saw Clara walk past. This time she was without the bag and coat she had been carrying before, which told me that she had seen Melissa. I leaned out of the waiting room and watched her disappear into the lift. Then I walked briskly down the corridor, looking as if I had every right to be there, until I reached the ward where the nurse in A&E had said Melissa was spending the night.

I had to exert every ounce of charm I possessed to talk my way past the ward sister, who had the free and easy manner of a prison guard and the eyes of someone who had seen too much, particularly on night shifts. Her expression was the opposite of encouraging as I explained who I was and what I wanted.

'And I won't stay for long. You see, I want to be able to reassure her son that I've seen her and she's OK. He's only eight, and I promised him I'd have an update for him in the morning when he wakes up.'

'She's in a ward for three but on her own. If it wasn't for the fact that she's alone in that room, I wouldn't allow you to see her.' She shuffled paperwork crossly. 'But she is awake, at the moment, and you won't be disturbing anyone.'

'So I can see her?'

'I'll ask her.'

That was that, I accepted; there was no way Melissa would hear the name 'Maeve Kerrigan' and lay out a welcome mat. I watched the ward sister walk impressively slowly down the hallway, and thought about leaving before she returned so I didn't have to deal with the humiliation of being evicted. When she emerged from the ward again, though, she stopped at the door and beckoned to me.

'You can see her. But not for long. She's tired. She needs to sleep.' The ward sister eyed me. 'And so do you.'

I currently felt as if I would never sleep again, as if my blood had been replaced with a caffeine-adrenaline cocktail. I nodded, though, and thanked her, and slid past her into the ward.

The ward was dark, apart from a single light above the bed nearest the window. I walked slowly towards the still figure in the bed. She was propped up against the pillows, looking small and fragile in the oversized hospital gown. It was a few months since I'd last seen Melissa. I had been expecting her to have visible injuries – I had seen the blood in the hall of Derwent's house, after all – but apart from an impressive bandage around her head, her face was unmarked. Her eyes tracked me across the room until I reached the end of the bed.

'Hi.' A breath of a voice, but she was alert.

'How are you?'

She lifted a hand and gestured vaguely at herself. 'Not my best.'

I had been expecting to feel angry and self-righteous, but all of my outrage collapsed like a deflating balloon as I stared at her. Round, reddish-blue and black bruises marked her arms, all the way up, disappearing under the sleeves of the gown, and there was nothing imaginary about them. 'God, Melissa. I'm so sorry. Are you in pain? Have they given you something for it?'

She waved her hand instead of answering me directly. 'What are you doing here?'

'I wanted to be able to reassure Thomas that you were OK. He was worried about you.'

'I called my mum just now, once I got hold of my phone.' She frowned and tried to clear her throat. 'So you can stay away from Thomas.'

'I was only trying to help,' I said quietly. I was staying at the end of the bed but I couldn't take my eyes off the injuries on her arms.

'You look shocked.'

'I am. I knew you were hurt, but . . .'

'Bruising like this all over my back and my legs.'

'That's . . . awful.'

'You weren't expecting it, were you?'

'No.'

'Does it remind you of what happened to you?'

I stiffened, shocked. 'I don't remember a lot of that.' *I've tried to forget it.*

She struggled to sit up. 'You didn't know he was capable of this, did you? Your Josh. Your knight in shining armour. The man of your dreams – and whatever else you think he is.'

'You don't have the first idea what I think about him.'

'I think you don't want to believe he did this. But it's true.'

'No.'

She gasped in outrage. 'How can you question me when you've been in this exact situation?'

I shook my head.

'You remember what it was like. The helplessness. The shame. You remember how you hated yourself. You couldn't trust your own judgement anymore. You were so sad and so alone.' Her voice was honeyed with sympathy but every word hurt, as she intended.

'Let's talk about you, not me,' I said. 'Because you're right, I don't believe Josh did this. It doesn't make any sense to me.'

'You see what you want to see. You get it wrong all the time – you should have learned better.' She closed her eyes. 'I didn't think he was like this either, at first. He's good at fooling people.'

A wave of doubt swept over me, leaving me dizzy. It was like a nightmare, where the impossible becomes real. I dug my nails into my palms, fighting for composure. Maybe I didn't know him – maybe I'd been mistaken to trust someone again . . .

But I knew better than this, didn't I? I squared my shoulders.

'I spoke to Mark.'

Her eyes snapped open. 'Mark? Why? Where did you see him?'

'He's here, staying nearby. For Thomas.'

'He shouldn't be anywhere near him.' She pushed at the covers, trying to free herself, and for the first time I thought her reaction was genuine and instinctive. 'Keep him away from my son.'

'Relax.' I looked at the door, worried about the ward sister coming back. 'He hasn't been alone with him, and he won't be. But he is Thomas's father.'

'Unfortunately.'

'He's a good father. He loves Thomas.'

'What would you know about that?' She gave a little huff. 'You don't even have kids.'

'Does that mean I can't recognise a loving parent when I see one? He seems kind. Thoughtful.'

She glared. 'God, you really have a type, don't you? If you want a full list of my cast-offs, you can work your way through them all.'

Bitch. I let my feelings show on my face and her eyes lit up: she enjoyed getting a reaction from me.

'Let me guess. Mark convinced you he was a decent person who'd been misrepresented. What a fantastic judge of character you are.' Her lip curled. 'You learned nothing from what happened to you.'

'You've created a whole fantasy where you were the brave victim twice over, but the details don't match up with the facts.'

'You've let Mark and Josh talk you into believing I couldn't be telling the truth, even though you can see with your own eyes that I am.' She dragged the gown off one shoulder, turning to show me the overlapping bruises that dappled her back. 'I'm not making this up, am I?'

I stared at her – at the injuries she couldn't have caused herself this time.

'Nothing to say?' She leaned against the pillows, triumphant. 'I didn't think so.'

'I don't know how that happened to you, but I know it wasn't Josh.'

'No, you *wish* it wasn't him. It's almost worth it to see the look on your face. You're always so superior, so smug, so *perfect*. But I'd be ashamed to be like you – obsessed with work, no husband or boyfriend, no kids. What sort of life is that? And you act as if it makes you better than everyone else.'

'I don't,' I said, stung.

'He talks to you, doesn't he? He tells you about how awful I am, how he wants to leave me but he can't, because of Thomas, or for some other reason that you have to respect.' She imitated his voice. '*Poor Melissa, I can't walk away at the moment. She's making me miserable. If only I had you to cheer me up, Maeve. You understand me. We have so much in common.*'

I shook my head. 'He doesn't talk to me like that.'

'I don't believe you.'

'He keeps it all to himself. He never talks about you at all.'

Her eyes hardened and she sat up straight. 'I feel sorry for you, you know. You've been making a fool of yourself over him, all this time, and he's never been worth it.'

'You're not going to make me hate him,' I said. 'You can't manipulate me the way you've manipulated Clara.'

She was a good liar, but not good enough to hide her surprise. 'What do you know about Clara?'

'You have her exactly where you want her, doing your bidding, sharing evidence with the police.'

'She cares about me.' Melissa examined her hand and the drip that was taped to it. 'She knows the truth and she wants to make sure justice is done. You should want the same.'

'Oh, I do. And it will be.'

She raised her eyebrows at me. 'We'll see, won't we?'

The door swung open with a clatter, and Melissa shrank back against the pillows, suddenly looking both terrified and frail.

Roz Fuller stalked into the ward, glaring at me. 'What the hell do you think you're doing?'

I tried to look innocent. 'Talking to Melissa.'

'For what possible reason?'

'I wanted to see if she was OK so I could reassure Thomas,' I said, wide-eyed.

'Please . . .' Melissa's voice was a wail. 'I want her to go away.'

'Don't worry, she's going.' The inspector waited, holding the door, and I walked out past her and Henry Cowell. His expression was a mixture of disappointment and concern, and I wished I could explain myself to him. I made eye contact with Roz Fuller instead, meaningfully, and she followed me out into the hallway. I turned to face her, bracing myself for her rage.

'Are you actually joking?' she hissed. 'I've been told you're a good police officer – highly regarded, according to your boss. Reliable, hard-working, trustworthy. What the hell is this?'

'I know how it looks.'

'Do you? Do you really? Give me one good reason not to have you suspended and investigated for tampering with a witness.'

'She's lying. That's one.' I was trembling. 'Look, I know I'm in trouble. But I didn't challenge her about her evidence or try to make her change her story. I let her talk to me about it, and about her ex-husband, that's all. Ma'am, you can't be taken in by her. She's not what she seems.'

25

Roz came back into the ward, shaking her head. 'I'm sorry that happened, Melissa. She shouldn't have been allowed anywhere near you.'

'I was wondering.' Melissa put a hand to her head, exploring the bandage that covered it as if she couldn't understand what it was. 'I thought she wanted to tell me about Thomas. I've been so worried about him. What did he see?'

'Nothing.' Roz sat down in the chair by the bed, which Cowell had left empty. He stood behind her, silent. 'By the time Thomas got to the house, you were already on your way to the hospital. He went off in the car with Mr Kerrigan, to his house.'

Melissa's mouth tightened. 'He likes the Kerrigans.'

'Well, he's still there, quite safe, and your mother is there with him.'

'I knew she was there. I called her a few minutes ago. She said he was OK but she didn't know if he'd seen me while I was unconscious . . .' She closed her eyes.

'I know it's late and ordinarily I would wait until the morning but I'm under pressure because of custody time limits.' Roz cut herself off and smiled. 'Which you don't need to worry about. If you aren't too tired to talk, can we ask you some questions about what happened to you?'

'I'm not too tired.' Her eyes fluttered open. 'But I don't remember everything. It's . . . patchy.'

'Start with what you remember clearly,' Cowell suggested. 'Start with yesterday morning, if you can. When did you wake up?'

'Around seven thirty. Josh woke me.' She shrank down in the bed. 'How . . . how is he?'

'No need to worry about him,' Roz said. 'You say he woke you?'

'He was on his way to work so he couldn't take Thomas to school. I usually do it but I was running late because I should have been up at seven. He'd turned my alarm off to let me sleep, he said.' She gave a tiny shrug. 'That's the kind of thing he does. He likes to be in control.'

Roz made a note and underlined it. 'What happened then?'

'We had an argument.' She shivered. 'I was rushing and he kept slowing me down, getting in my way. I was panicking. I lost my temper with him. I knew there would be consequences – I just didn't think . . .'

Melissa pressed her hand against her mouth to stifle her sobs. Roz nodded understandingly.

'Take your time. When you're ready, carry on.'

'Um . . .' she sniffed. 'Well, he left. Then I calmed down, because he wasn't there being annoying anymore. I got Thomas to school. I came home and tidied the house. I cleaned the kitchen. Josh prefers it to be immaculate. Then I went to the gym. He – he likes me to look a certain way. I got home not long before eleven thirty, when I had my first therapy session of the day, online. I made a salad for lunch. I got a text from the mum who was supposed to have Thomas for a playdate, cancelling . . . and then I had a call from a client who really needed help. They were going through a difficult situation.' She frowned. 'My head hurts. Why does my head hurt?'

'You hit it on the post at the foot of the stairs. You have eight stitches.'

'Oh.' She flattened her fingers against it for a moment. 'Will it scar?'

'I don't know, I'm afraid.' Roz shifted the notebook on her lap, the tiniest giveaway that she was impatient. 'Tell me about this client.'

'I can't tell you anything. It's confidential. But I knew I needed to clear my afternoon for them. It's one of my regulars, you see – and they've been struggling. They really needed me. I had two other appointments so the only time I could see them was when I needed to pick up Thomas. I called Josh and asked if he could do it and of course he couldn't – no surprise, it's never convenient for him to help when I need him to do it.'

'His job is demanding.'

'My job matters too.'

Roz smiled. 'Of course. Of course it does.'

'Was this appointment a phone call? A video call?' Cowell asked.

'No. He came to the house.' Melissa blushed. '*They* came. I wasn't going to say – I didn't want you to know who it was for the sake of the client's privacy.'

'We're going to need to talk to him anyway,' Cowell said, his voice reassuring. 'We're used to being discreet, don't worry. We won't ask about the session and what you discussed.'

'OK.' She closed her eyes. 'I'm so tired.'

'I know. Nearly done.' Roz leaned forward. 'Melissa, what happened then? You and Josh arranged for someone else to pick up Thomas, is that right?'

'Josh got one of the Kerrigans to do it.'

'How did you feel about that?'

'I was annoyed that Josh didn't change his plans. Thomas hasn't been well and he's on a restrictive diet. I was worried the Kerrigans would feed him things that might disagree with him. But they love Thomas and he has always adored them. They were pleased to be asked.' She gave Roz a lopsided smile. 'I was generally irritated by Josh. I wasn't in the right frame of mind to deal with him. All of this – what he did to me – it was really my fault.'

'You mustn't say that. Any kind of domestic violence is never justified. Never.'

'Thank you,' Melissa whispered.

'Thinking again about what you were doing during this time, you saw your client,' Roz prompted.

'From three until . . . probably getting on for five. It was very intense. I wasn't looking at the clock. I'd switched off my phone so we wouldn't be interrupted. I'd told the client they couldn't stay any later than that because I didn't want Thomas to be there at the same time – I try to keep my personal life and professional life separate as much as possible. So it was a shock when I realised how late it was. I brought the session to a close, said goodbye, let the client out, and what I didn't know was that Josh was there, outside the house. Josh saw him leave. He was jealous, I suppose. And I knew I was in trouble when I saw his expression.' Her calm demeanour fractured, her face twisting as she struggled with her emotions. 'I don't remember anything else.'

'Don't remember, or don't want to remember?'

Melissa gave a shaky laugh. 'Maybe both. It was all a blur. I was so scared. I thought he was going to kill me.'

'Did he say anything?'

'Something like "I've had enough of this". I was begging him not to hurt me, reminding him about Thomas coming home, apologising, but once he started it went on and on and he didn't seem to want to stop. Then I must have hit my head and passed out.' She sighed. 'I tried everything to distract him, when he walked through the door. I knew straight away that I'd made a terrible mistake and I was going to have to deal with the consequences.'

'Was it the first time this happened?'

'No.' She said it in a small voice, looking down, ashamed. 'I should have left a long time ago. I was scared to leave and scared to stay.'

'I understand.' Roz turned a page in her notebook, checking something. 'Do you remember the first time it happened?'

'The first time he punched me with a closed fist was Christmas three years ago, but he'd been rough with me from the start of our relationship. At first it was playful – pushing me out of the way, dominating me physically. Then it was sort of irritable. Then it became scary.'

'Did you tell anyone about it? A doctor? A friend?'

'Not then. I never had injuries, in the beginning. It was stuff I could shrug off. I only told one person about it and that was my friend Clara, and I didn't do that until last year. I needed to talk to someone about it but I knew she wouldn't make me confront him. She knows how to listen. Sometimes you want someone to push you into changing things and sometimes you want the comfort of talking over what's happening in your life. I wasn't ready to make a change yet but I needed someone to know what was happening to me in case . . .'

'In case what?'

'In case he hurt me and no one knew what he'd been doing,' Melissa whispered. 'In case I couldn't tell anyone what he'd done.'

'I've spoken to Clara,' Roz said. 'She's given me a lot of material – photographs and messages. She kept a record of everything you told her.'

Melissa's eyes widened. 'Did she? Wow.'

'It was very thorough.'

'She's like that.' Her voice was flat. Her face looked pinched, sharp instead of pretty and frail.

'We showed it to someone who pointed out that the dates don't match up with times that you and Josh were together.' Roz's voice was quiet. 'He was away for a long period the summer before last, wasn't he? And some of the incidents that Clara recorded date from the time when he was away.'

'He came back.' Melissa sounded sulky.

'Briefly. But he was certainly not here when some of the reported incidents are alleged to have taken place.'

Her face was red. 'I wanted a record of what he'd done. I didn't know she was listing the dates.'

Roz waited. Behind her, Henry didn't move. He was barely breathing.

'What happened was that I was afraid to tell her all of that when he was around. When he was away – that was the first time I got the courage to speak up about it. I told Clara about it as if it was happening then because – well, it was easier. It was all things that genuinely happened, but from the previous year. I was . . . reliving them. I was safe, because he was gone, so I could let myself remember and it came out as if it was then, at that precise moment. I didn't think that would ever matter.'

Roz leaned back, relaxing. 'So you can match up those incidents with the correct dates.'

'Absolutely.' Melissa blinked at her. 'It was an honest mistake on Clara's part. And on mine. Does it ruin everything?'

'It's something we need to address if we're putting a case together for the CPS.' Roz paused, steeling herself. 'Another thing that has come up is that we've read the statements you made to police about your husband, Mark Pell.'

All the colour drained out of Melissa's face. 'And?'

'There are . . . similarities. In terms of incidents. Language.'

She laughed, a shrill sound this time. 'And you think I've made it all up. Twice. God, I don't know why I thought it would be different. I should have known I wasn't going to get a fair hearing, *again*. Of course you were always going to look after your own. He's one of you! You were never going to listen to me.'

'I have to ask about it.' Roz's voice was steady.

'Well there's a simple explanation, isn't there?' She looked from Roz to Henry, her lower lip trembling. Her words tumbled out in a rush. 'He'd read those statements too. Josh, I mean. He acted it all out. It was a way of taunting me. He wasn't just hurting me himself – he was showing me that what Mark had done to me wasn't over. It made everything he did so much worse for me, and now you're punishing me for the fact that he was copying Mark. I can't believe this is happening.'

'Melissa, calm down,' Roz said.

'I've done nothing but tell the truth and it's not going to work, is it?' She was crying openly now. 'He was always one step ahead of me. He knows how to play the system. I was always going to lose.'

It took quite some time to soothe Melissa, to reassure her that she was still entitled to justice and that they hadn't written her off. She was settling down to sleep when they finally took their leave.

Roz set off down the corridor.

'Well, I believe her.' Cowell caught up with his boss. 'He played her, didn't he?'

'Did he?'

'Wait – you think she was lying?' Cowell frowned. 'Isn't that what we're supposed to think?'

'Yes. No. I don't know anymore.'

Uncertainty wasn't something that Roz Fuller liked and it certainly wasn't something she ever allowed herself to show. Cowell couldn't remember the last time he'd heard her say 'I don't know'.

'Well, what do you want to do? What's next?'

'Honestly? I'm not sure.' She glanced over her shoulder, down the empty hallway. 'But I am sure of one thing. We have a big problem.'

26

I had done what I could to shake Roz Fuller's faith in Melissa as a victim, including showing her the evidence that Melissa's dates were wrong, but I left the hospital weighed down with the knowledge that it wasn't enough. The bruises on her body worried me too. They couldn't have been self-inflicted, and they were brutal – the result of a long, sustained assault, as if someone had been determined to hurt her. No one was looking for that person, except me, and I didn't know where to start.

I wondered about Mark Pell, who might have done what his ex-wife wanted, if she made it worth his while – not out of anger, but love. He hated Derwent. He wasn't all that keen on me, if it came to that, but then I'd taken Melissa's word for it when she said he'd hurt her before. And if it wasn't Mark Pell who had conspired with Melissa, who else could have done it?

If Roz Fuller was trying, she might have a chance of finding out. But that would require her to see past Derwent, who was undoubtedly digging his own grave in every single interview. He would come across as the kind of police officer who belonged to the bad old days of the Met. I couldn't blame her if she thought he needed to be removed from his job at the earliest opportunity, and it would be good for her career if she was the one who made that happen.

Melissa would be selling her story to Roz even now, I thought as I paid the hospital parking charge. She would be playing up the fragility that had attracted Derwent to her in the first place – the need for help, for support, for gentle handling. I was exactly, precisely the opposite to her, hiding my vulnerability as best I could, trying to rely on my own inner strength instead of borrowing from someone else, determined to succeed no matter what it cost me, and a lot of good it had done me.

That refusal to give in, though – that meant that I couldn't walk away. I headed for the car, shivering from tiredness. It was a clear night, the air as hard as iron. The plummeting temperature had left a faint rime of frost on the tarmac around me and dusted white powder on the car roof. The windows were clouded and I set about wiping the windscreen with a gloved hand. I could go home, I thought. No one would blame me if I stopped, now that it was the grim, quiet time of night when everything looked hopeless. I could go home to the other side of London and shut myself away from all of this. I would hear the outcome from Una. I had an actual job to do and she would expect me to be ready to carry on with it in the morning. Ilaria Cavendish in her bath felt extremely remote, like something that had happened in another country, another world.

I thought about what I knew, and what I could prove, and then I drove through the sleeping streets to my parents' house where I let myself in silently, with the care and focus of a career burglar. I headed to the kitchen. The ceiling light was a long fluorescent tube that hummed loudly as it flickered into life, a fixture since long before I was born, the ultimate in 1970s technology. There was no question of using it. I might as well shout to tell my parents I was there. I took out my phone instead and used the torch to look at the board where the family keys hung, looking for one in particular. With a small hiss of triumph I found what I was looking for: two keys on a toy tank key ring, hanging there since my parents had watered the garden in Jena Road for Derwent and Melissa while they were on holiday. There was a framed photograph on Derwent's desk in the office from that trip, holding Thomas in a swimming pool, heads together as they stared at the camera, their eyelashes starry with water. Thomas had been smiling; Derwent was not but there was something soft about his expression that I didn't usually get to see. Melissa had taken the picture.

I tried not to look at it when I was at work.

I unhooked the key ring and slid it into my pocket, then tiptoed to the hall where I jumped out of my skin.

'Maeve.' My mother was in her dressing gown and slippers but otherwise looked as composed as if it was broad daylight and not the small hours of the night. 'I thought that was you.'

'My *heart*.' I had my hand to my chest, trying to hold it in as it battered against my ribs.

'Well, what about mine? It put the heart across me when I heard the front door open and close.'

'You should have been asleep.'

'How could I sleep when you weren't home?'

'I don't live here, and anyway, I'm not a child. You don't need to listen out for me.'

'I haven't slept properly since the day your brother was born. It's a mother's job to worry about her children. That doesn't stop when you're an adult.' Only in the most technical sense an adult, her tone implied, and a very flawed one at that. 'Where have you been?'

'Everywhere. The hospital, most recently.'

'Did you see Melissa? How is she?'

'Infuriating.' I sighed. 'She's lying about everything, Mum.'

'Well, of course. You knew she would.' She tightened the belt of her dressing gown. 'What are you doing about it?'

'Everything I can.'

'It'll all come out in the end. She won't be able to keep up the lying. She'll give herself away.' She looked me up and down. 'Have you eaten anything?'

'No.' It was impossible to dissemble with her. I should have brought her in to see Melissa, I thought. I actually wasn't ruling it out.

'And you're going out again?'

'I have to. I have one more thing to do. I don't even know if it will help.'

'Will I make you a sandwich to take with you?'

With difficulty I warded off the sandwich, and the offer of a thermos of coffee. I did accept a hug that made me feel a little better, and a buttered homemade scone wrapped in tin foil, and I promised I'd let her know if anything happened, good or bad.

'I worry about you,' she said, from the doorstep.

'I know, but you shouldn't.'

'You of all people should know you can't help worrying about the people you love,' she said tartly, and I was all the way down the road before I thought about what she'd meant.

I parked a distance from the house as before and walked quietly down the street, looking around at the silent houses, windows and curtains firmly closed. I was trying not to draw attention to myself. I wasn't forbidden to go into Derwent's house but I knew Roz Fuller would disapprove, so I kept a low profile, in the shadows.

When I let myself in I waited for a moment, standing on the doormat. There was no alarm, which was lucky for me but somehow also typical of Derwent, as if he was daring anyone to try breaking into his house. With Roz in mind I left the hall light off. I had my proper torch out now, the one I used for crime scenes, small and powerful and very bright. The heating had been on and the house was still noticeably warmer than outside. A sweet scent of orange hung in the air, overlaying something darker, something metallic that I recognised as blood. I let the torch play over the area at the foot of the stairs where a thick smear of blood had coagulated, but not for long. I needed to be strategic and focused about this.

I started in the kitchen, at the back door, and moved forward, scanning every surface. I wasn't entirely sure what I was looking for, but it helped to think of the house as a crime scene rather than Derwent's home. In fact, for whole minutes at a time I forgot it was where he lived, where he relaxed, where he sat on the sofa and watched TV and mowed the lawn . . . I knew exactly how he behaved when he was at home, having spent weeks living with him, and I could see traces of him everywhere, from the way the chargers were organised on the counter to the regimented line-up of cleaning products under the sink.

Melissa liked interior design – there had been a time early in their relationship when Derwent had flecks of paint in his hair more or less constantly from redecorating the house – and the kitchen was magazine-perfect as well as tidy. The sitting room was immaculate too. There was no sign of a burglary, or of a fight that had spiralled out of control apart from the bloodstains in the hallway. I stepped carefully around the blood, noticing Derwent's running shoes neatly placed next to the stairs, side by side with a pair of women's trainers that had to be Melissa's. I frowned, remembering how my flat had looked after I'd been attacked: blood on the walls, furniture tipped over, the pictures askew. This had been a very orderly incident, to say the least.

There was something in the shadow cast by the stairs, near the end of the hall. I thought it was a ball at first, but as soon as I touched it, I recognised the cool, dimpled rind of an orange. It was pulpy, as if it had been used for cricket practice, and I wondered with a pang if Derwent regularly bowled oranges at Thomas down the long hall, or if it had escaped Thomas's lunch box. I set it down on the hall table and went up the stairs, my torch sweeping over the treads.

I had never been anywhere in the house except the ground floor, apart from when I was being shadowed by Henry Cowell a few hours earlier and I hadn't dared to look around then. There were three bedrooms on the first floor – two doubles and a tiny box room that was evidently Melissa's study. It took me a bare minute to inspect it: the room contained two chairs and a low table with a box of tissues on it, and a desk with a Mac, and wall shelves full of textbooks, but no paper, no notebooks, nothing that allowed me to see who had been there or anything about her patients.

Thomas's room was crammed with toys and decorated with Star Wars artwork. A large train set took up most of the floor, a locomotive halfway through an enormous accident as it fell off a bridge onto a line of traffic below. In the distance a fleet of emergency vehicles responded to the scene – various police cars and ambulances, from different sets, in different sizes. I recognised a couple I'd given him over the years.

The front bedroom was a guest room which had the kind of obsessive tidiness I recognised instantly as a hallmark of Derwent's occupation. The duvet was flattened and folded as he had left his bed when we shared a house. I opened the wardrobe and saw familiar suits hanging there, organised by colour, and shirts crisply ironed. The old soldier habits were hard to shake. I wanted to press my face into the cotton and inhale the familiar smell of him – I wanted it so badly I ached – but I settled for straightening a sleeve that was twisted in on itself before I shut the wardrobe door.

I ran up to the top of the house, where a bedroom and bathroom had been added to the loft. This was a very different space, feminine and floral, with a hundred cushions on the bed. It felt very much like Melissa's room, and the sense that I was intruding was stronger here than anywhere else.

I took a quick tour through the bathrooms, finding Derwent's shaving kit and toothbrush in the bathroom on the first floor, with Thomas's toothbrush and children's toothpaste. The medicine cabinet over the sink in Melissa's room contained a beauty counter's worth of anti-ageing creams and serums, a variety of painkillers and antihistamines, a bottle of mouthwash to ward off gum disease and an array of prescription medicine that surprised me. I hadn't thought Melissa was prone to ill health, but then again I didn't know her well at all. I remembered what her mother had said about her succumbing to illness when she was upset about something else in her life. The situation that she and Derwent were in – knotted together, in his case unhappily – couldn't be helping her mental state. She would hate that I'd seen it. I could barely meet my own eyes in the mirror. This was crossing all sorts of lines.

Based on the house, the two adults led separate lives. He kept very different hours to Melissa, I reminded myself. But she had complained about him not sleeping with her when she talked to Mark Pell. Celibacy wasn't her choice.

None of my business.

I went down and looked at the hall again, sure that I was missing something, not sure what it was. My head was throbbing and my whole body ached, which was exhaustion. I walked around aimlessly, frustrated, then headed upstairs and found myself in the front bedroom again. It was where Derwent seemed closest, somehow. I sat down on the edge of the bed. I wanted to get warm, I told myself, kicking off my boots. I needed to rest for a few minutes, to see if it helped me make sense of everything. There was the faintest hint of lime and mint and cotton: the smell that was such a comfort when he held me, on the rare occasions when he allowed himself to touch me. This was second-best, but it would do.

I settled myself into Derwent's bed, fully clothed, covered myself with the duvet, and plummeted, instantly, into a deep sleep.

And when I sat bolt upright at six in the morning, I knew what I'd forgotten, and what I needed to do about it.

27

I met Roz Fuller on the drive outside Derwent's house at ten to seven, when it was still dark and the street was deserted. She was huddled in her coat and her eyes were rimmed with red.

'This had better be good,' was how she greeted me, which could have been more encouraging.

'Did you get any sleep?'

'A couple of hours on a sofa at the nick.' I believed her; she looked as if she'd come off a long-haul flight. She rubbed her neck as if it ached. 'What about you?'

'About the same.' *Don't ask me where*, I thought. 'I have to be at work in two hours.'

'That hotel case? The one Josh Derwent was supposed to be running?'

I nodded, shivering.

'I would have thought it was straightforward. You must have CCTV.'

She had a slightly abrupt, dismissive way of speaking, I thought – her brain going faster than everyone else around her, most of the time. Instead of minding the implication that I was making a big deal out of nothing, I sighed. 'That's part of the problem. I can't get my head around how what we can see corresponds with what happened. There wasn't time for my victim to die the way she did. It feels impossible.'

'I don't imagine it helps that you've been up most of the night trying to help your colleague.'

'Maybe not.' I shoved my hands in my pockets. 'Thanks for coming to meet me. I wasn't sure you would.'

She raised an eyebrow. 'I do want to find out the truth, you know. I haven't made up my mind.'

'I thought you might be angry about me speaking to Melissa.'

'I was.' She looked away from me. 'I'm not going to discuss Melissa with you now.'

But the very fact she had come when I asked her to made me think Melissa hadn't made a very good impression on Roz Fuller. No matter how sternly I tried, I couldn't repress a tiny flutter of optimism.

'Presumably you have a good reason for bringing me here,' Roz said.

'I don't know yet. I wanted you here so there's no question of me interfering with any evidence. In fact, you should probably pretend I'm not here.' I bit my lip. 'If I'm wrong, this is going to prove the case against him.'

'And if you're right?'

'You'll let him go.'

She thought about it. 'That feels like a risky strategy.'

'Not if you know him like I do.'

'What if you're wrong?'

I shrugged. 'Then we'll find out together and you can say I told you so.'

There was one light on in the house across the street when I rang the bell, and it was in an upstairs room. It took a long time for someone to come to the door.

'Hold on . . .' the words were shouted over the sound of lengthy unlocking, as a dog barked with a shrill, hysterical sound. In the front window a white terrier was braced on the back of the sofa, its eyes shiny with indignation.

'That bloody dog.' The man was in his sixties and resplendent in striped pyjamas, his hair wild, his face creased with sleep. 'What can I do for you?'

'I'm sorry for disturbing you so early. We're police officers.' Roz held up her ID and I did the same.

'There's nothing wrong,' I added quickly, seeing his eyes widen. Police officers coming to your door unexpectedly was never a good sign.

Roz moved in front of me, a matter of millimetres but reminding me that she was in charge and I wasn't even there on official business so could I please shut up and let her take the lead.

'We're here in connection with the incident that happened yesterday. I don't know if you're aware of it.'

'Oh I am, I am.' He looked down at himself. 'I'm a bit embarrassed to invite you in when I'm looking like this. I could get dressed.'

'No need at all. We can talk out here.'

I felt as if the cold was sinking into my bones. A fine rain was falling, little more than mist, but it was making the dark morning even bleaker. 'Maybe we could talk in the hall.'

He let us in and we stood listening to the dog having a rage-stroke on the other side of the – thankfully – closed door.

'Shut up,' the man bawled eventually, and then shrugged. 'He's a good guard dog.'

'He certainly is,' Roz said.

There was a final, frenzied scrabble of claws on wood and then the dog subsided to the canine equivalent of swearing under his breath.

'I shouldn't need to keep you for long,' she said. 'Were you here yesterday during the day?'

'No.' True regret in his voice. 'I missed everything. I got home when they were taking the bloke across the road away in a police van. Handcuffed and everything. Not what you expect on a nice street like this. We all know each other. Time was, that kind of thing was overlooked because it was nobody's business. Goes to show you how the world is changing, doesn't it?'

Roz and I agreed that it did. I chose not to investigate whether he thought a decrease in tolerance for domestic violence was a good thing or not. I wasn't there to pick a fight.

'Can I ask . . .' I said, 'are you Derek?'

He raised his eyebrows. 'How did you know that?'

'I work with Josh, from across the road.'

'Oh yes?' Suspicion was uppermost in his voice.

'He mentioned you had security cameras.' Derwent's voice echoed in my head, as it had since I woke up.

Bloody Derek across the road has new CCTV cameras in case anyone wants to nick his 2001 Skoda Felicia. I wouldn't mind but one is pointed straight at my house. You'd think he had a Bentley parked on his drive.

'That's right. My son helped me to install them. We put them inside, in the windows, to protect them from *sabotage*.' He pronounced the word with relish. 'You'd never know they were there.'

'Do they record?'

'Oh yes. I get a week at a time, straight onto the app.'

'Timestamped?'

'Yes. No point in it otherwise, is there?'

'So you would have the footage from yesterday,' Roz said.

He looked surprised. 'The arrest?'

'Before that. During the day. Anyone coming and going.'

'Oh yes. I'd definitely have that.' He looked defiant. 'The way they're adjusted, you see – I wanted to be able to see the drive and the road. Well, as it turned out, to get that view, the house opposite is in the background.'

'Josh mentioned that.' I'd said it as diplomatically as I could, but Derek's face darkened and swelled.

'I did get complaints off the neighbours but then, as soon as someone's car gets dinged, they're straight on to me. "Oh Derek, could you check your cameras to see who did it?"' he mewled in a high-pitched voice. 'Funny how they don't care about privacy when they need me.'

'Very true,' Roz agreed. 'Um . . . would it be possible to see the footage from yesterday?'

He frowned, considering it. There was almost no chance Derwent hadn't clashed with him at some stage. I waited, holding my breath.

'My grandson's bike was stolen.'

'OK,' Roz said, preparing to interrupt the anecdote. I pressed my elbow against hers and she fell silent.

'It was stolen from the garden here. They came in down the side of the house. Brazen, you know.' He rasped the stubble on his cheek thoughtfully. 'Told Josh and he went and got it back. No questions asked, if you see what I mean.'

'I can imagine that.' I could also imagine that the thief had regretted taking the bike in the first place. I hoped Roz wasn't adding it to the list of Derwent's crimes.

'Yes. Well. I appreciated it.' He sucked in his cheeks. 'I should have thought of checking the cameras to see what happened yesterday.'

'Can we see the footage now?' Roz was clearly running out of patience.

'Give me five minutes to put some clothes on and then we'll have a look.'

28

Half an hour later we were standing on our second doorstep of the morning, preparing to ring the bell. Before I reached out to it, the door swung open, as if Clara Porter had been watching for the car. She looked exhausted, with black shadows under her eyes.

'What do you want?' Her eyes slid from Roz to me and back again. 'Why are you here together?'

'Following up some leads,' Roz said smoothly.

'I didn't think you were on the same side.'

'We're all on the same side. We want to find out what happened to Melissa.'

'You know what happened.' She gave me an unfriendly look. 'Josh hurt her.'

'Maybe he did. We still need to prove it.'

'What were you doing at the house yesterday?' The question burst out of me. Roz turned and looked at me with a quizzical expression, but she didn't cut me off. Clara looked startled.

'I wasn't at the house.'

'You were, you know.' I was looking at another piece of evidence that I hadn't known about. 'That's your car on the drive, isn't it? A silver Nissan Micra. I parked behind it on Jena Road when I went there yesterday evening. You'd driven there at some stage, earlier in the day, and left it there. I should have realised something was off when you told me you went in the ambulance with Melissa. You told me you saw her lying there, covered in blood. But how did you know anything was wrong? You don't live near Jena Road. You weren't scheduled to babysit Thomas. You had no reason to park there.'

Her eyes were wide. 'Melissa needed me.'

'How did you know that?'

'She – she called me.'

'Before she was hurt?'

Clara was silent.

'She was unconscious, afterwards. She couldn't have called you.'

'I don't know.'

'Did you know something was going to happen?' Roz asked.

'I – no. I'm not sure.' Clara put a hand to her head. 'I don't want to get in trouble.'

'The best thing you can do for yourself is to start helping us.' Clara was shaking and I could have felt sorry for her, in different circumstances.

Roz took out her phone. 'I've got a video I'd like you to watch for me. CCTV from outside Melissa's house, from yesterday. I'd like you to tell me if you recognise anyone in it.'

Clara backed away, shaking her head. 'I don't want to look. I can't help you.' *And you can't make me.*

Roz held up her phone and played the video she had taken of Derek's CCTV. On the screen, a figure walked up to Derwent's front door carrying a canvas bag over one shoulder. The timestamp was from two o'clock the previous afternoon.

'That's—' She cut herself off and looked at us nervously. 'I don't know.'

'Are you sure? Look again.' Roz played the video again, pausing it when the person glanced around and there was a reasonably clear shot of their face.

'I don't know.' She fidgeted, looking down, indicating with every aspect of her demeanour that she was lying, which I would have known anyway because she was clearly recognisable in the image.

Roz tapped the screen. 'You went into the house at 2 p.m., when Melissa said she was with a client. What were you doing there for two and a half hours?'

She shook her head, pulling her sleeves down over her hands.

'You left about twenty minutes before Josh came home,' I said.

Roz played her the footage. Taping it off Derek's screen hadn't done much for the quality, but it was recognisably the same person who had gone in earlier. She came out quickly, hurrying down the driveway, her head bent. She had zipped up her jacket and one hand was in her pocket. The other held a black bin bag.

'No canvas bag this time. You seem to be carrying rubbish.'

'She looks furtive, doesn't she?' I said. 'Like she's trying to hide. And she doesn't know about the camera.'

Clara bit her lip.

'Did you sit in the car and wait for Josh to come home? And then magically reappear when the paramedics arrived?'

Her expression told me I was right.

Roz lowered her phone. 'What's your relationship with Melissa? Be honest.'

'She's my best friend.'

I swallowed, trying to control my anger. 'At the hospital, you told me you'd do anything for her. What did you do?'

'I only wanted to help her.' Clara was starting to tear up.

'What happened, Clara? What were you doing in the house for two and a half hours?'

Roz held up an evidence bag so Clara could see through the plastic window on the side.

'What's that?' Clara said.

'What does it look like?'

Instead of answering she began to moan. 'What have I done? What have I done?'

I had been right. I kept the relief out of my voice, sounding matter-of-fact. 'Well, what have you done?'

'I didn't know – it wasn't my idea.' She lifted her head. Sweat was prickling on her forehead and across her upper lip. 'You have to believe me, I didn't want to do it.'

'What's in the bag, Clara?'

'An orange.' She whispered it. 'I thought I'd got all of them.'

'You missed one,' I said. 'What's the significance of the orange?'

'It was used to hit someone.'

'Interesting use of the passive voice, there. Who used it?'

'I did. I – I hit her. I hit Melissa.'

Without missing a beat, Roz arrested Clara on suspicion of perverting the course of justice, and cautioned her. Clara didn't even seem to notice. Her eyes were fixed on me.

'I knotted it inside a sock. That's what she told me to do. I – I've washed the sock. It's in the tumble dryer.'

I wrote off the sock for forensic purposes. I was desperate to ask her questions but that would have to wait for interview now; there were formalities that had to be observed. As long as she kept talking though, and Roz kept noting what she was saying, I would stand there and listen.

'She told me to come to the house, and why, but I wasn't sure if I could go through with it when I got there. I'd bought the oranges, but I thought I'd talk her round – that I'd be able to convince her it was madness. She persuaded me it was the right thing to do – I didn't seem to have any control over my own actions. I lost my bearings, somehow. She talked me into it. She wouldn't stop – I mean, I begged her to let me off. She said it was essential, and I had to do it and if I loved her I would, but I – I didn't want to hurt her. But I mean that was the point, wasn't it? She wanted me to bruise her to save her from worse pain. And I started, and stopped, and she talked me into going on, even though she was crying, but she said that was how it should be. I was crying too.'

She was still white and shaking but a certain resolve tightened her mouth. 'I *hate* Josh Derwent. I wanted to help her. She needed evidence that he couldn't argue about and I – I wanted her to be safe. She told me he'd never let her go.'

'I see.'

'She's special.'

'Very.' I tried not to sound sarcastic, and I almost managed it.

'She's been kind to me. She understood me.'

She understood Clara Porter was a weak woman who she could make dependent on her, I thought. She understood that Clara was useful.

'I didn't mean to hurt her so badly. You have to believe me. She overbalanced and fell.' Clara clasped her hands. 'I didn't know what to do. I've barely slept. The sound of her head hitting the stairs – I don't think I'll ever forget it. It was a mistake. I checked she was breathing. I wanted to call for help but I knew Josh would be home so I thought – I thought I'd go. I mean, what was the point if I didn't see it through?' She wiped a snail trail of mucus from under her nose. 'But then I was afraid he'd be late home. I was supposed to leave – that was the plan – but I stayed to make sure she was going to be OK. When I saw her, I knew I couldn't leave her to go to the hospital alone.'

'You're going to have to go to the police station, Clara,' I said. Roz was already on her radio, summoning a van.

Her eyes were wide. 'I'm scared.'

'I understand that.' *But you should be scared of me.* Whatever she saw on my face made her jerk backwards.

'Am I going to prison?'

'The best thing you can do for yourself is to confess to everything you've done and cooperate with us,' Roz said, returning to the conversation and taking charge. 'You're on camera going in and leaving. There will be forensic evidence.'

True to form, Clara turned to me for guidance. 'What should I do?'

'I can't tell you that.'

Roz's phone rang and she moved away to answer it. Impulsively, I leaned towards Clara and lowered my voice.

'I know you love Melissa, and I'm sure she cares about you, but you need to be absolutely clear about what happened and stick to it. If she says she didn't want you to hit her, do you have any evidence to contradict her?'

She looked staggered. 'That didn't occur to me.'

'Of course it didn't. You trusted her.'

'She left me a voicemail, telling me to come over. I haven't deleted it.'

'That's good,' I said. 'That will help.'

'So everything will be all right?'

I couldn't quite bring myself to say yes.

29

I dropped Roz off at Jena Road after a van arrived for Clara Porter. Roz wanted to pick up her car and, I presumed, make some phone calls without me as an audience. I made it to the police station first and found it deserted apart from an elderly man standing at the counter. The receptionist slid out at the sight of me and after a moment returned with Henry Cowell who strolled into the reception area, his hands in his pockets.

'I hear you made an arrest. What does Clara Porter have to do with this?'

'Quite a lot. Roz knows about it.'

'She does?' Cowell looked baffled. Evidently she hadn't bothered to fill him in.

I handed Cowell the evidence bag. 'You're going to need this too. I picked it up without a glove when I found it, but my DNA is on file if you need to rule me out.'

'An orange? Where did this come from?'

'I'll tell you all about it, Henry,' Roz said from the doorway behind me. 'Clara Porter will be giving us a prepared statement. We're just waiting for a solicitor to join us.'

'Right,' Cowell said uncertainly, lost.

I stood still, feeling the weight of every single hour of sleep I'd missed. If I hadn't got some rest I'd have been on the floor. As it was, if I sat down I would probably have drifted off.

'I wanted to ask about my son,' the elderly man at the counter said, his voice wavering.

'Course you do. Hold on.' The receptionist slid off his chair again and walked away. The man leaned over the counter and called after him.

'Please. I need to know.'

I felt like joining in. The need to know. To be sure. To prove what had really happened. It was unbearable.

Roz beckoned to me. 'I want to talk to you. Come with me.'

She led me through the secure door and down a hallway to an interview room that was set up for four. The atmosphere had changed, somehow, from when we had been hunting the truth together, and I couldn't work out why.

'Take a seat.' She went to one side of the table and I moved to the other, stopping with my fingertips resting on the back of the chair.

'What?' Roz was watching me.

'Is this where you've been interviewing Josh?'

She nodded. 'So?'

'Nothing. Just . . . it must be odd for him. Being treated like a criminal.' I didn't want to sit down in the chair, I discovered. I didn't want to be on the wrong side of the table. 'Can I see him? Are you letting him go now?'

'No. And no.'

'Why not?'

Roz looked away from me, evasive. 'We don't know that he didn't hurt her on other occasions.'

'You're not still trying to make this work, are you? Melissa is going to end up going to prison for perverting the course of justice, with any luck. She set him up. The CPS aren't going to go near this and you know it. It would never get to court. And it never happened.'

'I wish I could be sure of that.'

'What more do you want?' My heart was thudding. 'What can I show you? What evidence do you want? Tell me what you need and I'll find it, but for God's sake, give up trying to make Josh into a villain.'

'I can find my own evidence, thank you. You don't need to investigate my case,' Roz rapped out, her jaw tight with irritation.

'Well, someone has to! You haven't looked beyond Josh from the first moment you started working on this. You came up with a narrative and tried to find the facts to fit it, which is what you learn not to do on the first day in the job.' I was so angry I didn't even care that Roz Fuller was a rank above me. 'You missed some very obvious things, like the orange I found in the hallway at Jena Road.'

The question burst out of her. 'How on earth did you know what the significance of that orange was? You couldn't have known.'

'Not immediately. But the hall smelled of orange – didn't you notice?'

'I – no. I didn't notice.'

'Once I started thinking about why that was, and Melissa's injuries, I put it together. I will admit that I had a head start because I knew Josh couldn't have hurt Melissa, and I knew Melissa was prepared to lie about that. You were too willing to believe the worst of him and the best of her. You're wasting your time looking for a way to punish him for something he never did. He's a good police officer.'

'He's a rule-breaker. Arrogant. Egotistical.'

'All of that,' I agreed. 'And he's still the best inspector I've ever worked with.'

She rolled her eyes. 'Oh my God, what is it with the two of you?'

I felt my stomach drop. 'What do you mean?'

'The way you talk about him, and the way he looks when your name comes up—'

'How does he look?'

There was a hint of compassion on her face now. 'Honestly? His eyes go dead when I say your name. He doesn't want to talk about you.'

I swallowed, hurt, trying not to show it.

'Look, never mind. Forget I said anything.' She paused. 'But what I find really annoying is watching someone who is exceptionally talented and hard-working sacrifice her career for someone who wouldn't lift a finger for her.'

'If you're talking about me—'

'Well done.'

'—you have no idea what he would do for me,' I said. 'Or what he has done in the past. I owe him far more than you can possibly imagine.'

'Is that a fact?'

'But even if I didn't, I would still be here, telling you that you're making a mistake, because it's true.' My voice was steady. 'If you want to lock up Josh Derwent, keep looking, because you don't have anything on him at the moment and I don't think you're going to find anything. If you want to find out what happened to Melissa, I've done what I can to help you, but you need to let Josh go. You've got no reason to keep him.'

30

'We've got to let Josh Derwent go. We've got no reason to keep him.'

Roz turned to frown at Henry Cowell, who was sitting on the edge of a desk with his arms folded. He had spoken with confidence but now his face changed: the instant regret of someone wandering through long grass who has just found a rake by stepping on it.

'That CCTV that Maeve found looks pretty conclusive . . .'

'I know.'

'OK,' Cowell said slowly. 'So you agree that he definitely didn't hit Melissa yesterday. He wasn't responsible for the way she ended up.'

'It seems not.' She was pacing back and forth in the small room they'd commandeered in the police station.

'So unless he was conspiring with Clara Porter – and that's not the story she's told us – he can't have been involved.'

'What if he's been beating her up at other times? What if this was Melissa's way of looking for help? She thought she had to stage something because otherwise no one would believe her.'

'And the dates in the diary not matching up with times he was around? We'll be taken apart by any competent defence brief, if it ever makes it to court, which it won't.'

'That's difficult,' Roz allowed.

'Even without Clara's evidence she wouldn't be a good witness.'

'No.' Roz tapped her foot. 'Did you know that Maeve Kerrigan recorded her conversation with Melissa in hospital?'

Cowell raised his eyebrows. 'Recorded her? That won't be admissible.'

'Maeve knew that. She told me that before I could tell her. She wanted me to hear what Melissa is really like.'

'And?'

Roz sighed. 'Everyone has different faces they turn to the world, Henry. I listened to part of it and it seemed obvious to me that she dislikes Maeve. But not liking someone is not a crime, and what Melissa actually said to Maeve didn't contradict anything she's told us.'

'No, but the facts do. The dates. The way it lines up with what she said about her previous partner.' Henry lifted the printout of her statement. 'This is more than a coincidence, isn't it? She's saying the same things happened in exactly the same way, twice, with two different men. And the ex-husband never got to court either, because there was no evidence that it was true.'

'Are we really going to let a potentially abusive police officer walk out of here because his partner isn't good at expressing herself?'

'Is that what this is? I think Melissa set him up, Roz. I think she wanted to get him in trouble and she talked Clara Porter into helping her. Clara said it herself, she went round there and didn't want to do it, so Melissa worked on her for hours, pressuring her until she did what she wanted. It was cold-blooded and calculated.'

'Why would Melissa do that?'

'Because the relationship with Josh Derwent isn't going well? Because she enjoys the attention?'

'No one would want to end up in hospital.'

'She banged her head by accident. She wasn't supposed to be knocked unconscious, according to Clara.' Cowell shrugged apologetically. 'Look, all of the evidence contradicts Melissa's allegations and supports Josh Derwent's story. And frankly, we're lucky to have the evidence we've got, or we'd be going after a good police officer who doesn't deserve it.'

'Is he a good police officer?' She was still walking, still restless. The room was airless, the heating was on full blast, and she felt as if her shirt was too tight, clinging to her arms and across her back. 'He has Maeve on his side, but I don't think she's the best person to decide whether he's innocent of everything. She's extremely biased in his favour.'

'And you're biased the other way, so that balances it out.'

'I don't want to miss something,' Roz said quietly. 'I want to know if he's cut corners in the past. I want to be sure he's the sort of person who should be a police officer, especially at his rank.'

Cowell frowned. 'What else is going on here?'

'Just a feeling I have. He clams up every time her name is mentioned. He wants to stop me from asking any questions about her. I admit that I don't have enough for a criminal investigation right now but I do have concerns about his conduct. I think he might have something to hide.'

'What kind of thing?'

'Being manipulative. Inappropriate. Maeve was up all night trying to find the evidence to get him off.'

'Which she did.'

'Yes. Which we would have found ourselves.'

'If she hadn't told us about the neighbour's CCTV—' he began.

'We would have canvassed the street. There wasn't time to do house-to-house enquiries because we had him in custody already. We would have got around to it.'

'You're not angry because she found the evidence you missed.'

'Angry?' Roz raised her eyebrows. 'Me?'

'You don't have anything to prove,' Cowell said quietly. 'Not to me or anyone else.'

'That's not what this is about. I've met the Josh Derwent type before, Henry. You might find him easy to work with – you might even like him – but I can tell you he would be very different with someone like me. He's arrogant and sexist and rude.'

'He does seem arrogant, but we're hardly seeing him at his best. He's definitely capable of being rude. He seems to have a reasonable working relationship with women – his boss was fairly complimentary about him – so I'm not sure he's a straightforward sexist either. None of that automatically makes him bad at his job.'

'What if he behaved inappropriately with Maeve on duty? He's a senior officer. She's vulnerable, being younger than him and junior to him. She's worried about him.'

'She's worked with him for a long time. That's loyalty.'

'It's devotion. Misplaced devotion.'

'If they do have a good relationship, professionally speaking, doesn't it make sense that he'd want to protect her from getting in trouble? It doesn't have to be because they're romantically involved.'

'We need to look into it.'

'Do we?'

She reminds me of me, Roz thought, but didn't want to say. *I have been the junior officer. I have been the vulnerable one.*

'Sometimes people don't realise they need help, Henry. Maeve is a good police officer and she's putting herself on the line for someone who doesn't seem to care about her at all.' Roz frowned. 'OK, you're right. We're going to have to let him go for the time being, but that isn't the end of my interest in him. I don't want to find out we missed something important because we didn't look at him carefully enough. Even though we don't have a criminal case against him at the moment, that doesn't mean there's no case to be made. You know me. I have to be sure.'

'I know.' Cowell looked at her quizzically. 'Is this because he annoyed you?'

'That didn't help.'

'Remind me to stay on your good side,' he said, with feeling, and Roz Fuller smiled.

31

The Porsche went past slowly, the driver looking for a space. He didn't see me – I was parked between a van and a large tree – but I saw him. It made all kinds of sense that Derwent would have called him, and I told myself I didn't mind, and it was a good sign anyway that he was there, and a lot of other things as I got out of my car and waited for him to turn off his engine.

'Maeve, what are you doing here?' Luke jumped out of the Porsche and slammed his door. He came straight over and hugged me. Squint and it was Derwent – that quick stride, the height, the broad shoulders, the brown hair and blue eyes, the way he settled into the hug with his head turned in towards mine rather than away, so he could finish it with a kiss on the side of my head. There was nothing flirtatious about it; he was there to comfort me, and nothing more, and for a moment it almost worked. Then I pulled away.

'He called you, I take it.'

'He wanted me to pick him up.'

'I could have done that.'

His eyes softened with pity, which instantly made him look a lot less like Derwent. 'Maybe he didn't know you were here.'

'Oh, he definitely didn't know that. He told me to keep my distance.' I shivered, hugging myself for warmth. 'But he would have known I'd come and get him if he asked me to, and he should have known I'd be a lot closer than you. Did you have to take the day off work?'

'Yeah, but it wasn't a problem. Owen was fine about it.'

Owen. I had forgotten all about him, which probably showed on my face. Luke winced.

'I'm guessing you didn't make it to your date, then.'

'I had things to do.'

He raised an eyebrow. 'Things like getting Josh out of trouble?'

'It would take more than one woman to achieve that. But I will take the credit for getting him out of the nick before he was charged with anything.'

'Really? That's cool.' Luke looked impressed. 'He's lucky to have you.'

'As he'd tell you himself, he doesn't *have* me. And I'd have done the same for anyone on the team.' Even as I said it I was thinking of the exceptions: I might have made a phone call for Pete Belcott, my least favourite colleague, but getting no sleep in favour of wringing the truth out of semi-cooperative witnesses? Unlikely. 'Do you know what time he's getting out?'

Luke checked his watch. 'In about half an hour, I think. Is there anywhere to wait in there?'

'Not really.' The small reception area wasn't the kind of place where you were encouraged to hang out. 'I was planning to sit in my car.'

'Come and sit in mine. It's probably more comfortable and I can show off about it.'

'How long have you had it?'

'Three weeks.'

'It's a bit flash, isn't it? I thought you were sensible about money.'

He ducked his head, embarrassed. 'Yeah, but I got a bonus and Owen told me I should make the most of having a bit of spare cash. He told me I was being too sensible. And it's eight years old. I'm its third careful owner.'

'And the others were little old ladies who drove it to the shops. I get the picture. What did Josh say?'

Luke grinned. 'He asked if he could borrow it.'

Too much to expect Derwent to be the sensible dad . . . but then again why shouldn't Luke have a nice car? He worked hard for it. And he was young. Maybe it was what Derwent would have wanted at Luke's age, if his life had worked out differently. One way or another, he'd missed out on so much.

'What's wrong?' Luke was looking at me, concerned.

'Nothing.' I tried to smile. 'I just drifted off for a second. I didn't get much sleep last night.'

'You can have a nap while we're waiting.'

'I don't nap.' I shivered. 'But I do want coffee. I've got time to run around the corner and get one, if we've got half an hour to wait. Do you want anything?'

'A macchiato would be good.'

'I think your choice is going to be more black or white.'

'White, then. I'll come with you.'

'No, stay here in case he comes out early.'

Reluctantly, Luke agreed, and I headed off. I was jittery enough without the caffeine, but I was tired enough to know I needed it.

I came back with the coffees, balancing them on top of one another precariously as I came round the corner so I could check my phone, which was buzzing with messages. Nothing important, I decided, thumbing through them, and I looked up again to see that I had missed the moment when Derwent walked down the steps from the police station. He was halfway across the road, heading towards Luke. I took a moment to assess how he looked: an up-all-night state of dishevelment, which was out of character, but his shoulders didn't have the defeated slump I'd feared. He was wearing a custody tracksuit – I assumed his clothes had been confiscated for forensics – and he must have been cold, but he didn't show it. He stopped a couple of feet from Luke, who shook his head, exasperated, and threw his arms around him. Derwent leaned against him for a moment as Luke thumped his back affectionately. I felt my throat tighten. This was what he deserved.

Derwent freed himself and held Luke's arm briefly, saying something that made his son laugh. Then he moved towards the car and Luke stopped him. Whatever he said made Derwent turn and look straight at me. His good mood evaporated instantly. He strode towards me, scowling. I quailed, trying to put my phone away while not dropping the coffees. My knees were trembling: it felt as if my ligaments had come unstrung.

'What are you doing here?'

'Good morning, how are you, Maeve?'

'Don't give me that. I specifically told you to stay away.' He took hold of my elbow, turning away to scan our surroundings, on edge. 'Which one is your car?'

'It's the blue one.'

'Come on.' He set off towards it. I leaned away from him, resisting.

'Why?'

'I don't want you out here in the full view of the nick and whoever might be looking out of the window.' He was still looking around, affecting to be casual, but his mouth was a line. 'I don't want you here at all. And I'm fairly sure I asked your dad to tell you that.'

'Yes, he passed it on. Obviously I ignored you.'

'It's not a game, Maeve. You don't want to be involved with this.'

'But they let you go.'

'That doesn't mean it's over.' His attention was on everything but me, and he was frowning. 'That Fuller woman isn't the type to give up. You don't know how badly she wanted to find something on me. I could see it in her eyes.'

In the circumstances, I didn't think I should mention that I'd talked with her, more than once.

'Mind you, she's brilliant at what she does,' Derwent said. 'I didn't like her but she did a good job. She found out who beat Melissa up.'

I made a small exclamation from sheer outrage, and he interpreted it as a question.

'One of the TAs from school. A woman. Mel asked her to do it, to frame me. They were friends, apparently.' He shook his head. 'She wasn't even on my radar. I wouldn't have thought of her in a hundred years.'

If I told him I was the one who'd found Clara, he wouldn't be grateful. In fact, I'd get in more trouble. I kept my mouth shut, but with difficulty.

'I was going back through my career,' Derwent said, still brooding on what he'd missed. 'I was trying to think of people with a grudge against me.'

'That must have been a long list.'

He glared at me. 'Seriously?'

'And then if you added in the ex-girlfriends . . .'

He drew himself up, hurt. 'None of my exes have any reason to complain.'

'I'm sure they all think of you very fondly.' We had reached the car and I put the coffee cups on the roof.

'From the number who've wanted a repeat performance, I'm guessing they do.'

'Jesus Christ.'

'It's a fact.' He shrugged. 'Sorry you don't like it.'

Off-hand, arrogant – why was it that I'd missed him? I couldn't recall. I gathered the shreds of my composure. 'Where are you going now? You can't go back to Jena Road.'

'No. I'm going there to pick up some things. Luke's bringing me to see Thomas after that – he's still at your parents' house, I take it?'

I nodded. 'With Melissa's mum. She's in the guest room. Thomas is sleeping in my room. I don't think my parents are ever going to let him leave and I'm not sure he's going to want to. They'll spoil him rotten between the three of them.' Then, with a sinking feeling, I added, 'And you should know that Mark Pell was there too. He's staying in one of the local hotels until Melissa is out of hospital.'

Derwent's face darkened. 'Is he fuck.'

'Leave it,' I snapped. 'If you have a fight with him, you'll wind up back here. And anyway, you might need his help.'

'I don't need anything from him.' His eyes were like chips of glacier ice. 'Give me strength.'

'He said he went through the same thing. A false accusation.'

Derwent laughed without any humour whatsoever. 'I bet he did.'

'Maybe he was right.'

'Maybe he should stay out of it.'

I looked at him for a moment, wanting to argue, knowing there was no point. Instead I sighed. 'Look, he helped you already, believe it or not. He's a big part of the reason you weren't charged.'

'I'll have to thank him when I see him,' Derwent said, very much as if he didn't mean *thank* at all, but something completely different.

'Where are you going after my parents' house? Do you have somewhere to stay?'

'Luke's putting me up for a while.'

'I thought you might want the flat.' My flat was, after all, Derwent's flat, even if I currently rented it.

'The flat's occupied.'

'I could make room for you,' I offered and he winced.

'Because that worked out so well the last time.'

But this time you and Melissa have split up, I thought, and didn't say.

'This didn't bother you at all, did it?' I gestured at the police station. 'I don't know why I was up all night worrying about you.'

'It was easily one of the worst nights of my life,' Derwent snapped. 'Do you have any idea what it's like to be arrested and processed? Your clothes taken? To be questioned? Not to be believed even though you're telling the truth?'

'It sounds awful—'

'Christ, Maeve, it nearly broke me.' He leaned an elbow on the roof of the car, for support, leaning closer to me. 'And the one thing that kept me going was knowing that at least you weren't caught up in it. My problem, my nightmare. My mistakes. Not yours. So please, stay out of it. Stay away from Roz Fuller, and stay away from me.' He looked down at his watch. 'And why aren't you at work?'

'I thought—'

'There's no reason for you to be here. I don't need you. Ilaria Cavendish needs someone to investigate who killed her though.'

I felt my shoulders sag. 'But—'

'You'll have a lot to catch up on.' He opened the driver's door and manoeuvred me into the seat. 'I'll be back at work in a day or two. I'll see you then.'

Slam. The door was closed. I started the engine so I could open the window.

'*Josh.*'

He lifted the coffee off the roof of the car. 'I'll take these.'

'One was for me,' I said, uselessly, as he lifted it in a last salute.

'Get to work, Kerrigan.'

PART THREE

Finale

'Sometimes I said: This thing shall be no more;
My expectation wearies and shall cease;
I will resign it now and be at peace'
                              Christina Rossetti

32

It seemed like a century since I'd been in the Governor Hotel, and a millennium since I'd slept. I walked carefully down the hall towards room 412, so tired that I felt as if the floor was sliding sideways. The room door was open and voices drew me in: Liv and Georgia, talking softly. About me, I discovered. They were standing with their backs to me, looking out at the view. Georgia was fiddling with the curtain tie.

'You know it'll break her heart.'

'That's not going to make Una want to keep him, even if he does get out of this one.' Liv, the voice of reason.

'You didn't see her face after she'd heard he was arrested. I mean, I thought someone had died. Then I found out what had happened and it all made sense.' Georgia shook her head, adding in a wondering tone, 'I've never seen Maeve like that. She's always so calm and in control.'

'Not always,' I said, putting my bag down on the bed. 'I don't know about in control but I certainly wouldn't describe myself as calm at the moment.'

Liv recovered faster than Georgia. 'What are you doing here?' She came over and hugged me. 'Are you OK?'

'You haven't been home,' Georgia said, following suit. 'That's what you were wearing yesterday.'

'Correct.' I smiled at her, amused that she'd noticed. 'But we have a murder to investigate. And this might be more information than you bargained for, but I did change my underwear.'

'Good to know.' Liv sounded cheerful but her eyes were worried. 'Did you know you're only wearing one earring?'

'Am I?' I put a hand up and checked. 'Oh shit. It was loose. I have no idea where I lost it. I *liked* these earrings.' It was a small tragedy, though, given the welter of shit I'd been dealing with, as Liv reminded me with her next question.

'What's the latest with Josh?'

'He's been released under investigation.'

'Surely that's just a formality.' Georgia gave a little jump for joy. 'It's over.'

'I don't think it is. He didn't make a great impression on the woman who was investigating him.'

'Josh? Really?' Liv rolled her eyes. 'Typical. What about Melissa?'

'Still in hospital but she's on the mend.' I had already decided not to say anything about how she'd ended up in the state she was in.

Liv was frowning. 'Do they know what happened to her? I mean, obviously it wasn't Josh, as anyone who knows him could tell them, but someone clearly had it in for her.'

'They've got some definite lines of enquiry.'

There was enough I-don't-want-to-talk-about-this in my tone and my expression that she backed off immediately, which I appreciated.

'Did you see Josh?' Georgia asked, less interested in the investigation but, as ever, a bloodhound for any hint of romance.

'For about thirty seconds. That's what I'm doing here. He sent me to work.'

Georgia and Liv were physically and temperamentally very different but for a moment they wore matching expressions of shock tinged with pity. I turned away.

'We do have a murder to investigate. And with that in mind, what's going on?'

Liv knew me well enough to understand that even if I wanted to be somewhere else, I needed the distraction of work. 'We're doing some follow-up interviews with members of staff who might have seen or heard something useful.'

'Like who?'

'The plumber who was working in 411, the room next door to this one, on the day of the murder. He's on his way up.'

I nodded. 'Before he gets here, Georgia, did you hear anything else about Sam Blundell's girlfriend? Is Lora OK?'

'I texted her this morning and she said she was feeling better.' Georgia showed me the message on her phone.

'*Sam wasn't involved please believe me,*' I read off the screen. 'Well, that's convincing.'

'He's still our best suspect,' Liv said. 'Our only suspect.'

'There's the husband,' Georgia suggested.

'How? When?' I looked around the room. 'Sam was the only one here.'

A clatter in the corridor was followed by a knock on the door and a man poked his head into the room.

'You were looking for me?'

'Come in,' Liv said, and ran through the introductions. The plumber's name was Jason. He was tall, Jamaican and about sixty, with greying hair. He wore clean, ironed overalls and his manner was courtly, if reserved. He stood instead of sitting in the chair Liv had indicated, obviously more at ease on his feet.

I leaned against the windowsill and watched rather than being involved in the questioning. Liv took the lead, guiding him through the events of two days before, and he explained he'd been called to the fourth floor to investigate a problem with the lavatory, discovered by Housekeeping.

'I was up here for about ninety minutes.'

'What was the problem?' Liv asked.

'It was blocked. Completely blocked. I had to take the whole thing apart.'

'What time did you start and finish? Is there a log of your work?'

The plumber shrugged. 'I go where I'm asked to go and do what I'm asked to do. They don't make me sign anything. They trust me. I've worked here for ten years.'

Liv looked apologetic. 'We have to ask.'

'I know, I know. Ask your questions. It was around half past eleven in the morning when I came up here and I finished at one.'

'And did you see anyone?'

Jason frowned, rubbing his chin. 'There was a member of the housekeeping team cleaning in the corridor when I got here.'

I nodded; we had seen her on the CCTV.

'Did you talk to her?' Liv asked.

'She came into the room but I was working and I didn't hear her if she spoke to me.' 'I was making quite a bit of noise. Usually Housekeeping want to know when we're going to be finished because they need to clean up after us and they only have a few hours where they're permitted to be in the bedrooms. But I'd told my boss it would take a while. You can't hurry that kind of work. They'd taken the room out of use for the day so I didn't have to rush, but it wasn't as bad as I had thought.'

'Well, thank you for taking the time to talk to us,' Liv said, closing her notebook. 'If you think of anything else, please give us a call.'

Georgia handed Jason a business card and he pocketed it, preparing to go.

'What was blocking the toilet?' I asked.

'Plaster.'

'Plaster,' I repeated, checking I'd understood. 'Ordinary builder's plaster?'

'I don't know about ordinary. It was some type of quick-drying plaster. Not much of it but enough to block the waste pipe. I had to chip it out by hand.'

'Was there any building work going on in the room? Any repair work?'

'There was nothing on the maintenance records,' Jason said slowly. 'But you can check.'

'When you said it was blocked, I assumed it was paper or a pad or something that had fallen in and got flushed.' Georgia was frowning. 'But that sounds like it was deliberate.'

He shrugged. 'I don't know why it was there. It was my job to fix it.'

'When was the blockage reported?' I asked.

'I don't know. You'll have to check with Housekeeping.'

After he left, the three of us looked at one another, nonplussed.

'Plaster,' Liv said. 'How could that have been an accident?'

'We need to talk to Jeanette Lee – that's the hotel manager,' I explained to Georgia. 'I need to know who was in charge of Housekeeping, and the name of the chambermaid who was on this floor, and I need to speak to Mo Ramzan, the head of security.' I felt wide awake for the first time, energy flooding back. 'I want to know who was staying in 411 the night before the murder and who had access to their room apart from the guests. Did they complain about the plumbing or was there something wrong with the bathroom when the chambermaid went to check on it? When did the blockage happen?'

'But what does it have to do with the murder?' Georgia asked plaintively. 'What am I missing here?'

'I don't know, but I know it's unusual and deliberate and it happened near room 412. I want to know more, don't you? If we find out what happened here then I think we'll have a better chance of working out why.'

We divided our efforts, in the end, because it was more effective. Liv and Jeanette Lee assessed one another swiftly and with mutual appreciation of efficiency. Jeanette took her off to go through the guest records to identify the last occupants of 411, while Georgia dealt with Housekeeping. I reacquainted myself with Mo Ramzan, who was just as genial as before, and just as helpful.

'So you want a record of everyone who was in 411 that day.' He looked sideways at me, eyebrows raised. 'Any particular reason?'

'A wild goose chase, probably, but I'm interested in it.' I shrugged. 'Call it a hunch.'

'Ooh, a hunch. I never got them.' He sighed. 'That's why you're a Met detective and I'm a hotel security guard.'

I snorted. 'We both know you could do my job, Mo, and that you get paid a lot more than a Met detective, so less of the self-pity.'

He was clicking through files on his computer as he grinned. 'Here we go. Room 411. When do you want to start?'

'The morning of the murder,' I said. 'It was occupied, I think.'

'What have we got . . . Right, well, we can see the door was unlocked at 7.51 and locked again straight away, which looks like the occupants leaving for breakfast, because at 8.37 it was unlocked with a guest key card. Each room has two cards issued, one for each occupant, and I don't have a way of telling which card was used, but it was one of the two. Then it opened and locked again at 9.12. Do you want me to check what time they checked out?'

'Liv's taking care of it,' I said. 'Stick with the door.'

'OK, it's policy for someone from Housekeeping to take a look at the room during check-out, in case the guests have nicked the TV and the pillows.'

'Surely that wouldn't happen in a place like this.'

'Rich people will take anything,' Mo said. 'Anything.' His attention was on the screen though, and he was frowning. 'That'll be this staff card at 9.23. I can find out whose ID this is.'

The head of security was a busy man and I was too impatient to wait for him to get around to checking the IDs. 'Actually, would it be possible for you to give me a printout of all the staff IDs and names? I can check them myself.'

'No problem.' A pause and the printer behind him whirred into life. 'Then . . . looks like there were two other staff cards used. One at 9.48, one at 10.44.'

'Which was what?'

'Housekeeping?' He sounded uncertain though, and he scribbled down the ID numbers on a yellow Post-it, which he stuck to the desk. It was clearly his to-do list: a field of them curled across the wood beside his keyboard. 'And then . . . 11.32 we have another staff key card opening the door, but it doesn't lock again.'

'That's when Jason the plumber said he got there.'

'Let's assume for now that's Jason's card. He must have wedged the door open.' Mo shook his head. 'The staff do it all the time, especially when they're coming and going, but Jeanette doesn't like it. The door locks again at 13.03. I opened it at 18.15 to make sure the entire floor was empty – that's my ID number.' He tapped the screen to show me. 'And that's it.'

'Can you print off this record along with the staff IDs?'

'Of course,' Mo said, gallant. 'Anything for you.'

I came out of his office with the printouts and ran straight into Liv and Georgia.

'What's new?'

'The occupants of 411 were Canadian honeymooners,' Liv said. 'Jeanette said they were model guests – quiet, uncomplaining, stayed four nights and checked out without any kind of fuss. The room was booked via a travel agent who was able to give me their itinerary and I tracked them down to Edinburgh. I spoke to the wife who said there was nothing wrong with the plumbing when they were there, at least that she noticed, and she said they didn't have anything like quick-drying plaster with them that could have blocked the toilet.' Liv grinned. 'I think she thought I was insane, for what it's worth.'

'Reasonable. Georgia?'

'I spoke to Housekeeping. The supervisor was in the room first and said it was neat and tidy, nothing missing, nothing wrong. That was Annette Pollock.'

'At twenty-three minutes past nine,' I confirmed, checking the printout.

'Right. And then Veronique Baptiste went in to clean the room mid-morning and the toilet was overflowing. She was the one who reported it. She said they have too many rooms to do and not enough time to do it so she was pleased to be able to leave one room out, but she went in to straighten it out and change the bedsheets before she finished her shift.'

'That fits with what Jason told us,' I said, scribbling a note to that effect on the printout. 'And here's Veronique's ID at a quarter to eleven. So unless Annette boobytrapped the toilet, we're looking at the middle visitor which was . . . let me check against the staff register . . .' I stopped, staring at it.

'What is it?' Liv asked.

'I know that name.'

'That's good, isn't it?' Georgia said. 'If you know who it was, that should help.'

'It should, and it doesn't. Not at all.' I led the way to Mo Ramzan's office. He looked up, surprised.

'What can you tell me about Abilo Braga?'

'Abilo?' He looked down at his desk and peeled a Post-it off it, holding it up so I could see the name written on it. 'You're the second person to ask about him today.'

'Why's that?'

'He didn't show up for his shift. I've been trying to get hold of him but he's not answering his phone. These things happen, but I wouldn't expect it from Abilo.'

'No?'

'He's a good lad, Abilo. I'd swear to that.' He looked up and saw the expression on my face. 'And . . . I'd be wrong?'

33

The one thing everyone agreed was that there was no reason for Abilo Braga to let himself into an unoccupied bedroom. We watched the CCTV together, and it was deeply uninformative. The waiter walked down the hallway, not hurrying but at a reasonable pace, looking as if he had every right to be there. He wasn't carrying anything and I couldn't tell if there was anything in the pockets of his close-fitting uniform, but then I didn't know how much plaster it had taken to block the toilet. I made a note to ask Jason the plumber about it. He let himself into 411 and we had a glimpse of his face that conveyed very little about his mood: he looked focused but not excited. A minute later, he emerged again and walked down the hall, towards the camera. Impossible to know what was going through his mind. Was this how a murderer walked?

And if it was, how had he killed Ilaria in the bare couple of minutes he'd spent in the room with her?

'Why didn't we see this earlier?' Liv asked.

'I called Colin. Apparently it's on his log of movements in the hallway on the day of the murder, but he didn't realise there was any significance to it because it was the room next door to 412. Also he didn't realise it was Abilo and he wouldn't have known he had no reason to be there.' I grimaced. 'Maybe if I'd looked at the log I'd have seen it.'

'I don't think you'd have thought anything of it,' Liv said, instantly supportive. 'You had no reason to think it was important.'

'And what is the significance?' Georgia was looking baffled, which probably matched my expression.

'I don't know. Why would vandalising room 411 be important if you were planning to commit a crime in 412? What was the outcome of taking what looks like a pretty significant risk?'

'No one could stay there when the toilet was blocked,' Liv said. 'Maybe they didn't want anyone to overhear the murder, in case she screamed.'

'But they didn't interfere with 410 on the other side,' I pointed out, 'and anyway, I'm not sure the risk would have been worth it for the sake of not being overheard. Then again, I'm not a killer and I've never planned a murder. Maybe it's the kind of thing that keeps you awake until you've dealt with it.'

'If we find Abilo Braga,' Liv said, 'we can ask him.'

I had already taken Braga's address when I interviewed him after the murder. He lived in North London, in what proved to be a small street of terraced brick houses that had so far resisted gentrification, a ten-minute walk from Hendon Central tube station. Number 18 was, like its neighbours, unloved and grimy, with an empty window box outside the single window. A young woman answered when we knocked, her attitude hostile for no reason other than that she was annoyed at being dragged down to answer the front door. She wore a peach-coloured tracksuit. Blonde hair hung down over her face, some of it curled, some of it straight, as if she'd given up on it halfway through the styling process. Zofia was from somewhere in Eastern Europe but I didn't ask too much about her origins in case she thought I was going to tip off immigration. Anyway, she was only sharing a house with Braga, who had lived there for eight months. She didn't even know him that well, she informed me. Enough to chat to, when they saw each other in the shared areas of the house. Not enough to go to the pub together. But she had liked him.

'And he's not here,' Zofia finished, triumphant. 'You've missed him.'

'When was he here?' I asked.

'He left last night and I didn't hear him come back. I can see his bedroom window from mine and there was no light on last night or this morning.'

'What time did he leave?'

She considered it. 'Around . . . eight.'

'Eight. Sure about that?'

'Sure.'

'Sure it was him you saw leaving?'

'Of course.' She looked offended. 'I said hello.'

'How did he seem?'

'He was . . . in a good mood. He made a comment about the stew I was cooking. He said it smelled delicious.' She blushed faintly. 'I asked if he wanted me to keep some for him and he said no, he was going to get something while he was out.'

'Where was he going?' Liv asked.

'I don't know. I didn't ask.'

'What direction did he go?'

'I didn't see.' Straightforward answers, no awkwardness; I believed her.

'Does he have a car or did he use public transport?' I was thinking of tracing him via an Oyster card or his bank card. Buses and underground stations had CCTV. It would be a big job for Colin and his team, but—

'He has a car. He bought it a month ago.'

'What kind?'

'I don't know. Small. Silver. Not new.'

'Two doors? Four? A hatchback?'

She didn't know; she didn't know anything about cars. She hadn't been in it. A wistful tone to that answer, as if she wouldn't have minded a drive with the Brazilian man. I possibly hadn't seen him at his best, I reflected.

'Was he carrying anything when he left?'

'He had a bag over his shoulder. A backpack.' She sketched the shape in the air. A small bag, not big enough for clothes or anything substantial, which suggested he hadn't been running away. On the other hand, the car might have been full of his belongings already.

'Does he stay out all night often?'

'No. Never.'

'Where's his room?'

'In the back.' She gestured with square-tipped acrylic nails that looked too long to be practical. 'Through the kitchen.'

The house was divided into units with a shared kitchen but individual bathrooms. It was a small galley kitchen where the residents were clearly expected to cook and go: no table, no attempt at conviviality. Everything was cheap and bleak, from the grey flooring to the white emulsion that coated every possible surface, but it was spotlessly clean. The door beyond it was Braga's, and he or someone else had put a sticker of the Brazilian flag on it. I knocked, then tried the handle.

'Locked.'

'Can we break in?' Georgia said.

I hesitated, considering it. The door was uPVC, the kind that flexed and absorbed a lot of energy when you hit it. I'd seen burly men armed with battering rams defeated by uPVC doors, and none of the three of us was particularly hefty. Besides, we didn't really have the grounds to break in.

'It would be more useful if we got permission from the homeowner. Then we'd be lawfully on the premises and we could search it without waiting for a warrant and take away anything useful.'

'Good old Section 19,' Liv said with a grin, referring to the relevant provision in the Police and Criminal Evidence Act.

'Exactly.'

'But what are we looking for?' Georgia asked.

'I don't know yet,' I said patiently. I leaned back to see the young woman was standing in the doorway. Her expression was troubled.

'Does the landlord live here in the property, Zofia?'

'No.'

That would have been too easy. 'Where can we find him?'

'Next door,' she said, as if we should have known, and I offered up a silent prayer of thanks that he wasn't miles away, that one thing had gone right, that we were at last making some kind of progress.

I had relaxed too soon, it became clear when the landlord was roused, and came in to unlock the door, leaning into the room ahead of us so that I had to yank him out of my way to see.

'He's not in there,' he announced, with a degree of satisfaction because we had interrupted his television viewing (a tennis tournament held somewhere hot, the female players glistening with sweat as they threw themselves around the court). Even Georgia's charm hadn't got very far with him. 'No one's home.'

The room took up most of an extension that someone – the landlord, possibly – had added to the rear of the house, complete with a window that gave a perfect view of the garden fence and not much else. It was neat and tidy, though, and the air was fresh: not unthinkable to live there, even if it was basic. An electric heater hung on one wall and the air temperature suggested it had been on within the previous twenty-four hours, but not recently. There was a tiny bathroom beyond it with a shower that was dry, as was the sink. It was looking as if Zofia had been right about when he left, and that he hadn't come back.

'Did you have planning permission for this?' Liv was asking the landlord, who looked shifty.

'Permitted development.'

'Is it? Are you sure about that?'

'It's a good bit of building.' He knocked on the wall. 'Insulated. It's cosy, isn't it?'

'Does that mean small?' I was working my way around the room: a double bed, with cushions to turn it into a kind of sofa during the day. A desk and chair. A cheap and flimsy set of drawers filled with neatly folded clothes. Paper-shaded lamps from IKEA probably made it look less grim at night than it was during the day, when unforgiving daylight turned the white walls grey. Someone – Braga, at a guess – had bought a rug for the floor that hid a lot of the cheap laminate. A corkboard hung on one wall, covered in photographs that sang with heat and light: blue skies, beaches, smiling faces. The life he had left behind, I thought, and wondered if grey Hendon and a small silver car and his job in the hotel had been worth it.

'What do you think?' Liv asked.

'There are clothes in the wardrobe and drawers, and his suitcase is under the bed.' I looked around, trying to see what wasn't there. 'If he had a computer he took it with him. There's a phone charger plugged in by the desk, but no phone so we can assume that was in his bag or on his person. It doesn't look as if he's run away, but he left last night and didn't come back, and didn't make it to work, so I'm not assuming anything at this stage. Maybe he has a girlfriend and forgot he was supposed to be working today. Maybe he's done a runner and he's taken the bare minimum with him.'

'Search?'

I nodded. 'Search.'

34

I didn't often get nervous at work – not the dry-mouthed, clammy hands variety of nervous, anyway – but my heart was thudding and I had to take a moment to steel myself before I knocked on the door. I was tossing a coin, socially speaking. Heads, sunshine. Tails, storms. The door opened: heads it was.

'Maeve!' Luke looked surprised and then delighted. 'I didn't know you were coming over.'

'I wanted to update Josh on the case.' Because what else would I want to do with my Friday night? It was a full week since I had gone to Braga's house, which meant it was also a full week since I had seen Derwent. 'Is he here?'

'He's out for a run but he should be back soon. Come in and wait. Do you want a drink?'

'No, thanks.'

He led the way down the narrow corridor, tall and lean in his shirt and suit trousers, in a post-work state of half-dress that involved not wearing a tie or jacket or shoes. I took a second to kick off my own shoes and edged past the expensive bike that was hanging on the wall next to the front door – a rich boy's toy, several thousand pounds' worth of carbon-framed aerodynamic perfection – before I made my way to the open-plan living area. Two low sofas stood at right angles to one another, with a huge TV mounted on the wall. Luke was standing in the kitchen on the left as I walked in, burrowing through a laundry basket full of clean clothes that he'd put on the island.

'Sorry, you don't mind, do you? I'm going to the gym in a minute.'

'Work away,' I said, perching on one sofa and looking out across the lights of London. 'Do you pay extra for the view of the river?'

'Probably.' He was grinning, though, when I looked around. 'It's smart, isn't it?'

'Very.' The flat was in a new-build high-rise complex in Nine Elms, one of the forest of developments that had suddenly appeared by the river where there had always been a lot of nothing. Battersea Power Station wasn't far away, with its new shops and flats and a shiny underground station. It had been derelict for my entire life and now it was the heart of Luke's neighbourhood.

'This is better than where I used to live when you first met me.'

'A box room in a shared house? Yes, quite a lot smarter than that. You used to be so careful about money. What changed?'

'I got a better job. And I paid off the rest of Mum's mortgage. Then I decided I could afford to enjoy life a bit more.'

'Hence the Porsche.'

'Yes, although it wasn't as expensive as you'd think.'

I regarded him with pleasure. It did my heart good to see him thrive. 'Well, you're not going to shake off the habits of a lifetime just because you make it big in the City, but it's nice to see you enjoying yourself.'

'And moving here meant I had a spare room, which was handy for Josh.'

'How has that been?'

'Having him here? Good.' He said it positively, without any suggestion of doubt. 'He's excellent company.'

If he was, he was making an effort and I wondered if Luke realised that. 'He's been a bit brief with me this week when I messaged him.'

'Really?'

I shrugged. 'I think he's frustrated.'

'He's still not allowed back to work, is he?'

'Not this week, not next week either.' Una had been clear with him, and with the team. He was taking time off, officially, which meant that he wasn't restricted to office duties while he was under investigation and she didn't have to deal with having him around all the time. 'I don't think it's a bad thing.'

Luke raised his eyebrows. 'He does.'

'Well, he would work until he dropped if he was allowed, just to take his mind off his problems, but that's not always the best approach.'

'Which you would know.'

'Ouch.' I went back to looking out of the window.

'Sorry. I didn't mean to upset you.'

'I know.' I could count the number of times Derwent had ever apologised to me; his son was a much more straightforward proposition.

'How are things going with Owen? Did you ever get around to rearranging that date?'

I winced. 'No. I should text him.'

'You could do it now, while you're waiting.'

I took out my phone and sent an apology message. The reply pinged immediately.

Drink tomorrow?

Did I want to say yes? I frowned at the screen, then put the phone down so I didn't have to think about it, and looked up to find Luke was watching me.

'Hmm.'

'What does that mean?'

'Nothing. Thinking, that's all.' He was folding clothes briskly. 'He's a good person, Owen. Decent.'

'I know.'

'I don't want anyone to mess him around, not even you.'

'I wouldn't,' I said, stung.

'You might not mean to.' He started unbuttoning his shirt. 'But you still might.'

'We haven't even had a first date,' I pointed out.

'He likes you, though.'

'I like him. What I know of him, anyway.' I paused, watching as Luke stripped off his shirt and started undoing his belt. 'What are you doing?'

'Getting changed.'

He was on the far side of the kitchen island so my view was cut off at the waist. He was a younger, whippier version of Derwent, but recognisably the same in terms of breadth of shoulder and length of limb. He stepped out of his trousers and then underwear, nonchalant. An aeon passed; he was in no particular hurry about getting dressed again. I was revising my opinion of Luke. He was more like his father than I'd thought. The actual living proof of nature being more important than nurture, given that they hadn't even met until Luke was twenty-five. He grinned at me, totally naked, his gym shorts in his hand, the kitchen island all that was protecting his modesty.

'What exactly is this?'

'Nothing,' he said. 'Just an experiment.'

'Well, the next time you conduct an experiment, try not to carry it out in a room full of reflective surfaces. The oven door is basically a mirror, you realise.'

He bit his lip and blushed, stepping into the shorts without any further delay. 'I didn't think of that.'

'Evidently not.'

He was putting on socks, concentrating on keeping his balance. 'Worth it, though.'

'Not that I don't appreciate it at the end of a long week, but I wasn't expecting the full Magic Mike routine. Do you mind explaining why?'

He laughed and was about to answer when the sound of a key turning in the front door made us both jump.

'Yo, in here,' Luke called and there was an answering grunt from the hall before Derwent appeared, looking around. For me, it transpired.

'I saw your shoes in the hall. What are you doing here?'

I took a second to answer. He was wearing running shorts and a T-shirt and both were saturated with sweat. He looked exhausted, and also not particularly pleased to see me. I wondered how far he had gone on his run, and how hard he had pushed himself. It didn't seem to have made him feel better.

'I wanted to keep you in the loop about Ilaria Cavendish.'

'She's still dead, I presume.' He glowered at Luke and went past him to fill a glass at the sink. Luke yanked his top on, his movements jerky and hurried. It was probably the first time he'd been on the receiving end of a trademark Derwent scowl.

I had been curled up on the sofa. Now I got to my feet, folding my arms even though I knew my body language would tell him I was defensive. 'I thought you'd want to know about developments in the investigation.'

'There's this amazing invention called email.'

'OK. Next time I won't bother. I'm going to go.'

'No, you're here now. You might as well stay. I'll get changed.' He downed the glass of water in one long swallow. 'Sorry if I interrupted you two.'

'You didn't,' I said, to his back as he walked out, and a few seconds later I heard a shower running.

'Interesting.' Luke had recovered enough to smirk to himself as he came to sit down on the other sofa, his trainers in his hand.

'What's interesting?' I was distracted, listening as the sound of the water changed once Derwent got into the shower. I pictured him washing his hair, lathering the shampoo irritably. 'How does he make water sound angry? He is the grumpiest man I've ever met.'

'What's interesting,' Luke said, doing up his laces, 'is that you didn't get excited when Owen messaged you, and you didn't even blink when I took off all of my clothes.'

I raised my eyebrows. 'Was I supposed to?'

'It's not the reaction I'm used to, put it that way.'

'I knew it was a test. What was I meant to do? Scream? Cry? Fall to my knees in awe?'

He grinned, moving on to the second shoe. 'Any of the above would have been acceptable, but no. Perfect composure. Very bad for my ego, for what it's worth. And then *he* walks in, and all he has to do is look at you, and you go to pieces.'

'I did not.'

'As an independent observer, I can tell you that you absolutely did. Blushing, stammering, the works. He didn't even smile at you.' He got up and started stretching out his quads, holding one foot behind him, his knee bent. 'Which is fine. But I think you need to tell him how you feel.'

'He's got enough on his plate at the moment. And anyway, I don't think he feels the same way.'

'Really?'

'Not any more.' I said it in a small voice that sounded desolate, even to me.

Luke dropped his foot, suddenly serious, and came over to put his arms around me. 'It'll work out.'

'I don't think it will.' It was the first time I'd said it out loud, but I had been thinking it ever since he'd come out of the police station the previous Friday. 'I think if it was going to be all right, I'd know that by now. There's always been a good reason for us to keep our distance from one another before. Now we've run out of reasons, and you saw what he's like. I don't know what I did or didn't do. Maybe it's just that he's tired of being in a relationship and he doesn't want to start a new one with me. Maybe the thought of being with me was always more exciting when there was no chance of it actually happening.'

'Maybe he's not in the right place to think about it now, with everything else that's going on. Do you want me to talk to him?'

'God, no. Don't get involved any more than you have already.' I leaned against him for a moment longer, then pulled myself free with a sigh, and realised a little too late that Derwent had returned, fully dressed in jeans and a T-shirt, with wet hair and a scowl like a black hole that was powerful enough to absorb all the light in the room.

'On that note, I think it's time for me to hit the road.' Luke picked up his gym bag. 'I'll be an hour, an hour and a half, something like that. Do you want to get a curry?'

'If you like,' Derwent said, without noticeable enthusiasm.

'Eat in or go out?'

'I don't care.'

'Cool,' Luke said lightly. 'I'll order in, I think. Maeve? Are you staying?'

'No. Thanks. But no.' I caught Luke's eye, and blushed because he was right. I couldn't even be in the same room as Derwent without falling apart.

He gave me a sympathetic smile, touched his finger to his forehead in an ironic salute to his father, and went down the hall to the front door, whistling.

Which left me and Derwent on our own.

35

'That was just a hug,' I said. 'Me and Luke, just now. He was just hugging me.'

'I didn't ask.'

'No, but you were wondering.'

He shook his head. 'Not me. Do you want a drink?'

I hadn't before, but I was starting to feel like I needed one. 'What have you got?'

He went to the kitchen and looked disapprovingly at the laundry basket, piling the clothes back into it and taking it down the hall to Luke's room, as if he couldn't bear the mess. When he returned, he reeled off, 'Wine, beer, tea, coffee, water, gin, champagne, whisky, vodka, Aperol . . .'

'Has he got a whole bar here?'

'More or less.'

'Gin and tonic, please.'

Derwent nodded and set about making two. I watched him slice a lime, and thought about saying nothing, and didn't have the sense to keep my mouth shut.

'Is this a peace offering?'

He paused with a tin of tonic water in his hand. 'It's a drink.'

'Oh.'

'A peace offering for what?'

'Being moody.'

The tin made a sharp sound as he set it down on the island, the better to frown at me.

'Never mind.' I turned and looked out at the view instead, trying not to fidget or give myself away any more than I had already.

A minute later he slid one glass across the island.

'Yours.'

I crossed the room and buried my nose in the glass to inhale the reliable juniper scent, as if that would clear my head. 'I only come here for the service.'

'You weren't planning to tip.' He moved past me and sat on one of the sofas, in the centre, making it very clear that he wasn't expecting to share it with me. I stayed where I was, leaning against the island.

'Well?'

'We haven't found Abilo Braga.'

Derwent growled in the back of his throat. 'Why not?'

'He turned his phone off when he left the house. No cell site.' I sipped my drink, which was strong, and the cold liquid burned on the way down, then spread warmth through my stomach. Neat trick. 'I found a second phone charger in his room.'

'He had two phones?'

'So it seems. We don't have a number for the second one and he didn't have a contract for either. Pay as you go for the main phone and I would presume the second too. No one at work saw him using anything other than the Samsung Galaxy, but the charger is for a Motorola.'

'A burner phone. Fuck.' He set his glass on the coffee table and pushed it away from him, leaning back with his hands behind his head. 'What about the car?'

'We found that today. It was parked in a small industrial estate in Wembley. Six units, two unoccupied. It was in the corner of the customer parking bays. No one in the units realised it was dumped there until we turned up.'

'CCTV?'

'Not great. We can see him walking away from the car but not where he went. He goes into a blind spot and we haven't picked him up again.'

'Maybe someone else picked him up.'

'Could be. We're looking at all the cars that were in the immediate area when he parked up. It takes time, especially when we don't know who we're looking for.'

Derwent was frowning. 'Was he carrying anything?'

'A small bag over his shoulder. Not a backpack or luggage. He left clothes, personal belongings, letters, bank statements.'

'What did he take?'

'I haven't found his passport or any cash.'

'Has he used his bank cards? Credit card?'

'No, unless he has an account we don't know about.' I sighed. 'One version of events is that he was planning to leave and made some financial arrangements that mean he's able to access funds. The other is that something bad has happened to him. His family say he hasn't been in touch. He hasn't been at work. He hasn't gone home. None of the friends we've traced have seen him, or they're not telling us if they have. One of them did say he was talking about having more money and going travelling, but she didn't know if he was expecting to get paid for something or if it was wishful thinking.'

'Do we need to go public on him?'

'I think so. I can't see any other way of tracking him down unless we get lucky and he pops up somewhere. If he hadn't taken the passport I'd feel a lot more worried about his well-being, but as it is . . .'

'Do we have an alert out for him at the ports?'

'Border Force are on it. If I was him I'd lie low, you know. Stay with a friend and wait us out. We don't have the resources to do surveillance.'

'He's a suspect in a murder investigation.'

'I know that,' I said patiently. 'But we don't have enough to charge him. Not even close. We can put him in the room next door for no apparent reason that morning, briefly, and we can say he was in the same room as the victim for a couple of minutes. That's not enough time to kill her and put her in the bath and run the bath and come out bone dry.'

He tipped back his head and stared at the ceiling. 'This case.'

'Mm. I know you're annoyed to be off work but it's not the most rewarding experience to keep running into dead ends.' I looked down at my drink to stop myself from staring at him and the way he was sprawling there, loose-limbed and relaxed.

Well, I could do something about the last part. 'I need to talk to you, Josh.'

He lifted his head, his expression wary. 'Go on.'

'About Melissa.'

Every muscle in his body tensed at the sound of her name. He sat up slowly, the gradual physical adjustment of a predator preparing to strike. 'What about her?'

'I've been talking to Mark.'

'Pell.'

I rolled my eyes. 'Yes. Mark Pell. I'm sorry for not giving him his full title. Mark Pell, your girlfriend's ex-husband.'

'Fuck's sake, Kerrigan—'

'Let me finish.'

He folded his arms and sat back, scowling. I put my glass down, feeling slightly sick.

'I talked to Mark. He was glad to hear you'd been released without charge. He's looking after Thomas.'

Derwent unclenched his jaw to say, 'I know.'

'Melissa has been released from hospital.' That got a twitch of an eyebrow which I guessed meant that he hadn't known her whereabouts. 'She's gone home with her mother. The house in Jena Road is empty.'

He inclined his head. 'Noted. Is that it?'

'The allegations that Melissa made against you are the same allegations she made against Mark. The similarities were so specific, not even Roz Fuller could ignore them.'

'You talked to her?'

I shook my head, which meant *I don't want to talk about that now* but I knew he would probably misinterpret it, and I felt fine about that, on the whole. I'd reached my quota for being shouted at that evening.

'It seems very clear to me, as an independent and impartial observer, that Melissa made false allegations against you, and Mark has always said he didn't do any of the things she accused him of.' Derwent began to speak and I held up a hand. 'Wait. I also talked to Melissa's mother. Ellen said she didn't believe that Mark had ever hurt Melissa. She thought Melissa ran away because she was in love with the idea of being a victim and she wasn't getting any sympathy from Ellen. That organisation stepped in to help Melissa find a new life and she got carried away and actually left for London with Thomas. Ellen thought she would have got bored and come home if it hadn't been for the fire.'

He frowned, thinking it over, looking away from me. 'Maybe.'

'Incidentally, Ellen also thought you'd definitely assaulted Melissa.'

'Thanks, Ellen.' His face was ashen.

'You should have spent more time charming her if you wanted her to like you.'

'Liking is one thing. Thinking I'd hit her daughter is another.'

'She believed Melissa, this time round.' I felt sorry for him and dug around for some scraps of comfort. 'But you know, I think a lot of that was guilt because she didn't believe her when she said Mark hurt her.'

'How very like Ellen to get it wrong twice over.'

I steeled myself. 'You've always believed Melissa's story that Mark hurt her. What do you think about it now?'

The blue eyes locked onto mine, his pupils pinpoints from rage. 'It's not the same as what's happened to me.'

'It's exactly the same, Josh. She had the same fantasy, the same vision of herself as a brave victim, and she got the same thrill from convincing other people she deserved sympathy and help. She took advantage of Clara Porter the same way she manipulated the charity that found her the flat in London. She swapped you into the story in place of Mark, the same way she swapped you and Mark in her life. You met her and fell for her and before you knew it you were living together, being a dad to Thomas, and I bet there was one morning when you woke up and had no idea how you'd ended up where you were. She manipulated you.'

'Leave it,' he snapped.

'Look, I'm not trying to upset you or – or *judge* you or anything like that. You looked after her and you loved Thomas and he benefited so much from that – and I think you did too.' I gave a helpless one-shouldered shrug. 'It was a good thing, some of the time. Same for Mark. He still loves Melissa, you know. She's the mother of his son. They share happy memories as well as the terrible ones. And because of that, Mark won't support a prosecution.'

'A prosecution?'

'Melissa could be charged with perverting the course of justice.'

His reaction was instant. 'Absolutely not.'

'If you and Mark made a complaint—'

'No.'

'—saying how it had affected your lives—'

'I said no.'

'—because there should be consequences, Josh. She can't tell lies about you and damage your reputation and get you in trouble at work and effectively have you *suspended* because she enjoys the attention she gets when people think she's a victim. It's not fair and it's not right.'

He shook his head. 'I'm not doing it.'

'They won't take it any further unless you ask them to.'

'They could prosecute her without us. There's enough evidence to prove she lied without a new statement from me or Mark.'

'Yes, but they won't. And you know they won't. If you asked, though, they'd have to look into it.'

'Is that what they told you?' The expression on my face told him that it was. 'I can't put her through it. Being arrested, being processed. I can't stop thinking about it.' He hesitated, then went on, 'I dream about it, you know. That feeling of being watched. Being judged. Being trapped.'

I wanted more than anything to cross the room and stand between his knees and hold him, to feel his arms around me so that we could both be comforted – but that stubborn part of me that believed in justice wouldn't stay quiet. 'The difference is that you hadn't done anything wrong. She has.'

'It's not worth it if the only reason is to punish her for what she did to me.'

'She did it to Mark too.'

That made him glower. He got up. 'Mark doesn't want her to get in trouble, and he's had a worse time than me. I certainly don't want to take it any further. Sorry to disappoint you, my sweet Maeve.'

'I'm not disappointed,' I said, flustered and annoyed in equal measure. 'It's about justice. She's been trying to destroy you, Josh. She's manipulated you seven ways to Sunday. Could you stop trying to be her white knight for a minute and acknowledge that she set out to hurt you?'

He leaned on the island, his hands gripping the sides so the muscles in his arms flickered. 'What will it take to persuade you to listen to me?'

'You don't owe her anything.' I was ignoring the warning signs. 'You should be using every advantage you have to prove she's not a reliable witness.'

His mouth tightened as if he didn't agree. 'It won't stop Roz Fuller from investigating me.'

'It might.'

He walked over and picked up my bag, handing it to me, then took my arm and guided me down the hall. 'I don't want you to come here again.'

'Why not?' I twisted, trying to free myself.

'It's not appropriate. I'm your boss, and I'm off work at the moment. If you need to get in touch with me, use work email and keep it professional.' We had reached the front door. He bent and picked up my shoes and tucked them into my arms beside the bag. 'It's late. Time for you to go.'

I stood my ground. 'Is this because you're worried about being investigated by Roz Fuller?'

I'd made it too easy for him. He gave me a humourless smile that showed off the tips of his teeth. 'No, it's not.'

I waited for him to open the door, went through it and took the lift down to the lobby, putting on my shoes on the way. I negotiated the revolving door to get onto the street, and walked away, and it wasn't until I was all the way on the other side of Vauxhall Bridge, in the genteel surroundings of Pimlico, that I allowed myself to cry.

36

After a weekend that I mostly spent, mindlessly, on leading the best possible kind of life – cleaning and going to the gym and batch-cooking healthy meals for the week and texting Owen, warmly, to arrange a time for that drink – I returned to work with a feeling of intense relief. Not thinking about Derwent was a full-time effort that ran in the background of my mind, draining me of energy. Work was the one place where, currently, I knew he wasn't.

This time I took Liv with me to the Soho offices of Cavendish Hickey, where Dally Field was sitting bolt upright at her desk, murmuring into the phone competently.

'Of course we'll be able to take care of that for you. All part of the service. No, it really isn't a problem. I know, a total nightmare. We certainly don't want to put your project on hold though.' She smiled, listening. 'I absolutely will. Thank you.'

The soft voice and diffident manner evaporated as soon as she hung up the phone. 'You're back.'

'That's right. I'm here to interview Jennifer. She should be expecting us.'

'Take a seat.' Dally waved at the chairs next to the water dispenser. I didn't make a move to sit down and Liv knew me well enough to remain where she was, beside me.

'You seem busy.'

'Things have been crazy. It's been such a trauma trying to deal with all the calls and requests for appointments.' Dally blew her fringe off her forehead. 'You wouldn't think people would want to work with a business where one of the partners was permanently out of action, but I suppose what they say about no such thing as bad publicity is a cliché for a reason.'

'People are strange,' Liv offered, and Dally smiled at her.

'It looks as if they're trusting you with more responsibilities,' I said. The desk in front of Dally was piled high with samples of fabric, Pantone chips and mood boards.

'It helps that Jennifer's been hungover a lot of the time,' Dally said in a stage whisper, one hand shielding her mouth. She dropped the act. 'But yes. More to do, at last. There's always a silver lining, isn't there?'

'Not always.' I looked around as the door opened to reveal a thin, harassed-looking middle-aged woman with grey-blonde hair. She barely glanced at us, heading for the water cooler where she filled a large bottle.

'All day,' Dally mouthed at me, and leaned forward. 'Anne, these are the detectives investigating Ilaria's death.'

'Oh.' She faltered, holding on to her water bottle with both hands. Round hazel eyes, open mouth. I thought she was doing the arithmetic of the working mother: *How is this going to delay me and does it mean I won't get home on time* . . . Her hands tightened and she spoke with resolve. 'I don't know anything, I'm afraid, and I don't really have time.'

'Just a few questions,' I said sweetly, and sent Liv off with her.

'Anne spends her life shuttling between the water cooler and the bathroom,' Dally drawled. 'Someone must have told her it was good for her to drink water, but my God, there are limits. It goes straight through her.'

There was a bang from downstairs: the front door closing. Dally cocked her head.

'Incoming.'

'Jennifer?'

She nodded, shuffling papers on her desk with renewed energy. The door burst open and a thin woman with a deep tan rushed in and balanced a coffee cup on Dally's desk. She was draped in layers and immediately began stripping off clothes.

'God, I'm late. I know I am. I'm sorry. And oh my God, I have to say sorry that I didn't manage to see you last week.

I was jet-lagged to *fuck*.' She had a warm, emphatic Dublin drawl, the vowels dragged out, a quick-quick-slow cadence to her phrases that was so different from the flat steady drumbeat of an English voice. Briskly, Jennifer removed two coats and a jumper that she was wearing as a scarf. She stripped off knitted wrist warmers and added them to the pile, her long fingers deft. A pair of Chanel sunglasses held her tawny hair back. One striking ring decorated her right hand: gemstones in pretty colours, like hardboiled sweets. 'I know, ridiculous. I feel the cold. It's worse when I've been away somewhere hot. I have no ability to cope with London weather when I've had a break. The last ten days have been hell.'

'I thought it was a work trip,' Dally said, and ducked as her boss pretended to swipe at her.

No one, it occurred to me, was much bothered about why I was there, or about the person who was not there, who was never going to be there again.

Jennifer had got down to a black cord boilersuit that showed off several inches of tanned chest. Her skin was stretched thin over her bones and I guessed she lived on coffee and stress. She stretched her arms over her head, leaning left and right as if she was warming up before yoga.

'Come into my office, I suppose. But I don't know what I can tell you.' She nudged the coffee cup. 'This is finished.'

'I'll put it in the bin, shall I?' Dally rolled her eyes and picked it up, but she was smiling. I thought the two of them would probably work well together. Maybe Ilaria's death wasn't the end of the business after all. Hickey Field had a certain ring to it.

I hadn't been in Jennifer Hickey's office before, and it was smarter than the reception area, with pale grey walls and an art deco desk. A huge painting hung behind the desk, sprays of pinks and blues that reminded me of hollyhocks in a garden. Twin lamps stood on a console table beneath the painting, as much for sculptural effect as for lighting.

'This is smart.'

'Zoom,' she explained briefly. 'Clients like to imagine themselves in this kind of space. I do all my consultations online or in person in their homes or I meet them somewhere we can have a drink. Everyone relaxes a bit and says what they really think, you know?'

Once the door closed, Jennifer Hickey switched off the slightly giddy positive energy and slumped behind her desk. She put her hands over her face and started massaging her skin, her eyes closed.

'Ugh. I'm screwed. I've got meetings all today and I'm going to be a zombie by the time I get to the last one. I mean, I'm a zombie now. It's not going to get better, do you know what I mean?'

I did, and I said so.

She opened an eye. 'You must be Irish.'

'My parents are but I was born in London.' I was feeling the familiar squirm of unease at being not quite one thing nor another.

'What was that like?' She leaned forward, curious.

'Like leading a double life. I was different in school and at home.'

'Isn't everyone?'

'I suppose so. How long have you lived in London?'

She rolled her eyes. '*Too* long. Nine years. I got married seven years ago. He's never going to move to Dublin so we're here, I suppose. Unless I leave him. But I don't want to do that. And anyway, London has been good to me. I have a nice home and a good job.' A frown struggled to dent her Botox-perfect forehead. 'For now.'

'Dally was saying that Ilaria was the source of a lot of your financial security.'

'Angus is.' She said it sharply. 'Angus has always been a huge help. I don't know why Dally said it was Ilaria. She didn't contribute anything.'

'Presumably his investment was for her sake, though.'

'No.' Jennifer shook her head, emphatic. 'He knew me before he ever met Ilaria. He met her through me, actually. I worked on his house when he was married before.'

'He was married before?'

'You didn't know that? Angus is a serial husband. He makes a five-year commitment, max. Or he used to. Ilaria was his third wife.'

I was surprised and trying not to show it. 'He didn't give me that impression.'

'No, well, he probably didn't want to draw attention to it.' Her tone was tart. 'I think he must know it doesn't reflect all that well on him that there are basically two things he wants in a woman: a thigh gap and an age gap.'

'Do you know his other wives?'

'Marika was his first wife and I never met her. She lives in Sweden. Married again, I think. I knew Devon – she was American. Gorgeous woman from Texas. Brilliant white teeth, like she wouldn't even know what red wine or coffee was. Flawless skin. Big hair. You couldn't fault her – she was always the perfect wife and hostess. But she aged out of the job. He got rid of her once she hit thirty-five.'

'When you say she aged out, was it because they didn't have children?'

'No, the opposite. He never wanted kids.' For the first time, Jen broke eye contact, clearly uneasy. 'She was the one who wanted them so he "let her go" in time to have them.' She added the quotes with her fingers. 'But he'd already lined up Ilaria to replace her.'

'Wow.'

'Angus is one of those men who likes things a certain way and if something isn't what he wants, he changes it. The reason he and Ilaria live in the mews house is because he gave Devon their place in the divorce. It was a gorgeous place in Hampstead. Dream house. Ilaria was hoping he would buy something similar for them but he decided he wanted to have less and travel more. He wanted a pied-à-terre type of vibe, so she had to make the best of it.'

'Does he fund this company?'

Jennifer nodded.

'And did he do that before he married Ilaria?'

'Indirectly. I had worked with him, as I said. But then I introduced him to Ilaria and things went to a whole new level. We were able to hire Anne and Dally. I started to feel like this was a business and not a sinking ship, you know? We had that security that if we didn't have enough in the business account we could call on him and get a loan or an investment or whatever he wanted to call it.'

'Did you know about Ilaria's affair with Sam Blundell?'

Jennifer pulled a face. 'Ugh. Yes.'

'Were you worried about it?'

She folded her arms and leaned back. 'Why would I be worried?'

'If she left Angus, your funding would disappear.'

'If Angus left her – which was far more likely – we were screwed too.' Jennifer shook her head. 'I was delighted for her to have someone in her life who made her happy.'

'But she wasn't happy all the time. Dally said she went through some ups and downs.'

'Oh yeah, well, there was always drama. And she did take drugs, but you probably know that already. A bit of coke. Recreational mainly. For someone who came across as a total bitch she was actually very shy and she used to load up before she had to do something that scared her.'

'She was clean when she died,' I said.

'Really?' Jennifer looked surprised. 'Then she'd changed. Although—'

I waited but the other woman had fallen silent. I had the sense that she'd withdrawn again – that this was territory she didn't want to enter, for some reason. I leaned forward.

'I know this is difficult but I really want to find whoever killed Ilaria. Anything you can tell me – especially if it's something that not many people might know – is really, really important.'

'Oh.' She rubbed her eyes, sniffing. 'Well, she had an abortion.'

'When?'

'August. I went with her to the doctor.' She was opening desk drawers, hunting for a tissue which she eventually found. 'She had to take some pills, that's all. Not very complicated. She spent a couple of days in bed.'

'Was she upset?'

'No, I was.' Jennifer gave me a tight smile. 'I can't have kids. Had IVF. Tried everything. No joy. We'd decided to give up and make the best of it.'

'I'm sorry.'

'Yeah, well, it is what it is. There are good things about it too, don't get me wrong. A child would have disrupted our lives completely. It's like a kind of madness to want that but it's overwhelming. Still, I thought it was ironic that Illy was able to have a baby and didn't want to.'

'And Angus didn't want kids.'

'Definitely not.'

'Was it his baby?'

Jennifer sighed. 'Yes, it was. She was sure of that. And actually it annoyed me because he wouldn't have a vasectomy even though he was so convinced kids were a bad idea that it was in their prenup. If she had his child, it would end the marriage. That child would receive certain benefits but Ilaria would have got nothing. That was the deal. But I wonder if she regretted the abortion after she had it. And I do remember her saying if it wasn't Angus's baby, the prenup clause wouldn't have applied.'

'But she didn't talk to you about having a baby.'

'She knew about my situation. For once she was tactful and didn't involve me.' Jennifer swivelled on her chair, considering it. 'Maybe she was looking ahead to Angus getting rid of her and had decided to take the initiative. From how she was behaving, I wonder if she was going to try again.'

37

'Welcome back.'

Derwent straightened up from where he had been crouching beside the bath in room 412 and clicked off his torch. 'Thanks.'

Which concluded the social pleasantries, as far as I was concerned. He was looking as if he'd spent his time off largely in the gym: lean, fit and dangerous. Not that it mattered. I was unmoved. Work was the only thing on my mind.

'Why did you want to meet here?'

'To remind myself of what happened.' He frowned, looking at the room, which was empty but ready for guests, the bed made up, the carpet marked with scuffs from a vacuum cleaner, the air smelling of polish and, in the bathroom, a reassuring note of bleach. 'It feels like a long time since I was last in here.'

'Two weeks,' I said.

He turned the frown on me. 'You haven't made much progress without me.'

'Of course now that you're back the entire case will start to make perfect sense. We were only missing your input.'

He raised his eyebrows. 'What's wrong?'

'Nothing.' I went over to the window and stared out at the building opposite, which was also a hotel, as it happened. A hundred rooms with identical mirrors on the wall, identical lamps in the window, identical curtains. It felt soulless and depressing, a definite step down from the Governor Hotel. 'I keep thinking I've missed something important. Something someone said to me.'

'Unless it was "This is how I committed a murder that seems completely impossible unless you can bend time", I doubt it was that important.' He came to stand next to me, shoulder to shoulder, looking out too. 'I thought maybe you were angry with me.'

'Angry? Why would I be?' I folded my arms. 'You know you upset me the last time I saw you.'

'Maybe I want to clear the air.'

'Do you?' I waited, and he said nothing. 'I thought so. Let's not start today with an argument.'

'How's Owen?'

That got me to look at him properly. 'Why do you ask? Oh – presumably Luke told you.'

'He might have mentioned it. What is it – two dates in a week? One of you is keen.' A shrug. 'Maybe both of you are.'

'Owen is . . .' I trailed off, struggling to put it into words. *Owen is straightforward. Kind. Thoughtful. Fun. Cheerful. No visible hang-ups. Owen smiles when he sees me. Owen makes me laugh.*

I never think about Owen unless someone reminds me he exists.

'He's fine,' I said in the end. 'He's nice.'

Derwent nodded. 'That's what I thought.' Then, as I turned away, he said, 'Have you slept with him?'

I paused, letting the anger surge through me. 'Why don't you ask Luke?'

'Fuck.' He said it softly, under his breath, as if he was annoyed with himself.

The answer was no, I hadn't. The two dates had been grown-up – sedate, even: dinner, and a weekend walk along the river that had ended in a pub, where Owen found us a secluded booth and kissed me. It hadn't changed my world, but it hadn't put me off him either. Maybe what I needed was the slow growth of affection and mutual appreciation. Maybe that was more likely to end in a proper partnership, instead of whatever on-again-off-again drama I could expect from Josh Derwent. And since currently it seemed I could expect nothing at all from Josh Derwent, it wasn't actually a choice and I didn't have to worry about it.

I walked away from Derwent, passing the bathroom door. Pristine, the bathroom was almost unrecognisable to me, even though I'd looked at the crime scene photos again and again. No one would ever know the horrible way Ilaria Cavendish had met her end there. It was becoming increasingly likely that no one would ever know who had done it to her, either, including me. I'd talked to everyone I could think of, more than once. Sam Blundell had come in for another interview and shivered throughout it, wide-eyed with terror, and I still couldn't see him as a killer, or make the timings work. No one had seen Abilo Braga since the day he failed to come to work, and I still didn't know how he fitted in, or why he had vanished.

I didn't want to go near Derwent. I took a turn around the fitted wardrobe area, checking shelves that had been looked at a hundred times before, knowing there was nothing to see. When I came out, the room door was right in front of me, and I stopped.

'What is it?'

'I'm just looking,' I said, vaguely. The door had always been propped open when I was in 412 before, I realised, and I hadn't seen the usual notices that hotels were obliged to display, by law, for fire safety. Under the peephole, there was a framed floor plan with every room on the fourth floor clearly marked, along with the lifts and stairs. The rooms at the end of the corridor, 411 and 412, were the biggest, with the extra wardrobe area and a larger bathroom, and I guessed that was why Ilaria had insisted on it.

Insisted.

To the point that she'd been furious when someone else had been staying in 412 and she couldn't.

She had turned down an upgrade to stay in 412. That didn't make any sense.

I took a step closer to the floor plan, frowning at it.

'Maeve.'

'Wait.' I looked from the plan to the room and back again. 'What's this?'

Derwent came to stand next to me. 'Where am I looking?'

'Here. Between 411 and 412.'

'A space. Some sort of cupboard, or a void or something.' He didn't sound particularly interested. 'Look, Maeve—'

'No, shut up for a second.' I moved past him, brushing against him by accident, but I ignored it. I was focused on something else. 'This bookcase.'

It faced the bed. The glass-fronted doors were clean and smudge-free, the better to show off the books and knick-knacks on the shelves. I'd noticed it when I came into the room first, and then I'd forgotten about it completely. Now I undid the latch that was holding the doors closed and swung them open, and instead of opening the bookcase it split the piece of furniture in two. Soundlessly, on oiled hinges, the doors came open, and revealed a small space behind them.

'What's that?'

'A hallway.' I could see light coming through from the other side. 'These two rooms have connecting doors.'

'Why didn't we know that?' Derwent sounded furious.

'We didn't ask and no one thought to tell us. Maybe they assumed we knew.' I was experimenting with opening and closing the doors. 'You can't even see it when it's closed.'

'So someone could have hidden in here and attacked Ilaria at their leisure.'

'I suppose so.' I turned to face him. 'Someone who didn't want to take the risk that 411 would be occupied, so they made sure it was out of use.'

'This room service waiter,' Derwent said. 'What's his name?'

'Abilo Braga.'

'He set it up and he was in the room around the time she died. So he's a killer or he's part of the conspiracy.'

'I interviewed him on the day of the murder. Based on how he was then, I'd have said neither.'

'But then he disappeared,' Derwent said softly. 'So maybe he was just really good at acting innocent.'

'We'll need to get forensics in here but it looks clean. What are the chances this hallway has been vacuumed in preparation for the next guests?'

'Good, I should think – and they'll have had guests in the room next door, which is bad news for us.' Derwent shone his torch on the floor and we both frowned at the marks in the thick pile that showed where someone had lovingly cleaned every inch of it.

'Can I go in?'

'Yeah, it's probably a write-off.'

I went into the small hallway behind the bookcase and pushed against the doors on the other side with a gloved hand. 'You can't open the other door from here. You have to be in 411 to open it.'

'What if Braga unlatched it when he was in blocking the toilet?'

'It's possible,' I allowed. 'I don't really know how it helps, though. Whoever was in here would still have to leave eventually, through 411 or 412, and we would have seen them. Unless someone hid in here and waited for us to finish our forensic examination and then walked out when we'd packed up and left and no one was looking at the CCTV anymore.'

'Risky.'

'This whole murder is risky. Why kill her in a semi-public place with cameras and security everywhere? Someone calculating did this. Someone who hated Ilaria and wanted her to die in humiliating circumstances, so her reputation would suffer.' I wandered over to the bed and sat down on it, staring at the connecting door.

'What is it?' He was watching me keenly. 'What are you thinking?'

'The way this room is laid out, with the connecting door opposite the bed, and Ilaria being so determined to have this room every time. She had a weekly booking, didn't she? Always the same time.' I crossed my legs and swung the uppermost foot, thinking about it. 'What if there was a matching booking for the room next door?'

It didn't take Jeanette Lee long to check. 'Hmmm. Well, yes, that room was frequently booked at the same time as 412, but it wasn't the same person every time and it wasn't booked every week the way 412 was. There are different names here.'

'Can I have a printout of the names?' I was leaning over the reception desk, trying to see the screen.

'Of course.'

'They used fake names to check in, didn't they?' Derwent said to me. 'Ilaria and her bloke. Who's to say the same wasn't true of the room next door?'

One of the elegant, long-stemmed receptionists had been standing to one side of Jeanette, dealing with a guest, her voice a competent murmur. She was looking over her boss's shoulder now, trying to be discreet about it, and what Derwent said made her jump.

'What is it?' I asked her, and she knotted her fingers together.

'I'm sorry – I wasn't trying to listen, but if you're talking about room 411 we had a running joke about that. With him, I mean. He used to get one of his secretaries to book for him. The room was never in his name – there were three or four different people who booked it. Then he'd turn up and check in *as them*. It was all pre-paid on their credit card. He was so nice to us.'

'Do you know his real name?' I asked, and she bit her lip.

'No. But I could describe him.'

I nodded and she ran through the most striking details of his appearance, and I knew immediately who she meant.

'Can you remember anything else about him?'

'Only that he always made sure it was room 411.' She smiled, remembering. 'He said he liked it because of the view.'

38

The Angus Cavendish who greeted us at his office was very different from the grief-stricken husk I'd interviewed at his house three weeks earlier. The office – a modern building behind the facade of a Georgian house in Mayfair – was a high-tech temple to making money, and from the way the staff behaved around him, Angus was the high priest. His office was at the front of the building, overlooking the street, and I recognised Jennifer Hickey's style: the same grey walls as in her office, the same console table with matching lamps. A huge modern desk sat in the middle of the room but, rather than sitting behind it, Angus ushered us to a seating area with three low armchairs around a small table. One of his assistants – a middle-aged, motherly woman who clearly adored him – brought in a tray without asking: three water glasses and two chilled bottles of mineral water, one still, one sparkling. Angus was wearing a suit that was so beautifully cut that even I noticed it: a miracle of tailoring. He was looking better than he had been when I saw him last, but he still looked too thin for his height, and tired.

'What exactly do you do?' Derwent asked.

'I run a hedge fund.' Angus's mouth twitched. 'I can explain what that entails to you until you pass out from sheer boredom or you can just nod and get on with updating me about the investigation. I presume that's why you're here.'

'Not exactly,' I said. 'We're here because you lied to me when I interviewed you before.'

He raised his eyebrows, not noticeably upset. 'I'm sure it was a mistake on my part rather than a deliberate attempt to mislead you.'

'I don't think it was a mistake when you said you'd never been in the Governor Hotel.'

Silence. Angus didn't move for a moment. Then he smiled.

'I should have known better. I thought I'd get away with it but I should have told the truth.'

'What is the truth?'

'I went there most Wednesdays and occupied room 411 while my wife was fucking her boyfriend.' He took out a cigarette and a lighter and drew an ashtray towards him. 'They let me smoke in here because it's my company and there's separate air conditioning for this part of the office. I'm not sure it's legal, so please don't arrest me for it. I've trained HR to turn a blind eye.'

'Fascinating,' Derwent said. 'Tell us about being in the room next to your wife.'

'While she was fucking her boyfriend.' Angus gave him a heavy-lidded glare. 'Don't leave that part out.'

'Did you open the doors between the two rooms?' I asked and he nodded, frowning, concentrating on touching the flame to the end of the cigarette.

'I liked to watch her, you see, but she didn't like being watched all that much, and the boyfriend was put off when I was in the room. That's how it was when we started. We settled on me being out of sight, as much as possible. I could see what I wanted to see and they could forget about me. Everyone was happy.'

'Were they happy about it?' I asked. 'Really?'

'My wife liked to please me, and it was hardly difficult for her. She enjoyed it. Sam's a reasonably nice chap.'

'You told me they'd fallen in love when they met. A *coup de foudre* was how you described it.' I folded my arms. 'Was anything that you told me the truth?'

'What do you mean?' He looked very slightly uneasy.

'They met last December. Then . . . nothing. Ilaria was unhappy. She was sleeping in her office. Avoiding you. You sent her presents.'

'Who's been talking? That little brat Dally?' He drew on the cigarette and the ember flared. 'We went through a rough patch. That happens.'

'It was your idea for her to sleep with another man in front of you. She didn't want to do it, did she? You argued and coaxed and eventually you wore her down.'

'I let her pick him. She was in total control, believe me. If she hadn't wanted to do it, she wouldn't have done it.'

'What I've heard from her friends was that she was shy. She had to steel herself to do it. She was using drugs to get through it.'

He grinned. 'Well, that's one version of events. I don't come out of it well, do I? But darling Ilaria was more than capable of coming up with a reason to dip into pharmaceuticals of one kind or another. It wasn't all shyness.'

'I checked with the Governor Hotel. She had a standing reservation there from January, but she and Sam didn't use the room until February.'

'That's right. The plan was to get started sooner but it took her longer than she'd thought to talk him into it. Very frustrating for both of us. I thought she'd gone for the wrong guy, to be honest. I thought he was too much of a wimp. I had someone older in mind. Bigger. More of a man.' As he leaned forward to stub out the cigarette he stared at Derwent, his eyes roving over his body. Derwent was as still as if he'd been carved out of stone, his expression forbidding. I had to resist the urge to snap my fingers in Angus Cavendish's face to get his attention, and settled for a question instead.

'Did you give Ilaria an ultimatum, Mr Cavendish?'

'What sort of ultimatum?'

'If she didn't sleep with Sam, you were threatening to end the marriage.'

He laughed. 'I'd have to be some sort of monster to insist on opening up our marriage like that, against her will.'

Monsters came in all shapes and sizes, as I knew well, and rich, successful men could be some of the worst.

'Look,' he drawled, when neither of us rushed to reassure him that we didn't mean *him*, 'I loved Ilaria. I wanted to stay with her. I have preferences and she knew that. She was quite happy about most of them. Some of them scared her and it took her time to come round. That was an issue of confidence, not coercion. She got into it as soon as she found Sam. He was easy. He went along with whatever she wanted.'

'Do you think Sam had much of a choice about it since you were giving him work?'

Angus shrugged. 'You can ask him, can't you? He's not dead. He can speak up for himself.'

'He doesn't seem the type to speak up for himself,' I said levelly. 'And you told me you invited him to dinner because he was working for you, but actually you gave him his first contract in February. Interesting timing.'

'There were three of us involved in this little scene. It was consensual, on all sides.' He shook a cigarette out of the packet but held it between his fingers, unlit, and gestured elegantly. 'We were all grown-ups and we knew the rules. I watched, they fucked. The end.'

'What if Ilaria got pregnant?'

His eyes went wide: genuine, unfeigned shock. 'She was pregnant?'

'No.'

'Well. You scared me there.' He rubbed his forehead with the heel of his hand. 'If she had been pregnant, it wouldn't have been mine or she wouldn't have been pregnant for long. I was clear that if she had a child, I would support it but not willingly, and I would regard it as unforgivable on her part. And she knew that I wouldn't raise another man's child within our marriage, so that would have been that, either way. She could have a baby, but not me.'

That was the story Jennifer had told me about the prenup. Ilaria had made that choice, I thought.

'Someone made it impossible for you to stay in room 411 that afternoon,' Derwent said. 'Someone made sure the bathroom was out of use.'

'I know. It was infuriating. They wouldn't relax the hotel's standards to let me have it when it hadn't been cleaned properly. They said I could have it at five o'clock, which would have been too late. I wanted to explain I didn't care about the bed being made up or the bathroom being available, but I couldn't really get into why I wanted the room with the failed Miss World contestants who work on the reception desk.'

It was such a good description I had to try very hard not to laugh. He spotted it, a sparkle of charm animating his thin face.

'You know what I mean, don't you? It would have been like trying to explain quantum physics to a small potato.'

I got my face under control. 'Who knew you were regularly there, Mr Cavendish? Who knew you had to be out of the way so they could harm Ilaria?'

'No one.'

'Well, that's not true.' I folded my arms. 'You're not even trying now.'

'Fuck it, isn't this your job?' With very bad grace, he counted on his fingers. 'Ilaria. Sam. That was it.'

'Someone booked the room for you.'

'Oh – my assistants. Patricia or one of the other secretaries.' Non-people, he seemed to imply. 'Patricia doesn't have a murderous bone in her body – although, having said that, I've heard her on the phone making restaurant bookings and I wouldn't mess with her. And the others are sweet.'

'Could any of them have told someone?'

He shook his head. 'They're very discreet. That's a key part of the job.'

'Who else knew?'

'No one.'

'Are you sure about that?'

'Whoever Ilaria told, I suppose, if she told anyone. Ilaria wasn't really a girl's girl. She didn't have close friends, apart from Jen Hickey. Whoever Sam confided in. I didn't tell anyone.'

'Where did you go, when you couldn't check in?' I asked.

'Home. I didn't feel like going back to work.'

Derwent gave him a level-five glare. 'You know, you should really stop lying to us. Maeve doesn't like it and I don't like her being upset.'

'I'm not lying.'

'We know you checked into the hotel opposite,' I said quietly. 'You asked for a room on the fourth floor, facing the Governor Hotel. They had a record of your credit card – I suppose it was an emergency and there was no time to get Patricia to book it for you. They remembered you straight away when I showed them a picture of you, because it was an unusual request. Their guests aren't usually so particular about where they stay in the hotel.' I paused. 'We will be able to find you on their CCTV, and we are in the process of checking it, so you might as well admit it now.'

He winced. 'You really are thorough, aren't you? How did you think of looking there?'

'Ilaria got undressed but she left the curtains open. That always bothered me. It was a grey day and the daylight was starting to fade. The lights would have been on. She would have been putting on quite a show for anyone who cared to look.'

'Some women like that. You know, don't you?' He appealed to Derwent, who was looking unimpressed.

'Regardless,' I said quickly, 'she knew you were watching. We can see a two-minute phone conversation with you on her phone records. It would have been when she was walking into the hotel. That's why she left the curtains open.'

'She knew I was there.'

'That means you're a witness. What did you see?'

'Nothing. I didn't have a good enough view. I tried to see what was happening in that room but I really couldn't see them in any detail unless they were right beside the window.'

For the first time I thought he was telling the truth. I'd stood in the room he'd occupied, and looked across, and the bay window of room 412 was unhelpfully deep. I'd been able to see Derwent when he was standing next to it, but when he was further back in the room it was hard to see anything other than a figure moving around, even with the lights on. He would have needed binoculars and he hadn't known that.

'Do you recognise this man?' I showed him the picture we had of Abilo Braga, which was from his staff ID. His face was impassive, his body cut off at the shoulders. It didn't look much like him in real life, I thought.

'I don't know.' Angus sounded uncertain. 'Should I recognise him? He looks familiar.'

'He works in the Governor Hotel.'

'Maybe. I might have seen him.'

'But you can't tell us what happened in room 412 that ended up with your wife being murdered,' Derwent said.

'I wish I had a different answer. Realising that I'd essentially watched her die was not a good feeling.' He appealed to me. 'You saw me. I was halfway to a nervous breakdown because of it.'

'Did you stay in the hotel across the way?'

'For a while.'

'Even though you couldn't see anything?'

'I stayed until I realised something was wrong. There seemed to be people coming and going, lights on, that kind of thing. I was alarmed. I went home and waited. I thought she would ring me if she was in trouble and I wanted to be ready. I was going to swoop in and fix whatever the problem was.' He looked pensive. 'I could always fix her problems.'

'I don't understand why you would stay for any length of time when you realised you had such a poor view,' I said.

'I didn't want them to be alone together. You can't understand that, can you? But she was still mine. He was with her because I allowed it. If I said stop, they stopped.'

'And if she said stop?' Derwent's voice was soft, which belied the fact that it was edged with lethal rage.

Angus shrugged. 'But she didn't.'

39

Angus Cavendish's words played on a loop in my head as I stared at Sam Blundell. *I thought she'd gone for the wrong guy, to be honest . . . I thought he was too much of a wimp.*

He wasn't doing much to challenge Angus's view of him. Sam had lost weight since Ilaria's death, and he was fidgeting constantly, his eyes darting around the room as he spoke. The flat was untidy compared to how it had been before. An ironing board was propped against the wall with a crumpled shirt draped over it, and the fruit bowl was empty apart from one shrivelled apple. A laptop lay open on the table flanked by an array of dirty mugs: the work of more than one day.

'Yeah, I mean, obviously I know I'm suspect number one.'

'What makes you say that?' Derwent asked.

'It's obvious. I was there.' He was flexing his hands, testing their range of movement. The skin looked new and painful. 'My own girlfriend assumed I'd done it.'

'How is Lora?' I asked.

'Yeah. She's OK. It wasn't ideal, with the pregnancy and everything, but she's calmed down. She didn't know about the affair,' he explained to Derwent. 'She found out.'

'And she's pregnant?'

'Again, I know it's not ideal.' He shrugged helplessly. 'I wanted to stop seeing Ilaria once I found out about the baby. I wanted to make a commitment to Lora. Change things. But it was difficult to stop.'

'You could have stopped turning up on Wednesdays,' Derwent pointed out.

'I'd have lost my job. I needed the money.' He shivered. 'And I couldn't tell Ilaria about the baby. She'd have gone mental because she really wanted a baby and she was going on and on at me about it.'

'You don't think she'd have understood?' I said.

'She'd have been furious.' He pulled a face. 'But then how do you end it? She was so fragile. I couldn't think of a way of telling her I'd had enough without sending her off on one.'

'What could she have done to you, really? You could have got another job,' Derwent said with a hint of scorn. Instead of getting angry, Sam dropped his head to his chest, submitting.

'I know. But with the baby . . . And then she said she'd tell Lora about it if I ever let her down. She sort of threatened me, I suppose. I was scared of her.'

He was giving us a good motive for killing her, I thought, and wondered that he didn't notice it himself.

'You didn't tell us about Angus watching you,' I said. 'That was a pretty big detail to leave out.'

He bit his lip. 'Fuck. Yes. I was not happy about it but it wasn't up to me. I tried to forget he was there.' Dawning realisation. 'Actually, he wasn't there that day, when I arrived. The door was closed. Did you know that?'

'We did.'

'Oh.'

'What else did you lie about, Sam? Or leave out?' I added, forestalling the protest that he was about to make.

'Nothing.'

'You said you never choked her.'

He raised his hands to his head, shifting miserably in his seat. '*Fuck*. I knew that was going to come back. I knew it would sound bad. How did you know?'

'Angus told us a few of the things you did with her. The things he liked.'

'I didn't *want* to do it.'

'You know she was strangled, don't you? That's how she died,' I said, conversationally.

'I didn't hurt her – we were careful. I made sure she was safe.'

'There's no safe way to choke someone,' Derwent snapped.

'I couldn't say no. I – I only did what they wanted. You don't understand.'

'No. I don't.' His voice was cold. 'You got yourself into a mess and you didn't lift a finger to help yourself, or her.'

'I should have handled it differently.' Sam was almost in tears. 'But I didn't know how.'

We came out of Sam Blundell's building and Derwent stopped.

'Unless I've lost my touch completely, I don't think he's our killer. Pathetic, but not a murderer. He'd never have the nerve.'

'I feel sorry for him,' I said.

'Why?'

'He was out of his depth. And you were mean to him.'

'I treated him like Angus Cavendish would. I knew he'd respond to a firm hand. You were being far too nice to him, I presume because he's pretty.'

Well, if that's how you want to play it . . . 'I thought Angus was going to ask for your number for his next wife.'

Derwent gave me a look. 'If you hadn't been there . . .'

'Oh please. You'd have said no.'

'I'd definitely have said no to *choking* his wife. What a stupid game to play.'

'I suppose. I wonder if she liked it or if it was Angus who wanted her to be degraded.'

'Even if it was her favourite thing in the world, Sam should still have said no. I've told Luke not to do it.'

I blinked. 'Fatherly advice has changed since the old days.'

'The whole football team come to me for advice.' Derwent favoured me with a slow smile. 'I have a reputation for knowing what I'm talking about.'

'I'm sure you've earned that through your long, long experience,' I said tartly.

'Yeah, all right. They need someone to tell them how to behave, even if it makes me feel old. There's too much bad information floating around on the internet. Anyway, I don't want Luke messing around with anything risky. All I need is for him to be charged with manslaughter. Coffee? There's a café over there.'

'Yes, definitely.' Anything to put off getting into the car with him when I was already blushing. *I'm so glad*, I thought, following him to the cute retro café with fifties styling and a window full of plants, *that this case has turned out to be all about kinky sex*. 'The affair with Ilaria was really for Angus's benefit, wasn't it? And Sam wanted to show off to him. Prove he was a great lover. He was never going to say no.'

'Whereas, actually, that just proved he was terrible in bed.' Derwent held the café door open for me.

'Because he did what she asked him to?'

'Because he— what do you want?'

I tried to focus on the purple-haired barista who was waiting patiently for us to order, wondering what Derwent was going to say next. He ordered his coffee, paid for us both and took up a position at the end of the bar, leaning on it. In his usual tone of voice, which carried more than I would have preferred, he said, 'Because he showed no imagination. She asked for what she wanted, if he's to be believed, and he did it.'

'He listened to her, though,' I objected. 'Women want to be listened to.'

'What she was telling him was that she wanted it to be exciting. If you can't make someone excited to have ordinary, everyday sex with you, you shouldn't be allowed to have sex. And the only advice I'll give *you* is that you shouldn't settle for anyone who doesn't make you feel special every single time.'

'You don't need to give me advice,' I snapped.

'I'm only looking out for you. If you ask me, your standards have always been far too low.'

'I didn't ask, and I can't even begin to count the ways this is inappropriate.'

'Worth bearing in mind though, if you like this Owen.' He moved on before I could come up with a reply. 'Anyway, if someone asks you to choke them, they're not actually asking to be throttled until they black out. That's no one's idea of a good time.' He picked up a packet of sugar and shook it idly. 'You have to think about what they really want, not what they say they want. It's your job to come up with something that makes them feel the way they want to feel, but you have to put some imagination into it. If you give someone exactly what they *say* they want, it's boring.'

Keep it about the case, I told myself. 'So what did she really want?'

'To give up control. But if you know what you're doing you can make someone completely helpless without even touching them.' He slid the sugar packet into the bowl and looked at me and I stared back, hypnotised, until the barista pushed two cups onto the bar.

'Here you go.'

'Thanks.' To me, he said, 'Where do we go from here?'

With an effort, I got my brain into gear. 'I know we were talking about Angus's next wife. I think we should talk to his last one.'

40

Jennifer Hickey was only too pleased to give me contact information for Devon Cavendish.

'What do you want with her? I suppose you can't say. You don't suspect Angus, do you? Or no, I shouldn't ask. But, like, isn't it always the husband in these situations? Except I can't see Angus getting his hands dirty, do you know what I mean?'

Sitting in the driver's seat of the car, Derwent blinked as Jennifer chattered away, blithely unselfconscious about being on speakerphone. I grinned at him before I answered her.

'You were right, I can't say. But it would be very useful to talk to Devon at this stage.'

'Oh sure. Like I said, she's gorgeous – you'll love her. Hold on . . .' A flurry of tapping, and then swearing. 'I can't find a fucking thing on this computer. I'm going to ask Dally.'

There was a clunk as her phone landed on the desk and I listened to her clatter out of the room.

'Is she always like that?' Derwent asked and I shushed him. Muffled conversation was barely audible at the other end. Then scuffling.

'All right, I'm back.' She reeled off the address. 'Thank God Dally had it in her phone or we'd have been here all day. Do you want me to ring ahead and tell Devon you're on your way?'

'No, thank you. I'll take care of that.' I hesitated. 'In fact, can I ask you not to get in touch with her until I've spoken to her?'

'Oh my God, of *course*. You don't know when that would be, though, do you?' A cackle. 'I'm absolutely going to call her once I have a green light from you guys. I am *dying* of curiosity here.'

'I'll let you know,' I promised, and ended the call.

'I really feel I've missed out by not being around for more of this investigation,' Derwent mused.

'Surely Jennifer is the one who's missed out.'

'Goes without saying.'

Devon Cavendish was more than happy to speak to us, it transpired, and not just because Derwent gave her the kind of appreciative smile that made most women blush. Devon took it as her due. She was tall and slim with the kind of grooming that simply didn't exist for most native Londoners: flawless teeth, expensive eyelashes, a bouncing blow-dry, an impeccable tan. The house was similarly perfect: set back from a quiet Hampstead street, big rooms, high ceilings, expensive furniture, an elderly housekeeper, everything redolent of luxury and good taste. But both house and its owner seemed somehow lifeless. Devon lived alone, she told us. It was a big house for one woman to occupy, and all the enormous flower arrangements in the world couldn't fill it.

'You've saved me from an appointment with my trainer. That man acts like he owns my ass. I mean, I appreciate that he wants to keep it looking good . . .' Devon leaned over, pouring tea from a china teapot into matching cups that sat on delicate little saucers. I had never seen a push-up exercise bra before, I reflected, as two perfect moons swelled out of her top a few inches from Derwent's face.

'Mrs Cavendish, we wanted to ask about your marriage to Angus. I appreciate that may be difficult.'

'Difficult.' She blinked at Derwent, sitting down. 'Yeah, because Angus made me sign an NDA as part of the divorce so I couldn't tell all our friends what he was really like.'

'This is a murder investigation, so you can forget about the NDA,' I said.

'Do you think Angus killed her?'

'We're keeping an open mind.'

'I guess that's British for yes.' She gave me a dazzling smile and picked up her cup and saucer. 'Don't let the tea get cold.'

'Do you think he's capable of murder?' Derwent asked.

'Probably.' She sipped her tea, composed. 'If he didn't get someone to do it for him. Angus is good at delegating. I spoke to his assistants more than I spoke to him when we were married.'

'When did your marriage end?'

'Officially? Four years ago. He married Ilaria straight away.' She smiled at me. 'I could have told her she was making a mistake, but she wouldn't have listened. I didn't listen when Marika tried to warn me.'

'Warn you about what, specifically?'

'Angus is easily bored. He's constantly in search of stimulation and distraction. He loves to push people beyond their boundaries. His first wife Marika couldn't or wouldn't fulfil his fantasies, he told me when we got together, and I thought that if I did everything he wanted, he'd stay with me.' She gave a laugh. 'I was wrong, obviously. He isn't in it for the long haul, with anyone.'

'And – forgive me – when you say you did what he wanted, what did that entail?'

'Oh God, everything you can imagine. He wanted to show me off to other men. He chose my clothes, which were kind of slutty. He joined a club for perverts in New York and dragged me there so he could have sex with me in public.' She was sitting very straight, perched on the edge of her chair, her ankles crossed to one side of her in the most demure and ladylike position. In the winter sunlight her skin had that unreal consistency that comes from constant professional treatment and an SPF addiction.

Beside me, Derwent was still, but I was acutely aware of him and the energy that seemed to charge the space between us. *If you know what you're doing you can make someone completely helpless without even touching them . . .* I pulled myself together.

'Was having sex in public something you were interested in?'

'No, not in the least!' She widened her eyes at me. 'I only did it because he gave me an ultimatum. That's how he operates. It wasn't fucking me in public that was the thrill, but making me go along with it when he knew it made me uncomfortable. It was his way of proving he had total power over me.'

'Did you know Ilaria?'

'Sure. She helped decorate this house. That's how they met.' The lovely face was serene.

'Did you like her?' Derwent asked.

'No. Of course I didn't. She took my husband! And you'd think I'd have been glad about that but you know, it broke this stupid heart.' One hand on her perfect breast, diamonds sparkling on two fingers. 'I don't think he made her happy, and that made me feel better about it. Bitch, huh?'

'Sounds reasonable to me,' Derwent said, and I resisted the urge to roll my eyes.

'They'd been together for four years, you said.'

'Uh-huh. She was about to reach her expiry date. Now he can walk away, which I'm sure will please him. He's learning as he goes. Marika didn't have a prenup. She got the best deal of all of us. I got this house and a nice fat bank transfer every year unless I marry again. Ilaria would have got less than I got. Now she gets nothing.'

'He could have afforded to pay her off, though.'

'If he wanted to leave her, sure. If she wanted to leave him?' Devon sat back. 'I don't think he would have been happy about that. Not at all. In fact, I think he'd have taken that personally.'

'Do you know for certain that she was planning to leave him?' I asked, curious.

'If she had any sense, she would have wanted to.'

'But you didn't want to end your marriage, in spite of everything.'

She shrugged. 'What can I tell you? I never had any sense where he was concerned.'

41

On Friday, two weeks after Derwent had been released from custody, and knowing it was a terrible idea, I went and knocked on Una Burt's door.

'What's happening with the investigation into Josh? Are they still looking at him?'

'I don't know anything about it.' She started tidying her desk, which was a massive giveaway that she was feeling tense. 'And there's a good reason for that. They need to be completely independent of me. I can't be seen to influence the DPS investigation in any way – and before you ask, I'm not going to try.'

'It would be useful to find out what the hold-up is, though. Don't you want to know what they're concerned about?'

'Useful?' She looked sympathetic, which was unusual enough for her that I flinched.

'It would help if Josh knew how worried he should be. He's . . . not himself.'

'He seems fine to me.'

'It's an act,' I said. 'When he forgets, you can tell he's worried.' I'd noticed him staring into space more than once.

'Maybe *you* can tell,' Una said gently. 'But you have to stop worrying about him. You don't want to attract any more attention from the DPS than you have already. I know you were heavily involved in finding out what happened to Melissa even though I told you to stay out of it.'

'It was on my own time,' I began, and she held up a hand to stop me.

'I've turned a blind eye to it because I know you meant well.' She frowned, not looking at me. 'I get the impression Josh has no idea you played any part in it.'

'I haven't told him. I don't think he'd be pleased. He likes to do the rescuing.'

'He wants to protect you, Maeve.'

'From what?'

'Getting dragged down with him. I probably shouldn't tell you this but Roz Fuller has requested files on every case you and Josh have worked on together.'

Every case? I was racing through the possible ramifications of that. 'Specifically cases that he's worked on with me? Or his cases in general?'

'The ones you worked on with him.'

I sat back, nonplussed. 'Why?'

'I can only guess but I imagine she's looking for some misconduct on his part.'

'But that's – that's not fair. I haven't complained.' I had *liked* Roz Fuller, I thought, outraged.

'I know.' Una rubbed her face, which was, as usual, make-up free. I would have ended up looking like I'd been painted by Monet, and after his eyesight started to go. 'Sometimes I thought you *should* complain about his behaviour. He pushed you to the edge.'

'It's how he works best.'

'Well, whatever it takes, now would be a very good time for him to find his form. Solving what happened to Ilaria Cavendish would be a big help.' Una flipped open the file in front of her and started reading, the traditional way she signalled that her interest in the matter at hand was at an end. 'So if you really want to help Josh, why not work out who killed her?'

I did my best to solve Ilaria's impossible murder but the mystery stubbornly failed to unravel itself before lunch. Frustrated, I went out to get a sandwich and some fresh air. I was deep in thought as I left the office, and it took me a minute to register that someone was hovering at my elbow while I waited to cross the road.

'Got a minute?' It was a mutter, deniably quiet. I nodded, the light turned green and Henry Cowell set off across the road a few paces ahead of me. He walked down the street to a small, ancient churchyard hemmed in by high buildings, a speck of green in the concrete and glass. It was a popular place for lunch on a bright, cold day and Henry took a minute to scan the groups of office workers and lone readers who were sitting on benches among the graves, wrapped in big coats. Satisfied, he perched on a piece of broken wall that was tucked behind a large evergreen shrub.

'This is a surprise,' I commented, sitting beside him. 'I take it this isn't official, since you're worried about being spotted.'

He was still looking around. 'I shouldn't be here.'

'So why are you? If it's to warn me that I'm about to get in trouble, I've already had one of those talks this morning from my boss.'

He winced. 'Look, I hope it won't come to that. Roz has concerns *for* you, not about you. She's investigating whether Josh Derwent has been abusing his position as a senior officer with you.'

'But she hasn't even asked me about it.'

'She will, but she thinks you'll lie to protect him.'

'So she won't believe me if I'm not telling the story she wants to hear?' I shivered. I had never been on the wrong side of an investigation before. 'This is a nightmare.'

He sighed. 'She's good at her job, you know. Thorough. She doesn't want to miss anything.'

'Anything *else*,' I said sharply. 'She missed plenty when it came to Melissa.'

'That's part of it, I think. You saw what she didn't.'

It was a fair point. The only thing worse than making a mistake was someone else knowing you had been making it.

'And Derwent got under her skin, in interview,' Cowell added.

'He would. But that doesn't mean he deserves to be kicked out of the Met.'

'That's why I'm here.' He leaned forward, his elbows on his knees. 'I've been reading the files. The cases that you've worked on with Josh Derwent. You're a bloody good police officer and so is he and I don't see what benefit there is to anyone in getting rid of either of you.'

'Is that a possibility?' I felt as if I was staring into an abyss that had suddenly opened up in front of me. 'For both of us?'

'You might get moved to a different bit of the Met, but there would be consequences.' He glanced at me, uneasy. 'A lot of officers find it so stressful to be the subject of an investigation they end up leaving instead of trying to wait it out. And it's not great for your career. People gossip. It affects your reputation. The Met is a big organisation but it's not big enough, sometimes.'

'Well, I don't want any of that.' And I didn't want to see Derwent leaving under a cloud. I could imagine it with great, pitiless clarity: he wouldn't look back. He would cut himself off from everyone and everything that reminded him of being a police officer, including me. 'What can I do?'

'You need to make it absolutely clear that Melissa isn't reliable as a witness. Roz still isn't convinced that the domestic violence accusations are false even if elements of them are faked. Melissa is trying to stick to the parts of the story we haven't disproved. It would be a tricky one to get past the CPS but you know the odds are in her favour these days.'

I did know. The very fact that Derwent was a police officer meant that everyone involved would be worried about accusations of trying to engineer a cover-up. There had been too many actual miscarriages of justice where investigations into police officers had mysteriously petered out, despite compelling evidence. The last thing the Met needed was another scandal.

'I asked Josh and he said he wouldn't cooperate if she was prosecuted for perverting the course of justice, but that would help, wouldn't it?'

'Very much so. The fact that he hasn't gone after Melissa for it makes Roz think she's telling the truth.'

'He wants to walk away.' There was a knot in my throat that was making it hard to talk. 'Being arrested was awful for him. He's not vindictive. He doesn't want Melissa to suffer just because it would help him out.'

'Unfortunately, that's a problem for him. And you,' Cowell added. 'But then that's the best card you have to play. If he had to choose between you and her, he'd choose you, wouldn't he?'

It was a good question. Unfortunately, I didn't know the answer.

42

I spotted Mark Pell immediately in the crowd of parents and caregivers at the school gate. He stood on his own, concentrating on his phone, solitary. As I watched, though, a pretty blonde approached him. I edged through the throng and was in time to hear her making arrangements for Thomas to come to her house for a playdate the following week.

'And would pizza and ice cream be OK?'

'Do you have to ask?'

'Brilliant. Tuesday it is. Pick him up around six.'

He agreed and returned to his phone. When I said his name he glanced up, and took a second to make sense of me being there, on a Friday afternoon.

'You.' Then, anxiously, 'What's wrong?'

'Nothing.' I smiled. It felt stiff on my face. 'I wanted to talk to you, that's all.'

'About what?' He looked suspicious.

'Probably better not to talk about it here.' We could be surrounded by Melissa's friends, for all I knew.

'Do you want to come to the house? I haven't really unpacked properly yet.' He ran a hand through his hair, looking frayed. 'I was going to do that this weekend.'

'I could walk there with you if you're on foot.'

'It's five minutes away. That was one of Mel's conditions. I had to rent somewhere close to the school if I was going to take over custody of Thomas, even if it's only until she's fully recovered.'

'It's a big upheaval for you.'

'I don't mind. It's better for Thomas. It would have been disruptive to make him come and live with me in my actual house. At least this way he can go to school as normal and spend time with his mates. And I get to be with him, so it works for me too.'

'I think my parents were hoping you'd stay with them.'

He brightened. 'They've been amazing.'

'He's the grandson they always wanted and I haven't provided,' I said dryly. 'I'm not sure there are formal adoption proceedings for grandchildren but if there were, they'd definitely sign up.'

A shift in the crowd: the gate was open.

'Time to get Thomas. Are you coming?'

I didn't want to intrude. 'I'll wait here for you.'

He returned a few minutes later, Thomas by his side, deep in conversation. Thomas was holding something made of clay with the solemn reverence that only an eight-year-old could manage.

'Maeve! Look.' He held it up for my approval.

'Science?'

'Art.'

'Of course it is.'

'Do you know what it is?'

'The moon?'

'No-o-o.' He beamed at me and I felt my heart creak. There was something unbearably tender about the sprinkle of freckles across his nose, the flush of colour in his cheeks, the long-lashed eyes that were still rounded, like a baby's.

'Do you want me to carry it home?' Mark asked, and slowly, grudgingly, Thomas handed it over, along with many instructions about taking care 'because this bit is wobbly and I think it might fall off soon'. He went into the bike sheds to extract his scooter, stopping to talk to a girl with plaits so tight, even at the end of the day, that her eyes were pulled towards her hairline. I had endured very similar plaits in my day and my scalp ached in sympathy.

'Who was that?' Mark asked when he came back.

'Bella.'

'Bella who's good at maths?'

'Da-ad.' Thomas swung the scooter around and sped out through the gate, insouciant about trivial factors such as other people, the camber of the pavement and gravity.

'Christ,' Mark said, hurrying after him. 'He goes like a rocket.'

'And never comes to harm, I bet.'

'Not so far.' He relaxed once he could see Thomas speeding along, scattering dead leaves with the wheels of the scooter. 'Don't go too fast, Tom. Don't cross the road.'

The boy stopped for that, and twisted to give him a withering look over his shoulder. I could read what he was thinking. *As if I would. I'm not a baby. I know the rules.*

'He's looking well,' I observed.

'He's happy.' Mark said it simply, a statement of fact.

'I'll tell Josh he's thriving. I think he'd appreciate some good news.'

Mark was frowning. 'Is he having a rough time?'

'He's been better, but it'll cheer him up to hear Thomas is OK.' I paused. 'Have you had any problems with Thomas's health?'

'Not a thing.'

'Really?'

'I'm as surprised as you. Maybe it was stress. I gather it wasn't a very happy house for the last few months.'

I wondered if Derwent had made that connection himself. I'd heard Melissa talking to him a couple of times in the last year, and it was the kind of vicious sustained attack that was difficult to listen to, especially if you cared about the person on the receiving end of it. I knew Thomas adored Derwent. It could have been enough to make the boy physically ill. With everything he'd been through – the blood tests, the uncomfortable procedures, the hospital stays – how guilty would Derwent feel if he'd accidentally been part of the problem?

'Was that what you wanted? To see Thomas and report back?'

'No.' I took a deep breath. 'I wanted to talk to you about Melissa and making a formal complaint about her.'

His reaction was instant and definite. 'As I said before, I'm not going to pursue her over something that happened so long ago.'

'Even though it's still affecting you.'

'It is what it is. I'm focused on keeping things stable for Thomas. Going after his mother won't help him.' We had caught up with Thomas and he fell silent until we had crossed the road and Thomas had set off again. 'He's my priority. I don't matter. He does.'

'I think you both matter,' I said quietly. 'And it's a huge problem for Josh.'

Briefly, because we didn't have long to talk before we reached the house, I told him what Henry Cowell had told me.

'If Josh thought he was helping you and me by making a formal complaint, he might take that step. He won't do it for himself.'

'Even to save his job?'

I shook my head. 'That's not how he is.'

'Look, I don't want to make a complaint but if it would help you, I'll talk to him about what she did to me. Maybe that will make a difference.'

'Would you do that?'

He gave me a lopsided smile. 'I do owe your parents a favour, as we discussed. Maybe helping you out would count. And I wouldn't mind if Thomas got to see Josh – he's been asking about him.'

'This weekend?' I suggested.

'We're free.' Mark stopped and I realised we'd reached the house he was renting. Thomas was sitting on the doorstep looking pleased with himself, his scooter capsized across the path. 'If you make the arrangements, we'll be there.'

I walked back to where I'd left the car, deep in thought. Something was bothering me and I couldn't quite grasp what it was. Something I had seen, or someone had said . . . I ran through the conversation I'd had with Mark and came up with nothing. I was getting a headache and it really wasn't helping.

It clicked for me when I started the car, as if my brain had been waiting for my attention to be on something else before it would unlock the answer. I switched the engine off again and sat, and thought, and then took out my phone. I probably wouldn't be able to get hold of him, I told myself, trying to calm my racing heart. I would probably have to leave a message, and even if I did get to speak to him, he probably wouldn't be able to help—

'Alex Brown.' The pathologist's voice was calm and utterly soothing. He was wasted on patients who didn't require a bedside manner, I thought.

'Dr Brown, it's DS Maeve Kerrigan, from the hotel murder – Ilaria Cavendish?'

'I remember. What can I do for you?'

'It's not about the hotel murder.' I pawed through my bag, looking for painkillers for the dull throb behind my eyes, finding only an empty blister strip that I shoved back into the pocket where I'd found it with a silent curse. 'And it's not really what *you* can do.'

He sounded amused. 'Then why are you calling me?'

'Because I need to talk to your wife.'

43

The closest thing I could get to neutral ground was Luke's flat, and the earliest I could get everyone together there was Sunday morning. Of course I got held up on a stalled underground train and arrived twenty minutes late. Derwent came to the door, his scowl essentially visible before he opened it. Silent, he walked down the hall to the kitchen, leaving me to shut the door. I found Mark leaning against the counter with his arms folded, glowering with much the same intensity as Derwent. Thomas, oblivious, was curled up on the sofa with Luke, burrowing into his side, watching cartoons. I couldn't tell which of them was happier to be there. As I walked in, they both laughed at Wile E. Coyote splatting at full velocity into a painted tunnel on the side of a mountain.

'You must have seen this before,' I said to Luke, who grinned.

'It's a classic.'

'He's going to blow himself up, look!' Thomas pointed at the screen, enchanted. 'He's got a bomb. Look, Dad! Look, Josh!'

They both looked, to their credit, and Derwent actually smiled as the coyote incinerated himself with an ill-timed match.

'Looks like your cooking,' he said to me.

'How dare you? I'm never cooking for you again.'

'Do you promise?'

'Should we get on with this?' Mark sounded tense.

I caught Luke's eye and he snapped off the television and jumped up. 'Let's go.'

'I want to see the end,' Thomas protested, and Luke bent down to tickle him.

'No spoilers, mate, but it's always the same. Roadrunner wins. Anyway, we can watch it when we get back.'

Thomas was giggling wildly. 'But where are we going?'

'How about getting a milkshake? There's a place in Battersea Power Station that does them.'

'Chocolate?'

'If you like.'

'Can I?' Thomas looked at his father, then at Derwent, as if he wasn't sure who was in charge.

'Go on.' Mark sounded resigned. 'I'll come and meet you when we're finished here.'

'Get your coat,' Derwent said, and we all watched Thomas hare down the corridor as if it was a race.

Luke turned around as he pulled his jacket on. 'Maeve, good luck. And you two behave yourselves. No fighting.'

'Were you leaving?' Derwent asked.

'When you're under my roof you play by my rules.'

Derwent gave him a filthy look, and since his general demeanour was prince-of-darkness-having-a-bad-day it was actually impressive that he managed to turn it up a notch.

Thomas zoomed in, again at full speed. Luke caught him and slung him across his shoulders like a shepherd carrying a sheep. The boy screamed with laughter all the way to the front door, bouncing with each long stride Luke took.

I waited until the door had closed behind them and the sounds of their conversation faded.

'They get on well, don't they?'

'Love at first sight. They haven't spent much time with one another up to now.' Derwent frowned. 'Melissa wasn't keen.'

'It's probably good for him to have Luke as a role model,' Mark said. 'He seems to have his shit together.'

It was an innocuous remark but Derwent bristled. 'Unlike me?'

'You said it, not me.' Mark stared him down.

'Stop it, you two. This isn't why we're here.' They were staring at each other like boxers at a weigh-in. 'I thought you could manage a few minutes of conversation without a punch-up.'

'All right,' Derwent said, his jaw tight with rage. 'Why exactly are we here?'

I gathered my courage. 'Well, originally, it was because I wanted to persuade you both to make a formal complaint about Melissa.'

'I'm not going to change my mind.'

'I won't either,' Mark said.

'That doesn't matter anymore. The situation has changed.' I had their attention now: unblinking concentration times two. I forged on, wishing I didn't have to. *Could this conversation have been an email?* If only. 'It's not up to you whether Melissa is prosecuted or not.'

Mark looked confused. 'What do you mean?'

'What have you done?' That was Derwent, suspicious now.

'Not what I've done. What she's done.' I was glad my voice didn't shake. I had worried I wouldn't be able to keep my composure. 'Have you noticed anything odd about Thomas since he's been living with you, Mark?'

He looked bemused. 'He's been a bit unsettled because of what's happened, but he gets on with things. He's fully occupied with school most of the time, and his friends. He's happy, as I told you. He misses his mum, of course . . . and Josh.' He said it grudgingly, but he said it. 'On the whole, I think he's enjoying being with me for a change.'

'And he's sleeping well. No nightmares.'

'No. He's out like a light every night.'

'But he's not falling asleep on the sofa after school.'

'No. He's got plenty of energy.'

Derwent was frowning. 'Where's this going, Maeve?'

I ignored him. 'What about his stomach issues? Has he been complaining about that? Being sick? Cramps and diarrhoea and all the rest of it?'

'Nothing,' Mark said.

'So presumably you've been keeping to his special diet. No dairy, no gluten.'

'Well. We've been busking it a bit. As I said, he's been fine.'

'When I went to talk to you on Friday, I heard you saying to another parent that he would be happy to eat pizza and ice cream. He's just gone out for a milkshake. He's been having all the wrong things. And yet no ill effects.'

'I should probably be more careful with him,' Mark began, and I shook my head.

'No. You've been doing a great job.'

'What is this, Maeve?' Derwent's eyes were on me.

I knew that what I said was going to hurt him more than I could imagine. 'When you were under arrest, I went to your house in Jena Road. I looked for evidence to make sense of what had happened there and how Melissa had ended up so badly injured. I treated it like a crime scene, basically.'

'I'd expect nothing less.' He frowned. 'Was it you who worked out what had happened?'

'I don't think that's important,' I said quickly. 'The point is, I found a large amount of prescription medication in Melissa's bathroom. Was she ill, Josh?'

'Not to my knowledge. She was always fit and healthy.'

'Right. Well, she had recent prescriptions for all kinds of things. I only glanced at the medications but they were things like Diazepam and co-codamol, blood-pressure medication, antihistamines, migraine medication – that kind of thing. They were all from the last few months. I put it down to stress about Thomas if I thought about it at all. It was . . . awkward, being there.'

'I'm sure.' Derwent folded his arms. He had adopted his alpha-male, feet-apart stance which he reserved for when he wanted to be intimidating.

'Then I was wondering about Thomas getting better so abruptly, and I thought of Dr Brown's wife.'

'Who is Dr Brown?' Mark asked, baffled.

'Our new pathologist. His wife is a doctor too, in emergency paediatric medicine. I got in touch with her on Friday to ask if there was something that would explain the symptoms Thomas has been coping with since May – which is, incidentally, around the time you told Melissa you wanted to leave her, Josh. She had tried telling you that you wouldn't be able to see Thomas if you left, but you'd decided that was better than arguing in front of him. She had run out of cards to play. So it was time for a new game.'

He scowled, but didn't interrupt.

'I asked the doctor if it was possible that medication might have caused Thomas's stomach cramps, the nausea, the weight loss, the general exhaustion. And she said that would pretty much do it. Melissa dosed him and then stopped once he was unwell. It would explain why nothing came up in the tests they did, which were not looking for the types of medication she used, and why he got better whenever he was in hospital. There was nothing wrong with him apart from the medicine that he shouldn't have had. It's not hard to fool a GP these days when you rarely see the same one twice and so many consultations are over the phone. We know Melissa is very convincing when she wants to be.'

'Melissa would never hurt him.' It was Mark who said it but Derwent nodded in agreement. 'She's a brilliant mother.'

'You only saw her with him when he was very young.'

'She didn't do anything to him then.' Mark sounded certain. 'I would have known.'

'Maybe not. But she enjoyed the attention she got when he was sick from time to time, and it brought the two of you closer together. I think it gave her the idea to make him sick when she knew Josh was planning to leave her.' I was not looking at Derwent, focusing on Mark's face instead. 'She wanted to keep him in their family unit. She wanted to be the fragile mother that he'd fallen for originally, when they first met, and she wanted Thomas to need her.' I looked at Derwent. 'She knew you'd never leave while he was sick.'

'I should have known.' He shook his head. 'I would have known.'

'The medication was in her bathroom, the bathroom you didn't use. You wouldn't have seen it and, if you had, it wouldn't have meant much to you. Also, I don't think she was dosing him all the time. She made him sick when it disrupted your working life. You kept having to rush home to be there when he was taken ill, in case she needed you.'

'In case *Thomas* needed me,' Derwent corrected. 'But recently I was in the house a lot more than I usually would be. And she would never have put him in harm's way to get at me.'

'I know you don't want to believe me, but Dr Brown's wife said if she encountered that set of symptoms in similar circumstances – especially given his return to health once he was away from his mother, and whenever he was in hospital – she would consider FDIA as a diagnosis.'

'What's FDIA?' Mark asked.

'Factitious Disorder Imposed on Another. It used to be called Munchausen's by Proxy.'

Derwent was white. 'I can't believe she lied to me.'

'She was good at it, because she believed it was real,' I said. 'It's the same thing she did with the abuse she said she suffered. The first person she convinces is herself. Then she convinces everybody else.'

44

Mark Pell didn't stay for long after that. I explained to them both that the wheels were already turning.

'There'll be a review of Thomas's medical records and then Melissa will be interviewed under caution. There are specialist officers who deal with this kind of thing, from the Sexual Offences, Exploitation and Child Abuse Command.'

'Child abuse,' Mark repeated. His face was blank with shock. 'I don't know what to tell Thomas.'

'Don't say anything to him. In fact, you have to promise me you won't.'

'They'll need to interview him,' Derwent said to Mark. 'We can't ask any questions until they do. But you'll be able to sit in the room with him while he's interviewed and the officers are trained to talk to kids about this kind of thing. He won't find it traumatic, especially if he doesn't understand why they're asking.'

'And if Mel gets sent to prison?'

'She probably won't be, especially if she pleads guilty,' I said. 'The doctor told me many of the people who do this aren't fully aware of why they're doing it. It's a mental health issue, fundamentally, unless they're doing it for money. If her story is that she genuinely believed he was unwell and in need of care, the court might accept that. He hasn't sustained any lasting harm. It would be at the lower end of the scale in terms of offence.'

'Melissa isn't going to say she's insane.' Derwent's voice was clipped.

'The people who do this are generally emotionally unstable and impulsive and prone to disturbed thinking – and she's always had all of those attributes as far as I can see. She needs a ton of therapy and that's probably what she'll get.'

'But she won't be allowed custody of Thomas again.' Mark sounded stunned. 'He'll be with me.'

'I'd have said so. I can't see any court agreeing to let her live with him in the circumstances.'

'I had no idea any of this was happening.'

'Arguably I was in a better position to spot it and I missed it completely,' Derwent said to him, and then, to my utter amazement, 'I'm sorry.'

'You can't blame yourself,' Mark said. 'You didn't have any reason to suspect her.'

'And you were worried about Thomas,' I added. 'That must have made it hard to think about anything else.'

Derwent gave me a brief shut-up-immediately-not-now glare and turned back to Mark. 'I let him down.'

Mark had been putting on his coat. He stopped. 'No, you didn't. You were there for him. You don't know how much worse it might have been if you hadn't been living with them.'

'I should have noticed it.'

'You'll always think that, but I don't. And I want you to be part of his life from now on, even if he's living with me. Especially if he's living with me. Luke, too. He'll need all of us.' Mark held out his hand and after a moment, Derwent shook it. Then Mark turned to me.

'You'll let me know what's happening with the investigation, won't you?'

'I'll give your details to the officers who are reviewing the medical records,' I said. 'I won't be involved myself.'

'She's done enough,' Derwent said to Mark, who nodded, and said goodbye, and headed out to see his son.

Once we were alone, Derwent ran a hand over his head. 'How did you see it when I didn't?'

'I didn't understand what I was looking at, at first. Then I did, but it took a while.' I hesitated. 'You know, even though

I think it's a sign of personal growth that you apologised to Mark, you didn't need to. This isn't your fault.'

'But she did it for me. I should be the one in trouble.' He was pacing back and forth, agitated.

'She did it for her own purposes. She made her choices. You aren't responsible for her actions.'

'I didn't see what was happening right in front of me. A child almost *died* and I didn't notice. She could have done anything to him and I was too wrapped up in myself.'

'Josh—'

He swallowed, fighting his emotions. 'There's a part of me that wishes you'd never worked it out.'

I could understand that. 'I know it must be hard for you. It will be difficult for Thomas.'

'Finding out his mother almost killed him? Yeah, I think that counts as childhood trauma.'

'Melissa isn't well. She had a terrible childhood and a marriage that ended horribly and a relationship that was in terminal decline, and she made some very bad decisions. She needs help and now she'll get it.'

He stopped pacing. 'I want to talk to her.'

'You mustn't.' I reached out and caught hold of his arm. 'Promise me you'll stay away from her.'

Something in my voice made him look at me. 'Why? In case I take out my feelings on her? Lash out? Get arrested for real?'

That was what I had been thinking. It must have been written all over my face because he pulled his arm away, quite gently.

'You thought I'd done it, didn't you? When you heard she was in hospital, and I'd been arrested.'

'No.'

'You thought you might be wrong about me. You weren't sure.'

'I knew you'd never hurt someone like that.'

'Then why are you worrying about it now?'

An unanswerable question. 'I – I don't know. But I know you love Thomas and I know you're devastated for him.'

'That's one way of putting it,' he said evenly.

'I think you need to stay away from her.' I was struggling to articulate why the idea of them being in the same space made me panic. 'She knows how to be hurtful. She might provoke you. It would make sense for you to be angry . . . and you do get angry . . .'

He was very still. The flat was so quiet I could hear music drifting down from the floor above, and the ticking of his watch, and my own heartbeat.

'Sometimes, Maeve, I think you don't understand me at all.'

I stared at him, unhappily aware that I had got it very badly wrong. He dug in his pocket.

'I have something for you.' He held out his hand. A gold earring sat on his palm.

'That's mine.'

'I know.'

'I thought I'd lost it.' I took it from him, puzzled. 'Where did you find it? At work?'

'No, Goldilocks. You left it in my bed in Jena Road.'

Instant, red-hot embarrassment swept over me. 'Oh.'

'I knew you'd been in the house. I just didn't know why.'

'I was trying to help you.'

'Very kind. And evidently you also had time for a nap.'

'I wanted . . .' I trailed off. I couldn't tell him what I had wanted when I wasn't even sure myself.

'It made me realise I need to talk to you.' He was looking away from me, his face set. It felt as if he'd already left the room, leaving a hollowed-out version of himself behind. 'Listen, Maeve. This focus on me – on us – has to end.'

Not what I had been expecting. 'Why?'

'What's between us was always something neither of us could have. It was a daydream for two unhappy people. A refuge from reality. I was unavailable so I was the perfect man for you, because you didn't want a relationship with anyone. I was your excuse.' He moved to lean against the wall, looking exhausted. 'I should never have encouraged you, but I was flattered.'

'Flattered,' I repeated.

'It was never really anything, was it? We're colleagues. And friends,' he amended quickly, as I glared at him. 'That's important to me. You know I'll be there for you when you need me. That friendship is what's real.'

I took a couple of paces towards him. 'Don't push me away because you're upset.'

'I'm not.'

'That's how it feels. Is this because you're angry with me about Melissa? Or because I misjudged you just now?'

'No.' He was watching me with something like compassion as I started to pick up my belongings with shaking hands.

'Nine months ago, you were kissing me on a street corner because you couldn't bear not to.' My mouth felt stiff. I was cold, my hands clammy. 'I kissed you on the stairs and you weren't the one who pulled away. You held me all night when I needed you, because I needed you. Six months ago, you told me you were going to end your relationship with Melissa so you could be with me. That was you. All you.'

'I'm only human, Maeve.' He folded his arms, unsmiling now so he looked arrogant and unfeeling. The alpha male, exactly as he was in the old days. It was if he knew what I was thinking. 'I thought I could be what you wanted, but this is who I've always been. You wanted to believe I was different, and maybe I did too.'

I felt as if I was going to faint. I walked down the hallway, not seeing straight, focused only on getting away. He followed me.

'It'll be all right, you know. You'll be happier in the long run.'

'Don't.' I stumbled away from him and collided with the bike that was hanging on the wall. The thin skin on the inside of my wrist dragged across something sharp. I held in a gasp of pain.

'Maeve . . .' He reached out for me and I drew back.

'No.'

His hand dropped. 'OK.'

'I'm going to go now.' I was holding my wrist. It stung but I didn't want to look at it in front of him. Thank God for anger, elbowing aside my hurt so I could keep my composure and look him in the eye. 'I want you to know that even if I didn't care about you at all, I would still have done the best I could to help you. I would still have found out what Melissa was doing, and I would still have stopped her.'

This time, when I got outside, I took a deep breath of the cold, grey air, dry-eyed. My mother's voice was echoing in my mind. *There's nothing wrong with wanting to be happy, Maeve.*

I did want to be happy, and this wasn't close to it. This was the opposite of happy. I took out my phone, barely thinking, and called Owen, who picked up on the second ring.

'Hello, you. What's up?' He sounded warm, his voice mellow and pleasant, like a log fire on an icy day.

'I just needed to hear a friendly voice.'

'Really?' He sounded pleased. 'You can rely on me for that. Any time.'

'Are you still on for tonight?' My wrist, I discovered, was bleeding. Blood had soaked into the cuff of my jumper, which was cream and cashmere and probably ruined.

'Very much so. I have something planned for us that I think you'll love.'

'Really.' I tried to sound enthusiastic. 'I don't need anything fancy.'

'We'll meet at the Delaunay at six for something to eat and go on from there.'

'Where are we going?'

'It's a surprise.' Owen was grinning, I could tell. 'Trust me.'

45

I didn't expect to have fun with Owen that night, but I did. First of all, the Delaunay charmed me completely, with its old-school Mittel-Europe feel. Owen kissed me when I arrived, ordered wine that tasted of sunshine in dusty French vineyards, and took charge of the menu so I didn't have to do anything at all but sit back and smile at him. I did find him attractive, I thought, watching him gravely discuss the specials of the day with the waiter.

As usual when we met, I had to take a moment to remind myself that he really existed, that he was a real person with feelings and thoughts and the capacity to make jokes, because he barely seemed to exist in my imagination when he wasn't right in front of me. I had the impression he felt the same way about me. He hadn't met my friends or my family, and he hadn't asked to. He hadn't needed anything from me at all: we were both busy and self-sufficient. This was not the sort of relationship that made you feel breathless, that made your heart flutter, that consumed every particle of your being. This was reason, not passion. I had taken full advantage of him being so detached because I didn't have space for him in my brain with everything else that was going on, but I wished he was a little more demanding. It would prove he cared.

I studied him. He had warm brown eyes, like tea before the milk, and a cheeky smile that had been getting him out of trouble, I guessed, since he was a child, and a quick mind that I appreciated. He was completely, utterly relaxed, as if nothing could ever go wrong, and if it did it could be fixed. He was neat in his movements, deft, intelligent.

I liked his confidence, and the way he smiled at me across the table as if we were already sharing a joke, and the fact that he could make me laugh without trying.

I liked *him*.

He had been to the gym that day, he told me, with a view to getting fitter so he could keep up with Luke and the other younger employees in his office. 'They go jogging at lunchtime. They're all seven feet tall and run marathons for fun. Do you know the French don't say "dad bod"?'

'Don't they?'

'No. They say "père-shaped".'

I giggled.

'When was the last time you were in Paris?'

'I can't remember.'

'That's a crime, for starters, when all you need to do is hop on the Eurostar.'

'I don't have a hopping-on-the-Eurostar lifestyle.'

'I do. Come with me.'

I laughed. 'As easy as that.'

'It can be.'

He asked me enough about my job that I felt he was genuinely interested in why I did it, but not so much that I felt uncomfortable. He didn't try to trip me up, or goad me into saying what I thought. He didn't challenge me, and if I found that meant the evening lacked an edge, that was all right too. I had wanted to feel happy. I had wanted this.

I had to stop comparing him to Josh Derwent, I thought, picking at the chocolate mousse that I'd chosen for dessert, demurring when he suggested a banana split. He deserved better than that. He was all the things he was, not all the things Josh Derwent was not.

Liv had said as much, when I called her that afternoon and told her about my argument with Derwent. She had been brisk.

'He's probably right, it's for the best.'

'Why?'

'Because he was right to say you were using him to avoid getting on with your life.'

'I don't think that's fair,' I began, and she laughed softly.

'No. You wouldn't. Look, he was honest with you. I'm actually impressed.'

'He was angry with me for misjudging him, and he was upset about Melissa.'

'Yes, but he was also aware that you've imagined a future for the two of you, and he was telling you that's not on the cards.'

'Why not?'

She sighed into the phone. 'I don't know, Maeve. Because he doesn't want another relationship now. Because he knows he isn't the one for you.'

'Sometimes he behaves like the one,' I said.

'And sometimes he behaves like he's not.' She sounded sympathetic. 'Maybe he just didn't want you to ruin something that might be good for you.'

'What would that be?'

'Owen?'

'You don't know that Owen would be good for me.'

'Mm, a solvent, mentally stable grown-up who's ready to settle down with someone. He sounds really problematic and unsuitable.'

'You should be on my side.'

'I am. But from what you've told me about your conversation with Josh, one of you got what you wanted and the other one got what they needed. And now you can stop wondering about what might happen with him, because you know the answer.'

'What are you thinking about?'

I looked up, startled. 'Oh – nothing.'

'Whoever upset you earlier?'

'How did you know?' I sat up straight. 'I was thinking about not thinking about him.'

'Him?' Owen's tone was casual.

'He's not important. It's the situation that's bothering me. But I can't talk about it.'

'Fair enough.' He smiled, and I felt my spirits lift.

'This is a lovely place.' I looked around, enjoying the soft lighting, the white linen and silver tableware, the shadowy corners and intimate booths, the other diners absorbed in their own small worlds.

'This is only the prelude to the main event.'

'Which is what exactly?'

He leaned over the table and dropped his voice. 'A magic show. I got tickets at a charity auction.'

'You are full of surprises.'

'The first surprise of the evening, but not the last.' He dug in his pocket, held up a pound coin, and then made it disappear.

'Don't tell me you do magic.'

'Badly. But enthusiastically.' The coin appeared again, shuttling back and forth over his knuckles. 'It's a real ice-breaker when I'm meeting foreign clients, especially if there's a language barrier.'

'What other tricks can you do?'

He spun the coin in the air and caught it, then put it away. 'A few. Nothing compared to the guy we're going to see tonight.'

'I've never been to a magic show.'

'You haven't lived.' Owen signalled for the bill.

'I don't know what I've been doing with my time.'

'Wasting it until you met me.' The gleam of amusement in his eyes made it clear he was joking.

Derwent would have meant it.

Stop thinking about him.

I lifted my glass. 'Here's to new experiences.'

'Here's to magic.' He clinked glasses with me, his eyes on mine.

The magician was a hot ticket, it transpired: the theatre was full, largely with young women who were smitten by his good looks and comedian-quality quips. He had been on television on a talent show where he had almost won, but dropped out before the final.

'Why didn't he go all the way?' I asked Owen.

'Drugs.'

'Oh.'

'Can't win a family show if the tabloids have pictures of you snorting coke off a stripper's arse. Or so I'm told.'

It hadn't put his fans off. In fact, I thought most of them were there because he had a touch of wildness about him, along with dark, soulful eyes and self-deprecating charm. His speciality was reviving old-school magic with a modern twist while working the crowd mercilessly, picking on the front row who seemed delighted to be victimised. I was glad we were out of range in the dress circle. In place of the classic magician look he wore low-slung jeans and trainers with a white shirt. He made a rabbit appear from a top hat and then turned the rabbit into a plume of smoke and transformed the top hat into a cloud of black butterflies. His running gag was that his assistant – tall, sequin-clad, with a plume of feathers in her hair – insisted on appearing in ever-skimpier outfits as he paused the show to lecture her about self-respect and making more of her brains and tried, with varying degrees of ineptitude, to cover her with drapes and curtains. She was down to a G-string and a tiny bikini top by the time she marched her fishnet-covered legs into a box to be sawn in half.

'I never liked this one,' Owen muttered in my ear.

'Don't worry. She'll be fine.'

'Do you know how it's done?'

'Yes.'

'Me too. Doesn't help. Just makes me claustrophobic.'

I patted his hand and he turned it, inviting me to put my hand in his. After a moment's hesitation, I did, and was distracted while the trick unfolded on stage. The feet kicked in their high heels, the plumed head screamed, and a cascade of red liquid spattered the floor under the box as the magician sliced through it with a paper-thin, razor-sharp katana sword. He bent and dipped his hand in the liquid, smearing it over his face and the white shirt he wore. He bent again and straightened and in the same movement flung a handful of red at the stalls. The audience screamed, then laughed as red rose petals drifted down on them instead of fake blood. The lights went out for a heartbeat, no more than that, the theatre so dark it felt as if someone had hooded me with black velvet. When the lights came up the stage was clean, empty, without a trace of the red mess or the box where the assistant had been sawn in two. The magician walked out from the wings, his shirt spotless and white, holding hands with his assistant, who was now wearing knee-high boots, tights, a pretty dress, glasses and no make-up. Her hair hung down her back.

'How?' Owen said, delighted, and let go of my hand so we could applaud. I thought about moving out of reach but that seemed mean-spirited and when he took my hand again, palm to palm, I didn't resist.

After a lengthy encore and a longer queue to retrieve our coats from the cloakroom, we made it out of the theatre in the tide of overexcited fans.

'Let's get out of here,' Owen muttered in my ear and I followed him, leaving the crowds behind.

It was one of those nights when mist tips into rain that drifts down in tiny specks, enough to keep people off the streets even if the temperature wasn't halfway to freezing. I wrapped my coat around myself, shivering a little. He stopped in a narrow, deserted street off Seven Dials. Christmas lights zigzagged above our heads and the shop windows were decorated with fake snow, lit up so non-existent shoppers could be tempted to splurge on glittering gifts.

'Happy?'

I smiled. 'I enjoyed the show. Not as much as the super-fans did, maybe . . .'

'They were terrifying,' Owen said. 'And I think they were more interested in the man than the magic.'

'Which was impressive.'

'Which was full of showing off.'

'Speaking as an experienced magician yourself,' I teased.

'Give me a good card trick any day.'

'Do you know any?'

'One. But if you want it to work, you have to pick the ten of clubs.'

'I'll try to remember,' I said, and he leaned in and kissed me, his mouth warm against mine, and I managed not to think about Josh Derwent for at least some of it.

46

I woke up in my own bed, alone. Owen had politely indicated that he would be happy for me to go home with him and I'd thought about it. I liked him. I thought he was attractive. There was nothing off-putting about how he kissed me. I stretched, staring at the ceiling. There was no reason to hold back, and yet . . . *I bet there was one morning when you woke up and had no idea how you'd ended up where you were.* I had flung those words at Derwent about Melissa, and now it felt like an increasingly likely outcome for me and Owen. I couldn't find any reason not to be with him.

That couldn't be enough.

I picked up my phone and thought about sending Owen a message to thank him for the previous night, then slid it back onto the bedside table with a sigh. If I sent him a message this early, he would know I'd woken up thinking about him. That was girlfriend behaviour and we certainly weren't there yet.

I took my time over getting ready, making coffee, dawdling over breakfast even though I knew I was going to be cutting it fine to get to work on time. I didn't want to go to work. Whenever I was in danger of forgetting about Derwent, my wrist would sting. I examined the graze and decided it didn't need a plaster, unlike my heart, which could have done with some sticking together.

I had got as far as putting on my coat when my phone rang. Derwent was calling. Tension made me curt as I answered it. I was already heading for the door, anticipating trouble about being late, but I was wrong.

'They've found Abilo Braga.'

'Where was he?'

'Underneath some rubble on a building site in Neasden.'

'Dead?'

'Very.'

'Fuck,' I said, stopping halfway down the stairs. 'That's not how I wanted him to turn up. Do you have the address?'

He reeled it off in a bored tone of voice. I scrawled it on the back of my hand, the phone caught between my ear and shoulder.

'Will I see you there?'

'Probably. It is my case.'

It had been a stupid question, I acknowledged, biting my lip.

'Better to get on with it, since we're going to be working together,' he said, not unkindly. 'If you can stand to be around me.'

'Josh,' I said, and couldn't think what else to add.

No, I'd rather not have to see you.

Yes, even being in the same space as you is better than nothing.

What if both were true at the same time?

The address was a building site near the railway lines that flowed west through North London like an iron river. Surrounded by hoardings, the site was tucked away behind a warehouse. The giveaway that it was where I needed to be, of course, was the collection of emergency service vehicles parked up along the roadway outside it, and the cluster of high-vis-wearing, hard-hatted builders standing around drinking coffee while their JCBs and cranes stood idle. It was a bitterly cold morning, the sky a heavy grey and so low it was hanging like gauze over the tops of tall buildings. I had gone back and changed, given that I wasn't heading for a heated office, so I was wearing jeans and lace-up boots, layers of jumpers and a down-filled jacket. I pulled a hat on, found some gloves and got out of the car, trying to convey I was getting a sense of the scene rather than searching for Josh Derwent as I looked around. I saw Liv instead, bundled up in a coat that covered her from chin to ankle. Her face was pinched from the cold.

'Where is he?'

'In the corner, over there.' She pointed to where a small digger was abandoned at an angle on a pile of rubble, and I realised she thought I meant Abilo Braga, which was probably what I should have been asking anyway. 'The builders weren't working here until today. They've been waiting for a safety certificate from the council so they haven't been on site for three weeks. This morning was their first day back.'

'They must be delighted.'

'They're still getting paid.' Liv snuggled down inside her coat. Her nose was pink. 'We basically have no idea when he was dumped here, but it could have been straight after he disappeared.'

'This isn't far from where we found the car,' I said. 'Was he buried?'

'Yes, but not very far down. Come and see.'

I would very much have liked to take it on trust, but I followed her across the uneven ground of the site, skirting a deep pit full of metal rods and inscrutable pipes that was securely fenced off. 'What are they building?'

'Apartments.'

'Here? Between an industrial estate and the railway line?' A train rumbled past, almost drowning out my voice.

'You know what it's like,' Liv shouted over the noise. 'Someone will buy them.'

Someone would, even with the obvious site disadvantages – even if they knew a body had been dumped there. You couldn't afford to be sentimental when it came to the London property market. I followed the makeshift rutted path created by caterpillar treads that had cut into the soft earth, looping up over the mound of rubble and down the far side where I could see the area that had been excavated that morning. One white-suited figure was Kev Cox, inevitably, and the other was – I waited for him to turn – the pathologist, Dr Brown. Nothing there to make my heart beat faster. They both waved at me.

'Can you see from there?' Kev called.

'Well enough.' The body was half-submerged in earth, his back arched, his arms spread wide, his head and legs lolling. He had begun to decompose, quite noticeably, but the cold weather had been a help: I'd seen worse. Still, it upset me. I thought of the life he'd left behind, pinned in pictures on the wall of his home. He had come a long way to end up dumped in cold earth under an iron-grey sky. There was no dignity in the way he had been discarded on the building site, but at least we could treat his body with respect now. Instead of complaining about the smell I tried to hold my breath and talk at the same time. 'Do you know what killed him?'

'Strangled,' the pathologist said. 'There's a ligature mark across his throat and under his ear. Someone right-handed who was behind him, if I had to guess, possibly while he was sitting down.'

'Like in a car?'

'Exactly what I was thinking. But consider that to be speculation until the post-mortem, which will be later on. I'll expect to see you there.'

'Can't wait.'

'We were lucky,' Liv said beside me. 'The digger disturbed the earth around him but it didn't touch the body. The driver lifted up a big scoop of earth and basically had a heart attack when he saw legs poking out of it. He dropped the body down where it is.'

'So where was it originally?'

Kev climbed up to join us, his face ruddy and sheened with sweat despite the cold. 'He was in that area there, to the left of the digger. We'll be sifting through all the rubble to make sure we don't miss anything that was dumped with him.'

'He had a backpack when he left his car,' I said. 'And we haven't found his passport anywhere.'

'If it's there, we'll find it.'

Liv had trotted off down the rutted path and I took the opportunity to ask Kev the main question on my mind.

'Is Josh here?'

'Haven't seen him.'

I felt a kick of disappointment in the pit of my stomach which was stupid and ridiculous. I smiled my thanks and went after Liv, who had cornered the site foreman. He was a large man in his fifties who darlin'-ed us and well-you-see'd until he'd explained that there was no usable CCTV on site, despite the signs about it, because the contractor hadn't actually paid to have it installed. 'Not when there was no plant here, which was the case until this morning. There wasn't anything to steal. The place was stripped out and levelled and that was more or less it up to now. Nothing but earth. They were planning to come today to put the actual cameras in.'

The good news just kept coming: there was also an unlocked vehicle gate not far from where the body had been dumped.

'Could someone have driven through the gate?'

'I suppose so. Nothing to stop them if they noticed it wasn't secured.'

'Why wasn't it secure?' Liv was looking severe.

He whistled and the builders looked around. 'Jimmy,' he called and a man detached himself from the group, jogging over to us. He was young, bearded and enormous, with soft dark eyes under his hard hat and tunnelled piercings in his earlobes.

'Why wasn't the gate secure, Jimmy?' the foreman asked, and he ducked his head, flushing.

'Because I lost the key to the padlock.'

'And why didn't you replace the padlock?'

He pulled his hat off and rubbed his head bashfully. 'Forgot.'

'Go on,' the foreman said, and Jimmy jogged back to the gang. 'It didn't really matter, or so I thought. This was all flattened earth apart from the area that has the metal fence around it, and that was secure enough. Nothing hazardous within reach otherwise. Nothing to steal. No reason to worry about people coming in, you'd have thought.' He shrugged. 'It was only supposed to be a couple of days until we got the go-ahead to carry on.'

'We might get tyre tracks,' I said to Liv, and the foreman pulled a face.

'Not now, you won't. We've had vehicles in and out of there this morning.'

'You didn't notice any unusual markings on the earth, I suppose.'

He shook his head and we let him return to his bacon roll.

'Not wonderful news,' Liv said dolefully. 'Braga was our best lead.'

'He was supposed to be paid money for something, wasn't that what his friends said? He might have had some already to pay for the car. If I had to guess, someone hired him to block the toilet and then thought better of it. They must have decided it was too risky to let him live.'

'So they arranged to meet him and strangled him to death.'

I shivered. A train rumbled past, the wheels shrieking with a metal-on-metal squeal that made us both wince. 'I wonder if he knew the whole plan. He might not have agreed to be part of it – even for the money – if he'd known it was murder.'

'Or he might have asked for more money.' Liv, ever-practical. 'In fact, maybe that's why they decided it was too risky to let him live.'

'I wish I'd asked him the right questions when I interviewed him.'

'You couldn't have.' She dusted off her gloves. 'We didn't even know about the blocked toilet then.'

I looked around at where Abilo Braga's body was still lying in the dirt, feeling guilty, and felt a whole lot worse as a man in a dark overcoat jogged down the mound of dirt, sure-footed. He was heading straight for us, or rather me, because Liv muttered something that I didn't catch and melted away. I thought about going to meet Derwent but dithered about embarrassing myself by assuming he was coming to talk to me and stayed where I was, so all I had to do was watch him stride towards me, his hair ruffled by the wind.

'Kev said you were looking for me.'

'Oh – no, I was just asking if you were here. Not for any reason.' Mortifying. Luke had been right: he had a terrible effect on my composure.

He looked around, frowning. Once he'd reassured himself that no one was within earshot, he said, 'Are you all right?'

'Yes.' Sort of.

'What did you do after you left the flat yesterday?'

'I met up with Owen. We went out for dinner and to a show.' The truth. I hadn't said it to hurt him, but I saw a muscle tense in his jaw.

'Sounds fun.' He wasn't looking at me. 'Is this going to be too difficult? Working together?'

'We've got through worse,' I said levelly.

'True.' He paused for a moment. 'The pathologist said the post-mortem would be today. I'll go.'

I brightened. Against the odds, my day was improving. 'Thank you. I was expecting to have to do it.'

'I was planning to be there as well as you, not instead.'

'Great.'

'Try to sound a bit more enthusiastic.'

'To be clear it's the dead body that's putting me off, not you,' I said, and he actually grinned, which took us both by surprise.

We could do this, I thought. We could be professional, and friendly, and still work together. It was bearable.

Just about.

47

This time it was my turn to be late for the post-mortem. I found Derwent, arms-folded grim, in the corridor when I hurried in to discover Dr Brown had already finished.

'Where have you been?'

'I got held up.'

Derwent frowned, unconvinced, and I realised he thought I'd avoided him deliberately.

'I spent all day looking for CCTV from near the building site and got basically nowhere. Everyone had their cameras pointed at their own premises, not the road or the building site.'

His scowl lifted very slightly. 'How dare they.'

'I know. You'd think they'd be more helpful.' I sighed. 'Whoever picked that spot to dump the body was inspired. We don't even know when they did it, let alone what car they were driving. There isn't any building close enough to have a view of the site, because of the railway line. They had all the privacy they could have needed.'

'I'm not seeing how this delayed you.'

'I went to Braga's house afterwards.' There had been a specially trained team searching it, for a second time. 'The POLSA team still haven't found the passport or either phone or his bag, even though Kev was at the building site sifting earth all day. Braga's housemate was there – Zofia. She was in bits. They'd been seeing one another, she told me. Off and on – when it suited him, as far as I could tell.'

'Did we know that?'

I shook my head. 'She also told me he had said to her that he was being paid extra money even though it was only to do his job, but he wouldn't give her any details. But listen to this – she said he told her it was a prank. A hidden camera thing.'

'No wonder he was shitting himself when it turned into a murder investigation.'

'No wonder he thought he could ask for more money. He took his passport with him because they told him he would need it for a bank transfer. I suspect that was so we would think he'd done a runner. All very calculating.'

'He should have talked to us. If he'd told us the truth he'd still be alive.'

'Zofia said he was genuinely scared of the police. He didn't think he'd be allowed to stay in the UK if there was any suggestion he'd been involved in committing a crime.' I leaned against the wall, exhausted. 'I wish he'd trusted me, and not just because I think we've lost our best hope of finding out what happened to Ilaria.'

'Usually having a second victim would be a help.'

'Did you get anything from the PM?'

Derwent shrugged. 'No surprises. He was strangled with some kind of ligature – more likely to be a rope than a belt, from the width of the mark on his neck. He died hard – he'd scratched his skin trying to loosen the ligature. It's unlikely that he managed to hurt his assailant but the doc took scrapings from under his nails so we might get lucky. No other injuries. He was fit and healthy.'

'Sorry I missed it.'

'Are you?'

'Well, no. But I wasn't having fun either.'

'Who says this isn't fun?' Dr Brown had appeared at my elbow without me noticing. 'How are you, Maeve?'

'Cold,' I said.

'How is that possible?' Derwent drawled. 'You're wearing half your wardrobe.'

'Layers keep you warmer, everyone knows that,' I said, defensive. 'And I'm always cold when I'm tired.' To Dr Brown, I said, 'Sorry I missed the big show.'

'That's all right. There'll be another one.' He looked at Derwent. 'Did you fill her in?'

'Yeah.'

'We'll see what comes back from the nail scrapings. That's your best hope for DNA, I'm afraid.'

'Thanks.'

'No problem.' He started to walk away, then turned. 'Oh, did you get that other thing sorted out? The factitious disorder issue? My wife wanted me to ask.'

'Yes. Thank you.' I was cringing. I'd thought I was cold before but now I was ice from the inside out.

'It was very helpful,' Derwent said, behind me. 'Thank her from me too.'

'Oh – good. Glad it was useful.' He shook his head. 'It's a nasty one, that. A difficult situation. And when you're in it, very hard for the other family members to see what's going on. You're so blinded by worry about the child, you lose all perspective on what might have caused the ill health. Then it's hard to believe the worst of someone you care about – that they would deliberately cause harm to someone so vulnerable. It goes against everything that you'd expect from a parent or caregiver. Unless you're a cynic, like my wife.' His chest broadened and he beamed, proud. 'She's happy to believe the worst of people.'

'I've never found that was a mistake.' There was a hint of amusement in Derwent's voice.

'Very true.' The pathologist nodded, said goodbye to us and walked away.

'Not often you come across someone who's so obviously in love with his wife,' Derwent said.

'Aren't you sorry you ever thought he was flirting with me?' I risked, and got a low *hmmm* as a response, which could have meant anything. I made myself turn around, even if I couldn't look him in the face. 'The factitious disorder thing – he didn't know you were involved.'

'So I see.'

'I kept it hypothetical.'

'Kind of you.' He put his hands in his pockets, frowning down at the floor. 'It'll come out eventually when it goes to court.'

'No. I asked about that. They'll want to protect Thomas's identity. If there's a trial there'll be reporting restrictions.'

His mouth twisted. 'That's something.'

'It was nice of you to thank Dr Brown and his wife.'

'I should have thanked you too.'

'That wasn't what I meant,' I protested, but his phone rang and he moved away to answer it.

I would go home, I thought. A hot bath. An early night, for once. I needed sleep. I needed to not have to think for a few hours.

The conversation was brief, and on Derwent's end comprised of short, borderline rude responses. He was facing away from me, and when he ended the call he stood still for a moment before he turned around.

I was shocked by his expression: despair. 'What's happened?'

'That was Roz Fuller. She wants to see me.'

'Why?'

'She wouldn't say on the phone.'

'That's the sort of trick I would pull,' I said, and he tried to smile. 'When does she want to see you?'

'Now.' He swallowed. 'At the nick where they held me.'

I understood in a rush of compassion. He wouldn't want to go back there. On the surface he had shrugged off the trauma of being arrested and interviewed repeatedly – the nightmare of being accused of something he regarded as unforgivable. The events of his arrest had been pushed into a dark cupboard, the doors slammed shut and locked, as if that was enough to get over it.

'I'll come with you.'

'You said you were tired. Anyway, it's not a good idea.'

'I didn't ask you if you thought it was a good idea. In fact, I didn't ask you at all. I'm coming with you.'

'Why?'

'Because you need someone to be there for you. And who's better than me?'

'Almost anyone.' He sounded deeply, utterly exhausted. 'I can't let you, Maeve.'

'It's not up to you. I want to be there for you – as a friend.' It seemed important to clarify that. 'I know where you're going. We might as well go there together. Otherwise I'll just have to tail you.'

His expression lightened for an instant, but then he sighed. 'I keep telling you to stay away from Roz Fuller. Coming with me is the height of stupidity.'

'Look, I'll stay in the car. She won't even know I'm there. But you'll know, and that's all I want. You shouldn't have to go there alone.' I took a step closer to him, clenching my hands in my coat pockets. 'Whatever it takes – whatever you need me to do – I'll do it.'

He straightened up, pulling his shoulders back, transforming himself, at least outwardly, into the Josh Derwent you couldn't break. 'All right. You win. Let's go.'

48

We pulled up outside the police station and Derwent reversed into a space with a grandstand view of the front door. He had driven – he was too tense to sit and watch me drive, he had explained when I tried to get the keys. I could tell he was nervous from the way he drummed his fingers on the steering wheel whenever we were stopped, and the monosyllabic efforts he made to reply to me, and the way his mouth thinned into a line when he was silent. I didn't force him to make conversation. Now and then he glanced across at me, and that seemed to be enough to soften his gaze, at least for a heartbeat or two.

I knew he would be worried that she planned to arrest him. He would be afraid this was the beginning of the end for his career. Melissa had set a fire blazing that I had put out, but the damage was done. Smoke could be as destructive as flames. The things she had said – the accusations she had made – tainted him, exactly as Mark Pell had warned me.

Now he switched the engine off and turned to me, his face grim. 'Right. You have no reason to get out of the car, so stay here.'

'Fine.'

'No matter what.'

'I understand.'

'If I don't come back—'

'You will.'

He went on as if I hadn't spoken— 'don't come in looking for me. I'll get a message to you. I'll leave you the car keys. You'll need to tell Luke where I am, and I suppose you should let Mark know in case Thomas is asking. I don't need to tell you how to get in touch with either of them, do I?'

'Josh . . .'

'Here.' He dangled the keys and let them fall. Without even thinking I reached out to catch them. The movement pulled my sleeve up my arm and I drew it down, but not quickly enough.

'What's that?' He reached across and caught hold of my hand, holding it up to examine it.

'It's nothing. It looks worse than it is.' Twenty-four hours later the injury amounted to some bruising and a scabbed-over graze like a coral atoll floating on the blue-green veins of my wrist. I looked away from it, staring out through the windscreen so I didn't have to look at Derwent either, or the way he was holding my hand with his thumb pressed against the palm and long fingers curled around my knuckles.

'When did it happen?'

'When we were talking yesterday in Luke's flat. I caught it on the bike. But I'm fine.'

'Tell the truth.'

I sighed. 'All right. It really, really hurt.'

'I thought so.' He sounded irritated. 'I told Luke it was a stupid place to put a bike.'

'Yeah, I wasn't talking about what happened with the bike.'

For a moment, he didn't react. Slowly, he pulled my hand across to hold it against his cheek. He closed his eyes and I didn't speak, didn't move, didn't breathe . . .

Then he was sliding out of the car, walking across to the squat, miserable police station with his head down. I bit my lip, watching him go. That wasn't how I had wanted to leave it with him. I had planned to say something reassuring – to make him laugh on his way in to face the music. Not for the first time, I'd made things worse.

Out of habit I checked the time – a quarter past seven – and started a clock running in my head. If he wasn't out in an hour, I would go in. Or forty-five minutes. In fact, half an hour was surely long enough for Roz Fuller to say whatever it was she had on her mind. I imagined him waiting in the reception area, pacing. You couldn't leave someone like Derwent hanging around. He would make his way through any locked door and hunt you down.

A jogger ran past the building, upright and fast, the reflective stripes on her running tights flashing as they caught the light. I judged her stride to be not quite as good as mine: I had worked hard on it over the last few months while I was humourlessly focused on being the best version of myself to take my mind off Derwent. Because that had worked so well . . .

A middle-aged couple strolled in the other direction, hand in hand, out with their elderly corgi who was in no particular hurry about his walk.

A teenage girl went by in school uniform, headphones on, her phone held two inches from her nose, oblivious to her surroundings. A walking target for people with bad intentions, I thought, and wondered if I should go after her and tell her so.

The door of the police station opened and a man came out but it wasn't Derwent – not even close: shorter, fatter, balder. I leaned my head against the head rest. He'd been in there for fourteen minutes. Unbearable.

A grey-haired man in a navy anorak, carrying a shopping bag, walked slowly up the police station steps past the bald man who was taking a phone call. The grey-haired man ducked his head as he passed, as if he was apologising for making Baldy move two inches to his left, and disappeared through the door.

I frowned.

I wanted to ask about my son.

The phrase floated through my mind, disconnected from context.

Please. I need to know.

I matched the words with the man who had been standing at the reception desk when Clara Porter had been arrested and I had hung around waiting for praise like a cat with a dead rat.

The same man who had been sitting outside the police station in the cold, his breath clouding the clear air on the night Derwent was arrested. I had trotted past him on my way to intercept Lesley Mackenzie. A man I had barely noticed because

I had been caught up with my own worries, who was haunting the police station because he wanted something that they couldn't or wouldn't give him.

Why was my mouth dry? I tried to make sense of it. Any public-facing organisation attracted obsessives. Usually there was nothing to worry about. This man was probably at the police station every day.

Why was I worried?

The answer came back: he didn't have a bag before.

And what was it about the bag that bothered me?

The bag was almost empty apart from something narrow and heavy that lay along the bottom of it – heavy because it was pulling the plastic taut as it dangled from his hand.

It could be anything.

Just because he hadn't had a bag before.

Just because he'd turned his head away as he spoke to the bald man, who was descending the steps now, who had been so much closer to him than I was and had noticed nothing out of the ordinary about him.

Just because I'd heard that note in his voice before that was uneasily close to desperation.

Just because I'd been right about that kind of thing in the past.

Just because the consequences for being wrong were unthinkable.

There was no harm in going in to check.

49

It was crowded in the small reception area and Josh Derwent didn't care. Politely, firmly, he looked Roz Fuller in the eye and said no, thanks, but he wasn't going to join her in the interview room where she'd tortured him.

'I'm here without my lawyer so this had better be an informal chat, and if it is an informal chat we can have it here. If it's not an informal chat then arrest me and I'll get my lawyer here and we can start the whole process again. Your choice.'

Roz sighed. 'There's absolutely no need to come here with that attitude.'

'There's no need to come here at all, as far as I can see.'

'It's how I like to do things.' She flicked through her notebook, unmoved, and when she looked up he was shaking his head at her.

'All right. Do it your way.'

'Not that you have a choice about it, but I will.'

'Sometimes,' Josh Derwent said idly, 'I feel as if I'm surrounded by women who don't listen to me.'

Beside Roz, Henry Cowell choked back a laugh.

The truth was that he was right; there was no great need for him to come to the police station. She had wanted one last look, to be sure she was doing the right thing. She had expected him to be unsettled, given that it was a place that couldn't hold many positive memories for him. Now that he was here, she could tell that even if it made the difference between him having a career and not having one, he wasn't going to grovel. He wasn't that kind of person and she found herself quite liking him for it.

A long, loud sigh came from the corner of the reception area, where a woman was sitting on the single chair. She was young, with badly dyed hair, and she was wearing a black tracksuit with fluffy slippers that were dirty enough to show it wasn't the first time she had worn them out of the house. A bullet-headed man was at the counter, arguing with the receptionist whose main job seemed to be explaining all the things they couldn't do for the general public at that desk. The man gave up, his hairless scalp shining with indignation, and elbowed past Roz on his way to the door. Off balance, Roz almost fell over – might have, if Josh Derwent hadn't reached out to steady her.

'Sorry, love.' The bald man held up his hands in appeasement, a phone clutched in one. 'I wasn't looking where I was going.'

'You should be more careful,' she snapped, and turned to see Derwent trying not to smile and Cowell pretending to cough to hide his own amusement. It was so nice that they were getting on, she thought, and gave Cowell a wounded look that pulled his face straight immediately.

The bald man ducked his head, scuttling to the door.

'Can we get this over with?' Derwent put his hands in his pockets.

The door opened again to admit an elderly man in an anorak, who skirted them with care.

Roz got a grip on herself. 'I wanted to see you to tell you I've reached the end of my investigation into you and your professional conduct. At this point I have not identified any major concerns relating to how you do your job. I'm also satisfied that you weren't involved with the attack on your partner, Melissa, despite her account of events. That investigation will be carried out by borough CID so they can decide what charges will apply, but as I have told them, you are not implicated in any way. You may be required to give evidence in their investigation but I'm sure you will understand the importance of cooperating fully with them.'

'Is that everything you wanted to say?' Derwent checked. Roz hadn't expected him to punch the air in triumph or anything so gauche but his face was unchanged.

'Yes.'

'So can I go?'

'I didn't realise you were in a hurry.'

For the first time during their acquaintance, Josh Derwent smiled at her properly, and it transformed him. 'I have to tell someone the good news.'

The door opened behind him and Roz understood immediately what he meant. It must have shown on her face because he turned to see Maeve standing by the door.

This should be touching.

Roz had time to think it before she noticed Maeve's pallor, or that she wasn't looking at the little group in the middle of the reception area. She was focused on something else.

'Maeve.' Derwent snapped her name as if he was really annoyed with her, Roz noted. Maybe she had been wrong about their relationship too. There seemed to be a lot that she had got wrong.

Maeve ignored him anyway, leaning to one side to see past the three of them.

Derwent turned, frowning, trying to guess what had caught her attention.

'If you want, you can go,' Roz began, then trailed off. She wasn't sure what was going on but she understood that some wordless communication had taken place between the two of them. They were both focused, both alert, and she had no idea why. Cowell was on her left, solid and still and apparently oblivious. A glance to her right: the tracksuited woman was half-asleep, leaning heavy-eyed against the wall. It had to be the man standing at the reception desk who was holding their attention, but Roz didn't understand that quite yet, even though she looked straight at him. He was fishing for something at the bottom of the bag he held. A small man, Roz saw, with wispy hair and stooped shoulders. She turned to see that Derwent was focused on Maeve again, watching her as she started towards the desk. A handful of seconds had passed since Maeve walked in, no more than that, but time seemed to have slowed, and it was what she was looking at that mattered, that was the danger... Derwent pivoted on one foot, reached out and pulled Roz towards him, away from the long knife that flashed silver as the man slashed through the air once, twice, and Roz still didn't understand what was happening.

'My son. I want to know what happened to my son.' The words were panted, distorted. Henry Cowell had caught on quicker than Roz. The edge of the blade snagged in his sleeve before the police officer dragged himself free and went low, driving towards the man to tackle him as if they were playing rugby. Derwent shoved Roz left, out of his way, and she collided with Maeve who went down under her, both of them sprawling on the floor. She was vaguely aware of Derwent stepping over them, taking a long stride to where Cowell had pressed the man against the reception desk. The way Cowell was bent, he had left himself vulnerable to a stab in the back or the neck, Roz saw with a rush of anxiety, but Derwent had noticed it too. He caught hold of the attacker's arm, twisting it up and away from Cowell, and that was better. His fingers slipped on the waterproof coating of the anorak: he didn't have a good grip. Roz watched the blade. She had no idea how Derwent would disarm the man: if he grabbed the blade, the knife would slide through his skin with that sharp serrated edge, and he still wouldn't have it under control. His left hand caught and covered the man's hand instead, gripping tightly where he held the handle, and Derwent squeezed as hard as he could, pressing the man's fingers against the solid plastic until he cried out, until he wanted to drop the knife, until it was impossible for him to hold on to it any longer.

On the CCTV afterwards it looked easy and inevitable. At the time, it was anything but easy. It was a fight, with all the awkward shifting of advantage and all the possible outcomes.

Cowell shoved his shoulder into the man's stomach, and Derwent twisted away from the rush of air that came out of his mouth. The man's eyes were wild behind thick glasses, his face contorted as if he'd had a stroke. Stubble coated his thin, lined cheeks.

'My son.'

'I know,' Derwent managed to say. Two of them and he still wasn't giving up. It wasn't as if Derwent was small, and neither was Cowell. What motivated this man was more powerful than either of them, and it was going to get someone killed, Roz thought, slipping sideways as Maeve squirmed out from under her.

'My son.' His eyes were watery now. 'My son.'

Derwent put his mouth next to the man's ear and said something.

It was like turning a key in a dusty, stiff lock; there was resistance, and the growing conviction that it wouldn't work, and then a sudden capitulation. The fight went out of him, and he sagged. The door by the reception desk came open and the cavalry arrived in the shape of some large uniformed officers who were ready to lay hands on anyone, everyone. Derwent took charge of the knife and stepped back, breathing hard, as Cowell unfolded himself.

'Make sure they don't hurt him,' Derwent said to Cowell, nodding to the uniformed officers who were grappling with the man. Then he turned towards Maeve and Roz, slipping on the tiled floor as he moved. He glanced down and his face went blank.

Blood.

A lot of it – too much of it – smudged and smeared where he had stepped in it.

'Maeve?' he said.

She was on her knees beside Roz, who held on to her.

'You're hurt?' There was something in his voice that made Roz want to cry. Maeve looked up at him.

'Not me. It's her. She's bleeding and I can't find where it's coming from.'

Who was bleeding? Roz wanted to look around, to see, but her arms felt heavy and her head was dull. Maybe the woman wearing slippers. She should go and help. That was what the police did. That was why she had become one.

Josh Derwent crouched beside Roz and put his arms around her, supporting her weight, cradling her against him. She felt as floppy as a rag doll. It should have been awkward that he was holding her, Roz thought hazily. She shouldn't have felt comforted.

'Check her back. He was behind her when he started waving the knife around.' He moved so he could see Roz's face, leaning away from her. 'Hey. Look at me. Open your eyes. *Look at me.*'

Her eyelids were so heavy. 'Leave me alone.'

'No, Roz. I'm not going to do that.'

She blinked, focusing on him. 'What's going on?'

'Josh.' Maeve's voice was low. He leaned to see and Roz watched his mouth tighten.

'What is it? Am I hurt?'

He shook his head. 'It's not bad.'

All Roz could see around them was blood – so much of it, streaks and pools on the tiles. 'Who else is hurt?' No one answered her. 'Is that all from me?'

'Give me your fleece,' Derwent said, low, and Maeve unzipped her top. He wadded it into a ball and pressed it against Roz's lower back.

'Come on. Let's get you onto the chair. Only one chair in here and I think you've earned it, Roz.'

'What?' She didn't resist as he lifted her and settled her onto the chair. He knelt in front of her, looking into her eyes as he kept up the pressure on her back.

'Just stay calm and breathe. The paramedics will be here before you know it.'

'Henry.' Roz was thinking of his neck, his skin inviting the blade. How vulnerable he had been.

'He's fine.' A glance over his shoulder seemed to confirm it. Roz couldn't see that far. The world was fading. She felt cold. There was only this man in front of her. His eyes were steady. Reassuring.

'Don't worry about him. Just look at me, Roz.' He sounded so sure of what he was saying. 'Everything's going to be fine.'

50

'Do you think she'll be all right?'

'Hmm? Honestly, I have no idea.' Derwent was standing on the steps of the police station, looking after the ambulance that was swaying away, lights on and sirens blaring. It was taking Roz Fuller to the nearest hospital at top speed, Henry Cowell in shock beside her.

There was a streak of dried blood on Derwent's cheek, and across his shirt, and the knees of his trousers were saturated from where he'd knelt in front of Roz to hold her together. He was standing next to me but he seemed remote, lost in his own thoughts.

'You sounded sure when you were talking to her.'

He blinked, coming back to me from wherever he had been. 'Funny. She thought I was lying to her from the start, and that was the only time.'

'You were so nice.'

He gave me a crooked smile. 'It was my last chance to win her over. I couldn't resist it.'

I shook my head. 'That wasn't it.'

'No?'

'You wanted her to go gently, if she was going. She was scared and confused and you wanted to make her feel safe, even if she wasn't.'

He looked down, as close to awkward as he ever got. 'You know me too well.'

'Well enough.'

'Come here.' He pulled me against him, wrapping his arms around me and holding me so tightly I almost protested. I could feel his heart beating through the thin shirt, the heat of his body warming me up for the first time that day.

'I thought it was you, you know that.' His mouth was buried in my hair.

'I know. But you'd made very sure I was out of harm's way. I hit the floor hard.'

'Sorry about that.' He didn't sound it.

'I should have expected it.'

'Why?'

'You don't remember the first case we worked on together?'

'I remember it.'

'I ended up with stitches thanks to you pushing me out of your way.'

'For your own good. Someone has to keep you out of trouble since you don't listen. You couldn't just stay in the car, could you?'

'I knew I was going to get in trouble for that – seriously, Josh, I can't breathe . . .' He let go of me and I dusted myself off, embarrassed. 'I had to do something.'

'Like run into the nick unarmed and tackle him without asking for help from anyone.'

'I didn't have time,' I said, defensive.

'Did you know he was armed?'

'I thought he was. That's why I ran after him.'

'See? Trouble. You can't resist it.' He was looking amused and a little sad, I thought. 'It makes you a good colleague, Maeve, but you are not a relaxing person to be around.'

'You'd have done exactly the same. You don't even like Roz Fuller and you'd have got between her and the knife if you'd had time.'

A fact. He acknowledged it and let it go. 'I think I could have liked her if she wasn't ruining my life.'

'Did you hear his story?'

'Who?'

'The guy with the knife. Peter Queensbury.'

I leaned against the wall to tell him what the receptionist had told me while the paramedics were shut away with Roz, trying to save her life: that his son, aged thirty-one, had died in custody from a previously undiagnosed heart condition six months earlier and he had been visiting the police station more or less daily to ask to speak to the officers who had dealt with him, to see CCTV footage, to make complaint after complaint. 'They've been nothing but supportive to him but there isn't any hidden information for him to uncover. Kieran Queensbury was left on his own because there was no reason to think he was in any danger. He wasn't taking drugs. He wasn't drunk. He had no risk factors for suicide and there's no evidence he attempted it. He was arrested on suspicion of stealing from his employer and lay down for a sleep once he was in the cell. When they went to wake him up for his interview, he was dead.'

Derwent sucked in a breath. 'Poor bloke.'

'Who? Kieran?'

'And his dad.'

'What did you say to him?' I asked.

'When?'

'You know when. Whatever made him give up.'

'I thought you were too busy to notice.'

'I noticed.'

'Of course you did.' He shoved his hands in his pockets, embarrassed, looking away from me. 'I said I'd die for my son too but he wouldn't want me to.'

'For Luke?'

'I was thinking of Thomas, but yes. Both of them.' He glanced up at me. 'I know he's not mine, and I know he has his real dad back, but Thomas feels more like mine than he ever did before.'

'He always will be.'

'I don't want to lose him, Maeve.'

And that was the whole story, in a nutshell: that was why he hadn't wanted to take Melissa on, why he had backed away from confronting her about the lies she had told. Melissa had him exactly where she wanted him. He hadn't stood a chance.

I tried to smile, to hide my thoughts, and said almost at random, 'Who else would you die for? Am I on your list?'

'Not if I could help it.'

It hurt more than I might have expected, and it must have shown because his face softened. He reached out and drew his thumb over my cheek.

'Come on, Maeve. I wouldn't think twice.' He looked down at my clothes, which were also stiff and damp with blood, as if he hadn't said anything remarkable. 'What do you want to do? Are you going to get changed?'

'I was going to go to my parents' house and find something to wear there.'

'Good idea. I'll make sure we're not needed here and then I'll drop you off.'

'You could come too. I'm sure Dad would have something you could wear. And they'd love to see you.' It seemed important somehow that he shouldn't go off on his own, after everything that had happened. He had been damned and reprieved. He had tackled Peter Queensbury without fear or hesitation, and held Roz Fuller while her blood pulsed out from the small, wicked wound in her lower back. He had absorbed a lot of punishment that day, one way or another.

'Well you can forget that.' Derwent stretched, as if he was waking up. 'I'm not wearing your dad's clothes.'

'What? He has some lovely slacks and sweaters.'

'He's a wonderful person, but his fashion choices are questionable.'

I snapped my fingers. 'What about Jena Road? You must still have some stuff there.'

'I don't want to go there.' An instant, unpremeditated reaction.

'She's not there. No one is.'

He shook his head. 'I can't.'

'I nearly died in your flat and you made me go back and live in it.'

That dragged his eyes to mine. 'Ouch.'

'Yeah, it was brutal of you.' I patted his arm. 'Come on. I'll even come in with you if you like.'

* * *

I came downstairs in my parents' house after a long shower and heard voices from the kitchen. I found Derwent leaning against the counter talking to my parents, who were sitting at the table. He had insisted on dropping me off before he went to Jena Road and I had said goodbye, not expecting to see him again.

He stopped talking to grin at me when I walked in.

'What are you doing here?'

'I forgot to ask you if you wanted a lift.'

'I'm going to stay here tonight.' I needed the comfort of home instead of being alone in the flat, thinking about the dazed look in Roz Fuller's eyes.

He nodded, as if he understood. 'How old is that sweatshirt?'

'Ancient.' I picked fluff off the Welcome to Maine logo. I had bought it on holiday in America when I was seventeen, which was not information he needed to know. 'The jeans are even older.'

He leaned sideways, eyeing the jeans that were at least a size too small so they clung to my legs as if they were sprayed on, and said nothing. He didn't have to. His expression was saying everything.

'Look, there's a reason I left these clothes here.'

'You could always get rid of them,' my mother said helpfully. 'Give them to charity.'

'I like them,' I said with dignity. 'They remind me of happy times.'

'Even though I'm enjoying this insight into young Maeve a lot' – Derwent put his mug in the dishwasher – 'I'd better make a move. Thank you for the tea.'

'Of course,' Mum said lovingly. 'You know you're always welcome.'

He nodded, and bent to kiss her on the cheek. His voice was gruff as he muttered, 'I appreciate it, Aileen.'

'Do you have to go already?' I sounded wistful and it made my mother peer at me, while my father cleared his throat and offered everyone – anyone – another piece of cake.

Derwent ignored me and said goodbye to them, declining the cake with real regret. I trailed out to the hall after him.

'I thought you might stay a while longer.'

'I should get home to Luke.'

'Why? Does he get upset if you're not there in time for his bedtime story?'

He raised his eyebrows. 'Tetchy.'

'Well, you hung around until I came downstairs.' I pushed my hair behind my ear, suddenly self-conscious about leaving it down. 'Then you suddenly had to go.'

'You used to hurry me out of here in case your parents shared privileged information about your childhood.'

'I'm not sure there's much you don't know at this stage.'

'There's always something.' He smiled at me and I felt my heart break.

'I'm going to miss you.' I blurted it out, and was immediately appalled. Ah, the familiar hot-cold horror of having spoken the truth without thinking of the consequences.

'We'll still be working together. You'll see me most days.'

'It's not the same.'

'No, and it shouldn't be. You know how it is. Things change.'

'Do they?'

'Sometimes they should.'

'But now that you aren't under investigation anymore, and you and Melissa have broken up . . .'

'I can't. I'm sorry.'

Can't. Don't want to. Whichever was true, the outcome was the same. It occurred to me with a lurch of unease that he had turned up because he wanted to say goodbye to my parents. Thomas would be living with Mark now. Derwent didn't need to live in that part of London anymore; he could go anywhere.

And he wouldn't be part of my life, outside of work. He would retreat behind a high wall and I would never see the real him again.

He took hold of my arm and pushed my sleeve back, looking down at the graze. 'I'm sorry about this, too.'

'It wasn't your fault. It's really nothing.'

His mouth tightened. 'I don't like you being hurt.'

'I'm fine. You can't protect me from everything, you know. I have to be able to live.'

'You're right. I should have let you take your chances with the bloke with the knife.'

I shivered. 'It keeps coming back to me that Roz is in hospital, in surgery.'

'I called earlier and spoke to Cowell. She's hanging on.'

'That might have been me. Or you. I think that's why I don't want you to leave. I can't talk to my parents about it – they worry enough as it is.'

He let go of my arm and tugged my sleeve down gently. 'You should talk to Owen. Let him look after you.'

'I don't want to.' I sounded sulky.

'Dressing like a teenager, behaving like a teenager . . .' He grinned. 'Is it being under your parents' roof or is this a reaction to danger?'

'You're so annoying.'

'Why don't you call your boyfriend and tell him about it?' He opened the front door. 'Goodnight, Maeve.'

Teenage me would never have allowed him to have the last word. Present-day me stood in silence and watched him leave.

51

I had not previously considered myself a vindictive person. However, when I got a phone call from one of the detectives investigating Melissa, asking me to make a statement, I couldn't have said yes with more enthusiasm. I had taken a day off already to prepare for Owen's Christmas party, so I didn't have to explain where I was going, to Derwent or anyone else.

Not that it was exactly difficult, currently, to get away with doing whatever I wanted under Derwent's nose. It was easier to swing that than it had been at any other time when we'd worked together, I thought with an unhappy sigh, watching the hairdresser blow-dry my hair into sleek, sleek waves. Ten days had passed since Derwent had let me down gently, and since then I'd barely seen him. He was burying himself in work, I understood, and I further understood that he had said all he wanted to say to me about us. The longest conversations we had were about Roz Fuller, who was still recovering in hospital. I had been to see her once, only staying for five minutes because she was clearly in pain. On my way out I bumped into Henry Cowell, who told me Derwent had been in touch with him every day, checking up on Roz.

'And on me. He told me to speak to someone about what happened. A counsellor.'

I thought that was a good call. Cowell had lost weight and his eyes were bloodshot. He tried to smile. 'He's been kind. But I should have done more. I didn't even know she was hurt.'

'It all happened so fast.'

'That's what they always say. I was more worried about whether Queensbury was going to get beaten up when the uniforms arrived.'

'Which was also worth worrying about,' I pointed out. 'You didn't let her down, Henry.'

'I feel like I did.'

I knew what he meant, and I knew it would take time to get over it. I still thought about it more than I liked. I still saw her face – her fear. You couldn't listen to that fear and do the job but we all had it, somewhere.

I had been on one further date with Owen, and found a reason not to go home with him, which he had accepted with obvious puzzlement. I still wasn't sure if I liked him enough to take things further, and I was going to have to make a decision soon. Still, I had bought a dress for the Christmas party, and I was putting in the effort by getting my hair done. I was giving it my best shot, because if Josh Derwent hadn't existed, Owen could have been making me very happy.

At a Met office building in Vauxhall, DC Sandra Bulling took my statement about Melissa with clear-eyed efficiency. She was a motherly woman with no make-up on her freckled, unlined skin and the kind of precision bob that needs redoing every four weeks. We were about three and a half weeks into the current one and little commas of hair stuck out here and there, which I found endearing.

When I got to the end of my statement, she nodded. 'That's all very helpful, thank you.'

'Happy to help. Is it going OK?'

A professional smile; I wasn't going to get anything out of her. 'I need to get one bit of paperwork finalised. Could I ask you to wait in the hall until I've got myself organised?'

'Of course.' I went out and leaned against the wall, thinking about Melissa, and how thoroughly she had baffled the men in her life. I'd tried to sound impartial when I was talking to Sandra Bulling – 'she comes across as very credible . . .' – while making it as clear as I could that she lied when it suited her. I had a fair idea that Melissa had been telling everyone who would listen that I was bitter and malevolent and had made the whole thing up. I had to try to counter that narrative somehow, while conveying that she was capable of lying to anyone, at any time, about anything.

The double doors at the end of the corridor swung open and two women walked through them, one carrying a briefcase and wearing a suit. Solicitor and client, I thought as I glanced at them, then did a double take as I realised the client was Melissa herself. She stopped dead when she recognised me.

'What are you doing here?'

'The same as you, I imagine.' I folded my arms, outwardly unruffled. She was looking terrible, with blue shadows under her eyes. Always petite, she was now edging towards gaunt. When I thought about all she had lost in the previous weeks, I could understand it. She had suffered. I felt suddenly, shockingly sorry for her, and hardened my heart, because she had brought about her own problems and, worse, inflicted them on people I cared about.

'We're not here for the same reason,' she snapped, 'because you're here to tell lies and I'm telling the truth.'

'Melissa,' the solicitor said: a warning.

Melissa put a hand to her head, her fingers trembling. 'I always knew you hated me, but I didn't know how far you'd go to destroy my life.'

Say something. Say nothing. I weighed it up. What did I have to lose?

'You did that all by yourself. You should be pleased. You've always wanted to be the victim and now you are.'

'Of course you're taking Josh's side, because you want him to pick you.'

'It's got nothing to do with that.' I gave a careless shrug, knowing it would annoy her. I wasn't arrogant by nature, but I could fake it when I needed to. 'Anyway, he already picked me. That's why you had to do something drastic to keep him. I didn't think you'd drag your son into it but I should have known you'd go to any lengths to get your own way.'

'This is inappropriate,' the solicitor said, and Melissa put a hand on her arm.

'It's all right, Barbara. I know it's hard to hear someone telling lies about me, but I'm used to it. The truth will come out.'

'I hope it does,' I said pleasantly. I had been taking in the details of her outfit: a short skirt, tights, ankle boots, a fluffy jumper. She looked delicate and unthreatening. It was hard to believe anyone so fragile could cause any damage at all. 'Did you hear that Thomas is doing much, much better? He hasn't been unwell at all since he started living with Mark. No more hospitals. No trips to A&E.'

'That's got nothing to do with being away from me. He needs me.'

'You were hurting him.'

'I wasn't.'

'I know what you did.' I peeled myself off the wall, abandoning the fiction that I was relaxed. 'It could only have been you, Melissa. You wanted him to need you. You wanted Josh to suffer, and Mark being miserable as well was a bonus. You were sick of coming second to the job, weren't you? And you tried to get Josh to put you first – I heard you talking to him on the phone, you know, so I know the way you used to scream at him – but he's not the sort of person you can bully. You had to find a different way to get at him.'

'It wasn't me,' Melissa said, sullen.

'It could only have been you. Just as you were the only one there all the times you pretended Josh was hurting you. If it wasn't for Clara's perfect record of when you showed her your bruises, you would have got away with it and Josh would have lost his job. He would have gone to prison. You know that, don't you?'

'Shut up,' Melissa said.

'You wanted him humiliated, publicly. You wanted to take away everything that was important to him. That was the plan. And if it wasn't for Clara, you might have succeeded.'

'But of course you were there to point it out. You've always been there, ruining everything.' Melissa's voice had risen. 'What chance did I have when you spent all day with him? Nights, too? You knew everything he was thinking, everything that was worrying him – all the things that he wouldn't share with me. He shut me out because he had you, and you *loved* it.'

I was aware of doors opening along the corridor. A man in shirtsleeves stepped out behind her, concerned. He was mid-forties, large, with the kind of complexion that made you worry about his blood pressure.

'We're just colleagues,' I said to Melissa.

She laughed. 'You've never just been colleagues. He was in love with you when he met me and he's still in love with you and I fucking *hate* it. I hate both of you. You're right, I wanted him to suffer. I wanted him to lose sleep over it, over me. I wanted him to cry. I wanted him to *care*. He never lets me see how he feels. Never. It drives me *insane*.'

We had that in common, anyway. I decided it wasn't worth trying to bond with her over it.

The door beside me opened, light spilling into the corridor. I willed Sandra to stay where she was.

'Then what? What was the plan once you'd broken him? Throw him away?'

She looked bewildered. 'No. I love him. I was going to be there for him, through it all. I wanted to look after him.'

'That's deluded,' I snapped.

'It was the only way I could make him need me, not you. He wouldn't have wanted to be around you anymore if you still had your police career and he didn't. That would have hurt him too much. It would have worked,' she added, sulky now. 'But you had to interfere.'

'Was it the same with Thomas? You wanted him to need you.'

'He's always needed me. I'm his mother.'

'But when he was sick he was like your baby again, wasn't he? You'd stay up all night with him. You got him through his bouts of sickness. Everyone commented on what a good mother you are.'

She smiled, thinking about it: a genuinely happy memory rather than the worst time in her life. 'People were kind. But I didn't mind looking after him. I'd have done anything for him. You're not a mother so you wouldn't understand.'

'I certainly don't understand how you could make him sick deliberately.'

She rolled her eyes. 'Stop going on about it. He wasn't that sick.' The change in her tone was like stepping out of the sunlight into deep, dark shadow. 'It didn't do him any lasting harm. I was *careful*.'

'You were careful,' I repeated, making sure everyone had heard it: the solicitor, the man who was standing behind Melissa, Sandra Bulling in the open doorway to my right with her hands full of paperwork.

There was a short, bruised silence while Melissa realised what she had said, and what that meant. She looked around at her solicitor, who was grey with shock.

'She's making it sound as if I hurt Thomas but I didn't. You know that, don't you? Don't let her turn you against me the way she's manipulated everyone else.'

'I think we need to have a conversation in private.'

'No, we don't. Don't overreact,' Melissa snapped.

I felt sorry for the solicitor. Melissa was like a sweet, huge-eyed bush baby until she sank her fangs into you and you realised she'd given you rabies.

Melissa caught sight of the man behind her and started.

'Oh – Geoff. I'm sorry. I didn't know you were there.' A hand went to her hair. 'I – I don't know what you heard, but—'

'You can talk with your solicitor in here, Ms Moore.'

'Ms Moore? That's very formal,' she said jerkily. 'I thought you were happy to call me Melissa.'

He held the door open, waiting for her, not a hint of a smile on his florid face. She walked past him slowly and the solicitor, who had recovered some colour in her cheeks, scuttled after her.

It hadn't been an interview. She hadn't been under caution. It wasn't a proper confession.

It was a lot better than nothing.

To me, the man said, 'I'm DS Cornell. And you are?'

'Maeve Kerrigan.'

'Ah.' Understanding and something that might have been shame. I was not what he had expected, I thought. 'Were you waiting for anything in particular, or . . .'

'I think I have something to sign before I go.' I looked at Sandra, who shuffled rapidly through the pile of forms in her hand and shook her head.

'No, that's fine. I was mistaken. We're all done.'

Geoff Cornell nodded to me and retreated to his office. I turned to Sandra.

'Thank you.'

'I think I should be thanking you.' She eyed the door Cornell had closed behind him. 'He liked her.'

'People do.'

She snorted. 'They shouldn't.'

I was inclined to agree.

52

The office was already emptying out for the day by the time I got back from giving my statement. The timings were tight so I had decided to get changed at work, and had brought my party clothes with me. I hurried into the bathroom, hoping a different outfit would make me feel like a party girl.

The run-in with Melissa had left me shaky. I had rarely seen such loathing in someone's eyes, even when I was an instrumental part in them going to prison for a very long time. And the things she had said burrowed under my skin like parasitic worms. I had done what was right. I had been trying to protect Thomas and Derwent. I hadn't been out to get Melissa – but I'd taken the opportunity to trap her, when I had it. I thought I'd done the right thing, but not necessarily for the right reasons. It didn't make me feel good about myself.

Georgia was in the bathroom, staring at herself critically in the mirror over the sinks. She brightened at the sight of me.

'Ooh, your hair!'

'Yep.'

'Is that your dress?'

'It is indeed. I only have twenty minutes to get changed.' I hung the bag on the back of the door and pointed at the closed cubicle door, mouthing, 'Who?'

'Liv.'

'I'll be out in a minute,' she called.

'What are the two of you up to?'

'Going for a drink with some of the team.' Liv emerged and went to the sink to wash her hands. 'They made arrests in the Russian case, did you hear?'

'No, I didn't. Well done them.'

'You're really pushing the boat out for tonight, aren't you?' Georgia was watching me, assessing my appearance with the kind of intensity she rarely brought to bear on the job.

'Mm. Kind of.' I had been going to get changed where I was, but I wasn't keen for a discussion about the lacy underwear I'd chosen, and why, so I slipped into the cubicle. Georgia would have no compunction about asking if tonight was the night with Owen. Maybe it was. I had no idea.

Climbing into tights was a challenge in a small space and I banged my elbow, twice.

'This is for Owen's Christmas party,' Liv checked.

'That's right. It's in Claridge's.'

Georgia whistled. 'Why don't we have parties in places like that?'

'Do you really have to ask?' I unzipped the garment bag and looked at the dress, wishing I'd chosen something longer, something that covered me from neck to ankles at least. I'd gone for brief and glittery and the opposite of subtle.

'How would Owen cope with drinks in a dingy pub with a load of coppers?' Liv asked.

'He'd be fine. He's good at fitting in. I've never seen him out of place.'

'Then why don't you ask him to come to our Christmas drinks?' Georgia's voice was honeyed with innocence.

I banged my forehead very gently against the cubicle wall. 'I can't believe I walked into that one.'

'Seriously, when are we going to get to meet him?'

I opened the cubicle door, contorting myself to zip up the dress over my hip. 'I don't know. Some time.'

'Wow.' Liv blinked. 'That is a *dress*.'

'Not much of one, considering what it cost.' The jewel-coloured sequins sparkled even in the flat glare of the bathroom lighting. Cap sleeves, a low back, a hem that ended six inches above my knees, a fit that was as snug as if I'd had it sewn to my body. My outfit was ready to party, even if I was not.

'I wish I had legs,' Georgia said.

'Last time I looked, you do.' I was patting on foundation, trying to avoid getting it in my hair. This was not how the get-ready-with-me girls on Instagram prepared for a big night out.

'I don't have legs the way you have legs. I have trotters,' Georgia said sadly, and untruthfully. 'On the other hand I know how to apply concealer.'

'I'm doing my best.' I rubbed at it. 'What time is it?'

'Ten to six.'

I swore under my breath; later than I'd thought.

'So, Owen.'

'I really don't have time for this,' I said, hunting through my make-up bag for mascara. I couldn't have left it out, could I?

'Let me.' Georgia took possession of the make-up bag. 'You tell us about Owen, and I'll do your face.'

'Thanks,' I said, genuinely touched, and she shook her head.

'I can't bear to watch you do it yourself. This is for me. Now close your eyes and tell us everything.'

It was a good thing I was tight for time so the interrogation-slash-makeover didn't last too long. Georgia and Liv headed off to the pub together, pleased with the minute amount I'd told them about Owen that they hadn't known already. I stepped into my heels, took a last look at the transformed me in the bathroom mirror, and went to my desk where I abandoned everything I didn't need for the party. There were a few people still working, dotted around the office. I put my coat on and checked, as subtly as I could, that the coast was clear: no Derwent. I told myself I was glad about that. I didn't want to see Derwent. The Russian mob had saved me from an awkward encounter. Thank you, the Russian mob.

I checked the time as I headed for the door. Three minutes behind schedule. Not bad, considering. I swerved the lift, which was always slow, and slower at that time of day when the building was emptying out. I pushed open the door to the stairwell instead. My heels echoed as I started down the stairs: five flights but it was better than standing around . . .

A door banged on the floor below and a man ran smoothly up the stairs, two at a time, so quickly that we were face to face before I could react – not that I had anywhere to go.

'Maeve.' Derwent checked himself, grabbing on to the handrail in a rare loss of balance. 'I didn't think you were in today.'

'I came here to get changed. I thought you were gone,' I blurted, and wished I'd said nothing. There was no possible follow-up to make it better. *I wasn't hoping to see you. I was glad you had left already.*

'You look nice.'

'Thank you. I was aiming for nice. Good to know I hit the mark.'

He smiled with a kind of superficial pleasantness that stung more than if he'd walked past without a comment. 'Have a good time.'

'I probably will. It's a party. That's what they're for.'

He nodded, and went to move past me, and stopped instead on the step beside me. I was acutely aware of him, of the empty space echoing around us and the gravitational pull he exerted on me. I longed to touch him, to press myself against him like a cat.

Oblivious, Derwent said, 'Just remember, you don't need to be nervous.'

'I'm not nervous,' I began, and stopped. 'I am nervous. You know it's in Claridge's. I don't think I'm going to fit in very well in that world.'

'You will if you let yourself.' He frowned at me. 'You don't have to apologise to anyone for how you are or what you do.'

'No. Thanks.'

His face softened. 'It'll be all right, you know.'

'Are you talking about the party?'

'What else?' He moved up a step, away from me. 'Go on. You don't want to be late.'

'I'm already late.'

'Then you'd better run.'

* * *

Claridge's felt like a fever dream compared to the office: vistas of elegant, understated luxury, disorientating levels of wealth and privilege, hundreds of immaculate staff steering guests in the correct direction given that there were several Christmas functions taking place in the building. I allowed myself to be steered as I compared the lobby and the welcome to the Governor Hotel. The Governor lacked the history and the grandeur of Claridge's – it was understated and international and anonymous in the luxury it offered. The Governor was a place where you could pretend to be anyone you wanted to be.

The party occupied two of the function rooms, an oak-panelled salon and a drawing room that connected to it. Because I was late, most of the guests had arrived already and it was crowded, with a genial buzz of conversation that almost drowned out the string quartet valiantly scraping in the corner. I accepted a glass of champagne from a smiling waiter and looked around for Owen, without success. After sidling through the crowd for a couple of minutes I arrived at the doorway between the two rooms, where I hovered, unsure if I should press on. A familiar dark head caught my eye: Luke, bending over to murmur in the ear of a short girl wearing glasses and a sardonic expression. He straightened and waited for her response, which was an eye-roll and a laugh. She said something else and moved away and he watched her go, his expression comically frustrated, before glancing around, touching his tie, his feelings masked again. When he saw me his face lit up. He hurried over and hugged me.

'You look absolutely beautiful.'

'Thank you.' I indicated the glasses-wearing girl with a wholly deniable gesture of my champagne flute. 'Who is she?'

'Emily. The love of my life.'

'Really?' She was pretty but not outstandingly so: normal, in fact. The dress she was wearing made nothing of her figure, fighting curves instead of showing them off. Her hair was in a ponytail and she had put on eyeliner without any particular skill or care and that was about it for party glamour.

'She's funny. The cleverest woman I've ever met. I love everything about her. I've been after her for months. I just want to . . .' His hands moved as if he was touching her: smitten in every way, I diagnosed, and had to try not to smile.

'And she doesn't feel the same?'

'She doesn't want to get involved because of office gossip. Also, her last boyfriend cheated on her. She doesn't think I'm any different.' He shook his head. 'First time in my life I've wished I was less good-looking.'

'I've lost my tiny violin,' I said earnestly, 'but if I find it I'll play for you.'

'Yeah, it's easy when you're all loved up and happy.'

The champagne in my mouth tasted sour all of a sudden. I put the glass down on a table and he frowned.

'What's wrong?'

'Nothing.'

'Still breaking your heart over Josh?'

'No,' I lied.

'I don't believe you.' Luke sighed. 'I should stay out of this, really. It would be far more sensible for me to pretend I didn't know anything.'

I narrowed my eyes. 'What do you mean? What do you know?'

'Nothing.' Luke jerked his head back in shock. 'Jesus, you're quick.'

'I don't feel quick,' I said. 'I feel as if I've missed something important.'

'You haven't, really.' He bounced on the balls of his feet, uncharacteristically awkward. 'I wish I'd had less champagne.'

'What are you not telling me?'

'Forget I said anything?'

'Not going to happen.'

He sighed. 'I'm going to get in so much trouble. Look, you were right when you said nothing was going to happen between you now.'

'That's what he said too. He said it was all a dream. But it felt real to me.' The sting of tears: I blinked, telling myself to toughen up. I couldn't cry at the party.

Luke winced. 'It's because of me.'

'You?'

'He can see the world I'm living in is different – the money, the lifestyle. He wants that for you. He knows Owen can provide it. As soon as he met him—'

'He *met* him?'

'After football a while ago. Must have been in September, I think. They got talking.' I stood completely still, rearranging my understanding of everything that had happened in the past couple of months. Oblivious, Luke went on, 'Josh asked me to invite you to my birthday drinks and make sure Owen met you. He liked you straight away.'

I felt as if the ground was sliding under my feet. 'Josh set the whole thing up.'

'Not exactly. He made sure the two of you were in the same place. Everything else that happened was up to you.'

Was it, though? I remembered him interrogating me after Ilaria's post-mortem, scowling, sneering at everything I told him. 'He made me defend Owen when he asked about him. And made sure Liv and Georgia and all of my friends knew about Owen so they could encourage me to keep seeing him.'

'Mind games. Did you really expect anything else?' The room went soft around the edges, the lights splintering into starry refraction as my eyes filled, and Luke put his arm around my shoulders. 'Hey, don't cry. He was trying to do the right thing. Thomas was sick and he didn't want you to wait around for him forever.'

'But that wasn't his decision to make for me.' And it couldn't be the whole story, either, because even though Melissa was out of the picture he had made it all too clear that he didn't want me now. I had too much pride to say that to Luke.

'I know it's hard to forgive him for interfering but he wants what's best for you.'

I could see Owen now on the other side of the room, talking animatedly to a couple who were laughing at whatever he was saying. Wealthy, charming, kind, handsome, easy to read, uncomplicated. There was a life for me, if I wanted it, and it would be straightforward. Happy, even.

And all I had ever wanted was to be happy.

'What's best for me,' I repeated, and smiled. 'Do you know what, Luke? I think I've just worked out what that is.'

53

At some point after I pushed through Claridge's elegant revolving door, it had started to rain, and it rained hard. By the time I got back to the office I was soaked to the skin, my coat so cold and damp I was glad to take it off. In the lift mirror I was able to confirm that my hair now hung in tails, the blow-dry a mere memory. I scrubbed the smudged mascara under my eyes and yanked off my wet shoes.

I walked into the office slowly, looking around as I put my belongings on my desk. There was no one there at all now. I scanned the room, seeing empty desks, chairs pushed in tidily. Christmas decorations hung from monitors, the straggling tinsel glinting in the fluorescent lights. The only sound was the low whine of a vacuum cleaner on the floor above. Everyone else was out at the pub, or at parties, or at home, or unlucky enough to be on call and out on a job. And Josh – Josh was gone.

Even as I thought it I realised his suit jacket was hanging on his chair, which didn't mean he was still in the building but it wasn't like him to leave without it. I tried the kitchen and found it was empty, the surfaces covered in crumbs, the sink full of dirty mugs. I hesitated outside the men's room, listening at the door to absolute silence from within.

He had gone.

He had left his jacket and he had gone.

He had—

I heard a small sound from the meeting room, more a disturbance of the air than anything identifiable, and all of my emotions tightened into a small, hard ball of resolve that sat in the pit of my stomach. I walked down the hall, silent with my shoes off, my heart thudding. I had walked down that hallway hundreds of times without thinking about it, but now every step felt significant.

Derwent was standing with his back to me, his hands in his pockets, staring out at the rain. The table was covered in files, one chair pushed away from the table as if he had been too restless to sit there for long. I stayed in the doorway for a moment, thinking about what I wanted to say and how I could say it. Before I was ready, he noticed my reflection in the window and turned.

'Maeve. Are you all right?' Then, with real concern, 'What happened?'

'Nothing. Nothing happened. I just left.'

'What time is it?' He glanced at his watch and raised his eyebrows. 'You can't have been at the party for long.'

'I needed to talk to you.'

'What's wrong?' His expression was guarded now: he knew me well enough to recognise the emotion that was making the sequins on my dress tremble: anger.

'I had a very interesting chat with Luke at the party. About how you met Owen, months ago. About how you decided he would suit me.'

'Maeve . . .'

'Luke told me it was all your idea.'

He looked bored and not remotely apologetic. 'I didn't do all that much. I let Owen know you were single and I told him you were worth the effort. Mind you, I didn't know how much effort he was going to have to put in. I actually felt sorry for him. What does the poor guy have to do to impress you?'

Be someone else. I kept the words in, with difficulty.

'That's not an issue anymore. I ended it.'

He glowered. 'You *what?*'

'Oh, does that annoy you?'

'It's stupid, Maeve.' He shook his head. 'He could give you what you deserve.'

'Because he's rich?'

'And decent. He's perfect for you.' Derwent's eyes were steady. 'Luke likes him, and I rate his opinion.'

'If Luke likes him so much, Luke can go out with him.'

His shoulders slumped half an inch, as if the burden he was carrying was too heavy for him for a moment.

'You lied to me, you manipulative *prick*,' I snapped, furious.

He leaned against the windowsill. 'So what?'

'First of all, how *dare* you? And secondly, what's wrong with you?'

'With *me*?'

'Why would you go to so much trouble to put me off? I know you have feelings for me. I know they're real, whatever you said.'

His expression was sceptical.

'There's no reason for you to keep me at a distance, Josh, except that's what you do. You think you've let people down, so you take the blame and go. You did it with your family, and you've done it in every relationship ever since. You cut yourself off before anyone else gets the chance to do it.'

A blink of surprise: for someone who was a master at keeping his face impassive, he had given himself away.

'You walk away,' I said softly, 'because you think everyone is better off without you.'

'I – well, maybe I do. But you'd have to be out of your mind to pick me over Owen. Or convinced that you owe me something, which you don't.'

I wasn't making any progress. Nothing could budge him when he'd made up his mind.

'You still think you're not good enough for me, don't you? If I had to guess, what settled it for you was when you got arrested. You're ashamed of what happened and how it made you feel to be locked up. And you wouldn't talk about it with me.'

'Leave it.' Anger made his eyes bright.

'Being arrested made you see yourself the way other people see you, and you didn't like it. But whatever you've been through – whatever you're carrying around with you – I'm not afraid of it. I don't think you have anything to be ashamed of.'

I paused, gathering my courage. 'You know me. You know I don't trust anyone. Except you. I trust you, Josh.'

He was completely still, but I knew his mind was racing.

'I don't understand why, because you're *so* annoying, and I'm still absolutely *livid* with you – but you're all I want. You want me to be happy. No one else is ever going to manage that.'

He frowned. 'What makes you think it would be different with me?'

An important question. The only question, really. I took a deep breath.

'Because when I think of the times in my life that I've been happy, it's always with you. Because you can tip the world sideways just by looking at me. Because you're the person I want to talk to about everything that happens to me. Because you're my best friend. Because I feel safe with you. Because when I stand next to you I can barely breathe for wanting you. Because for some stupid reason I'm in love with you, and I can't stop being in love with you no matter how hard I try.'

Halfway through my last sentence – after the first 'love', before the second – he took his hands out of his pockets and started towards me, and by the time I finished he was close enough to kiss me, but instead he moved me back until I collided with the wall behind me. He curled a hand behind my left knee and drew it up, then smoothly slid his palm along my thigh until his fingertips grazed the curve of my bottom. I shivered, clinging to his shirt, wordless.

'You know this is going to change everything, Maeve.' He murmured it, his mouth next to my ear.

'I know,' I managed.

'It's only worth doing if we both want the same thing.'

'What do you want?'

He leaned away so he could look me in the eye. 'Everything. I want everything. And not one day. Right now.'

I'd wanted honesty from him. I'd wanted him to tell me how he felt. I hadn't expected him to be so direct about it.

'That's what I want too.'

'Are you sure?'

I felt as if I was on a roller coaster. Straight to the next stage without a pause for a breath or even a kiss – how absolutely like him.

And he was watching me, I realised – he had deliberately taken things further than I expected. He was waiting for me to pull away, to panic, because no matter what I said, he wouldn't believe me until I showed him I loved him. I gripped his collar, drawing him to me, and I kissed him.

I couldn't help comparing it to the other times he'd kissed me – not many, the memories like treasure I hoarded. The time it was a joke, his mouth on mine to win an argument. The time he was in despair and needed comfort. The time I'd set out to teach him he couldn't resist me and found my own resolve lacking. This was different, I thought. This time there was no reason to pull away – in fact, it was essential not to. One hand was still curled under my thigh, pulling me against him, and the other was holding my face so I was exactly, precisely where he wanted me. He leaned in, pressing me against the wall. My heart thudded and the only coherent thought I had was that I wanted him, even if we were in the office, in the meeting room – there was a floor, wasn't there? A table? A chair, even? Or where we were, against the wall; it was solid enough . . .

A lot of things might have happened next if there hadn't been a noise – the lift doors juddering open, followed by a rattle as the cleaner pushed his trolley down the hallway. We sprang apart and stared at one another, breathless.

He recovered first. 'Not the ideal place for this.'

'No.'

'We should go somewhere else.'

'Your place is nearer.'

'Your place is quieter. Luke will be home at some stage and I don't want to be interrupted.'

'God, no,' I said, and for a moment amusement sparked between us before it faded and we were back to good old-fashioned longing.

He looked me up and down, decisive now. 'Where are your shoes? Did you have a coat? Get them. Come on, hurry up.'

Not the first time he'd ordered me around, I thought, darting to my desk, but the first time it had ever made me feel this fizzing anticipation. I grabbed my things, fumbling my way into my coat while I gave up on the heels and swapped to the flat ballet shoes from my desk drawer. Even though I was rushing he was ready before me, and I was acutely aware of him watching me from the hall, a still, focused presence.

'OK,' I said at last, and pulled my bag onto my shoulder. 'I'm coming.'

'Not yet. Soon,' Derwent said, and grinned.

'*Josh!*'

He was gone, heading to summon the lift. I heard him say goodnight as he passed the kitchen. The cleaner, rattling cups, incurious about us and where we were going. I glanced in as I passed the door and got a nod: he was older than I'd thought, dark-skinned, silent and discreet. I would mention the state of the place to the office manager, I thought; it wasn't fair to leave it like that just because the cleaner was coming in. He had a lot of ground to cover and people were surely capable of washing their own crockery . . .

'OK?' Derwent checked as we stepped into the lift.

'Yep.' I risked a look at him and felt my stomach flip, and the doors closed so we were actually alone, and I wanted . . . I wanted . . .

'CCTV,' Derwent said. He leaned against the wall of the lift, watching me, and his face was serious but his eyes were laughing.

'You're not helping,' I said tightly, and turned away, and then the lift ground to a halt and the doors opened: the fourth floor. A man stepped in, a stranger to me. He glanced at me and nodded to Derwent.

'Josh. How are things?'

'Not bad, Ken,' Derwent said, as if it was an ordinary evening. 'Busy?'

'Always. Actually, I'm glad I saw you. I had a question about something that's come up in a case and I think you might know more about it than me.'

'Happy to help.' Derwent's voice was bland.

The two of them talked work for the rest of the journey to the lobby, and for a couple of minutes afterwards, and I didn't hear a word of it. I kept my distance in the lobby, looking for absolutely nothing in my bag, and at long last Derwent said goodbye to the other man, and held the door open for me, and the two of us headed away from the building together.

54

The rain had stopped but water still coursed through the gutters and sat in puddles on the pavement. The world was turned upside down in each one, shimmering at the edges, gleaming with reflected light.

'We'll get a taxi around the corner.'

He sounded calm, sure of himself, and I was caught between irritation and admiration: was this not a big deal for him? Did he care? Or was he just better at this kind of thing than me? Certainly more used to it . . . I glanced at him again and saw amusement in his eyes, as if he could hear my thoughts.

And my nerves kicked in. I'd understood that he was hiding his feelings from me, no matter what it cost him. I'd understood his self-doubt. What I hadn't anticipated was the split-second change to this single-minded confidence. It was as if I'd gone into the office intending to rescue a timid cat and come out with a fully grown lion. I hadn't expected that he would be so instantly, fearlessly in control, which was stupid. And it was also stupid of me that I hadn't thought about how different he might be if he wasn't holding the world at bay.

When we reached the corner, he stopped. 'What's wrong?'

'I was wondering if I've ever met the real you before.'

He slid a hand inside the collar of my coat, his palm against my neck, his fingers tangled in my hair, and dropped a brief kiss on my mouth. 'Once or twice.'

A warm feeling blossomed in my chest, and I couldn't speak. For an instant he allowed himself a smile of pure, heart-shaking triumph. Then he turned to flag down a black cab, ushering me into it and settling at the other end of the back seat. I put my hand down on the seat for balance as the cab moved away, and my little finger brushed against his. The contact was electric and I snatched my hand away instinctively. We stared at one another. The cab was accelerating through the streets, a small dark space suddenly humming with tension, and anticipation, and impatience. The same thought, shared. *I want you.* He looked away first, staring out of the window, his profile frustratingly uncommunicative. I turned away myself and watched the streets sliding past in a haze of bright lights that dazzled through the wet glass.

I lost track of where we were or how long we had been in the cab, as if time and distance had no real meaning anymore, and it was a surprise when the driver pulled in and flicked on the interior lights.

'Go and open the door,' Derwent said to me. I slid out past him, leaving him to pay. The night air was cold on my skin and smelled of rain. All down the road Christmas lights swung in the wind, spangling the trees, and sparkled inside windows, but no one else was around. I dug in my bag for my keys then dropped them and had to grope for them in the darkness. The hum of the engine drowned out the conversation between the two men, and at last Derwent said something to the cabbie that made him laugh. He tooted his horn before he drove away at speed, and I found the bunch of keys but still couldn't manage to find the right one for the first lock, and Josh was coming up the path behind me, and then I had the key but I was shaking too much to use it . . .

He was shaking his head.

'What's wrong?'

'The driver asked me if we'd had a row because we didn't talk to one another.'

'I couldn't.'

'I know.'

'What did you say to him?' I was half curious, half suspicious.

'I said it was the opposite of a row.'

'And what did he say?'

'He told me I was a lucky git, which I knew already, and to wear a condom.'

'Helpful.'

He shrugged. 'I knew that already too. I told him to mind his own business. What's the problem here?'

'Lack of coordination.' I held out the keys to him and he made no move to take them.

'Pull yourself together and open it.'

I wanted to argue with him, to throw the keys at his chest and see if he caught them, but I thought about why he was saying it, and what he meant.

If you really want this, and you're sure, make it happen.

I took a deep breath, calmed my racing heart and opened the door, the keys turning smoothly in the locks, and I stepped inside and made it as far as the other side of the hallway before I had to lean against the wall.

'Now.' My voice was a whisper. 'This will do.'

He shut the door behind him and switched the light on. 'Absolutely not.' A conversational tone, as if we were discussing whose turn it was to make tea.

'Why not?'

'There's a perfectly decent bed upstairs.'

'Please,' I found myself saying. And then, 'The first time's never good anyway.'

He raised his eyebrows politely, shrugging his coat off and hanging it on the end of the stairs. 'Isn't it?'

'Everyone's too nervous to enjoy it.'

I could have kicked myself after I'd said it: I could tell from the way his expression shifted to something more gentle that I'd given myself away – assuming he had ever been fooled in the first place.

'But it doesn't matter. I mean, I don't mind if I don't – if you . . . it's fine. I don't expect – because it might not be easy for me to . . .' I stopped, aware that I was making it worse. 'It might take me some time to get used to this.'

'I'm not in a hurry.' He slid his jacket off too and hung it on top of the coat, then held out his hand. 'Let's go upstairs.'

'I can manage the stairs by myself.' My worst quality, spikiness, surfacing at the wrong time. I was going to ruin this for us, I thought, and knotted my fingers together from sheer anxiety. What if it wasn't how I wanted it to be? What if I wasn't what he wanted after all? 'Also, you don't have to take charge.'

He let his hand drop to his side. 'I know.' As if he'd said it out loud, I knew what he was thinking. *But I'm going to.*

He let me go past him and followed me up the stairs, leaving a respectable gap between us. In the bedroom, he went over to the chest of drawers and started taking off his watch, concentrating on it as if his mind was elsewhere. I stood by the bed, uncertain. I watched him unlace his shoes and pull them off, putting them neatly side by side. He wasn't following the script I'd had in my head. I had counted on him to hurry us both through this next part, because I wanted to get it over with.

'Josh?'

'Mm.' He glanced over his shoulder, rolling up one sleeve. 'You look as if you're steeling yourself to do something unpleasant.'

'Well,' I said. 'No. But you're not making it easy for me.'

'In what way?'

'You aren't sweeping me off my feet.'

'I know you said you wanted this now, but I wanted you to know' – he moved on to the second cuff, frowning down at it – 'if you want to back out, you can. You can call a halt at any time if you're not sure. We can do this another time, or never if you prefer that, and I won't mind.'

'Because you don't care?'

A glance up at me. 'Because I do.'

'I am sure,' I said, trying to sound it, and failing. 'And I've never been afraid to say I don't want to do something.'

Another look, one that made me blush. 'Then take your clothes off.'

My choice: up to me how far I went.

Everything. And not one day. Now.

I slid my coat off, then unzipped my dress and left it on the floor with my shoes and tights, but stopped there; I wasn't ready for full nudity. He turned around to face me, and smiled in appreciation of the lace underwear which did something to help my nerves.

'You don't seem to be getting undressed, I notice.' I was striving to sound calm.

'Not yet. I have something else to do first.' He crossed the room – a few steps but they were as conclusive as if he was walking off a cliff.

No way back.

I put my arms around his neck so we could fall together.

55

Not very long after that, more or less as soon as the rest of my clothes came off and Josh touched me, I was caught out by a light ripple of sheer pleasure that left me flustered.

'Told you so.'

'That – that doesn't count.'

'Oh really.' His mouth was muffled against my skin. 'Are we keeping count?'

'Yes. And that was too easy.'

'Too easy.'

'Too quick.'

'That' – he reached to kiss my neck under my ear – 'was the result of years of anticipation.'

'Years of what? Years of you being maddening, maybe—'

He moved his hand and I forgot what I was going to say next, which was one way to win an argument.

'Let's see if we can make the next one count,' he murmured.

'You're quite good at this, aren't you?'

'Only quite good.'

'Very good. Gifted. Talented. Thorough.'

I felt him laugh. 'I've practised.'

'Of course you have. They say it takes ten thousand hours to become an expert at anything.'

'It's been at least ten thousand hours. Maybe more.'

'Well, thanks for putting in the time and effort.'

'With any luck I'm going to spend the next ten thousand hours becoming an expert on *you*.'

'Fine by me. Now will you take the rest of your clothes off?'

'In a minute.'

'Josh, I'm losing patience.'

He chuckled. 'Standard.'

Well, if he wouldn't cooperate . . . I managed to get two buttons of his shirt undone before he caught my wrists and pinned them against the bed.

'Not yet.'

'Why not?' I tested how firmly he was holding me: like he meant it. 'Don't tell me you have a thing about making me beg.' Not that it was completely out of the question . . .

He shook his head. 'You still want to hurry. That's not what I want you to be thinking the first time.'

'Oh. What should I be thinking?'

'Absolutely nothing.'

Doubt caught me. I felt exposed in a way that had nothing to do with being naked. Maybe I couldn't do this after all. 'That's – that's not easy for me.'

'I know.' He let go of me, watching me gather myself together. 'So we're doing this slowly.'

I focused on the top button of his shirt, unable to look him in the eye. 'And this involves you still wearing most of your clothes because . . .'

'I don't trust you not to try and hurry things up.' He grinned lazily. 'And I don't trust myself not to go along with it if you do.'

'Oh, I see.' I felt better. 'It's a you problem.'

'It's not a problem at all.' He kissed me and sent his hand skimming over my skin. My body responded instantly, aching for him, taut with longing as soon as my brain got out of the way.

'Leave it to me,' he said, very quietly. 'I know what I'm doing.'

Gradually, I coaxed him out of everything he was wearing and discovered, to my delight, that he was easy to distract, that I could make his eyelids flutter and his breath catch if I chose, that he sometimes made a low sound at the back of his throat from pure pleasure as I explored new territory. And eventually, I understood what he meant about not thinking, because I was fully occupied with feeling.

'Now.'

He waited. 'Sure?'

'Very sure. Extremely sure. But *now*.'

Oh.

My.

God.

'Fine. You were right.'

'Of course I was. About what?'

'It's possible for the first time to be good.'

'Oh, that.' His arm tightened around me, pulling me even closer. 'What's your theory about second times?'

'There's generally too much showing off. It's not until the third time that you find out how it's going to be between you.'

'I see.'

I twisted to look at him. 'Don't tell me you're actually agreeing with me.'

'No, but I've no objection to testing the theory.'

'Not yet.'

'No?' There was the faintest hint of concern in his expression, and I smiled.

'Nothing's wrong. I want to ask you something first, that's all.'

'Go on.'

'When did you decide this should happen?'

He lay back to stare at the ceiling, considering it. 'The first time I saw you, I wanted you, obviously.'

'Obviously,' I agreed.

'Then there was what happened the first day we worked together.'

My main memories of that day were one horror after another, not least the music he'd chosen to listen to. 'What happened then?'

'I fell absolutely, totally in love with you.'

So straightforward, after years of hiding his feelings: no equivocating, nothing but honesty.

I laughed. 'Why did you fall in love with me *then*? The way I remember it, you were terrifying and I was sulky.'

He settled his head into the pillow, contented. 'Just you being you. I'll tell you the details some other time. The only thing that really matters was that I knew it was for keeps.'

'You hid it well.'

'You were off limits.'

'Because the boss had told you to stay away from me or because I was already in a relationship?'

'As if either of those things would have stopped me. No, because I wasn't right for you then either.' He reached out and traced the curve of my waist, his fingers trailing up over my hip and down my thigh. 'I had a long way to go.'

'Did you deliberately behave badly to put me off?' I was thinking of the sexist jokes, the sneering, the ceaseless needling and all-round poor attitude he had displayed.

'Sometimes. I couldn't risk you falling for me.'

'Because otherwise I wouldn't have been able to resist.'

He glanced down, examining the way I was wrapped around him. 'Evidently not.'

'You were obnoxious because you like being obnoxious.'

'That too.' A fact, simply stated. What had I said? *I was wondering if I've ever met the real you before.* I had, and in spite of it, or because of it, I wanted him. I wriggled, trying to get even closer to him. Amused, he slid a helpful hand behind me to pull me against him. 'What about you? When did you know?'

'Well, it wasn't love at first sight.'

He grinned. 'No, it was not.'

'On the other hand, I would have denied it if anyone had asked, and I even denied it to myself, but I thought you were extremely attractive from the beginning.'

'Did you?' The grin widened.

'Too attractive. Risky. A bad idea.'

'Sounds about right. And then?'

'I didn't like you.'

'I remember.'

'But even when I didn't like you,' I said, wanting to be fair, 'I knew you'd never let me down. Even when you were being maddening, you were on my side.'

'Always.'

'Then . . . I don't know. When I was with you, I was happy, and when I wasn't with you, I was counting down until the next time we would be together.' I sat up so I could look at him, leaning on my elbow with my chin on my hand. His eyes were narrowed with affection this time. I luxuriated in the full sweep of his lower lip, the deep contentment that had transformed his face. 'When you found me, when I was hurt, I knew everything was going to be all right, because you were there. And in the hospital, do you remember I said I loved you?'

'I do remember that, believe it or not. But I knew you didn't mean it.'

'Oh, I meant it. I just didn't know what to do about it. And you weren't free to be with me then, so it didn't matter anyway.' I traced the line of his cheek with my fingertips, still almost awed that I could. 'I really tried not to fall in love with you.'

'I promised myself I wouldn't tell you how I felt.'

'Total failures.'

He kissed my shoulder, working his way along my collarbone slowly, and I edged away from him.

'What now?' He sounded both resigned and amused.

'I want to ask you something else.'

'Anything.'

'It's work,' I clarified. 'It's about Ilaria Cavendish.'

'Of course it is.' He slid his arm under his head, readying himself to listen.

'You don't mind?'

'I'd have been disappointed if it wasn't.' With his other hand he tucked the duvet around me. 'That's so I can concentrate. But I warn you, if you want to have sex with someone else while I watch, I'm not keen.'

'Ugh. No, it was something that happened earlier, when we were leaving the office.'

'Ken, the guy in the lift?'

'Before that.'

He frowned. 'You told me I was an emotional failure who ran away from difficult relationships.'

'After that.' I watched one eyebrow slide up and nudged him. 'After *that*.'

'You got your things. We left.'

'You said goodnight to the cleaner.'

'Oh.' He thought about it. 'He was in the kitchen.'

'What did he look like?'

There was a short silence. 'IC3 male, about five foot six. Slight build. West African accent. Probably fifty-five or thereabouts.'

'Features?'

Derwent shook his head. 'He was turned away, working. I didn't give him a lot of thought.'

'You noticed more than most people would.'

'What did you notice that I didn't?'

'Nothing, actually. And that's the point.'

He sighed. 'Maeve . . .'

'I know.'

'Tell me why it's important.'

'Not yet. I'm beginning to have an idea, that's all.'

'Is that really what you've been thinking about?'

'Not most of the time. In the cab, a bit. Not during.'

'I should hope not.' He pulled the duvet free. 'Now I want your full attention, Sergeant.'

'You can't pull rank on me here,' I protested, and he slid his hand along my leg from my knee to my hip, his thumb tracing a straight line down the inside of my thigh.

'You're the one who brought work into it.'

'My mistake,' I managed to say before I forgot about everything except him.

I had set my alarm at some point, with a vague awareness that tomorrow would come and with it responsibilities like work, but I opened my eyes a minute before it was due to ring and switched it off. I didn't want to disturb Josh. He was fast asleep beside me, sprawled across two thirds of the bed. I looked down at him as I slid out from under the covers, feeling a new, enjoyable sense of ownership. The scars, small and large, the muscles that shifted when he moved, the faded tan lines from the summer: his body told the story of his life and I wanted to hear it again and again. A story that was only for me, I thought, suddenly possessive. *Mine.* My own body hummed, every inch of me tingling. Not enough sleep – not nearly enough – but I didn't care.

I pulled on a dressing gown and went to the kitchen: two mugs, two teabags, a smile I couldn't seem to wipe off my face. I looked at my reflection in the window, where the darkness of night was lightening to navy blue, and felt made new. He wasn't like anyone else I'd been with. I'd expected it to be difficult at first, or awkward, and he had found a way to make it easy. It was his sense of humour, his surprising tenderness, his determination, his refusal to compromise, his unwavering focus, his confidence: all the different things I loved about him, but in a new context. I felt as if I understood his particular kind of self-possession now. Put it this way: he had earned the right to swagger.

His arms went around me when I was pouring the water into the mugs.

'I was going to wake you up in a minute.'

'Why are you wearing clothes?'

The question suggested he wasn't. I investigated and flinched.

'Why are you naked? What will the neighbours think?' The flat was at the end of a terrace so the kitchen window looked out on the backs of houses, and if I could see them, they could see us, especially with the lights on.

'They've seen it all before.'

'I know I'm one of many but I don't want to think about that,' I said primly.

'Maeve.' He tilted my head so he could kiss my neck and I found myself gripping the edge of the counter. 'It's different. You know that.'

'I suppose . . .'

One hand slipped inside my dressing gown while the other found the belt and undid it.

'Do we have time?'

'Nope,' I said, pressing against him.

'Are we going to do it anyway?'

'Yep.'

And the third time – the third time was the best.

56

It should have felt strange, getting ready for work while Josh Derwent was lounging around my flat, but it didn't. He wasn't going in for a couple of hours, he told me, so I was on my own, which I was surprised to mind, quite a lot. When I had been with someone for the first time I always needed my own space afterwards, except now, when I could barely bring myself to leave the room he was in, and when I was in the same room as him I longed to be touching him, and it was all unmanageable when I had to get to work instead of falling back into bed. I forced myself to go and shower alone. *Control yourself.*

When I was getting dressed I pointed out a mark on my hip that would turn into a bruise, a thumbprint from where he had held me down, ruthlessly, exactly as he'd once promised. He was sitting against the pillows, lazily watching me, bare-chested.

'Let me see.' I went over to him and he pressed his mouth against it. 'Better?'

'Oh sure. Fixed.'

He held on to me, frowning. 'I'm sorry, though. First your wrist, now this . . .'

'It's not the same.' I sat on the edge of the bed. 'But you know I'm tougher than you think. You can't hold back, Josh. We have to be equals or this will never work.'

'You thought I was holding back. I see. I'll have to raise my game.'

'I mean in general. You can't spend your life worrying about me. You were overprotective enough before.'

He covered my hand with his, solemn. 'I promise to be completely self-centred.'

'Josh. I'm serious.'

'Seriously, I think you're tougher than pretty much everyone I've ever met. You're certainly tougher than me. I will never, ever underestimate you.'

'Better not.'

'But I will also try not to leave marks.'

I leaned in and kissed him. Something like hope was fluttering in my chest, and it was a long time since I'd felt anything like that.

On the verge of leaving at last, I stopped. 'Are we going to tell people?'

Derwent stretched. He had made it out of bed and into the shower, but he was still only wearing a low-slung towel and a contented expression. 'I'd be happy to put it up in lights at Piccadilly Circus but I presume you want to keep it to ourselves.'

'I don't care if other people know. In fact, I want them to know – I just don't want to have to tell them.' I pulled on my coat. It helped to have another layer of clothing between me and him. 'Mind you, everyone will have an opinion about us – whether it was a one-off, whether it's true love or Stockholm syndrome, whether I should run for the hills or you should, whether I took advantage of you, whether it was mutual insanity or inevitable, whether it's going to end badly and if so how . . .'

He put his arms around me. 'And what's your opinion?'

'I don't have one. I'm happy and that's about it.' I shook my head. 'Maybe it's better not to say anything for the moment.'

'They'll work it out if you keep looking like that.'

'Like what?'

He laughed before he kissed me. 'Go on.'

I hadn't planned it that way but it was a huge advantage that the team had been out the night before. No one was operating at full strength, and the person who was most highly attuned to romantic developments, Georgia, could barely manage to sip her full-sugar Coke as she slumped over her desk.

'Why did I do that to myself?'

'I don't know.' I dragged her to her feet and steered her to the small room where Colin Vale spent most of his time watching CCTV. 'Because it's Christmas?'

'I must have been out of my mind.' She sat down in one of the two chairs that faced the monitor, closing her eyes. 'When someone offers you a tequila shot, you say no. You know that. I know that. But what I actually said was, "I'll get the next round". And I did.'

'You do look like someone who had two tequila shots,' I said sympathetically.

She held up a trembling hand with four fingers extended.

'Four tequila shots? Oh, Georgia.'

She opened one eye. 'What about you? Shouldn't you be in a similar state to me? You were going to that swanky party.'

'Good champagne,' I said quickly. 'No hangover.'

'If only I had been drinking champagne. Actually, I think there was a glass of champagne in there somewhere, but it was between cocktails, which is always a mistake.' She dragged her other eye open and focused on me. 'You look revoltingly well. Like you've been to a spa or something.'

'Never mind how I look. Concentrate on the screen.'

'What's this? CCTV footage from the Governor?' She sat up, a degree of professional interest kicking in at last. 'Is this from the day of the murder?'

'It certainly is.'

'Where's Ilaria?'

'Not here yet. This is from the morning.' We were watching it on double-speed because for long periods nothing moved in the corridor. Every so often a door opened and a guest waddled up or down the hall, their movements jerky. I checked the timestamps against the chart Colin and Liv had made: names, addresses, useful information they had contributed to the investigation. There was very little in the last column.

'Tell me when you see the chambermaid,' I said, and Georgia groaned.

'Is this like that video of the basketball players? You're so busy watching the ball you don't even see the guy in a gorilla suit walking across the court?' She glanced at me. 'Sorry, I ramble when I'm tired. Hardy sent it to me when I was trying to improve my observational skills. Naturally, I missed the gorilla. Do you even know what I'm talking about?'

'I do, incredibly.' I pointed at the screen. 'No gorilla, but a chambermaid any second now.'

'Oh, there she is!' Georgia watched as the woman moved into view, bent over, sweeping the carpet with a small handheld vacuum cleaner, neat in a long-sleeved navy top and trousers.

'Those elderly American guests, the Glazers, said they heard this while they were having their usual nap between midday and one.'

'So?'

'So it was unusual for someone to be vacuuming the hall at that time, and that's why they mentioned it. I should have picked up on it.'

'On what?' Georgia was staring at the screen, baffled.

'I know she hasn't turned around,' I said, watching the navy-clad figure on the screen work her way up the hall, 'but you interviewed Veronique Baptiste who was the chambermaid on that floor of the Governor that day. Is that her?'

'No. Veronique is a Black woman.'

'Could it be her boss, Annette Pollock?'

'Too thin, too short.' Georgia sounded definite and, for the first time, wide awake. 'Who is that?'

We watched her disappear through the door of room 411 without looking back.

'I have a fair idea,' I said. 'All I have to do is prove it.'

Una Burt was not hungover, but she was extremely keen to solve the murder of Ilaria Cavendish and she was only too pleased to come and watch the CCTV when I summoned her.

'So that's our suspect.' Una leaned in, peering through her reading glasses. 'Do we have a full-face image of her from the CCTV?'

'No.'

'What about when she comes out of room 411?'

'She doesn't.'

The glasses came off so Una could fix me with her pale, slightly protuberant eyes. 'What do you mean?'

I had paused the video. 'That's the last time we see her, walking through the open door. Jason the plumber was in the room, working. He saw her, but he didn't think anything of it. He barely glanced at her – just enough to see that she was a chambermaid and not a guest or a manager or his boss. He didn't recognise her but it didn't occur to him that he should mention that to us.'

'And he didn't notice she was still in the room when he left?'

'I think she was probably hiding in the area between the two rooms, behind the fake shelving.'

'Then what? She disappeared into thin air?'

'More or less. I think I know how. I'm nearly sure.'

Una dismissed that: *how* wasn't as important as *who*. 'Does anyone know who she is? The housekeeper? They must have a record of all the members of staff who were at work that day.'

'She's not a member of staff,' I said. 'She looks like one at a glance, but that's not the right uniform. She's wearing navy blue, like the housekeeping staff, but there's no white edging on the sleeve and the trousers should have white piping down the side. She was holding a vacuum cleaner like a chambermaid, although actually they use proper full-sized ones, not the small handheld variety, which was another reason we might have been suspicious about her earlier. She was behaving like a chambermaid, so no one looked at her in any detail. They *saw* her but they didn't notice her.'

'That was a huge risk, wasn't it?' Una said.

'The hotel industry has a relatively high turnover of staff, especially in the kitchens and housekeeping departments. If anyone wondered who she was, they would have assumed she was new. But no one did.'

'Maeve thinks she knows who this is,' Georgia said. She was standing in the doorway with Liv, both of them looking the worse for wear and sulky to boot. 'But she won't tell us.'

'Not until I'm sure.'

'What will that take?' Una asked.

'I need to interview someone, and I need to be sure I've chosen the best way to do it.' I flapped my notes, thinking. 'And I need to check two more details. I have an idea at the moment and I'd need to back it up with some actual evidence, but I think I know how to get it.'

'Then go ahead.' Una stood and surveyed me. 'This really makes you happy, doesn't it? Nice to see someone getting job satisfaction.'

For a wild moment I thought about telling her it wasn't the job that was putting a smile on my face, but I nodded. Then I braced myself to run the hungover gauntlet of the twin guardians flanking the doorway. In more ways than one I felt I was on the right track at last.

57

'I don't see why I can't be the chambermaid.' Chris Pettifer stood with his hands on his hips, his bulk more or less blocking the corridor on the fourth floor of the Governor Hotel. 'It's sexism.'

'You won't fit in the uniform,' Liv said crushingly. 'And it involves bending over while you vacuum. You know how that makes the blood rush to your head.'

'I do get dizzy.'

'You're Abilo Braga, Chris,' I said. 'You're delivering the champagne. That's an important part of the process. And Georgia is doing a very good job as the chambermaid.'

Georgia dropped a curtsy. She was wearing the actual hotel uniform, her hair tied back, her make-up removed in accordance with the housekeeper's instructions. Colin Vale and Una Burt had walked past her without recognising her when they arrived, which proved my point.

'Liv, you know what you have to do.'

She nodded. She was playing the part of Ilaria Cavendish, although without the dressing up. Jeans and a jumper would do fine, I had assured her. It was better for clambering into the bath.

'Why are we acting this out?' Mo Ramzan asked. He was standing in for Jason, the plumber. Jeanette Lee had been reluctant to allow us back to the fourth floor, and it was only Mo – as well as the fact that it was mid-morning and all the guests were out – that had persuaded her.

'To check the timings,' I explained. 'It's all about the timings. That's why Colin is here.' Colin waved the clipboard he was holding, along with a stopwatch. Never let it be said he wasn't taking this seriously. 'He'll keep track of what's supposed to happen when. We'll film two versions. One is the story we were told, and one is what actually happened.'

'OK.' Mo sounded uncertain.

'This entire murder was about misdirection, like a magic show.' I was thinking of the magician I'd seen with Owen, and how brilliantly he'd focused the audience's attention where he wanted it. 'We were nudged in the direction of making certain assumptions and that meant we had the wrong idea all along. We thought we knew when everything happened and how, but we were relying on what we could see, and what we could see was deliberately misleading. We just didn't know that. All we knew was that it was impossible for Ilaria Cavendish to be dead in a bath full of boiling water, and yet she was. I think I've worked out how they did it, but I want to be as sure as I can be before I show my hand.'

'What if it doesn't work?' Una Burt asked.

I sighed. 'Then I'm out of ideas. I can still make arrests but I don't have anything like enough to make the CPS agree to charge anyone. And I wouldn't count on getting a confession. But if they taught us one thing, it's that what you see can be more compelling than anything anyone tells you. I'm going to film this as we go along and see if that helps jog their consciences.'

'So it was more than one person.'

'That I do know for sure. It couldn't be done with one person.'

'Shall we get started?' Una looked around. 'Places, isn't that what they say in the theatre?'

'Isn't Josh here? He should be standing in for Sam Blundell.' Georgia looked around vacantly, as if she was expecting him to step out from behind a flower arrangement. The very sound of his name made me blush.

Una to the rescue, incredibly. 'He's got some personal business to take care of. He'll be in later.'

Personal business. I stared down at my phone, letting my hair fall forward, and discreetly checked through messages, emails, voicemail. Nothing from Derwent.

A curl of worry spiralled through my stomach. It was, of course, entirely reasonable that he hadn't been in touch. But I had expected *something* by now. And I'd thought he was out of the office for work. I'd got the wrong end of the stick, I told myself, and put my phone away. I had worried about him being overprotective, and here I was, panicking because he hadn't called me.

Would I ever stop worrying about him getting himself in trouble? Probably not, came the dispiriting reply.

I took out my phone again and sent him a lightning-quick message before I could second-guess it.

How are things?

Neutral. Undemanding. Easy to claim it was a colleague's question and not a baited hook lowered in front of him by a far too keen new lover. He would know the difference, though. Maybe he had minded the way I had behaved, as if I needed him like air. It occurred to me with a thud of dismay that he had asked me what I wanted out of our relationship, but he hadn't told me how he felt about it.

'Maeve, are you ready?' Una asked, and I snapped back to what I was supposed to be doing.

'Absolutely. We'll start with the plumber arriving at half past eleven.'

It took three tries to run through it perfectly so the timings matched up, but in the end I was satisfied that we'd worked out a version of events that was close to what had actually happened. Pettifer wheeled the trolley up and down the hall with aplomb and a bit too much of a sashay. I followed him into 412 on the final take and filmed him pretending to open our prop bottle of champagne. He poured a glass, accepted his tip and headed out into the hall. Una Burt was our Sam Blundell and stumped down to the door with precisely none of his elegance. She was grim-faced as she bent over Liv, who was lying in the (dry) bath, and followed my directions. When we were finished, she walked out, shaking her head. I pursued her into the hall.

'You don't think it works?'

'No, it does. They were very clever.'

'Very,' I agreed. 'The CCTV should have been a problem and they turned it into an asset.'

'Are you happy you have everything you need?'

'I think so.' I pulled a face. 'I wish I knew why, that's all. I'd feel happier going into an interview knowing that. I can understand they wanted Ilaria out of the picture, but not to the extent of committing murder twice over.'

'Who are we arresting?' Georgia asked, and I showed her the photograph on my phone, taken from social media. It was a good likeness, but I wasn't expecting her reaction.

'Jesus.' She'd gone pale.

'What is it?'

'I *know* her.'

'She's a friend of yours?'

'No. But I met her.' Georgia bit her lip. 'That's Lora's sister.'

And just like that, I had my motive.

58

I opened my laptop and set it up on the narrow console table as Jennifer Hickey fussed over the arrangement of chairs.

'Just as long as everyone can see the screen,' I said. 'I thought this would be easier than trying to see the video on my phone, but don't get too excited. It's not exactly professional quality. And it's not edited.'

'I'm sure it's great.' Jennifer slipped easily into her cheerleader role, generous and positive. She threw herself into the middle chair. Dally, beside her, was picking at her manicure: long, milky nails that I slightly envied. The third chair was occupied by Anne Pusey, the bookkeeper, who was fidgeting as if she had somewhere better to be.

Behind her, casually blocking the doorway, was Chris Pettifer, who had looked around the Cavendish Hickey offices with an unimpressed expression but warmed up when he met Jennifer. I also had Georgia, who had recovered from her hangover in the nick of time.

'This won't take too long.'

On the screen, Georgia vacuumed her way up the hall.

'This was at noon on the day Ilaria died. This person went into room 411, where the door was wedged open by the plumber who was working there,' I narrated.

The camera followed her. I had paused by the bathroom to show Mo Ramzan tinkering with the plumbing.

'The plumber in room 411 saw her, but he didn't think anything of it. She was just another chambermaid. He didn't notice that she didn't come out again, and neither did we, at first.' The camera tracked to where Georgia was opening the false doors and slipping through to the hallway between the two rooms. She drew the doors closed behind her.

'Oh my God,' Jennifer said, enthralled. 'Is she hiding?'

'That's right. Now we'll skip ahead to 2.13 p.m. This is my colleague, Liv, but she's standing in for Ilaria.'

'Ilaria would never have worn those jeans,' Jennifer said. 'She was not a jeans kind of girl.'

'I don't think that's the point,' Dally snapped. She was watching, though, her foot tapping.

The camera followed Liv into room 412. 'We know Ilaria was expecting Angus to be in the room next door so she opened the doors to the connecting hallway. My guess is that the person we'll call the chambermaid had returned to the main bedroom once the plumber was gone, because Ilaria carried on as usual. She took off her dress and put on one of the hotel bathrobes, ready to receive the waiter with the champagne she had ordered. While she was distracted, the chambermaid came through the hallway between the two rooms and looped a dressing gown belt around her neck.'

'She murdered her?' Anne Pusey's eyes were wide.

I nodded. 'With a weapon that she returned to room 411, I suspect. A hotel laundry is a good way of getting rid of evidence.'

On the screen, Georgia towed Liv into the bathroom.

'Ilaria was very slim but she would have been a dead weight. We know that she was bruised around the time of her death by being dropped into the empty bath. I think this was the hardest part for the murderer, apart from the actual killing. Once Ilaria was in the bath, the killer stripped off her remaining clothes, which we'll let you imagine, and dropped them on the floor. She put the plug in and ran the water as hot as she could get it, letting the bath fill up around Ilaria.'

I had stopped filming with Georgia's gloved hand on the tap as Liv lay in the bathtub, her eyes closed. 'So then there's a short break and we return to the hallway at 2.32. Abilo Braga appears with the champagne Ilaria ordered from room service.

Someone knew that she always did this – maybe someone who made the bookings and checked the bills.'

Anne Pusey flinched, very slightly, a movement so small I might have missed it. Dally was still looking irritated and Jennifer was open-mouthed.

'Abilo had been paid some money to help with various aspects of the plan – putting 411 out of use, bringing the champagne. I don't imagine it was very much money, considering what he was doing, but it was enough to make him risk his job. He thought he was helping out with a prank. When he realised it was murder – which I think was around the time I interviewed him – he was horrified. But here, he's enjoying himself.'

Chris trotted down the hall with the trolley, the starched white cloth immaculate, the champagne sweating in the ice bucket. He knocked on the door and Georgia opened it. He pushed the trolley in and the camera followed.

'Things had to happen in a certain order. The champagne had to arrive before Sam did, because of the trolley.' I paused the video. 'Someone told me early on in this investigation that the secret to a good hotel is hiding everything ugly and functional. The trolley is an ordinary metal catering trolley with a lower level for hiding the things they don't want the guests to see, like dirty plates. The tablecloth hanging down gives the illusion that everything is clean and immaculate.

'We know when Abilo walked into the room and when he came out. There was only enough time for him to open the champagne and pour out a glass. The chambermaid took it and put it in the bathroom, and either she was wearing gloves or she wiped it because there were no prints on the flute. Abilo left the bottle and the unused glass on the table, as usual. The chambermaid tipped him, not knowing that Ilaria never bothered, and Abilo didn't tell her that was unusual because it was money, after all. She climbed under the trolley, presumably with her little vacuum cleaner, and Abilo wheeled her out, down the hall, into the service lift. I think she probably got changed and walked out of the hotel looking very different from the chambermaid she had been, and very different from how she usually looked, and we didn't notice her at all. Meanwhile there's a dead body in room 412, in a bath that's filling with very hot water, but the person who did it was invisible, even when she was in plain view all along.'

'Oh my God, it's mad,' Jennifer breathed.

'Do you know who the chambermaid is?' Dally asked, and I nodded.

Anne Pusey jumped to her feet. 'You can't think it's one of us. You can't.'

'This is ridiculous.' Dally stood as well. 'You've made up this whole thing. Why would you do that?'

'Because I wanted to make it clear we know what happened.' I clicked on a still from the actual CCTV on the day Ilaria died. It showed the chambermaid bent over, vacuuming the hall, anonymous in the long-sleeved uniform. 'Who is this, Dally?'

'I don't know.'

'Strange. I'd have thought you'd recognise yourself.' I folded my arms. 'You didn't tell me you knew Sam Blundell. You didn't tell me he was your sister's boyfriend.'

She thought about running – I saw her turn to assess her options while I cautioned her – but Chris Pettifer gave her the no-chance look along with a tiny shake of his head.

'But I don't understand,' Jennifer wailed.

'Don't worry,' I said. 'Dally does.'

59

Dally: bolt upright, furious, uncooperative.

'Why didn't you tell me that Lora was your sister?'

She said nothing. Her solicitor typed furiously, noting everything.

'Or that you knew Sam. It's a pretty big detail to leave out.'

Silence.

'Unless you have a reason for wanting to hide the relationship.'

Silence.

'Did you set him up with Ilaria? Or was it unintended consequences? I spoke to Sam. He told me you knew he was looking for work and you got him invited to the dinner Angus was hosting.'

Nothing.

'What did Lora think about him working for Angus?' I leaned forward. 'What did she think about Sam sleeping with Ilaria? Did she know? Sam thought she didn't.'

Dally picked up the cup of water in front of her and took a tiny, measured sip. Her hands didn't shake.

'Lora works in the theatre, doesn't she, backstage? She's produced a few plays. She's good at timing things, at planning out where people should be and when. She's good at making things appear a certain way for the audience. Was this her plan?'

Nothing.

'You knew Ilaria was pregnant. You knew she had an abortion. Did you know she regretted it? Did you know she wanted to try to get pregnant again?' I put the cap on my pen, taking my time over it. 'Did you think that Sam would have chosen Ilaria over Lora, if both of them were having his children?'

She might as well have been a mannequin in a shop for all the emotion she was showing.

'Were you envious of Ilaria? Did you want what she had? Did you want her job or her husband?'

Dally's mouth tightened a fraction and it was the very first sign that what I was saying hit home.

'I think you hated Ilaria. You envied her the life she had. You could have done so much more with all that money and all of those opportunities. You could have made the business a success instead of relying on Angus's money – but you did spend a fair amount of time charming Angus, all the same. Ilaria was reaching her sell-by date and you were ready to take her place.'

'He would never have gone for me,' Dally said scornfully, and stopped.

'Oh, I don't know. He likes you. He called you a little brat when I was interviewing him.'

Dally blushed, but rallied. 'Nothing ever happened. Again, you're making things up.'

'Am I?' I took out an evidence bag and slid it across the table. 'I'm showing you a photograph in a frame. Can you tell me who is in it?'

A shrug. 'Me.'

'Who are you with?'

'My boyfriend.'

'What's his name?'

'James Rayne.'

'He looks different with a beard, doesn't he? I didn't recognise him when I met him. But they called him Jimmy on the building site.' Jimmy, the big man who had lost the key to the padlock. I remembered his guileless stare, those soft brown eyes.

She had gone pale again, her lips parted in shock.

'I suppose the hard hat didn't help. I might have recognised the piercings, but I didn't. I was a bit distracted by the body that we were there to recover.'

Dally looked as if she was about to faint.

'Did he help you dump Abilo Braga's body? Was it his idea to put it on the site because he knew no one was working there, or did you come up with that plan on your own?'

'He didn't know.'

'He pretended to lose the key for the gate so you could get in.'

She shook her head.

'We think Abilo died in a car. Someone strangled him from behind. We've got forensic investigators looking at Jimmy's car now. If Abilo was in it, we'll know.'

'No.'

'And if he was, and that's where he died, we know that someone was in the driver's seat and someone else was in the back seat. Two people. One of them was you. Was the other one Jimmy? Or was it Lora?'

'No.' Tears were brimming in her eyes as she stared at me. 'No.'

'She's not going to confess,' Una Burt said to me in the corridor. 'And we don't have any evidence that isn't circumstantial. We can't identify her from the CCTV we've got. She managed to hide under a hat or behind a face mask in everything Colin has turned up, where she isn't facing away from the camera. Unless you can get the boyfriend to talk, this is looking too thin to take it to the CPS.'

'He's not talking,' Chris Pettifer said heavily. 'No comment all the way. It's not his first time being arrested either. He knows the drill.'

'What about Lora?' I asked Liv, who shook her head.

'I don't think she knew anything about it. She keeps crying.'

Dally: shifting in her seat, uneasy.

'Can I talk to my sister?'

'No. Why didn't you tell me you were sisters?' I asked.

'How did you find out?'

'You met my colleague Georgia when you went to comfort Lora. She only knew you as Lora's sister. I only knew you as Ilaria's assistant. But I had already worked out it was you on the CCTV.'

'It could be anyone.' She looked up at me, her eyes challenging.
'But it isn't. We know all about it, you see.'
'Obviously you don't.'
'Why not?'
She pressed her lips together and said nothing more.

I walked around the office, trying to pull my thoughts together. Everyone I passed seemed to have an opinion about the case, and wanted to share it with me.

'Probably acted alone—'

'She wouldn't have been able to carry him, but if Lora helped—'

'How much money was Lora on at the theatre? Thirteen k a year? That's starvation. How did she live?'

'The boyfriend. Not in her interests to look too closely about what he was doing in his spare time on a Wednesday, was it? He was keeping a roof over her head and food on the table. So what if she had to share him? Maybe she was into that. If you ask me, he's the one who was being conned.'

'Shut up, Pete,' I took the time to say, eyeing him with disfavour as I passed Belcott's desk. He hadn't even been involved. The Russian gangsters had taken up all of his time.

'I'm just saying.'

'Well, don't.'

'What's your problem?' He gave me a piggy-eyed look, but it was uncomfortably shrewd. 'You should be happy to have those two in custody. Is it because JD isn't here to pat you on the head?'

'No one calls him that,' I snarled, and walked away, before I realised I should have pretended I didn't know who he meant.

And my phone was still silent.

I found myself going to the meeting room, which was empty. I shut the door behind me and closed the blinds. It was quiet in there, so I could hear my own thoughts instead of everyone else's. I pressed my fingertips into the arches above my eyes, trying to concentrate. I hadn't had enough sleep for this. I had been reckless, careless, caught up in the moment. In Josh. Moments from the night flashed through my mind like stills from a film, details out of order: his eyelashes dark against his skin as he closed his eyes, his profile against the streetlights slipping past in the taxi, his fingers wrapped around my knee, the gleam of a smile in the half-light of the bedroom, the muscles taut in his shoulder as he buried his head in my neck, his stunned expression in this very room when he'd realised what I was saying, and that I meant it . . .

Concentrate.

Sam Blundell had all the substance of a plume of smoke. I didn't believe he was capable of lying about the murder, let alone committing it. I could have sworn he was in the dark about the whole thing.

Jimmy Rayne had a record of committing impulsive, poorly planned minor crimes. I couldn't see him coming up with the plan for a murder that depended on precision timing and sophisticated psychology.

Someone with money. Someone who hated Ilaria. Someone who wanted to destroy her reputation along with her beauty.

I found Jennifer's number and called her. She was only too happy to answer my questions with the sort of instant, helpful honesty I rarely encountered.

I came out of the meeting room with a smile on my face that had nothing to do with Josh Derwent, this time, and everything to do with being very good at my job. I still had that.

'Something that bothered me, Dally, was that you and your sister don't have money, do you? Neither of you earns much. Your parents are dead and as far as I can see you didn't inherit anything from either of them. I asked Jennifer about you. Your mum was a costume designer but she was also an alcoholic. She drank herself to death. Your dad was a failed actor who killed himself. Not exactly a stable upbringing. Where did you get the funds to bribe Abilo Braga?'

She said nothing, her face mulish.

'There has to be someone else. Someone who funded this. Someone who made sure they had an alibi. Someone who didn't want Ilaria to get a big payout. Someone like Angus.'

Dally flinched.

'I don't think it was him, as it happens. I think he's capable of it but I don't think he knew anything about your plans. He was genuinely shocked that Ilaria was dead. Someone involved with the plans for this murder went to great lengths to give him an alibi because they wanted to make sure he wouldn't get in trouble. He didn't deserve that care and consideration, but that, again, doesn't make him a murderer.'

'No.' Her voice was low, barely audible.

'Someone else is letting you take the blame for this. Someone who paid Abilo Braga. Someone who might even have paid you. If you had money, you could have set up your own business. You could do the designing and Jimmy could do the building work. You didn't need much to get started but you didn't have it.'

She jumped; I had hit on the truth.

'You probably wouldn't have done anything to Ilaria if you hadn't been thinking of your future as well as your sister's happiness. This was your one chance. But what you didn't realise was that you were being set up to take the fall.'

Dally swallowed, looking down at her hands. 'It's not fair.'

'No, it's not. So tell me who it was.'

She looked up at me, her pretty face blank, as if she was facing a firing squad with no way out and nothing left to her but her composure. 'Do you know already?'

'I do. But I want to hear you say it.'

60

It was the housekeeper who opened the door to us this time. She was small and elderly, with a heavy Russian accent. She had been welcoming when she brought out the tea tray on my last visit to the house in Hampstead. Now she couldn't meet my eyes.

'Mrs Cavendish is not to be disturbed. She's sick.' It didn't sound convincing.

'I'm afraid we need to speak to her urgently,' I said.

'She's in her bedroom.' Behind the housekeeper, the hall was shadowy and cold. The vases were empty. 'She wants to be left alone.'

'What's she doing? Packing?' The house already felt deserted. The lights were off in the rooms on either side of the hall. I half-expected to see suitcases in the hall.

'No. Of course not.' A pause as the housekeeper gave me a small, sly smile: she had superb comic timing. 'She never packs for herself. She asked me to do it.'

'Where is her bedroom?' Chris Pettifer was looming behind me, practically pawing the ground.

'Upstairs, on the right. But the door is locked.'

'She'll open it, or we will,' I said grimly, and started up the stairs with Chris and the two uniformed officers we had been allocated as muscle, their body-worn cameras chirping.

Disappointingly, from the point of view of the officers who had been looking forward to kicking the door down, Devon let us in to her bedroom. The curtains were drawn and the lights were off, so at first all I got was a vague impression of chaos. There were clothes flung over chairs and piled on the floor. Shoes littered the carpet. Devon, wrapped in a dressing gown, her hair in a silk turban, shuffled back to bed as fast as she could. She pulled the covers over her head without speaking to us.

'Come out,' I said. 'We need to talk to you.'

'Go away.'

'That's not very polite, is it?' Chris managed to sound deeply offended, and sad about it.

'Do you know why we're here, Devon?' I asked. 'Did you know we've arrested Dally and her boyfriend, James?'

The bedclothes remembered their manners. 'I'm so sorry, I don't know who that is.'

'Dally works for Jennifer Hickey.'

'Oh, does she? I don't think I know the name.'

I leaned over so my mouth was close to the approximate area where Devon's ear might have been. 'We have her phone records, Devon. We can see how often you called her, and when, and for how long. And we're here to arrest you, so you can come out from under the covers now, of your own volition, or we can drag you out.'

I caught one of the PCs checking his camera was on, in case it turned out to be option two.

'Devon, don't lose your dignity here.'

There was a sniffle from the bedclothes. 'Can I put some clothes on before we go?'

'Yes, of course.'

'And make-up? And do my hair?'

'Don't push it,' I said, not unkindly, and Devon sighed.

'I'm going to need to get hold of my solicitor.'

I patted the pile of fabric. 'I think that's a good idea.'

Devon's solicitor was Barbados-tanned and incredibly posh. He talked so much I began to suspect he was paid by the word, but he went quiet after the first few minutes of her interview. Beside him, Devon sat in a doleful heap, one leg tucked up under her chin. She stared at the table, unblinking. Her hair was dishevelled and her eye make-up, which looked like yesterday's, was inching down her face.

'As you said, you had no reason to know Dally Field. She didn't work for Jennifer Hickey or Ilaria Cavendish when you were their client, before your marriage ended.'

'Right. I didn't know her.'

'Jennifer recalled you coming into the office about six months ago because you needed a replacement for a lamp she had sourced. It wasn't available anymore and you were hoping she could find it for you.'

Devon shrugged. 'Sure.'

'You got talking to Dally. Somehow, Ilaria came up and you made it clear to her that you weren't a fan.'

An eye-roll. 'OK, but so what?'

'Dev . . .' her lawyer said and she flicked her hair back over her shoulder, irritated.

'When I rang up looking for your number, Dally had it in her phone.'

Devon held up her hands. 'Nothing to do with me.'

'So we knew you were in touch with one another and when I checked Dally's phone records I found that you had called or messaged one another with increasing frequency right up until Ilaria's murder in November. At that point, communication dropped off. There was a period of several weeks where you made no contact with one another, at least by phone. Then, when you came up in our investigation, Dally called you – presumably to make sure you knew what to say.'

'I only say what I think, not what other people tell me to say.' Devon's expression was haughty.

'You told us Angus asked you to do humiliating things and made you dress in an exposing way, but I found pictures of you from NY and London and your clothes are beautiful. You were featured in gossip columns and complimented on your style. So I spoke to Angus.'

Devon looked down, her face red.

'There was no sex club in New York, according to Angus. He told me he loved you very much but he didn't want children and that was a deal-breaker for you. You left him and he was devastated.'

'Was he?' She bit her lip.

'Nevertheless, he arranged a very generous settlement for you – so much so that you avoided going to court over it. You and he had an agreement and you trusted him to honour it. A couple of months ago he warned you that if Ilaria wanted to end their marriage, he would have to give you a smaller share of his income.'

'I don't need much to live on,' Devon said, her voice husky. 'I didn't care about the money.'

'But you did care about Ilaria. Specifically, you cared that life was much more boring for you once you were divorced. You hated being on your own. When you found out from Dally that Ilaria had cleaned up her act, you realised she was trying to get pregnant, and it made you furious. You had discovered, after you left Angus, when he had remarried and it was too late, that you would rather have him than a child. Now Ilaria would have your place in society, your husband and, potentially, a baby. She was going to make sure she had everything she needed before she left him, unlike you, or she was going to make him go along with what she wanted. Simply, she was better at gaming the system than you were, and you hated her.'

'Ugh.' Devon looked away from me, her lovely face twisted with anger.

'You knew very well that Dally disliked Ilaria too. She was open about her feelings and what was going on in her life – she's frank about her worries – and you recognised someone who had a good reason to want Ilaria gone. Maybe it started out as idle conversation to test the water, but soon you were actively planning to commit murder. Dally and her boyfriend worked to come up with the practical elements of the plan, but it was your idea to kill Ilaria, and you made it possible. You were the third part of the conspiracy – you provided the money and the motivation. It needed all three of you for the plan to come together, and arguably you were the key player. You were determined to destroy her.'

'No.'

I folded my arms. 'If Angus had let her keep a baby, it would prove what you always feared – that he cared about her more than you.'

'He did not,' Devon said hotly. 'First of all, Angus would never have changed his mind. He really does not want kids, I assure you, and certainly not with her. He would have dumped her ass and she would have been a single mom.'

'People can change as they get older. They get more sentimental. They have less of a stomach for divorce, especially when it would cost them too much money. Angus thought he controlled Ilaria, but you were worried it was the other way round.'

'She was manipulative. She had him exactly where she wanted him. You know he was trying to get rid of her? He kept pushing her to do more and more degrading things because he wanted her to leave him. But she loved it because she was a little *whore*.'

'He preferred her.'

'No. He just couldn't get free of her. I knew if she wasn't there anymore, he would want to marry me again and we could go back to how things were before. That was all I wanted. I was so stupid to leave him.' She put her hands up to her face. 'It was such a mistake.'

'I think I need a word with my client,' Devon's solicitor said, half-rising, but he was too late.

'Angus missed me. He told me so. He was so unhappy with her. He wanted me instead and we would have been happy this time.' She blinked away tears, sniffing piteously. 'You have to understand, I did it for him. And I know it was wrong, and I know I was stupid.'

'Devon,' the solicitor said, appalled. She looked at him.

'I'm making your job hard here. But I have to face the consequences.' She turned to me. 'I was a fool. We're all fools for love, in the end.'

61

At the best of times, the end of a complex investigation felt like spinning hundreds of plates. I rushed from the interview room to Una Burt's office, then to a quiet corner where I called the CPS for charging authority. After that I begged Chris Pettifer to share out a list of tasks to the team – a list that was getting ever longer while I went back to the interview rooms and spoke to Dally one more time. Liv was organising the evidence we'd already seized, and making a further list of what we needed.

In the middle of everything I had a call from Sandra Bulling, the police officer who had been investigating what Melissa had done to Thomas, to let me know she was going to be charged with child endangerment.

'How is she taking it?'

'Badly,' Sandra said, with great satisfaction.

I could imagine it. She would be desperate for someone to come to her rescue. Someone with a white-knight complex at the best of times, perhaps.

Halfway through the afternoon, I retreated to the kitchen to catch my breath and check my phone once again. No messages from Derwent. The alarm bell that had been ringing in the back of my mind was shriller now. How was it possible to go from total elation to this sharp, agonising worry in a few hours? He had been so determined not to reveal his feelings and I'd forced him into it. I had told him he was – how had he put it? – an emotional failure who ran away from difficult relationships. Maybe he had decided to run away from this one.

I was stirring a mug of tea, staring into space, when a clatter behind me announced that Georgia had arrived in the kitchen. No preamble.

'Did you see Josh's email?'

'No, I haven't been at my desk.' What had he done, I wondered with a lurch of uncertainty.

'It's a save-the-date email. He sent it to the whole team.' She came closer. 'Maeve, he's getting *married*.'

I looked at her blankly, and then past her at the flurry of movement in the doorway that was Liv, moving at speed.

'Did you see it? Did she tell you?'

'I didn't see it but I've heard.' The hope I'd been nurturing gave a forlorn flap as it died. 'Sorry, what was the date?'

'The end of June next year.'

'June,' I repeated. Six months away.

'That's what the email says. It doesn't say much apart from that.' Georgia's eyes were glassy with tears. 'It seems so unfair, Maeve. I know how you feel about him. And you've waited so long, and you've done so much for him . . .'

'Oh Georgia, shut up. She knows all that. Can I just say I'm glad nothing happened between you?' Liv had folded her arms, her body tight with anger. 'I know he was unfinished business but imagine if you *had* slept together, when all the time – I mean, I understand why he wouldn't want to tell anyone that he was seeing someone new, but not even to *hint*.'

'If it is someone new,' Georgia said. 'It could be Melissa.'

I would not be able to bear it, I realised, if it was Melissa.

'Obviously you have Owen and he's probably an upgrade on Josh,' Georgia said, very much as if she didn't think he was at all but she had to say something.

'Owen and I broke up.'

'Oh *shit*.'

Maybe people like us didn't get a happy ever after, I thought. Maybe that was too much to ask.

But I had trusted him, and he knew that.

'We were all hoping you and Josh—' Georgia broke off and blew her nose dolefully on a sheet of kitchen paper. 'I can't believe he's done this.'

I put my mug down. 'Has he come in yet?'

'Just now. He was in Una's office for a few minutes, then he came out and he must have sent the email straight away. At least we were able to warn you before you saw it.' Liv put her hand on my arm. 'Did you know he was seeing someone?'

'I – I had some idea. Is he in the office?'

She nodded.

'OK.' I would know as soon as I saw him, I thought.

I went out of the kitchen, Georgia and Liv trailing behind me. Derwent was sitting on the edge of his desk with his arms folded, looking innocent, surrounded by a circle of our colleagues. He nodded to me in a friendly way.

'Hello.'

'Hi,' I said, and tried to take a deep breath before I went on, feeling as if my lungs were being squeezed. 'I understand you have exciting news.'

'Only if you like weddings. I heard you've had a busy day. Well done.'

'I thought I'd achieved a lot, but not as much as you, apparently.'

'He's getting married in June but he won't say who the lucky lady is,' Pettifer complained. 'Maeve, did you know about this?'

'Not really.' I leaned against my desk, matching Derwent's position exactly. 'June doesn't give you much time. Have you been planning this for a while?'

He shrugged. 'I made most of the bookings today. Spoke to the bride's parents first, obviously.'

'You—' I broke off, unable to put my feelings into words.

'I didn't think you were ever going to get married, Josh,' Georgia said, sounding deeply wounded. 'And if you were, I didn't think you'd find some random person to marry.'

'Not random. I chose her very carefully.'

Liv was frowning at him. 'What's going on? Why are you looking so smug?'

'He's looking smug because he thinks he's thought of everything,' I said. 'But he hasn't.'

'Details,' Derwent said, unmoved.

'Details like actually proposing.'

He unfolded his arms to pull a small black velvet box out of his trouser pocket. 'I have a ring.'

'Shouldn't the bride have that?'

'I'm getting around to handing it over.'

'Here? In the office?'

He grinned at me, the troublemaking glint very much in evidence.

'Wait,' Liv said. 'Hold on.'

'What's this?' Chris Pettifer was swivelling on the spot, looking from Josh to me and back again.

'I don't believe it.' Georgia's voice was as squeaky and high-pitched as a dog whistle.

'I'm not going down on one knee,' Derwent warned me. 'Not on this carpet.'

'I can't say that's not disappointing. And before you go on, I want to clarify something.'

'Of course,' he said gravely. 'Be my guest.'

'You started off with the bride's parents,' I said. 'You asked them first.'

'I had to ask permission. I wanted to do it properly.' He snapped his fingers, remembering. 'Your mother wants you to call her, by the way.'

'I bet she does. She'll be lucky to get a call twice in one day.'

His chin lifted with a quick jerk; he was too surprised to hide it. 'Twice?'

'I phoned her this morning on my way to work.'

He frowned. 'She didn't mention it to me.'

'You'd better get used to that.'

Liv was the first person to recover enough to be outraged. 'You haven't *proposed*, Josh? You made all the arrangements and told Maeve's parents and you haven't even *asked* her?'

'I knew what she'd say.'

'You couldn't have known.'

'And I didn't have time,' he went on, as if Liv hadn't interrupted. 'I had a lot to do.'

'You would have had plenty of time if you hadn't tried to organise a whole wedding in a day,' I pointed out.

'When did all of this *happen*?' Liv again. 'The two of you, I mean.'

I checked my watch. 'About . . . eighteen hours ago.'

She waited for the chorus of catcalls and whoops to die down. 'And you didn't think to mention it, Maeve?'

I shrugged. 'I was busy.'

She glared at both of us. 'You two . . . Sorry for being the voice of reason here, but this is the last thing that you should be doing. I can see why you'd do this now, Josh. Of course you want to hurry her into making a commitment now that you've finally talked her into sleeping with you, but it's not fair.'

'Actually,' Derwent began and I cut him off.

'No, Liv. I was the one who persuaded him.'

Once the cheers died down again, Derwent smiled at Liv. 'Don't worry. She can say no.'

'Because it's that easy when you're making a public proposal in front of everyone.'

'Liv,' I said gently. 'It is that easy.'

'Sorry for not getting carried away, guys, but it all feels a bit rushed.' She folded her arms.

'Rushed is the one thing it's not,' Derwent said. 'It's been years, and I'm not waiting one second longer than I have to.'

Georgia turned to scrabble for something on her desk.

'Hang on, mate.' Pettifer was shaking his head, paternally disapproving. 'I don't mind you proposing—'

'Good of you.' Derwent grinned at him.

'But you can't do this *here*. Maeve deserves moonlight and champagne, not the office on a rainy Thursday.'

'She doesn't need moonlight and champagne. There are more rainy Thursdays in life than moonlit nights.' He stood up and looked at me. 'And I want to be there for all of them.'

I felt my heart flip over. A tiny squeak came from Georgia's direction; I hoped she wasn't going to faint.

The way he spoke was as if there was no one else in the room. 'Maeve, I want to spend the rest of my life with you. I've spent long enough without you. Will you marry me?'

Yes or no. He was watching me carefully; how I answered was as important as what I said.

'June, did you say?' I leaned back and picked up my diary. 'I have to check. I might be busy that day.'

'You aren't,' he said with quiet triumph. 'I've booked it as holiday for us both.'

Una Burt poked her head out of her office, beaming. 'Did she say yes?'

'Not yet.' He hadn't taken his eyes off me. 'Any second now.'

'You're asking me to make a decision like that, with no warning, when you're the person who said I could never even decide what to have for lunch.'

'That's right.' He paused for a moment. 'And I stand by that. But this is easier than lunch, isn't it? You just have to decide if you want to marry me or not.'

Complete silence: a room full of people holding their breath.

'I can't imagine why,' I said. 'But I'm absolutely sure that I do want to marry you. In fact, I've never been so sure of anything. So yes. The answer is yes.'

'Go on, kiss her,' Pettifer growled. For once in his life, Josh Derwent did what he was told without arguing. Georgia emptied the contents of her hole-punch over the two of us in a drift of confetti and he kissed me as if he really meant it, as if it was forever.

Author's Note

Dear Reader,

Thank you for reading *The Secret Room*, the twelfth Maeve Kerrigan novel. If you haven't finished it, don't read this note yet! Save it for the end.

That's because what I want to talk to you about is the end of the book. I've spent the last year reading your comments on *A Stranger in the Family*, and listening to readers at events, and you've all been very articulate about That Ending and what torture it was and how you'd never forgive me if . . . And I loved it, mostly because I knew what was coming next for the characters. I am absolutely delighted that Maeve and Josh have such passionate supporters in the real world. But I also came to realise that I'd written another That Ending here, even if it's a different kind of ending, and I didn't want any of my readers to jump to conclusions.

To be absolutely clear, this is not the end of the Maeve Kerrigan series. I'm already thinking about what happens next for her, and I'm very excited about it.

I would love readers to be surprised by how this book ends, so please, if you want to talk about it in reviews or on social media or in real life – and I'm so grateful if you do! – remember that some readers are a few books behind, or haven't started the series yet, or have spent the last year waiting patiently for *The Secret Room* to come out. Please keep the secret of *The Secret Room* for their sake, and for me.

With much love,

Jane
xx

Acknowledgements

This is the last writing I do for every book and in some ways it's the most important, because without the following people I wouldn't ever have written this book. So huge, huge thanks, as ever, to my wonderful agent Ariella Feiner, Amber Garvey, Jen Thomas and all at United Agents.

At HarperCollins the brilliant Julia Wisdom guided and encouraged me and unerringly identified the places where the first drafts of *The Secret Room* needed more work. Her imprint, Hemlock Press, is a very happy place to be. I'd also like to thank Kathryn Cheshire and Jo Thompson in particular for editorial excellence, along with Lizz Burrell, the genius copyeditor Anne O'Brien and proofreader Sarah Bance. If there are any mistakes left, they're entirely my fault. The entire team at HarperCollins excels at what they do but I'd like to single out Philippa Cotton and Fliss Denham for publicity efforts that go above and beyond hard work, Maddy Marshall and Tanuja Shelar for marketing excellence, and Kate Elton and Frankie Gray for their insightful support. The new look for the series is thanks to the inspired vision of Sean Garrehy; it makes all the difference to have creative people engage so brilliantly with my writing. I'd also like to thank Patricia McVeigh and Tony Purdue for their superb efforts in running my Irish publicity and sales. From Charlie Redmayne to the newest members of staff, I always have the sense that HarperCollins are entirely committed to me, celebrating when things go right and fixing anything, no matter how minor, that isn't quite perfect.

As ever, I must mention some of my best writer friends because I'm so lucky to have them in my life: Sinéad Crowley (my ideal reader), Liz Nugent (my guru on just about everything) and

Catherine Ryan Howard (my perfect partner in crime). They are my first port of call for emotional support, writing advice and sheer entertainment. Catherine Kirwan, Edel Coffey, Andrea Carter, Andrea Mara, Amanda Cassidy, Karen Perry and Sam Blake are also part of the formidable and ever-growing gang of Irish crime writer pals who make events so much fun. Cressida McLaughlin and Sarra Manning always know how to make a day – and a book – better. Colin Scott is essential for just about everything to do with life, crime writing and publishing in general. Much love in particular to Sarah Hilary, Erin Kelly, Elly Griffiths and Ruth Ware for their very special friendship and camaraderie.

Love as ever to Alison Gleeson, Claire Graham, Sarah Law, Emma Kershaw, Nadia Wilkinson and Vicky Lloyd-Roberts for the book chat (and the everything-else chat which is just as important).

My thanks to Andrew Mackenzie who won the chance to name a character in this novel at the International Arbitration Charity Ball auction in aid of Save the Children and made it a gift for his remarkable mother, Lesley. It was a very great pleasure to use her name in this book.

I'm immensely fortunate to have such a supportive close and extended family, particularly Kerry Holland and Philippa Charles. Edward and Patrick are at the heart of everything I do. Writing involves a lot of staying in when everyone else is out, and Felix and Rory are my perpetual companions (which sometimes helps and sometimes does not, but I forgive them). James is the best and most important person of all, always.

Last but not least, I would like to thank my readers. *The Secret Room* is dedicated to you all with love and gratitude for your support. Every writer wants to be read but very few of us find such dedicated, clever, funny, determined, astute and committed readers. I hope this book – which has required enormous patience on your part, and on mine – lives up to your expectations.